AHEBBAN

Ages of Claya – Book 3

Whitney H. Murphy

'Ahebban'

To elevate—

when life's winds

seem to choke

the hope from your veins;

when the wounds

and imperfections

in your bones

seem too deep to heal;

when your mistakes come down

with the weight of a mountain

on your shoulders,

on your breaking heart;

when the world seems too cracked to be mended

and all that was lost can never be replaced—

yet you stand again

on trembling feet,

eyes to the dawn,

and rise

above it all.

Whitney H. Murphy

'Ahebban'

To elevate—

when life's winds

seem to choke

the hope from your veins;

when the wounds

and imperfections

in your bones

seem too deep to heal;

when your mistakes come down

with the weight of a mountain

on your shoulders,

on your breaking heart;

when the world seems too cracked to be mended

and all that was lost can never be replaced—

yet you stand again

on trembling feet,

eyes to the dawn,

and rise

above it all.

Whitney H. Murphy

Part 1

1

-Common Year 152-

They say that in ages long past, the land of Igretho had a different name. They say the hills were once so parched and treeless that no creature cared to roam them—that the stones lay alone like dry, dust-laden bones on the fruitless earth, cold and sharp-angled against the winds that beat relentlessly over them. It was an empty land. Desolate. Barren. Forsaken. They say Igretho was a *kravón*—a wasteland.

Until six generations ago, when the Nakuë was born. The river that appeared in a single morning.

No one can tell how it happened. Some teach their children that it was the ancestors themselves who brought the river with them—the legendary people of King Rand. A people so mighty that the very earth obeyed the shout of their voices. Others say it was the gift of a powerful spirit that once dwelt in the inland sea of Emér, which feeds the waters of the Nakuë—that it was a gift of water and life to a land that was starved for both. Some say the river was paved overnight by the fingers of the gods.

Igretho. It means "inheritance." The ancestors praised the land as a paradise, a haven, a gift. A healed land. The legends of the river are endless. But one fact is certain among them all: the Nakuë is the heart of the Igretho nation. Its birth marked the start of the common calendar, which the surrounding nations have since adopted. In six generations the people of Igretho have hunted and mapped the river's every turn. They've counted each bend and branch in its course like precious pearls in their collection. They've ridden its waters to the young forests of the southeast and followed its winding fingers to the seashore, where the wind whips like hot silk on their faces. They've traced each of its narrow westward veins until the current slows and its banks melt low into the sand. The river is the spout of life. The gift that quenches the thirsts of all people along its endless flow. And all their cities and villages have risen beside its waters.

That is, all but one.

Built in the southernmost sweep of the Igretho plains near the feet of the mountains, the settlement of Kasántos has always been a place of solitude. A place away from the bustling riverside capital and its lively markets. A village divided from its neighbors by no less than a week's travel over hills and dales. The first settlers came south looking for timber to build their cities along the first branches of the river in the northwest. But when they found the secluded young forests in the shadows of the mountains, they never left. And so Kasántos became unique among the settlements of Igretho. The only village south of Emér where children are raised without the memory of the crowded cities, the riotous voices of the festivals, and—above all—the sound of the river.

2

-Common Year 152-

He's about eight years old when he discovers the keepers of the woods. He spots them when the afternoon has already begun to fade along the horizon, at that hour when all the day's smells have baked long in the summer sun and become a single, heavy taste in the cooling air.

Some say the forests will eat up aimless wanderers who venture into them without a plan. But the trees have never frightened young Skéisono. Each one seems to carry an aura of its own. Living energy that he can feel when he lays a hand to their thick trunks— energy he can *see*, when he pauses to watch them in the afternoon light. The spirits of the trees are subtle flames. Warm and glowing, like the warmth of the lanterns the townspeople hang at the start of the new year. No tree is exactly like the next. And with so many recognizable markers in his path, how could Skéisono ever become lost?

This day, he begins with the same route as always, bolting down the hill from the cottage and keeping a northwestward path until he reaches the slumping tree with the deep violet glow at its core. Then, turning south, he steps through a little forest of thickets until the young tree with the amber-golden glimmer in its leaves comes into view. And heading straight west from there, Skéisono's more than halfway to the next marker before he notices an odd stillness in the air. Most days, the trees are no less alive than the birds that nest in their branches, shifting their auras and seemingly chattering to one another just beyond human hearing. But today, they've fallen still. Watching. Waiting. Pausing among them, little Skéisono suddenly finds himself waiting along with them. But for what?

He hasn't waited long when the keepers of the woods appear. They come soundlessly, as if their feet never touch the leaf-and-stick-carpeted earth. They come creeping with heads lowered and backs arched, with only dark fur to clothe their slender, humanlike bodies. Four of them. They're close. Close enough for Skéisono to glimpse the vibrant hues in their massive, shining eyes. Close enough to leap and capture him for their evening meal, if they choose. The boy becomes helpless at the sight of them. His limbs seem to harden into place, and he finds himself suddenly holding his breath at his teeth. Unable to blink, to move. Unable to think at all.

Maybe they could slay him on the spot. Maybe they could maul him to pieces. But they don't. They only stare back at Skéisono with their broad ears tilted forward to frame their emotionless faces. When they turn away at last, vanishing into the distant foliage without leaving any trail in their wake, Skéisono's thrumming heart nearly drops out onto the forest floor. He doesn't wait for his breath to return. He turns and dashes homeward through the trees with all the speed his quaking legs can muster—all the while, a single instinct sounding an unending chorus through his young mind.

Run!

The evening's closing in like a dark cloak at his back when he reaches the house at last. He throws the door open and pauses at the threshold, feeling lost. Speechless. His mother rushes to his side, shuffling him in and pulling the door carefully shut behind him.

"Thank the gods!" She leaves a kiss on Skéisono's head as she drops to her knees, looking him thoroughly over. "Where have you been?"

The boy turns his head from side to side, as if it's all too difficult to remember, too strange to describe. And when he speaks at last, the words feel clumsy and disjointed in his mouth. "Th-they're real. I saw them," he mumbles. "But I escaped."

The answer's barely audible above Skéisono's breath, but Mother's expression changes at the sound of it. The lines fade from her brow, and a cold shine floods into her widened eyes. It's something young Skéisono's seen in her face only once before, when a massive tree notched for chopping fell and nearly crushed his elder brother, Marntrei.

"Skéisono." Father rises from his usual chair beside the fire and crosses the room with a hand at his belt. "Were you in the woods again? Alone?"

"They didn't come after me—" Skéisono braces himself, ready to present a myriad of excuses, but Father shakes his head, raising a hand to silence him.

"I won't be angry with you, son. But I need you to listen." He glances to the floor, as if the words he's searching for are somehow hidden between the woodgrains. "The keepers of the woods were always real. But they've only just begun to appear in these lands, in the north and western forests. We know little about them. But you've heard the old tales as well as anyone. If provoked, they can be very dangerous. Even the huntsmen are avoiding those lands these days." He pauses, kneeling beside Mother to look more directly into his son's eyes. "If you've really seen them, you must never enter those woods again. Especially not alone. Do you understand?"

Little Skéisono stares back at his father's face, at the way the lines around his eyes have somehow set into place, and he gives a slow nod. He'll obey.

Or at least, he'll *try* to obey. He tries for days, looking for little adventures around the garden and the empty hills east of town, remembering the fear that gripped him in the woods that day. Remembering how terrifying Father can be when he's angry. He tries for nearly a week. But the woods bring a kind of solace and relief that Skéisono can't seem to find anywhere else— the only place where the frowning townspeople can't find him. In time, he can't stay away. In time, he *needs* the woods.

Six days have passed when Skéisono begins to sit at the edge of the trees after supper each evening, staring through the branches and planning how he might slip into their midst—quickly, silently. He should be helping in the garden. But it won't kill Marntrei to do a bit of weeding on his own for once. Chores are already tiring enough; toiling away with a brother nagging at his back is even worse.

"What I'd give to have an ordinary brother," Marntrei's always said. "Is it the curse that made you so weak and lazy?"

He's always going on about "the curse"—no matter how often Mother chides him. As if it isn't already bad enough to be known as a cursed child among the neighbors. *Neighbors*. That's what Mother and Father call them. As if the people of Kasántos were actually *likeable*. Skéisono's never understood how Mother can manage to smile at the strangers in the market. For as long as he's ever remembered, the neighbors are hardly people at all. They're little more than staring eyes. Eyes that watch his every step beyond the cottage. Eyes that glower when he follows Mother into the general store. Eyes that lose all light and laughter when they see the boy of the curse.

They say the curse that came to Skéisono on the day of his birth was first seen generations ago, when the ancestors lived far away to the north of the inland sea. The curse of the black eyes. Wherever it appears, a child is born with entirely black eyes—eyes that stay black as the night sky from corner to corner for the first days of life, before fading to a more natural color. The blackness never returned to Skéisono's eyes again. But they say the settlers of the village where it last struck vanished without a trace, and their homes have remained empty and abandoned ever since. The curse has taken what it wanted before. Some fear it will strike again. And who can stop it? It's no wonder that the neighbors have never trusted Skéisono among them. In the woods, he can forget them. After all, the trees don't care about curses. Sometimes, when he sits quietly enough, he can almost hear them saying so. The woods are his sanctuary—one he could never bear to truly abandon.

Eight days have passed when he dares to venture as far as the tree with the violet aura before darting back to the hill where the family cottage sits, lowering himself to the tips of the prairie grass and watching carefully for any sign of Father. By the twelfth day, young Skéisono forgets all hesitations. He spends long afternoons exploring new groves to the north and splashing through the tiny creeks he discovers there. He even finds the courage to revisit the place where the keepers of the woods frightened the breath out of him. But in all his wandering, the massive-eyed creatures never reappear.

And so after less than two weeks since Father's admonition, the woods become a sanctuary once again. A haven, where no one will dare to follow—not his nagging brother, not the mistrusting townspeople. Not anyone.

3

-Common Year 152-

The night is almost pitch. Mother's putting out the lanterns for the evening, and the air is thick with silence. Oppressive. It's the sort of stillness that compels people to whisper for no apparent reason. The silence that sometimes wakes Skéisono in the night and leaves him wondering whether there's anyone else awake in the world.

He's still awake in the loft, watching the soft flutter of the firelight along the roof beams, when a subtle shuffling echoes up from the room below. It's Father, stepping slowly over the floorboards. He pauses by one of the north-facing windows, unlatching and tapping the shutter open until a sliver of blackness can be seen along its edge. And he leans with his ear to the night. Listening. Near the edge of the loft, Skéisono props himself up on stiff elbows and attempts to catch sight of the trees beyond the window. The woods must be a different place entirely when night comes. Full of shadows, hidden from the cool light of the twin moons overhead. Perhaps at night, the forest is lit by only the colorful auras of the sleeping trees. Skéisono wonders, leaning for a better view. But the moment's cut short. Father pulls the shutter abruptly closed and returns to the kitchen. He lets out a mild sigh as he settles down to finish the last of the evening dishes while Mother mends an old belt.

Up in the loft, Skéisono flops back onto his blanket, mind full of thoughts. If only he could visit the woods at night! He closes his eyes and makes an effort to imagine what the tree with the amber-golden shimmer would look like now, with its glimmering leaves sending warm rays of light in every direction, piercing the darkness. It must be amazi—

A loud, hollow sound erupts outside the cabin walls and jolts Skéisono from the sleep that had just begun to creep stealthily over his mind—the same sound the stacked wooden crates alongside the house made when Skéisono tried to climb atop them weeks ago. Near the hearth below, Mother's risen to her feet. She stares wordlessly toward the rear door that sits directly below the loft. Skéisono waits in desperate stillness. Has someone come to the door?

"I'll have a look."

Father's whisper can be heard—cut off in part by the low whine of a hinge in need of oiling. He's opening the rear door. What will he find? The question drives out all hope of sleep from Skéisono's mind. He tosses his blanket aside and scrambles for the ladder. But his foot's only just reached the first step when a second, thundering crash nearly sends him tumbling to the floor below. Now another loud knock strikes the north wall of the house. And another. Mother rushes out into the night, bending to snatch the fire rod from the hearth as she goes. Are the neighbors attacking? Is Father hurt?

The pounding falls abruptly silent as Skéisono reaches the ground floor. And then all is still. Beneath the loft, the rear door is wide open to the night beyond. A gaping wall of blackness that seems to beckon and threaten all at once. Skéisono stands motionless before it, watching the shadows, waiting for whatever might come creeping over the threshold to meet him. For a moment, it brings a terrible chill to his bones.

Mother and Father return without warning out of the night, both pale and looking as though they've held their breath from the moment they left. Mother glides across the room to the front door, checking the lock, while Father starts toward his chair with his largest garden shovel still clutched in his hand. Then he spots little Skéisono standing beside the ladder, and his gaze seems to lock into place, hardened into stone.

"You've gone into the woods, haven't you?"

How does he know? His voice is a single, level tone. Skéisono stares back at him, holding his jaw tight as the sweat springs up along his brow.

Father lowers into his chair, and the firelight plays across his features, accenting the curving lines and shadows there. "Why did you do it?"

Skéisono swallows, suddenly unable to bring any words to his lips—somehow believing that the problem might float away in the night air if he delays long enough. As if his silence can somehow outlast his father's temper.

But now Father lets his shovel clamor to the floor as he returns to his feet. "Did you ignore what we told you?"

Up in the loft, Marntrei stirs. He's probably awake, listening in. Glad to be excluded. He and

Skéisono always know that Father's especially upset when he can't stay seated. And somehow his height is always intimidating, despite the fact that they see it every day.

"Do you want to endanger us all?" Father's voice swells as he holds his hands out from his sides. "They've seen where you *live* now. They followed you here! I had to chase them off!"

"No," the boy beside the ladder replies through clenched teeth, tight fists forming at his sides.

"No?!"

The silence that follows is unbearable. Like stifling humidity on a merciless summer afternoon. A stillness broken only by the sound of Mother dropping into one of the kitchen chairs and letting her head fall into her hands.

"Answer me, Skéisono!"

Father's voice resounds like an unyielding gale at Skéisono's ears. Sharp and relentless, like the scowls of the people in Kasántos. And the boy with the curse has heard enough.

"I wish I *lived* in the woods!" he shouts with all the breath in his chest, not caring if everyone in town can hear it. "No one bothers me there!"

He tries to stand tall and unafraid—to be something stronger than the quaking boy that he is. But the hot tears are already welling up in his eyes, about to betray him. Tears he can't possibly let anyone see. There's only one place to hide them. And so without any plan, without saying anything at all, little Skéisono dashes to the rear door, yanking the lock out of place and flinging the latch before his father's outstretched hand can stop him. The night air is a cold burst at his face as he rounds the corner of the house and bolts for the black wall of trees to the northwest. Father's thundering footfalls follow close behind, so heavy that for an instant Skéisono's sure he can feel the vibrations in the earth. But the boy's fast. And he knows where he's going. He leaps through the leaves at the base of the hill and flies into the shadows without slowing down. He runs until his legs can go no further, and the sound of his father's calling voice has faded to echoes at his back.

4

-Common Year 156-

"*Alarei!*"

It was a sunny day, wasn't it? Or perhaps there was rain in the afternoon. It's difficult to remember exactly . . .

"*Hey, are you coming?*"

A late summer day—no, it was in the spring. Yes, the breeze was cool. Everyone was wearing overcoats . . .

Alarei sighs, unable to concentrate. The memory's become so foggy over the years. Maybe the details don't matter. But the sight of the tree always seems to bring them back. The tree beside her father's house. She's sat in its lower branches for nearly an hour now, trying to remember. But the memory seems to tease her, dancing just out of reach. Blurred, incomplete images that hang like little weights at the edge of her mind.

"Are you sleeping over there?"

She isn't. But Seva's nagging voice almost convinces her to give it a try. She loses her balance and nearly falls to the ground when she moves at last—saved only by a thick limb that catches under her right arm. Nearby, Seva lets out a cackle. She's still bent over with laughter near the crest of the hill when Alarei looks up.

Seva. She's a meditation instructor from the east and is nearly twice Alarei's age. But she's rarely serious. She straightens up now, waving a hand in the air. "Let's go! Are you ready or not?"

"Yeah, I'm coming," Alarei calls back as she snatches her bag from the foot of the tree, not bothering to swat the bits of leaves and bark from her hair.

"Sorry to keep you waiting," Seva calls down. "Looks like we've got about eighty *sirlene* for the return trip. Not bad! We can buy all the food we want when we reach Firal. And—*oh!*—I wonder if that bakery's still around!"

Seva gives an excited little clap, words pouring like an endless fountain from her mouth. But Alarei scarcely listens. She reaches the top of the hill and turns to send a final glance to the house she's leaving, to the city that's fallen into view behind it. The city of Jaker, built along the northern shores of the inland sea, resting at the southernmost edge of the nation of Tayd. The city where she was born, and where her brother still lives. Years may pass before she'll see it again.

The oxen are harnessed and nibbling idly at the grass beside the wagon. A boy with fiery red hair stands beside them, running a gentle hand down their necks. He's pale, like someone from the far west, beyond the Atayu Sea. And he's thin. Maybe *too* thin.

"Oh, I nearly forgot." Seva comes to a stop near the heads of the oxen, gesturing loosely at the stranger who stands beside them. "This is Asei. He'll ride back with us this time. He's eleven." A year younger than Alarei. He looks up, and his silvery-gray eyes somehow complement the vibrant waves of hair that frame his slender face.

Alarei tosses her bag into the wagon bed before turning back to the newcomer. "You from here too?"

The boy shakes his head. "Up north."

His voice carries an accent Alarei's never heard. Maybe he comes from the far north—from Old Sketza, or beyond.

"This your first time to Clevyan?" Alarei asks.

"First time."

Alarei nods, satisfied.

Beginning in the far east, the trail from the clifftop sanctuary of Clevyan stretches east and west across three nations' borders. Most travelers need five to six weeks to complete the journey with oxen. Sometimes more. Alarei's walked the path to Jaker and back once before—leaving Clevyan for nearly half a year to visit her brother at a time when their father was visiting him from the north. She was ten years old that summer. And she had been certain that the endless days of walking in the merciless glare of the sun would be the end of her. But this time, the long road seemed to lose its hard edges. Maybe it was the way the desert sands in the far east seemed to glimmer like fallen stars in the moonlight, or the way the black mountains stood like lonely, jagged watchtowers at the desert's edge. Maybe it was the blinding shimmer of the Emér Sea when it came at last into view, near the borders of Tayd—or the sight of seabirds circling and gliding over the tossing waves. Somehow, in the roughly two years since young Alarei traversed it last, the long path between Clevyan and Jaker has learned to take her breath away. Now, she'll follow it back to the east once again.

The elders of Clevyan say it's good for the foreign youth to return home now and then, to see their families. But it's difficult for Alarei to call the city of Jaker—a place she's only visited a handful of times in her young life—home. The wide marble halls and open colonnades of Clevyan in the largely-desert nation of Ketsa have been her home for ages. Rising atop the far-eastern cliffs that overlook the rolling dunes of the Sand Sea, Clevyan was built by immortals at a time when the power of the gods still existed on the earth. Or at least, that's what the traditions say. Whether it's true or not, Alarei can at least agree that Clevyan is old—and unlike any other structure built by human hands. Every massive brick of it.

The people of the cliffs have taught Alarei everything she knows. From reading and writing to gardening and meditation. They say that with careful concentration, anyone can learn to sense the living spirit of Claya, the earth itself. It's an ability the elders of Clevyan have used to discover the coming of countless dangers through the generations. Droughts, sand storms—even occasional marauders from the desert. Someday, they hope to use their gift to detect the return of the immortals themselves.

The wagon jostles lightly as the oxen begin to heave it along at Seva's direction, and Alarei leans back against the supplies in the bed to watch the sky slide by.

Everyone was wearing overcoats . . .

The thoughts that filled her mind as she sat in the tree moments ago come slipping quietly back. It's the same tree. She's almost certain of it. The same tree she was playing beside in Jaker when her father first told her about going away to Clevyan. It was springtime, and she was sprinting aimlessly around the hillside. Running and running with some little girl from town. It was the year she turned five—or was it six? Then her father came out from the house and said something about going to stay someplace far away. She didn't understand it then. When she's asked him since, whether in letters or in person, her father's always given the same answer: "Those wise folks at Clevyan can give you a better future than this poor fisherman."

Maybe he's right. After all, Alarei's never envied her elder brother's life as a shipbuilder's apprentice.

A soft tap at the wrist pulls Alarei from her thoughts. Kneeling less than an arm's length away with a handful of jerky clutched in his slender hand, the new boy stares at Alarei with unblinking eyes. How long has he sat so close?

"We can eat this now?" He nods as he asks, as if trying to convince her to give the answer he hopes for.

"Well, yeah, but don't get too greedy. We've got to make sure it lasts. We've only got enough money for a few supply stops."

She tips her head to the crates and little sacks that fill the wagon all around them. A broad smile breaks across the boy's face. He settles hurriedly back into his place between two sacks of vegetables, shoving nearly an entire strip of meat into his mouth at once. Such bony shoulders, such skinny limbs. He probably hasn't eaten in days. What was his name again? Asei? Alarei watches him feast like a starving animal. And she smiles. He's a little strange, but at least he'll be someone new to talk to.

* * *

The greater moon is bright that night. Like a massive street lamp looming over the trees, bold and unafraid among the shadows. Alarei lies watching it for ages. Ordinarily, she'd claim a space to sleep in the wagon with the cover up, away from rain and dew and crawling things. But when the greater twin rose up with such a vibrant display along the horizon, Alarei couldn't resist spreading a blanket in the grass. Now, after what may have been hours of tracing the gray valleys on the moon's face, she's unable to fight the heaviness at her eyelids.

Until a sudden commotion erupts between the trees nearby—a soft rustling of leaves, then a series of rapid footfalls.

Alarei sits abruptly upright with her humble traveling knife in hand, still blinking away the dream that had just begun to cloud over her mind. It isn't unheard of for travelers to be ambushed on the road to Clevyan. But nothing seems out of place when she glances around the camp. Seva lies beside the fire only a few paces away—an odd lump of blanket with a dark tuft of braided hair visible at one end. The wagon is unmoved. Untouched. And the oxen are still resting peacefully in their places, tails swaying soundlessly at the gnats that buzz nearby. Everything's fine. But where's the new kid?

The air's grown chill. Alarei rises wearily to her feet, with her blanket wrapped tightly across her shoulders, and peers into the trees.

"Asei?"

Her voice sounds thin and pitiful against the night's oppressive silence. The boy probably just needed to pee. And if someone was going to rob them, they would have done it by now. But Alarei can't seem to quell the odd tension that's risen in her lungs. And another mild commotion echoes out from the leaves nearby. Leaves and branches swaying and colliding as if a sudden wind had passed through them.

"Asei? Is that you?"

She unsheathes her little blade. Clouds come drifting over the moons as she steps toward the trees, and the woods grow dim in uneven patches. Alarei stands breathlessly at the edge of the shadows. Listening. Wondering how far she should dare to wander, wondering what creatures may lurk in the night forests of Tayd. But now the clouds drift on, and when the light falls anew into the trees ahead, it lights a little patch of red between the leaves. Waves in Asei's sunset hair. The boy sits with perfect stillness, staring off into the distant night like a long-forgotten statue between the trees. Alarei opens her mouth, about to question—but before she can speak, the boy darts from his place. He shoots through the leaves and vanishes into the shadows. And when he reappears a moment later, carrying a limp rodent in his hands, Alarei can't withhold a sharp gasp. Asei nearly leaps into the air at the sound of it.

"Oh! You! I-I was just—I got—" He fumbles helplessly for words, quietly tucking the rodent behind his back.

"Did you just catch that? With your *bare hands*?!"

Asei waves his free hand in the air, glancing frantically in all directions. "Not so loud! And please, don't tell anyone."

Alarei stares back at him in disbelief, unsure which question to ask first. Before she can decide, they all begin to pour out at once. "Don't tell anyone what? How'd you learn to do that? And how long have you been out here, anyway—in the middle of the night?"

"I got hungry. Just don't tell anyone. If they knew, they might not let me into Clevyan."

- 23 -

"If they knew what? That you can catch things like that?"

"No, no. If they knew I'm . . ." Asei shakes his head, turning in a little circle before suddenly pausing in place to look back to Alarei with his silvery stare. A stare that seems oddly bright in the partial light. Almost glowing. Then, abruptly, he smiles. "I mean—yeah, just don't tell anyone about me catching things. Those fancy cliff-top people probably wouldn't like it. I hear they hate to get their hands dirty."

Alarei pulls her blanket tighter across her elbows, blinking. What just happened? Wasn't this boy speechless a moment ago? Suddenly, he shows nothing but smiles. It's strange. But wondering takes more energy than Alarei's sleep-robbed mind cares to manage.

"All right, all right, I won't. I won't tell. You don't have to be so weird about it."

"Thanks."

Asei holds up his fresh kill in the air between them and gives a little bow. Maybe it's some kind of formal gesture where he comes from. A gross one. The unanswered questions gather in a little pile in Alarei's mind, stored away for later. The road to Clevyan is long. There'll be plenty of time for questions. She sighs, turning back to the glow of the fire beside the wagon. Next time the strange boy goes adventuring in the night, she won't bother to follow.

5

-Common Year 156-

He's become accustomed to spending long nights away from home, tucked into the safety of the woods—sometimes as many as three nights in a single week. Morning tends to find him curled in the lower branches of an ancient tree or slouched in the mossy gaps between boulders. And there's something wonderful about waking to the sweet melodies of the birds in the canopy. But he can't say exactly what it is that wakes him this time. Whether it's a change in the air, a leaf brushing against his shoulder, or simply the subtle sensation that creeps into his dreams—the haunting awareness that he's no longer alone.

The dew is cold when Skéisono opens his eyes. It drops from the leaf tips all around and showers down in an almost soundless barrage onto his shoulders before slipping down to the soil, where the air shifts and stirs like cool mist between the bases of the trees.

When he notices it at last, the creature is watching from scarcely an arm's length away. A keeper of the woods. It sits directly ahead of him, crouching low to the earth—blended almost perfectly into the shadows beneath the bushes. Its short fur is the color of Father's old spade. Rusted. And its stare is as bottomless as the massive eyes that paralyzed Skéisono in the woods once before. But it's unmoving. It sits as motionless as the trees and stones surrounding it. And until it opens its mouth, the boy almost convinces himself that it isn't alive at all.

"Don't be afraid." Its voice is small, quiet. Female. "I would never hurt you. Neither would any of my clan." She lifts her hand, showing Skéisono a dark palm. "Do you know what you are?"

Skéisono might answer if his voice wasn't trapped somewhere deep in his chest—if he actually *knew* the answer. But instead he sits in wide-eyed silence, saying nothing at all.

The creature tilts her head to one side, gaze unbroken. "I don't believe you do, child." She comes crawling closer over the forest floor, moving like a predator on the hunt, somehow as silent as the morning that surrounds her. "Do they treat you differently?"

Skéisono's heart begins a wild thrumming in his chest. And as the creature with the massive eyes and rust-colored fur raises her little hand in the air between them, he wonders for a helpless instant how death's final grip will feel. But the killer's hand only brushes delicately along his cheek before falling away again. And her whisper is warm.

"You don't really belong with them. Not for long. You are unlike any one of them."

* * *

The morning's giving way to a blustery afternoon as Skéisono comes stepping out of the trees. Mother's the first to spot him. She's out on the hill on the west side of the house, hanging laundry out to dry in the rising wind. She runs down the hill to catch him in her arms, her hair pulled back in the same braided bun as always. And she smells like the garden.

Father stays hunched over his work in the back shed all afternoon, smelting screws and bolts for the plowshare he's mending. Mother doesn't insist that Skéisono confront him after vanishing into the woods for yet another night. And so he doesn't. When evening comes sliding along the tops of the trees and edging over the hills, he finds Marntrei lying prone along the lower bough of his favorite tree. The older boy clings like a lizard to the coarse bark, squinting at the grass below with his slingshot pointed at some unseen target.

"Back already? Aren't you always saying you want to live in the woods forever?" He pulls a little stone from his pocket and readies his weapon without taking his eyes from the hillside.

"I want to tell you something." Skéisono glances momentarily over his shoulder at the house in the distance, at Mother's silhouette in the garden. "About last night."

Up in his perch, Marntrei lets his stone fly from its sling. It hits the earth with a solid clap before rebounding at a random angle into the tall grasses. He curses. Missed again. "You're scaring off my targets," he growls.

"Just *listen*! I have to tell someone."

"About what?" He fishes another stone from his pocket.

Below, Skéisono's hands fiddle anxiously in his pockets. "I saw one of them again. In the woods. But this time it talked to me." He can't seem to dispel the urge to whisper. "Did you know they can talk?"

Marntrei looks up from his hunt at last, letting his aiming wrist fall limp. "Skéisono, do you *want* Father to run you through with the pitchfork? He told you—"

"Father doesn't know—and she didn't hurt me! She said none of them would."

Marntrei folds his arms under his chin. Unconvinced. "Oh, really? I bet they're just pretending to be your friends so they can catch you more easily, once you're fattened up for their dinner." He says it with a sneer and a wrinkled nose, clawing at the air like a ravenous animal.

"*No!*" Skéisono kicks the foot of the tree, sending a little plume of dust into the dry air.

"They're beasts, Skéisono. Why do you think they're interested in you? Maybe they'll use you to somehow get to the rest of us. Maybe they'll slaughter the whole town!"

"You're just scared!"

Marntrei sits up now, letting his feet dangle below the bough. And he gives Skéisono the typical look: the slanted eyebrows, stiff frown—like he knows better. It's a look that always ignites rage like a little flame in Skéisono's young heart. "Fine, then keep going to them. See if I care when they eat you up."

"I *will!*" Skéisono spits as he turns away.

But he doesn't return to the woods. He charges to the northeast until the cabin sinks out of view behind the hill, eventually collapsing into the swaying grasses and gazing up at the yellowing clouds in the afternoon sky. Marntrei doesn't know. He only hates that his little brother's braver than he is. *He* would never go exploring in the woods. *He* would never have the courage to talk to the creatures there.

High above, weaving in and among the clouds, a flock of white birds passes by. Their wings seem to flicker and fade against the failing blues of the sky beyond, gliding toward the south until they fade out of sight altogether.

You are unlike any one of them.

The creature's soft words and dark face come drifting back into Skéisono's memory. She told him to discover who he is. She told him to *search*.

6

-Common Year 158-

The instant the last candle of the morning ceremonies is lit, Alarei's racing out the corridor and down the wide steps—wisps of incense still trailing from her long, embroidered robes. It's the path she's followed at the start of each week for nearly two years now: down the steps from the gathering hall, through the north courtyard, and down the first corridor to the right. Then up the stairs and down the long hall beyond. Past several dozen storage chambers, four classrooms, and the north entrance to the bathing fountains—until the corridor takes a sharp left and opens into the grand west hall. There, the wide face of the Sand Sea can be seen rippling out to the west— golden dunes by day, shimmering silver waves by night. Set high atop the cliffs, the west hall of Clevyan is the perfect place to settle down between the columns and watch sandstorms rage in the desert below.

It's also the perfect meeting place.

Alarei rounds the final corner of her path, nearly losing her footing along the slick marble floor, and claps a hand to the dark statue that stands watching the Sand Sea from a curved nook. It's a life-size carving of Kehljen the Philosopher, the first teacher of Clevyan. It marks the meeting place. And at the moment, it's the only other human figure in the long, open stretch of the west hall.

"*Balayë!* Victory!" Alarei exclaims softly, wiping fresh moisture from the sides of her face. But the celebration's cut short.

"Almost. But not quite."

The voice seems to materialize at her shoulder. Alarei nearly leaps out of her skin at the sound of it. She whirls around, hoping to land a solid shove on the boy it belongs to. But he isn't standing beside her when she turns. She glances in all directions, letting out her breath in one loud exhale before spotting a single red wave of hair along the edge of the dark statue's robes.

"What?! How long have you been hiding there?"

There isn't much space in the statue's nook, but there's enough. Enough for a slender boy to settle down with his knees to his chest and vanish from sight.

"Beat you again, priestess." Asei's grin is as broad as always. He rises to his feet and leans on the revered statue beside him with a sort of casualness that would horrify the scholars of Clevyan.

"You cheated! This time you *had* to. There's no way you ran here all the way from the east wing—and got here first." Alarei scowls, bringing her hands to her hips and turning in place—the same way the grandmothers of the sanctuary often do when they're about to scold a herd of misbehaving children. "And I'm only dressed like this for the morning meditation ceremonies. I had to ring the chimes."

Asei swats the dust from his clothes before stepping out into the hall. "Well, apparently it makes you even slower than usual." He starts down the hall with his hands tucked contently into the folds of his belt.

Alarei follows after him, grabbing her skirts in fistfuls. "Oh, yeah? Well, what's with you hiding back there?"

Asei laughs. Or at least, he attempts to. But the angle of his smile's all wrong. Forced—as if a foul smell's suddenly drifted by in the morning air. "I had to," he tells her flatly, silvery eyes bright like the candleholders in the ceremonies. "They don't like it when—when I . . ."

"Who doesn't like what?"

For a moment, it's as if Asei didn't hear her at all. He only continues walking, staring down the massive length of the hall and through the corridors beyond. What trouble has he gotten into now? Last week it was the chief groundskeeper who was enraged at Asei's attempt to string a rope swing between the two most massive trees in the orchard. But the last few days have had little excitement. At least, as far as Alarei's seen. What did she miss? She nearly opens her mouth to ask when Asei's smile returns, and he leaves a soft shove at her shoulder.

"Oh! I almost forgot!"

He reaches into the little pocket that's strung to his belt, pulling out two carefully wrapped twists of colorful paper. And the questions that floated in Alarei's mind a moment ago are gusted away by the sight of them.

"Sweet cream twists?! There were *two* of them for us?" They're the most coveted treat in the head librarian's secret stash of candies. They're a rare find— even for the librarian, who has his sweets specially ordered from the western merchants. Ordinarily, if a sweet cream twist appears in the stash, it's far too risky to snatch. "You sure he won't notice they're missing?"

Asei shakes his head. "He must've had thirty in there! Trust me. He won't miss these two."

The librarian has more than one hiding place for his sweets in the central library. And in the two years since Asei first came to Clevyan, he and Alarei have managed to find them all. It's a kind of tradition of theirs, to check the stashes at the start of each week and enjoy their spoils in the west hall. Some days they sit for ages between the hulking columns, planning their next adventures, the dazzling glimmer of the Sand Sea reflecting across their foreheads. Some days they talk of faraway lands, of exploring the isles of the Atayu Sea, or of wandering the ancient forests of Sketza in the north. And Alarei often finds herself drifting away in daydreams too marvelous to abandon. One day, she and Asei will see it all. Or at least, that's the plan.

* * *

They say the eastern cliffs of Ketsa capture all the ocean winds from the shores beyond and hold them captive—depriving the vast desert to the west of nearly all life-sustaining moisture. Unlike the Sand Sea that rolls in golden dunes far below the sanctuary walls, the lands atop the cliffs are vibrantly green. Full of life, full of trees. Another world entirely.

Lake Ivehlith sits at the heart of the sanctuary lands. Fed by three rivers, it flows with waters as pure as that found in any of the greenest nations of the eastern continent. The sloping hills that surround Ivehlith have long been a favorite spot for the meditation instructors to hold their classes. They call them the Listening Hills. Young students can be seen there at almost any hour of the day, sitting cross-legged on thick rugs in the grass, with their eyes closed or fixed on the distant skies. There they learn to listen to the hills, the wind, and the sky—to hear the spirit of Claya that stirs all around them. But for Alarei, the concentration is rarely easy. Especially out on the wind-dusted hills, where her short hair is relentlessly gusting into her face and tickling her nose.

Today, as the rugs are spread over the hillside and the instructor urges the students to quiet their minds, Alarei's too restless to try. She settles down on her rug with her eyes to the distant shores of Lake Ivehlith, a smile at her lips. The lake's very best swimming shore isn't far, and the summer sun is intensifying. Moments from now, it'll be easy to slip out of view and steal away into the cool waters there. Asei's probably already planning the route. She turns to give an excited glance over her shoulder, ready to leap up at the slightest opportunity. But Asei isn't watching. He sits instead with his head in his hands, frowning down at nothing in particular with the same stare that momentarily filled his gaze in the west hall that morning. A dejected stare that plants an almost frightening heaviness in Alarei's heart. Something must have happened. Something he has yet to tell her. But what could it be? She watches her friend a moment longer, waiting for him to look up with his usual grin, waiting for the right words to come to her mind. But he doesn't move. And the words she'd ordinarily say seem suddenly out of place.

She turns back to her lakeside view with a sigh in her chest. Maybe tomorrow Asei will be back to himself. He probably just has a headache. Alarei runs through the explanations in her head, trying to let the wind carry away the stiffness that's grown in her breath. Trying to convince herself that everything's normal, despite the odd gnawing sensation at the back of her mind.

Maybe tomorrow.

7

-Common Year 158-

Skéisono doesn't need to look over his shoulder to know his father's come for him. Vayeka looks up from her stitching, sending her calm gaze to the trees at his back.

"Your father seems weary. You should go to him." She lays her work momentarily down on the grass as she grips his hand, and a soft stirring flows from her palm where it touches his. Like warm static spreading into his veins. Energy. "Our camp will be here when you need us. Remember, child: always come to us if danger rises."

Skéisono nods, watching the shifting shades of his own reflection in Vayeka's wide, scarlet-black eyes. He rises to his feet. He could've sat for hours by her side, watching her little fingers work dark and delicate patterns, asking her more questions about the way her people live without money or cities or markets in the depths of the woods. But he can feel Father's stare like a ray of sunlight at the back of his head. He can't stay.

"*Eidyá*," he tells Vayeka as he turns away. It's a word she taught him years ago, the first time she spoke to him. A word her people use when parting ways.

Father's standing quietly at the edge of the clearing. His hands have vanished into the pockets of his worn *jolden* tunic, and his mouth has settled into an oddly slanted line across his face. He shifts his weight as his son comes to meet him, doing his best to look comfortable. He's not very good at it. He's seen Vayeka and other keepers of the woods before. Many times, in the past two years. But their presence still makes him visibly unnerved.

It's the fourth time Father's followed Skéisono to the clearing, a place hidden deep in the maze of the woods. From Kasántos, it's more than an hour's hike away. Vayeka's clan has used the clearing as a gathering place for months now. Some days, Skéisono finds them tending their little gardens there, or preparing the meat from the stags, birds, and rodents they've slain in a morning hunt. Other days he finds them sitting together in the grove, weaving dark fabrics into blankets and shawls. And now and then, when the morning is still young, the clearing is full of tiny children. Furred, broad-eared children who squeal and leap as they chase one another through the tall grasses. All colored in varying shades of red and brown and gray fur. All dressed in simple tunics or waistcloths. They always gather around Skéisono's knees like curious little animals when they spot him—chattering incessantly up at him in words he's still learning to understand, and framing his entire figure in their massive, vibrant eyes. *Voránjevin* children. Vayeka says her race overcame countless hardships in generations past. And so for as long as any clan can remember, they've called themselves "voránjevin." *Overcomers.*

- 38 -

The voránjevin camp has become a home for Skéisono. A place where he seems unconditionally accepted, despite the fact that he lacks fur and stands a full head-and-shoulders taller than any other being he's met there. A place where no one glares or flinches as he passes by, where no one mentions a curse. Among Vayeka's people, he isn't cursed. He isn't an ill omen or sign of bad fortune. In the woods, he's free.

Skéisono's nearly reached his father's side when he turns to send a final glance over the clearing. Still sitting with her stitchwork in her lap, Vayeka raises her hand in a silent farewell. Vayeka. In the past several years she's taught Skéisono all about her clan—about their language, their traditions, and the way they channel their physical energy at will. Sometimes they share energy to strengthen each other. To mend wounds or soothe pains. Other times, they draw energy from the bodies of their prey, stilling living hearts without using any weapons at all. Vayeka's taught the boy from Kasántos more about her kind than he could ever record. But most fascinating of all, she's told him about *him*. She's told him that he carries the sign of deity in his eyes—that one day, he'll rise up to his full potential as a steward of the gods. Skéisono's clung to every word of it, not caring if it made any sense at all. Maybe it's all nothing more than idle folklore. But it's far more than the people of Kasántos have ever given him.

"We'd better get home before your mother has a breakdown." Father's hands slip out of his pockets as he turns away from the clearing, talking over his shoulder. "She doesn't eat when you disappear for too long, you know. Doesn't sleep either."

"I'm sorry," Skéisono tells the ground.

The two of them duck away into the trees, Father walking in the lead. He must've memorized the way by now. They walk in silence, accompanied by only the rhythmic thump of their steps through the foliage and the sporadic melodies of hidden birds in the treetops. Skéisono eyes a loose rock in his path and kicks it free as he passes by, sending it toppling away through the leaves and out of sight.

"Skéisono, you know you can tell us anything." Father's voice breaks the silence. "This month you're fourteen years old. You're old enough to make your own decisions." He steps over a fallen tree and sends a fleeting glance back to his son. "We just need you to talk to us."

Skéisono follows behind and watches the way his father walks with his back stiffened and his elbows never relaxing entirely. For a time, he has no answer. But the words come a moment later, as the two of them come within sight of the massive boulder that's always marked the presence of a little brook in the path ahead.

"I'll leave a note next time."

Ahead, Father pauses his steps to look back at Skéisono with one eyebrow raised. And a thin smile spreads along his ordinarily stern face.

"Fair enough, son."

* * *

The heat of the sun seems to linger especially long into the afternoon. As the evening rolls in, Skéisono throws back the shutters in the loft to let the hot air escape in a rush of dry warmth. And he smiles at the soft breeze that gusts in to replace it. Perhaps he and Marntrei won't bake in their sleep after all, when night comes. For once. He shakes the dust from the blankets before returning to the ladder, leaving them crumpled and askew in the corner. He's just stepped out the back door and into the garden when Mother's voice comes hiccupping over the next hill. A sharp, breathless shout. She's walking back from the south fields when Skéisono spots her, coming along the way she and Father have always taken to and from the market near town. But this time, something isn't right. Skéisono can feel it before they're close enough to tell him—before he sees the way Father hobbles along with Mother's strong shoulder supporting him.

"Skéisono, get out of sight! Go!"

They've come closer now, and he can see the wide ribbon of redness soaking down Father's leg. What happened?

"Go!"

Father's loud bellow jolts the boy into action. He races back through the garden and rounds the corner of the house, nearly toppling over Marntrei— who catches him by the arm and tosses him toward the back door.

"Get inside."

Marntrei grips the largest of the shovels from the work shed in his other hand. Skéisono scarcely has a moment to find his balance before he notices the company: a pack of boys—looking mostly Skéisono's age and older—gathered beside the house. They stand with rocks and clubs and dirty fists at their sides. Some glowering, others showing off wicked grins. All staring at Skéisono. He's seen a few of their faces before, around Kasántos. But he's never known their names. One of the tallest among them raises his pointing finger abruptly in the air before him.

"There he is! The cursed one!"

It all happens so quickly. The mob of boys lunges forward like a pack of wild animals closing in for the slaughter. Skéisono flinches sharply sideways to avoid a stone that comes hurling at his face—then shuffles backward to clear the swing of a makeshift club that's flying at his stomach. His back claps hard into the wall of the house, and he reaches out instinctively to catch hold of his attacker's weapon, shoving it away.

"Hey!" The stranger scowls, winding up for another swing. But the motion's interrupted when the flat end of a shovel meets his unsuspecting forehead.

Now other boys leap over the stumbling figure of the first, one of them raising a rock-wielding hand high above Skéisono's head. Marntrei's shovel comes down from nowhere to pummel the enemy's knee, and a sharp cry rips into the air. The assailant doubles over, clutching his knee and unconsciously tripping two others at his back. Marntrei charges after them, landing the shovel with a merciless clap across both their heads. The fifth boy only narrowly ducks out of harm's way before turning to run.

"LEAVE MY BROTHER ALONE!" Marntrei roars.

The first attacker scrambles back to his feet and flees down the next hill with a hand to his bloodied forehead. The second rises and hobbles desperately behind, cursing loudly. Now the others are running for their lives, and Marntrei stomps after them, shouting and spitting and kicking dirt at their heels. Only one scoundrel remains—a tall boy who snatches a garden hoe from the corner of the work shed and rushes at Marntrei's back.

Skéisono leaps to trip him, shouting breathlessly to his brother, *"Behind you!"*

The dulled blade comes angling down as its wielder stumbles forward. Marntrei scarcely manages to raise an arm to shield his face from the incoming blow. The tool's shaft hits with a sickening snap on his arm, and he lets out a terrible shout. But the enemy has little time for another attack. He's still struggling to regain his footing when Marntrei's shovel knocks him clean over. Then Skéisono can hear the shouts of distant voices over the hills. More of them.

"To the woods! Go!" Marntrei cradles his arm as he turns to the northwest.

"But—Mother and Father—"

"They'll meet us there! Just go! Go!"

The two of them bolt for the start of the trees as though a fire were lapping at their heels, and Skéisono doesn't question. There's no time for questions. The townspeople have gotten angry before. Have yelled and accused—even forbidden Skéisono from entering their properties. And they've made awful threats. But their intimidations have always been empty, idle hissing. Until now.

The sun's already begun to set when they find Mother and Father at last. Father's lying with his right leg wrapped and propped gingerly in the fork of a young tree. Mother's using a canteen of water to rinse a bloodied rag, and when she looks up, her eyes are red but tearless.

"Thank the heavens!" She leaves little kisses on her boys' sweltering foreheads, then gasps at the sight of Marntrei's mangled arm. "*Iat veinin!* What in Claya— sit down! I'll find a splint. Skéisono, there's spare wrapping beside your father's foot."

Marntrei sits reluctantly down, raising his good arm to swipe pearls of sweat from his temples. "They've lost their minds, those idiots. They've gone absolutely insane."

Mother returns, frantically snapping the limbs from a short branch she's collected and comparing its length to her son's arm.

"What happened?" Skéisono asks as he hands the wrapping to Mother and moves to steady the splint.

"It's been a dry summer, son," she tells him without looking up from her work, without slowing the swift circular motion of her wrists. "Too dry for a good harvest. The neighbors are just getting desperate. They want something to blame. And your father was having trouble turning away, in the market."

Skéisono breathes, glancing from his mother's face to his brother's, then back again. "They think it's the curse, don't they?" He uses the word that Mother's always so careful to avoid. His parents have crept around it for years—all his childhood. But there's no reason to soften the reality now. Not anymore. For a moment, no one answers.

Father sits watching the distance with a stubborn straightness in his jaw, mumbling to no one. "Should've gone. Should've left as soon as we knew . . ."

"As soon as you knew what?" Skéisono rises to his feet, talking more loudly than he should. "Is the curse real? Am I some kind of demon?"

Mother shakes her head. "No, Skéisono." Her voice lowers. "People simply fear what they can't understand."

"They've *made* it real! Those—"

"*That's enough!*" Father's shout shocks the silence of the trees and startles more than a few birds overhead. Then he lets the air out of his lungs, and his voice falls back to its usual volume. "All of it, enough. Kasántos was the home of my grandfather, but it's no longer a home for us. We've got to leave it behind."

"Westward?" Marntrei chimes in.

He's always talking about going west to the capital to become a physician's apprentice, like Mother once was. He's been preparing for ages, training with

Mother as well as he can while still aiding Father with the smelting work. But it's difficult to practice a physician's skills in a town where he and his family are considered untouchable. The plan was to bid Mother and Father and Skéisono farewell and head west in several months' time. But that was before today. Before the teenage mob and the violence in the market.

"Anywhere but here." Father runs a weary hand through his hair and leaves it standing partly on end.

"We can head north for Berkerin for now, live near my sister." Mother looks up as she finishes the wrap on Marntrei's arm. And Skéisono wonders at the thought. The idea of leaving Kasántos comes like a fresh breath to his chest. One he's been waiting to take for years.

"We've got one lantern. We can return to the house tonight once everything's settled down and gather what we need. We'll leave behind everything we can spare." Father leans into the tree at his back, closing his eyes. "Never thought it would get like this."

Skéisono peers off through the trees to the northwest. "I'll go get my friend Vayeka. She knows how to help heal—"

"No, son." Mother takes his wrist before he can turn away. "It'll soon be dark. We've got to stay together for now."

Ordinarily, Skéisono might try to reason with her. But there's a sharp light in Mother's stare that somehow grips him by the heart. And so he nods, sitting down between the leaves at his brother's side and letting his chin fall onto his knees.

Marntrei leans into the tree at his back and moves his injured arm to his lap with a mild wince. "It's not your fault, Skéisono. None of this is."

Maybe he's right. But Skéisono can't seem to dispel the awful sourness in his stomach. The terrible feeling that he should've run away with the voránjevin clan and abandoned Kasántos long ago. *Years* ago. Either way, it's too late now. He sighs. There won't be any sleep tonight.

8

-Common Year 158-

The night sky is cloaked and blackened behind a veil of clouds when they come creeping back to the cottage by the light of a single lantern. They slip in through the back door like panicked thieves, fumbling for bags and shoulder packs, snatching breads and fruits and canteens for filling. Skéisono's racing to stuff spare clothes into a sack when a flicker of orange light catches his eye through the open southern windows. In the kitchen, Father pauses with a cup in his hand, staring wordlessly out into the night. He sees it too. Now he turns to catch his son in his gaze.

"Skéisono, we can't let them find you here. We'll take the path to your friend in the clearing. You go on ahead. We'll gather the supplies and follow behind."

"But that's them, isn't it? They're coming back—"

"There's no time, Skéisono! They're just coming to threaten us again. But they shouldn't see you. We'll be right behind you—now get out of sight!" Father's voice quavers as he struggles to force his shout into a whisper.

Mother rushes across the room to push a lantern into Skéisono's hands. "Be swift!"

She leaves a kiss at his cheek and rushes him out the back door, failing to hide the bitter tears that have begun to spring up in her eyes. The night closes its cool embrace on all sides as Skéisono steps out into the darkness. But it seems colder than usual. Stagnant. It brings an almost suffocating numbness to his breath, his hands, and his spinning mind.

Everyone will follow behind. They'll be right behind you.

He plays the thought like a simple melody across his mind as he steps into the trees. In darkness, the soft hues of the forest are left to glow with more brilliance than the daylight would ever permit. The colorful path to the clearing is easier to see at night. But it's still long. First straight west to a tall tree with a tannish-pink glow in its upper branches. Then northward to the sapling with the blue shimmer, and onward. All around, trees of every color sit like idle candles in the shadows. And the longer Skéisono walks among them, the more rapidly the night forest seems to meld into one blurred scene before his eyes. It's a path he could follow in his sleep. One he'll soon leave behind, along with all the troubles of Kasántos—including the curse.

Walking, creeping. He moves like a fugitive in the darkness, constantly glancing over his shoulder. He walks for ages, until he's more than halfway to the clearing—until the silence at his back begins to brew a sour sinking in his heart. He pauses near the base of the next tree and turns back to the southeast. Listening. Waiting. But the soft chittering of rodents in the leaves is the only sound. High overhead, even the winds have ceased their dance along the treetops, cloaking the night in unsettling silence.

They were supposed to be right behind him. They were supposed to be close. But the woods are empty. And young Skéisono stands entirely alone in the shadows. At first, he waits. Maybe he was simply moving too swiftly and got too far ahead. Maybe Father's bandaging needed replacing. Maybe they forgot something important. The possibilities float and clutter Skéisono's thoughts as he waits, and he fights desperately to believe them. *Any* of them. But the wrenching in his stomach has reached an almost nauseating intensity. He can't wait any longer. He must go back.

He begins slowly, retracing each step through the sleeping forest with eyes wide open. Searching, watching. All along his path, the silence of the woods persists. There's no one waiting in the leaves ahead. No swaying lantern lights. No one rushing to meet him in the shadows. No one. And in time, Skéisono begins to run.

The dawn has begun to paint shallow gray hues along the horizon when he reaches Kasántos at last. The smell of the smoke meets him first. A thick, bitter taste that chokes the air and stings his sleepless eyes. Then he sees it rising in dark plumes over the trees. It twists and ripples as it rises over the canopy, scattering feathery embers through the leaves. They must be burning thistles at the edge of the fields again. It's the wrong time of year for that—but Skéisono tries to forget, doing all he can to shrug off the tremor in his bones. The smoke is too black. Too near. And there's only one house on the hill ahead. A hilltop that was once his home.

The hill that's now cloaked in a raging curtain of flames.

Skéisono stops where the leaves still conceal him and stares up into the blaze—suddenly too numb to think, to feel anything at all. The flames billow up in brilliant amber clouds, curling and lapping over the eaves of the cabin and clawing wildly at the cold night air beyond. Skéisono stands motionless at the sight of it. Deep in the blaze, the cabin's front door hangs open like the gaping mouth of a dying beast, full of yellow-red and orange-white ribbons. A handful of men still saunter in slow circles at the edge of the burning chaos, stooping now and then to gather stones and hurl them into the blaze. And slumped on the blackened earth beside the front doorstep, the glowing outlines of two lifeless figures can be seen. A man and a woman. Human figures with flames wrapped and clinging like vibrant, flowing blankets over their motionless shapes. Then Skéisono's heart seems to seize up and fall from its place. The world begins to reel on every side.

Mother! Father!

He stumbles rigidly through the trees, searching aimlessly in every direction for any sign of them at all. Maybe the bodies aren't theirs. Maybe they escaped into the woods again. Maybe they ran another way. And what about Marntrei? Did the mob take him away? Skéisono calls out into the woods, voice hoarse and quaking. Calls for his brother, for the mother and father who were supposed to be right behind him all this time. But no one answers. No shouts, no waving hands. At his back, the hillside lets out a loud and merciless roar—the voice of collapsing roof beams and snapping timbers. The remains of the cabin hurtling down into ruin. Any hope that persisted in Skéisono's young heart comes crashing down along with it.

And so he runs. He turns to the cold darkness of the woods and runs the way he ran as a little child. Blindly, randomly. He runs until his lungs burn and his heart rises to a deafening thunder in his ears, forcing him to collapse at last at the forest's feet.

The curse! It couldn't be satisfied, could it? It couldn't possibly allow the boy in its grasp to escape without a toll. The curse has taken what it wanted before. And now, it's taken again.

* * *

He's sat in a blur for ages when the visitor arrives. It comes with a tide of silence in its wake, somehow hushing even the tempest in Skéisono's fevering young mind. It comes without footfall or rustling, without moving a single leaf in its path. A spirit. Or perhaps a living creature. When Skéisono looks up to see it floating effortlessly in the air before him, he isn't sure which it could possibly be. But he can feel the warmth that radiates from its presence—can see the white light that pours from every surface of its slender, limbless body and floods like shimmering waters between the trees. The creature is tall, like the rod of a powerful king, and its single eye drifts weightlessly within the open crescent shape of its head. Its gaze shifts and glints like a precious stone in the rising light. And when the being speaks, its words seem to resonate into the very core of Skéisono's bones. It calls him a child of gods—speaks of a call from the heavens, of fate and eternity. The words are ancient, and all the world seems to fall silent in reverence of the sound. They make no sense. But they wrap Skéisono's breaking heart in an overwhelming calm, like a sudden gap in the storm that's raged until now. And for the very first time in his young life, he knows where he belongs. Vayeka was right. He was never meant to belong in the world that made him an outcast. He was meant for something higher. Now someone—or some*thing*—has come to take him there.

It feels entirely natural. Instinctive. Without any thought at all, Skéisono reaches out his hand to the radiant creature that waits in the air before him. A blinding burst of light erupts where his fingertips meet its shining surface, flooding the scene and streaming like marvelous flames through every bone and vein and living thread of Skéisono's being. Surging, purifying. Then it fades as swiftly as it came, and Skéisono's left standing between the trees. Changed. The hunger and aching weariness that tormented him moments ago have vanished altogether, and the radiance of his visitor now flows out from his own presence, as if he stood cloaked in the rays of the setting sun. Somehow, he's reborn. Changed into something less mortal, less limited or vulnerable. Something stronger.

Someone more capable of vengeance.

9

It comes like thunder before the dawn. Sharp, sudden. It pulls her from the very deepest valley of dreams, from a place where the waking world is little more than an old and faded memory. It jolts like lightning through her mind—wrenching her abruptly awake. A vision. But more than a vision.

The dawn has yet to peer over the eastern slopes when Alarei sits sharply upright in her bed, awakened by the vivid image that comes mercilessly down upon her mind. The sight of a boy whose countenance glows like the face of the sun. A boy cloaked in fiery light, with eyes like shining embers. Then, like a wisp of dust in the rising breeze, the vision is gone. Vanished, leaving Alarei sitting breathless in the pre-morning shadow of her little room. Hopelessly awake.

10

-Common Year 158-

The flames are still raging over the blackened bones of the cabin when Skéisono returns to Kasántos.

He appears like an angel of light at the edge of the fields, gazing down at the miserable place that once held him captive. Its muddied streets, its cramped cottages. Its inhabitants that creep like vermin throughout every lane. Foul place. Home of a mindless mob. It was a prison to him once, not long ago—in a time that seems like another life to him now. A tortured memory. The cruel superstitions of Kasántos no longer have any power over him. But the ashes of the dead beside the cabin have yet to cool. The boy of the curse remembers every detail of this loathsome place—every detail of the men who stood watching the flames consume the bodies of his mother and father. He alone will remember.

There was a time when only the trees let him see their auras. Now their voices join those of the earth and winds and waters in an unending chorus at his ears. All living, all full of light. And they obey his voice. He calls to the stones first, bidding them rise. They leap and collide at his command, gaping open beneath Kasántos and swallowing up an entire neighborhood in their jaws. Others jut sharply skyward, tearing through every house and barn and shop in the central lane. Cries of terror crack the air in every direction. Screeching, wailing. But the boy who stands robed in terrible light at the edge of the fields doesn't flinch. Doesn't blink. He draws the rage from deep in his bones and sends it out in tumbling fire over all he sees, blanketing the ruined rooftops and scalding the fields until the earth glows red beneath them. He pours his wrath over the land until soot and ash return the rising day to night, and glowing embers drift like snow in the seething air—until every heart and every breath in Kasántos is stilled. And the boy who stands on the north hill—the lord of the flames— stands gasping and wild-eyed at the edge of the ruin. The ruin that he alone will remember.

11

They sit without blankets on the rough scalp of the Listening Hills, plucking wildflowers and letting the breeze carry the fragments away. The grass pokes easily through Alarei's thin dress, prickling her ankles and making them itch. But she doesn't mind. She leans back on open palms and watches the shaded silhouettes of birds against the sky.

The two of them came for the silence. To enjoy a little supper away from the crowds of the sanctuary. To the south, Lake Ivehlith has just fallen below the reach of the sun's sinking rays. It captures the image of the spotty clouds above and repaints the scene on its near-motionless face. To the west, the towering walls and colonnades of Clevyan rise above the trees like a silhouetted fortress, outlined sharply against the sunbaked shine of the Sand Sea beyond the edge of the cliffs.

"Do you think it's getting too late?" she asks the clouds.

"Never." Asei's voice rises from slightly down the hill, hidden behind a curtain of prairie grasses. He's probably lying on his back the way he always does, with his limbs sprawled out in all directions.

Alarei turns to peer at him through the blades, hardly able to glimpse his shadow. "Don't get too cozy over there. I might not bother to wake you up later."

"I wouldn't mind spending the night out here."

"I've heard that beasts roam these hills when the sun sets."

Asei's slender arm rises up out of the grass, holding a clenched fist in the air. "I could take 'em."

Alarei laughs and snatches a runaway hair out of her face, tucking it safely behind her ear. Beyond the cliffs, the sun is threatening to sink behind the desert mountains and set the horizon ablaze.

"I wonder"— Asei's voice strains against a yawn—"if the view from the north fields wouldn't be better?"

"Are you kidding?"

"It's clearer over there. No trees and such in the way, not like this." He waves his hand lazily at the scene.

"Well, *I* say it's amazing right here. The trees make it better, don't they?" Alarei gathers the little dishes that carried their supper and packs them gently back into the bag at her side.

Asei sits up to show her a calm smile, shreds of grass clinging to his hair and dark robes. "If you say so."

Even in the failing light, his eyes seem to cast back the full force of the sun. Shining like the eyes of some night-stalking creature. It's a wild light in his eyes—such bright, silvery eyes. They're no different than usual. But tonight, the boy's vibrant gaze seems to stick in Alarei's mind. It turns over and over in her memories, and the longer it churns, the more it dredges up the details of a memory she had buried away. Details from a night she's tried desperately to forget. She crosses her ankles in front of her and begins to smooth the creases from her skirt, wondering. Remembering.

They came like ravenous animals that night. With bright eyes. *Immense* eyes. Eyes like lanterns in the moonlight.

"Summer sunsets remind me of that night. The night my mother died." The words seem to slip out before Alarei can stop them.

"How old were you?" Asei's voice falls to a softer tone.

"Five years old." Alarei swallows down the tightness that forms in her throat. "We were visiting the beach just east of Jaker. We played in the sand. Built canals and little seas. It would've been a perfect evening."

"What happened?"

Alarei's never told him the details. Never told anyone at all. It's a night no one's ever asked about. But in all the world there's no one she's spent more time beside than Asei—and no one she can trust more. She draws the evening air deep into her chest, then lets it out in one long sigh.

"They attacked us as we walked home that night. Came like ghosts out of the trees." She watches the shrunken, shifting shadows of figures walking along one of Clevyan's distant southern balconies. "Some people call them *parafa*—beasts. Predators that live out in the wild. They walk upright and sometimes wear clothes, like people. But they're more like animals. I don't know why they came for us that night. They went for my brother first. My mother stopped them, charged at them—and my father moved to help. But it all happened so fast. I hardly saw them touch her. She collapsed to the ground and was gone before we could even realize what happened to us."

Asei has a look that's difficult to place when Alarei finds the courage to look back to him at last. His eyes carry an odd shine she's never seen, and his usual smile has melted into a tight line across his face.

"Does it still hurt?" he nearly whispers.

"Sometimes. But I was so young. More than anything, I wish I could just forget the way my mother looked when I ran over to her. It was . . . it was such an empty, lifeless stare."

The image has clung like frost at the center of Alarei's memories for ages. Never fading. It's a memory that's driven her to do everything she can to avoid attending the occasional burial ceremonies across Lake Ivehlith. Death itself can be unsettling enough. But the vacant gazes it leaves in its wake trigger a sting in Alarei's young heart that's almost impossible to define.

She shakes her head, hoping to move beyond the cold thoughts that momentarily held her mind captive. "You've never told me about your own family. Only that you aren't an orphan."

The words don't seem to reach Asei's ears. He's still sitting up, staring off toward the north. Probably drifting off in daydreams of his own.

"Asei?"

Alarei leans into his view. But the boy's gaze only briefly meets her own before darting off again.

"There's not really anything to tell you about," he murmurs.

"What do you mean?"

"Just trust me. You wouldn't want to hear about it. I . . . I'm sorry, about your mother."

Asei rises to his feet without warning and starts off toward the sanctuary, making a new path in the wildflowers that sway and dance at his passing. He leaves without a single word more, without any trace of the grins and teasing eyes that are always such reigning features of his face. As if the Asei Alarei's known for six years was suddenly torn away, leaving a silent stranger in his place. It's a hollow feeling, watching him walk away. An unsettling feeling—like the earth has shifted underfoot. Is he angry? Was it something she mentioned? Something she's forgotten? She's *got* to make him explain. But by the time the plume of questions settles down in Alarei's mind, she finds herself sitting entirely alone on the hillside.

For the first time in months, she walks alone to her room that night. There are some who find the stone halls of Clevyan too chilled for walking after sunset. Others say the sanctuary's corridors are far too eerie to traverse by moon and lantern light, when the shadows stretch long murals between the pillars, and the wind transforms the open stairwells into massive stone flutes. But Alarei's always found peace in the stillness of the empty halls and courtyards. The sort of peace that clears the mind and speaks rhythms to the heart. She's nearly reached the south wing when the echo of hurried footsteps comes hiccupping along the corridor, reflecting and resounding off the stone walls like ripples in a dark pool. Alarei pauses midstep to listen, then glances down the length of the hall she's just crossed. It's empty, occupied by only the shadows of the people who've crossed at the far end—shadows that sway and bob steadily over the polished floor as their owners hurry away toward the north wing. Elders in ceremonial gowns. Or night robes.

Where could they be going at this hour? Alarei wonders, and any drowsiness that may have been creeping in at the edges of her mind is suddenly pushed away. She glances to the south, to the flight of steps at the end of the hall that would lead to her quarters. Her bed isn't going anywhere. Tonight, she has time to be curious.

The little crowd heads northward along a mazelike path through the sanctuary. Through courtyards, past curving stairs and sweeping balconies. Alarei follows casually after them, rounding corners and climbing steps just beyond the reach of the lantern light. The way is long. But the elders traverse it in total silence. Even now, as they gather near the center of the Hall of Prayers in the north wing, none of them speak. Alarei slips in through the wide entrance at their backs and leans along the edge of the first towering pillar for a better view. It isn't difficult to identify the faces that have gathered. From her spying place, Alarei can easily spot the high priestess Kávukrei and her apprentices, along with each of the fifteen teachers of Clevyan and the librarian. Most stand in simple night robes. Some without shoes. Whatever this gathering is for, it's far from official.

Standing between the tall stems of two silvery-black candelabra, the high priestess looks over her audience. Her long graying braids rest like coiled serpents over her shoulders—loosed from their usual ties at her back.

"I welcomed a guest into my study this afternoon." She doesn't bother to whisper, and her voice seems amplified against the vastness of the hall. "A young man endowed with the gift of sight beyond time. A seer. His gift came to him very suddenly, five years ago—on a morning that I'm sure you all remember."

The elders exchange glances, some shuffling awkwardly on their feet. A seer? Alarei's heard of the seer who once lived at Clevyan, generations ago. A man who seemed to be the first and last of his kind. But now Kávukrei talks of another. Is it possible?

"It was five years ago when we gathered in this very hall for our morning meditations and felt a terrible shift in Claya's balance. We felt the earth mourn for the loss of many lives, and felt a burning presence on the face of Claya. The presence of a being full of power and rage." The high priestess brings her hands together, hiding them beneath the long sleeves of her robe. "We were aware of these things because of our diligent study of meditation and communion with the spirit of Claya. But the seer who visited me today has seen far more than the elders of Clevyan. I'm afraid he has confirmed our very worst suspicion."

The little circle of once silent elders now bursts into a mild commotion of gasps and exclamations and shaking heads.

"It can't be!"

"What can be done?"

One man raises his hand to silence his fellows before turning back to Kávukrei. "High Priestess, you mean to say that the presence we felt that morning was indeed a sasarian immortal?"

"Yes," Kávukrei answers without blinking. "He has turned to darkness. The records have warned us that this is possible."

"We're not prepared! The *world* is not prepared! He could—he might—"

The circle erupts again, and all the elders begin to chatter about fear, about the tales in the old records, about the safety of the people. But Alarei no longer hears them. Still kneeling behind a pillar, her mind seems snagged—captured by the words the high priestess spoke only moments ago.

A burning presence. Full of rage.

It was five years ago when an image more vivid than any dream woke her at the stillest hour of the morning. The nightmarish vision she's shared with no one—of a boy robed in flames, with eyes like the setting sun.

Sasarian immortal. It's a term Alarei's heard often since the day she first entered the vast halls of Clevyan. The name of human beings endowed with power from the goddess, whose voices the very elements obey. Undying beings who can cross the earth in a single breath, who can step beyond the barrier of death. They say it was a sasarian immortal who led the first families to these cliffs. And the library is filled with records of the glory of the immortals. Every child of the sanctuary is taught of the godlike beings who once protected the free will of all people. They're taught to reverence them. And it's said that all the wisdom of the elders of Clevyan came from the sasarianë. But the immortals have always been something mythical to Alarei. Something that exists in records and songs alone. Now the high priestess talks as though they still exist— as if the boy Alarei saw could be somehow related. But what does it all mean? And why did *Alarei* see it, of all people? Even after thirteen years at Clevyan, she's never once tried to clear her mind and meditate as the instructors have always urged her. And she's only ever pretended to sense the spirit of Claya.

Why me? she wonders, and the strangeness of it all brings a sudden aching to her mind. *Forget it.* It's late. Too late for heavy thinking. She pushes her thoughts aside and slips softly away into the night without looking back to the circle of elders in the Hall of Prayers.

* * *

The rain falls softly the next morning, blanketing the hills and filling the air with its cool breath. She stands at their meeting place in the grand west hall, her arms wrapped tightly in a knitted shawl. At her side, the philosopher's bust sits with a thin layer of morning dew collecting like sweat on its stony face. But it's a chilled morning. Almost too chilled.

"Who are you waiting for, Miss Alarei?" The man's voice comes unexpectedly. It belongs to one of the older priests.

Alarei tips forward to glance down the otherwise empty hall. Then, looking back to the inquirer, she attempts to smile. "Just for a friend."

"If you're still spending your days with that pale, silver-eyed boy, you'd best be careful," the man tells her, raising a single, furry eyebrow. "You know he's got an odd aura about him. A smart young lady like yourself would be even wiser to keep a distance from his type. Strange boy, that one."

His type? Alarei resists the urge to wrinkle her nose.

"He seems perfectly all right to me," she answers, and she watches as the old man saunters away around the corner, shaking his head in dismay.

Alarei sighs. Some of the elders are so opinionated. She bends to give the hall yet another peek in each direction. Where is he? Asei's never been late before. Most days, Alarei arrives to find him waiting, leaning against the stone columns with the usual smirk on his face. He would tease her for being slow, and they would head down the corridors together, joking, laughing, and planning their day like always. Most days, she *knows* him. She twists her arms in her shawl, willing them to hold in the warmth. He isn't coming. She can feel it. But she still gives the hall one final glance before slipping away. Just to be sure.

The shawl isn't enough. As she reaches the stone archway that opens into the orchards, she can feel the shivers bubbling up in her lungs and rolling along her spine. It's too cold for summer. The rain that falls over the orchard lands in a frigid mist over her shoulders. She pulls her arms tightly together and stomps through the wet grass, frowning as it clings to her calves and paints the hems of her skirts in dark, sopping blotches. Her shawl is already drenched. Ahead, the ancient trees of the orchard stand like shadowed giants in the mist. Alarei squints to see beyond the rain that clings to her eyelashes, scanning the outlines of the trees for any human shape, any motion beyond the stillness of the scene. Somehow, she knew to look for him here.

She finds him leaning against one of the largest trees, slouching and entirely soaked, staring off through the rain. His robe droops heavily over his slender shoulders, threatening to slip off and hang in a dripping clump from his belt. Alarei pauses just beyond the reach of the tree's vast canopy and wonders how soaked she might be before he notices her. Perhaps, with a little patience, she could wait there until nightfall. But the rain is picking up now, relentless and cold. And she's grown tired of waiting—waiting all morning.

"What's going on?" She nearly shouts to be heard above the pattering of the leaves.

When Asei turns his head at last, the rain is running like tears along his near-expressionless face. He must be freezing.

"Nothing." His voice is oddly tuned. Forced.

"Nothing? You just wanted to spend your day out here in the cold?"

"I should leave you out of this, Alarei. It really shouldn't concern you." He stares idly down at the mud at his feet.

"How can it not? Am I supposed to continue on as usual when my best friend goes silent and hides? Just *disappears*? Right after I tell him about losing my mother?"

She nearly begins to laugh. But Asei doesn't look at her. He's gazing off into the mist now, and Alarei can see the subtle shifting in his jaw, the tension in his dripping shoulders.

"They've gotten suspicious of me. I'm sure you know by now too," he mumbles just above the rising voice of the rain and dancing leaves.

"What are you talking about? What's happened?"

He steps away from the tree, turning to face her at last. "Is it really that difficult?"

"Asei, I have no idea what you want me to say right now." Alarei holds out her hands from her sides, out of words. And for a moment, the scene falls entirely mute beneath the onslaught of the rain. The two friends stand motionless, letting the rain spatter in their faces.

Then Asei turns in his place as if searching the trees for something he's forgotten, water flicking from the ends of his hair as he turns his head. "Isn't it obvious?"

The rain has risen to a torrent. A gray, thrumming curtain that hangs like an impassable barrier between the trees.

Alarei shakes her head. "No, it's n—"

"It's what I *am*, Alarei! Don't you see? It's what I am!" Asei's hands rise up to his temples. "The elders don't want me here! They don't trust my *kind*."

A smart young lady like yourself would be even wiser to keep a distance from his type.

His type. His kind. Alarei's shawl has slipped off her left shoulder, clumping in a wet pile at her elbow, but she scarcely notices. "What do you mean, your 'kind'?"

Asei stares back, bringing a hand to the back of his neck the way he always does when there's something waiting at his teeth that he'd rather not say. Now he comes stepping toward her through the grass, red hair darkened and clinging to the sides of his slender face.

"Do you really not know? After all the years you've known me?"

He pauses a single pace away, and Alarei stares back at him. Wondering. Asei's different. That's no mystery. His vibrant hair, his pale complexion, his uniquely silvery eyes, and the slight, unidentifiable accent that still lingers at the edges of his words are evidence enough. And he's undoubtedly the fastest runner Alarei's ever seen. But is that really so different? So different that the elders of Clevyan would want him sent away?

"Asei, you belong here as much as anyone else does. Why would anyone think otherwise?"

A mild grimace spreads along Asei's face. He runs a hand through his dripping hair and shakes the water off into the grass. "Because Clevyan was built as a haven for people who came from Tayd. *Human* people," he tells her, and he looks carefully into her eyes. "And I'm not human."

Not . . . human? Alarei blinks, momentarily unaware of the cold rain that trickles down her neck and between her shoulders. "What are you saying? Wh-what are you, then?"

The boy standing before her says nothing at all. He stares back with a face Alarei knows better than any other. A face that's been a part of every waking day of her life for years. A face more dear to her than any in the world—now tainted by a shadow she can no longer recognize. What could it possibly mean?

"You don't want to know." Asei's answer falls like a discarded leaf to the wet earth as he turns away. He takes several steps to the northeast before Alarei catches his wrist.

"Asei, listen to me. Whatever you are, it doesn't matter. Not to me. You don't need to tell me. Above all else, you're Asei. *My* Asei. Nothing changes that."

The smile he sends over his shoulder leaves a bitter flutter in Alarei's sinking heart. As if the warmth and splendor of the years they've spent together until now are somehow drifting away—fading, like the sun behind rain and clouds. Out of reach. What's happening?

Now Asei continues on his way without looking back, vanishing into the gray mist between the trees. And Alarei doesn't follow.

12

-Common Year 163-

The remains of the morning's dew run along the eaves of the shrine like minnows in a pond, pausing at the edges before darting off again along the damp wood. They catch the hanging ribbons and trickle swiftly to the swinging ends. A thick cylindrical bell hangs like a heart at the center of the shrine. Perfectly motionless. She could use the little mallet resting beside it to strike a resounding toll into the air—a sound that would echo far over the hills and into the distant city lanes. But she doesn't. It's a *tautsu* shrine—one of many found throughout Jaker and the cities surrounding it. The bells of the tautsu shrines are awakened in times of rejoicing, when the people wish to offer gratitude. They say the sound of the bells reaches up into the heavens, into the ears of the goddess herself. But watching the morning settle over the outskirts of the city, Alarei isn't certain what brought her to this one.

It was six weeks ago when the elders of Clevyan called her to the study of the high priestess. They rose to their feet when she came to the door that morning. High Priestess Kávukrei sat like an ancient queen at her carved stone desk at the center of the room. Her long braids were carefully looped and gathered in a bloom of silvery white at the back of her head. She alone remained seated.

"Miss Alarei, you seem to be recovering well, after last week's incident. I hope your walk here wasn't too exhausting." She spoke as if she understood. As if everything were simple.

Alarei gave only a slight bow in response, keeping with tradition. "Elders of the sanctuary, what may I do for you?"

The high priestess let a mild furrow appear in her already wrinkled brow. "Since the beginning of Clevyan, our people have anticipated the return of the sasarian immortals. We've always hoped that if the immortals returned, they would bring the same miracles and wonders as their predecessors—that as the keepers of Clevyan, we would greet them with joy and celebration, as our ancestors once did." She sat forward, leaning into the well-polished stone at her elbows. "But we can no longer hope for such things. Five years ago, a sasarian immortal appeared somewhere in Claya. We have reason to believe that this being was responsible for the deaths of many. But before we could learn anything more, his presence vanished entirely. None know where in Claya he has gone since. Now there's a tremor in the heart of the earth. We fear he may return. And that he will bring darkness with him."

Darkness, lives lost, and a powerful immortal. Alarei had heard it all scarcely a week before, in the shadowed Hall of Prayers. But this time, the strangeness of it clamors like dissonance in her ears. The children of Clevyan have always been taught that the sasarian immortals brought goodness into the world. They blessed the ancestors with new lands and protection from all kinds of threats and danger. How could this one, if he really did appear, bring death and terror? There was no time to ask before the high priestess rose from her seat.

"Alarei, since the day we first became aware of this new sasarian, we've gathered morning and night to listen to the earth. We've listened for any hint of his whereabouts, any clue to his intentions. But Claya has given us only one response. The immortal is tied to only one person in this world. You."

Alarei allowed herself to look politely confused. She stood for a moment in silence before raising a hand to point to her own stomach. "Me? But what does it mean?"

"The records tell us that the last immortals to visit Claya were born as mortal beings, but were changed to their angelic states sometime in the course of their lives. Is it possible that this sasarian was a member of your family, in his mortal life?"

The question revived an image that remained stained in Alarei's mind since the moment it appeared five years before. The sight of the boy cloaked in fire, who stood with the glory of a thousand sunsets shining from his countenance. The vision that still sparked like a living flame at the back of Alarei's thoughts, demanding significance through the years. But the boy in the flames was no one Alarei could name.

"No." She shook her head. "I didn't recognize him."

The elders exchanged glances, and Kávukrei's eyes grew suddenly round. "You mean to say you've actually *seen* the immortal?"

The elders were all listening in before, but now they leaned toward the young woman in their midst with eager ears and widening stares. Alarei found herself abruptly pressed beneath the full attention of every face in the study, and the hairs on her neck stood suddenly on end.

"I—I saw," she stammered, wondering if she even knew the answer herself. "I don't know for certain who it was. But I did see a boy in a dream, five years ago. He was like an angel . . . or a demon."

"And you didn't recognize him in any way? Did you see where he was?"

"No, no. All I saw were flames. Flames all around him."

The high priestess sank slowly back into her seat. "Claya has spoken well, then. You must have some connection, indeed, to the sasarian who has risen."

"But how could that be? What does it mean?" Alarei didn't care to wait any longer. Of all the people of Claya, only the elders of Clevyan could give her the explanations she lacked. Or so she hoped.

But Kávukrei only bowed her head. "I trust you will find the answer in time, young priestess. Only you can find it. This is why we have called you here today. You must leave the cliffs and these lands behind you."

"Leave Clevyan? For what reason?" Alarei made a desperate attempt to sound at ease. A miserable attempt.

The high priestess shook her head. "Your connection to the sasarian would ordinarily be something to celebrate. But it seems our days are not fated for the blessings our ancestors once enjoyed. We know little about this immortal. But we do know that he has already used his power to destroy. We know he carries great malice in his heart—enough to sicken the spirit of Claya itself. Your connection to him is a danger to our people." She sat forward again, framing Alarei in her weary gaze. "If you focus, I'm sure you'll be able to sense that connection. You can reach him, find him— maybe even persuade him to show kindness to the people of Claya, as his predecessors did. But if you remain here, and if the immortal comes for you, you'll endanger all who dwell at Clevyan. And besides, the past week has been especially troubling for you. You'll hear the earth's voice more clearly if you find a place that won't remind you of the worries you've experienced here."

Alarei looked down to the elaborately stitched rug at her toes, breathing deep. Troubles? Worries? Is that all they thought it was? The events of the past week left her world in ruin, knocked her free of everything that once seemed stable and secure in her life. Now they wanted to send her away from the only real home she had.

"But where should I go?" She struggled to keep her voice level.

"Long have you lived as an exemplary young priestess here in the cliff sanctuaries. Now you are free to follow the paths the earth has paved for you. Claya will guide you. Remember what you've learned in this sanctuary."

Alarei walked back to the south wing that day with questions pouring like fountains from her ears. The words of the high priestess repeated hopelessly in her thoughts, resounding with maddening exactness. And they only deepened the questions. The sasarianë were never more than old legends. Now, one had come to Claya—and was somehow connected to Alarei? But how? How could that possibly be? And what did it mean? No answers came to her as she had prepared to leave Clevyan that morning. Or as she made her way down the long, jagged path to the foot of the cliffs, where the Sand Sea gusted and danced in the evening light. She walked for days to reach the city at the desert oasis. Walked alone, at a time when she needed Asei more than ever before. If he were still with her—

The sound of a heavy shoulder pack dropping into the grass pulls Alarei sharply from her memories. It wrenches her back to the outskirts of Jaker, where the tautsu shrine is still losing the last dewdrops from its ribbons. A dark-haired man stands only several paces away when she looks up. A young man, with a jolden tunic more decorated by discolored patches of varnish and black tar than with the stripes it was sewn with. The mark of a shipbuilder.

"Alarei, is that you?" His voice has aged since she heard it last, nearly seven years ago. But it still carries the same swinging Tayd intonation Alarei's always remembered.

"Lorith! You've gotten so tall!"

"They say that's what happens to boys who eat the hearty fish of Emér." He steps closer, grinning shyly in a way that nearly transforms him into his father. *Alarei's* father. "Did you just arrive? How long will you be visiting Jaker this time?"

"They've kicked me out of Clevyan. I can stay as long as I like," she tells him.

"What? What'd you do?"

"It's a long story." Alarei kneels to lift her bag from where it leans against the shrine. "Is Father still living in Hadón?"

Lorith nods. "He tends to visit Jaker every few months."

Alarei raises an eyebrow at the thought. Ever since Mother died, Father couldn't bear to stay living in Jaker. That was when he sent his daughter away. He's always said in his letters that the place holds too many memories. Memories that tug at old wounds in his heart. But Mother's passing was over fourteen years ago, now. Maybe the memories are losing their sting.

"*Setait*—come on, you can stay with me as long as you need." Lorith snatches the bag off Alarei's shoulder to throw it over his own. "I've got a place in town. Can't let my little sister be homeless."

Lorith. Alarei's glad to find him. Somehow, finding her brother makes the earth feel a little steadier beneath her feet. More predictable. As if everything will somehow straighten out and make sense in the morning. Few things have felt stable in the past weeks. Now, Alarei only hopes for something to hold onto— something *real* that won't slip away in her sleep. Real like the sights and sounds in the streets of Jaker; like the warmth of the early autumn sun on her shoulders; like Lorith's hearty laugh.

The two of them do their best to fill in all the years they've missed as they walk into the narrow streets, talking of long winters and busy summers, of the endless road to Clevyan and the vast face of the Emér Sea.

Lorith's home is humble. A shrunken cabin wedged between a busy lane and an alleyway. But it's a place where Alarei can breathe—can look forward to sleeping without fear of road thieves or wild animals in the night. And for now, that's more than enough. She finds herself slumping down on the bench beside the fire well before sunset, watching the way its feathery limbs dance and flicker over the logs. The flames seem to send a gentle hush throughout the room, urging stillness and calm on all present. But even as the evening closes in, Alarei can't seem to still the subtle quake in her heart. Lorith settles down in a chair nearby, with a little cup of soup in his broad hands, and glances up.

"You all right?" The reflections of the flames play tiny scenes in his eyes.

Alarei nods. The past weeks have been full of questions. But one question has tugged and twisted in her heart more than any other—has robbed all her concentration by day and stolen her sleep by night. Where has Asei gone?

It all comes back to her at night—like a hopelessly recurring dream. But she's never sleeping when it comes. She lies awake for hours in the darkness as the scenes play relentlessly over again in her eyes. Scenes from her last days at Clevyan.

It was a gorgeous afternoon the day Asei left. It was little more than a week before the elders called her to the study of the high priestess. The sky was wide open. A bold, unashamed blue with only a few wisps of cloud lying low on its horizons. The Listening Hills were tinted almost yellow in the evening sun. The two of them sat in the golden light there for hours. Alarei was watching the sky and wondering if Asei would go with her on a hike to the lake. It was a good day's walk, and they both needed a break from the people of the sanctuary. A place where they could talk freely, where she could convince him to tell her everything that was bothering him. He'd been unbearably silent since the morning she found him in the orchard. Silent for too long. It was time to resolve things. Alarei had cleared her mind, ready to listen to anything he'd be willing to tell her—if he'd say anything at all.

But Asei's spot on the hillside was empty when she turned to see him. When did he move? Alarei glanced toward the sanctuary, then down toward the shores of Lake Ivehlith, and to the distant orchards. But there was no one. She was standing when she finally spotted him several hilltops away to the north. He was leaving. She could see it in the firmness of his steps, in the tightness of his shoulders. He wasn't coming back. He was leaving the cliffs the same way he once came, carrying nothing.

She was running after him before any plan could form in her mind. She ran without bothering to replace her sandals, without understanding the fear that was suddenly gripping her lungs and shortening her breaths.

"Wait! Asei! Where are you going?"

He took several steps more before glancing over his shoulder with a kind of resolution in his face that she couldn't recognize. "Go back, Alarei. It's time I leave Clevyan. You can't let them see you coming after me like this." He continued onward, each step falling mechanically to the ground, each beginning to feel like an irreversible motion.

She had nearly caught up to him. "Then let's leave *together*, like we've always talked about!"

Asei stopped at last to look back at her. "Alarei, you have a spectacular future ahead of you, and Clevyan is the very best place for you to stay until then. The elders should know how to help you better than anyone. But they won't let you live here much longer if I stay by your side. They'll evict you. Make you an outcast."

She caught up to him and reached out to take his hands in hers. "Why should it matter what anyone thinks of us?"

Asei's gaze sank momentarily down to the grass. "Because humans only trust humans." There was redness at the corners of his gray eyes when he looked up again. "You've told me it doesn't matter what I am, that you don't really need to know. But Alarei, when you truly realize what I am, I promise you won't want me around anymore either."

"Why don't you let me decide that for myself?" Alarei fought desperately to swallow the growing tremble in her voice as Asei leaned to leave a little kiss on her forehead.

"It's better for your future this way." He said it as he pulled his hands out of hers and turned away, about to continue northward.

Words like a winter wind on Alarei's heart. She blinked through the wet blur that was rising up in her vision. "Better? Asei, you mean more to me than anyone. How could I possibly be better off without you? Don't leave like this—please just tell me what I did to—"

"They're called the Iftav." His voice cut off her words without warning, and Alarei stared speechlessly after him, feeling stiff.

"What?"

"The creatures who killed your mother. They came from the clan of the Iftav. No other clan would do that." He was looking away as he spoke—was staring down the hillside to the rolling lands beyond.

"Clan? Y-you know about those creatures?" She didn't need to ask. The answer was obvious. It dropped like a hulking, merciless stone on Alarei's breaking heart, despite her very best efforts to bury it quickly away.

Asei gave a single nod. "They were once my family. I refused to become a murderer like the rest of them. But no matter how long I stay in this human form, I'll never be able to change the fact that I'm not human. I'm a voránjevin, a runaway from a ruthless clan. The elders of Clevyan can help you find your path in this world. But they would never accept you with someone like me by your side. Don't you see?"

He spoke, and the words nearly shook Alarei from her feet.

One of them? All this time, he was one of *them*? It can't be possible, but somehow it is. Only that morning, he was just Asei. The boy at the center of her world. The boy with the fiery hair and invincible grin. The boy with a knack for sneaking, who loved sweets and long hikes and midnight swims in the lake. The boy who was Alarei's very best friend—the one whose company felt like home. Only moments before, he was Alarei's Asei. Now, he stood before her as a stranger whose humanity was only as thick as his skin. But had he really changed? Had *anything* changed? At that instant, Alarei didn't have the time to wonder. But one fact was certain. She didn't need the world's acceptance.

"Asei—" She opened her mouth, about to tell him that none of it mattered, about to tell him that a life without him would be hopelessly incomplete—but Asei only shook his head, raising a hand to silence her as he turned away.

"No, don't say it. I'd rather leave before I have to hear you send me away." He started walking, and she followed at his heels.

"No, Asei, wait—"

The memory of the moment that followed has grown hazy, like a fading dream. But the throb it brings to Alarei's heart never dulls.

She reached out to grasp his arm, hoping to stop him, to pull him back and convince him to stay. And he *did* stop. But not for long. He turned sharply around and took Alarei into his strong arms—locked her in too tightly to move, to *breathe*. She scarcely had a chance to gasp before a shock traveled down her spine. A surge of static that rolled down her arms and back and left every muscle limp and aching. Drained. Her strength vanished. Her back slumped, her legs buckled, and her arms became wilted and useless at her sides. She was suddenly overwhelmed by such consuming fatigue that even the air seemed to weigh down like thick waters in her lungs. Then her heart shuddered, the world began to tilt and sway, and in the midst of it all she thought she heard his voice whisper.

"I'm so sorry, Alarei."

Then his hands lowered her gently, soundlessly down to the grass. And he was gone. She can still perfectly recall the way her tears painted cold streaks from her eyes to her ears, the way the grass prickled her arm where her sleeve was bunched at her elbow—and the way the varying hues of the sky seemed to brighten and blend more vibrantly toward the east. Asei was gone. And Alarei was left lying helpless in the grass, unable to crawl or move. Silent, confused, and afraid.

She could feel the footfalls coming before she heard them. Subtle, solid drumming in the earth. People from the sanctuary. They came running, shouting and calling after her. Alarei listened to the steady pounding of their feet on the earth as they came nearer, watching the sky through her watering eyes. Even now, over six weeks later, she can still hear their voices—speaking to her the way they did at her bedside the next morning.

"We suspected all along. We never should've let that creature enter our sanctuary!"

"I bet that beast would've dragged you away for his dinner if we hadn't come running!"

"He was one of *them*—those horrible creatures who change their shape to fool their prey."

"They hunt human beings in some places, you know. Savages!"

"It was only a matter of time before his true nature would emerge. We should've recognized it sooner, should've known . . ."

Eight days. Alarei lay recovering her strength for eight days. And every day the elders would visit to tell her again how terrible the shape-shifting creatures from the woods are, recounting what a shame it was that they didn't do more to get rid of Asei at the start. But to Alarei, their words were little more than an unending buzz at her ears. A buzzing that did little to distract her from the aching wound in her heart.

* * *

The house is bright when Alarei opens her eyes. The morning light falls pleasantly in through the southern window panes and paints pale cream-and-yellow squares along the floorboards before the fire. The room is empty. Alarei peers through the fireplace and into the cramped sleeping quarters on the other side. No one. Lorith must have gone out. The fire is small, with only a few smoldering bits lying in the hearth to keep it alive. Only a light sprinkling of sawdust rests in the little box where fresh tinder ought to be stacked. At Clevyan, a dying fire and empty kindling box would mean a walk to the wood-keep near the central courtyard. But this isn't the cliff sanctuary in eastern Ketsa. This is Jaker. And like any city in Tayd, the wood bearers deliver kindling to the alley troughs at first daylight.

Alarei rises wearily to her feet and shuffles to the back door, snatching her shawl from the back of a chair as she goes. The air that meets her at the edge of the alley is chilled. Crisp—and surprisingly clean. The scent of autumn *feithya* blossoms floats like a gentle perfume along the lane, drifting from the vines that climb along cabin walls and dangle playfully into the streets. It's a quiet morning. Away toward the south, the heart of the city can be heard waking. Creaking gates, bouncing handcarts, and the muffled shouts of shopkeepers to their assistants. But here, the city still sleeps. Alarei leans out from the stoop, hoping to peer farther down the vacant alley in either direction. But it curves and bends quickly out of view between the jagged bodies of the houses. Jaker is a labyrinth.

The kindling lies waiting in a trough beside the door. Alarei stacks two little logs into her arms and is reaching for a third when the sound of a single footfall breaks the stillness of the empty lane.

Suddenly, the alley isn't empty anymore.

Alarei nearly drops the stack in her arms when she catches sight of the creature that now waits there. A hairless, leathery-skinned beast sits hunched over in the center of the path only several paces away. Pale, and sickeningly thin. Its almost-featureless face hangs at the end of a neck as long as Alarei's arm—a blank mask with two sinking, shrunken black eyes. Horrible, beady black eyes, like little stones pressed into tortured clay. Like the eyes of a demon. The sight of the beast seems to freeze the blood in Alarei's veins. For an agonizing instant, she can't seem to move, can't seem to think at all—as if the repulsive creature before her eyes has somehow taken hold of her every nerve. Only her heart continues to race in its place, throbbing madly in her throat and threatening to burst in her ears. When she finds her feet at last and turns back into the cabin, she's helpless to stop a terrified cry from escaping her lips. She stumbles over the threshold and lets the kindling logs crash and tumble across the floorboards, whirling around to shove the door shut with enough force to send a tremor through the cabin walls. She's only just secured the lock and rushed to the far corner of the house when the front entrance swings abruptly open. Alarei grips the metal fire rod from the mantel and nearly sends it hurling at the shape in the doorway.

"You all right? I heard—ah!" Lorith flinches and ducks instinctively behind the door he's just entered through.

Alarei lets her weapon clatter to the floor at her feet. Lorith. It's just Lorith.

"What in demons' fires is going on?" Lorith glances in all directions before slipping in and closing the door at his back. "Did someone try to break in?"

"No, I just—I saw—it was—" Alarei's hands float up in front of her as she struggles for the right words—words that couldn't possibly describe the sight in the alley. "It was in the alley."

"What, a rodent?" Lorith steps across the room and reaches to unlatch the back door.

"No—*don't!*" Alarei nearly shouts, and Lorith pauses with his hand in midmotion, eyes wide.

"What is it, then?"

Alarei doesn't answer. She crosses the room on her toes and leans to peer soundlessly out through the weather-stained glass in the little window there. A window to the alley—to the very spot where the beast may still be hunched over and waiting.

But the back street beyond the window is empty.

Part 2

1

-350 years before the start of the Common Calendar of Glesia (513 years before Common Year 163)-

Rehda Mihinehn had served as the school's headmistress for nearly fifteen years. It was a position as admired as the gold-plated eaves of the schoolhouse she operated—which was the grandest, most prestigious school in all the Ten Regions. A school that only the most privileged families could afford for their children, while all others were regrettably forced to be satisfied with the amateur instruction of volunteer institutions. Unlike the government-established schools in the land, Mihinehn's Boarding School required lofty payment for its services. And with good reason. A greater education could be found nowhere else in all of East Ataran—or perhaps the world. Scholars from all nations came to teach within its broad lecture halls. Located near the heart of Tekéhldeth, the capital of the Ten Regions, it was encircled by all the richest aspects of East Ataran culture. From its windows, the students could count each of the eight towers that surrounded the city. From the eastern balcony they could watch the crowds roam beneath the glow of the great torches that rose like towering, golden trees along the Grand Way, or listen to the minstrels sing their sweet, solemn melodies beneath the blowing banners of the marketplaces. From the windows of the dining hall they could glimpse travelers entering at the city's celebrated southern gate—the same gate that was built by the kings of old and etched with the signatures of every leader since. And from the towering window of the school's north-side library, the students could gaze at the shining domes and twisted spires of the House of Voices, where the wisest and most powerful men and women from all the Ten Regions were elected to govern and represent the will of the people. Only the very best and brightest youth were permitted to enroll at Mihinehn's Boarding School. And only excellence was expected of each graduate who left its halls. Because, after all, to live in the City of Glimmering Lights, one must be accustomed to nothing short of excellence.

Rehda became the headmistress in place of her own father, whose family established the school in generations past. And in the course of her fifteen years in his stead, she had seen every kind of talent and wit that any child of the Ten Regions could possibly possess. Or so she supposed.

It was a cloudless night when the nanny of one of Tekéhldeth's wealthiest families brought a boy to the steps of the boarding school. The only son of the Sekýnteo family.

"Headmistress, ma'am." The young caretaker gave a courteous nod when the school's broad, rustic-red doors were opened to her. She was smiling in a way that seemed strained—almost forced. "Our apologies, calling on you at such an hour. The young sir was simply too zealous to wait until morning."

Rehda waived her hand calmly in response. "It's no trouble at all, my dear. If anything, I'm honored to welcome such a motivated new pupil into our classes."

She turned to the footmen in the lobby at her back. "Come now, take our new student's case to the fourth floor, the first year boys' quarters."

Then she brought her attention back to the boy who waited beside his nanny. He stood about as tall as any other ten-year-old, though he was dressed in the finest style of silk the Ten Regions could offer, with a matching embroidered coat and cross-shoulder sash that were clearly tailored to his exact size. His dark hair was combed and slicked flawlessly into place, as if it were painted there—the perfect frame for his slender face. He was as sharp-edged and clean-cut as any child of a wealthy family could possibly be. But it was his stare that Rehda would always remember most vividly. The boy stared with a piercing gaze—a solid, unnerving gaze. And he wore a hidden grin at his lips. Not the typical mischievous, boyhood grin the headmistress was accustomed to seeing in many of her young male students. But something different. As if the boy carried some sinister secret behind his well-mannered appearance.

"And what is your name, young pupil?" She made an effort to act as though it were all ordinary.

"Kyvóike Sekýnteo," he answered without breaking his stare, and Rehda couldn't help shifting in her shoes.

"Welcome to Mihinehn's school, Kyvóike. I know the Sekýnteos are a very accomplished family. Your mother and father each obtained their educations in these very halls, you know. If you're anywhere as clever as they are, I suspect you'll make a wonderful addition to our classes."

Young Kyvóike was quiet as Rehda led him to the fourth floor. He glanced only briefly at the priceless artwork on the walls and the masterfully carved banisters of the west staircase. When they reached the door to the quarters where the first-year boys were preparing for the night, Rehda stopped and put a hand on his shoulder.

"You and your classmates will room in this wing of the school for the first year of your studies. I'll introduce you. Don't worry about trying to get everyone to like you. Focus on your studies, and you'll find friendships in time."

"I'm not worried." The new student's secret grin came out from its hiding place. And for some reason, it sent a cold chill through Rehda's heart. "They'll all know me soon enough, when I've become king."

King? For a moment, Rehda wasn't sure how to respond. The boy must have been joking. She knelt down to get a better look at his face. "Oh, I see. Do you hope to serve as a representative in the House of Voices someday? A very respectable goal."

But the boy shook his head.

"Before the House of Voices, there were kings. My father carries the blood of the kings, and so do I. He says our line was robbed of their royalty. But I'll be king over all the Ten Regions someday. I know so."

"And how is that?"

"Because I've already seen it. In visions. I'll be king, and I'll control them all."

He spoke with unshaken certainty, and his stare was so sinister that Rehda found herself momentarily speechless, staring into the seemingly emotionless eyes of the child before her. In some bizarre, almost incomprehensible way, it was a terrifying moment. One she would retell many, many times in years to come. One that would haunt her until the very end of her days.

2

It's night on the hills. Dark. The earth seems so rough and cruel as she's dragged over it—pulled by one arm like a fresh kill through the tall grass. She struggles, kicking and clawing with the last of her breath, fighting to break free. But her attacker only turns and sends another startling jolt like fire through her spine, tearing all the strength from her body and shocking the breath in her lungs. She falls limp. Defenseless.

Overhead, the stars and twin moons flash sharply into view. Such gorgeous, silvery-white lights! They stick like gemstones in the dark face of the sky, entirely apart from the world below and its endless troubles. Untouched. In a way, the sight of them gives her peace. She should be afraid—*terrified* to know that her life may very well end before the dawn returns. But on all sides the world is suddenly so very calm. Even the wildflowers are motionless as she's dragged alongside them, their petals clinging delicately together in the moonlight. Mother's always loved the wildflowers.

Loved them enough to name her eldest daughter after the rarest kind. *Hamara.* A good name. She smiles. It was a short life. But at least it's been a good life. A very good life.

The attacker pauses now, chattering in an odd language to his companion as he turns to lift Hamara from the grass. He tosses her like a rug over his shoulder in one smooth heave and knocks out what little breath remained in the girl's aching lungs. And the world turns to blackness.

* * *

The air has lost its chill. And the light that peers through the leaves overhead is mercilessly bright. It must be morning. But then, maybe it's always morning in the realm of spirits. Hamara lies watching the gentle sway of the treetops as the wind passes through them, wondering what sort of place she's come to. Wondering what happens next—until she tries to move, and a thousand sensations come cascading into her nerves.

All at once, the dull pounding in her head, the raw sting at her calves where the grass and earth must have worn through her fitted trousers, and the startling heaviness in her breath—all aside from the horrible throbbing in her chest—become overwhelmingly obvious. It's an aching, choking sensation, as if her heart beats far too slowly. But it *does* beat. Somehow, she's still alive.

"Why'd you let your guard down?" The voice is calm. A man's voice.

Hamara struggles to bring the air into her chest. "I thought . . . they were human."

"You're certainly not the first to think that."

Is he one of them? Hamara fights to quell the little trembling that sprouts in her stomach and makes an effort to turn her head. There's a stiffness in her spine that brings water to her eyes as she bends through it, hoping to catch a better glimpse of the stranger who speaks from somewhere nearby. But only a handful of trees and a rigid wall of rock fall into view. It's likely one of the many low, stony plateaus that dot the Igretho plains. Perhaps one not far from home. How far did they take her?

"It's unfortunate, really, the way their clan treats your people. They were even willing to break a covenant to come murdering in these lands. They say the humans deserve it." The man seems to rise to his feet, and Hamara can hear the dry earth shifting beneath his steps. "Makes me sick, to be honest. But most of us aren't that way, you know."

He *is* one of them. Hamara struggles to move as his footsteps come closing in. She fights with all the strength that remains in her dying body, and by some miracle manages to flop over onto her stomach. She props herself up on one elbow, arms quaking uncontrollably, desperately hoping to crawl away. To do *anything* at all.

But now the man—the stranger, the creature— speaks again. This time, from directly behind. "I'm glad to be what I am. At least it means I can help people like you."

Hamara throws her fist over her shoulder, aiming for the voice. But the stranger catches her arm mid-swing. Before she can scream or struggle or react at all, she's pulled backward into a complete embrace. A strong arm holds her tightly across the shoulders, and a hand lies over her throbbing heart. Another appears at the back of her neck, palm to her skin. The sudden warmth and relief that surges out from where they lie melts every tension in Hamara's bones. All at once the pain is erased from her aching, shuddering heart. Her lungs open with newfound ease, and a jolt of life returns to the limbs that were useless only an instant ago.

Then the stranger backs away as abruptly as he came, letting Hamara stumble forward onto her knees. "Seems like they drained you pretty badly. I'm actually a little surprised that you endured this long. They must've dragged you half the night before I caught up."

Hamara takes a moment to breathe, testing the strength in her back and looking herself over. Aside from a few little tears and grass stains below her knees, her clothes are entirely unchanged. And her stinging calves are the only visible injury. But how could that be? A moment ago, she was certain her heart was circling death—that every fiber of her body was failing. How could there be no injuries to show for it?

She looks up to see a bright-haired man sitting among the boulders at the base of the plateau, several paces away. But he isn't a man, is he? His oddly gray eyes give him away, if the strange wrap he wears over his shoulder doesn't do that already. They were wearing dark wraps over their left shoulders as well when they attacked—the ones who dragged Hamara like a captured stag over the hills. But this creature seems different. For some reason, this one has somehow brought her back from death's doorstep. With only the touch of his hands.

"I . . . don't understand." Hamara blinks.

The stranger nods in response, as if he had expected her confusion all along. "The strength I just gave your heart won't last long. You'll need to regain it naturally, with food and rest. Y'know what I mean?"

Hamara tries to stand, but her knees quaver awkwardly beneath her weight.

"Take your time. Your balance will come back in a while. Oh, and before I leave—" The bright-eyed man lifts a sheathed weapon from the stones beside him and lays it gingerly in the grass at Hamara's feet. "I saw them rip this from your belt."

It's her *sénsin* rod. The weapon her father's trained her to use from the time she was old enough to write her name. The weapon that should've prevented all this.

"Thank you." Hamara reaches unconsciously for the sénsin, momentarily dazzled to know that it wasn't lost. Then she looks up. "Wait, who are y—"

Her voice leaps off the empty stone face of the plateau, bouncing back to her ears alone. Whoever he was, the stranger's gone.

3

-Common Year 178-

The chalked calendar on the slate beside the wash basin has never looked so disheveled. Nearly half of the ordinarily neatly drawn and numbered days are marred by the slashes Hamara's drawn through them at the end of each evening. The marks she's left for the past eleven days. Today, she doesn't bother to mark the twelfth. Today—nearly two weeks since the night her life nearly ended—she finally has the strength to stay on her feet.

She has yet to explain her escape to anyone, simply because the right opportunity never seemed to arise. Mother, Father, her sister—*everyone* was so overjoyed to discover her stumbling toward the northern boundaries of the city the morning after the attack. The relief and excitement seemed to override all else. She was found. She was *alive*. The details just didn't seem to matter. And in a way, Hamara's glad. Her memory of her bright-eyed rescuer seems to lose a little more clarity with every waking morning. Now, twelve days later, she almost wonders if it was real at all.

But one detail is certain. The attack *did* happen. And it's taken ages for Hamara to recover.

The strangers were wandering like lost foreigners at the edge of town when they came. It isn't uncommon for travelers to stop in the riverside city of Remertrei on their way southwest to the capital, or on their way north to the inland sea and the nation of Tayd beyond. But these two were light-skinned, unlike the earthen-toned people of Igretho. They wore clothing Hamara had never seen, and they spoke with an accent so thick that she found herself stepping closer to make sense of their poorly constructed questions and gesturing hands. One of them reached to touch her shoulder—or so she thought. He clapped a hand to her back instead. And for some incomprehensible reason, her spine seemed to melt. Her legs turned limp and buckled beneath her before she could so much as gasp, and the attackers were dragging her halfway across the next hill before her father's shouts could be heard following from the edge of town.

Mother says Father ran after them for hours. Ran with a lantern in one hand and a dagger in the other—with his sénsin rod clipped to his belt at his lower back. A handful of men from Remertrei trailed close behind. All searching, all racing. But the strangers who took Hamara were fast. Unbelievably fast. And when they slipped into the trees, they left no trace. The men were still out searching when Hamara came wandering home the following morning.

Hamara sighs, stacking the afternoon dishes on the dining table. It was good fortune that her little sister Elein was inside when the attackers came. If she had seen it all, months would have had to pass before anyone could convince her to step outside after sunset again.

In truth, hardly anything so exciting has happened in Remertrei for as long as Hamara can remember. It sits enveloped in fields of gold and amber grain at the fork of the second and third branches of the Nakuë River, which many call the life-vein of Igretho. But despite being the last significant stop along the oft-traveled northward road to the Emér Sea, it's a decidedly quiet town.

Mother was the first in the family to come to Remertrei. She was only a child when she came with her father, a silk tradesman from an ocean-side city in the west. Father came from the south nearly twenty years ago. He was nineteen years old, filled with grand plans to explore every branch of the Nakuë and the inland sea beyond. Remertrei was only a supply stop along his path. But he met Mother in the town's main market that year. And he never left.

It was Father who sparked Hamara's interest in traditional sénsin defense. Originally used by soldiers in the far northern nation of Sketza, the sénsin rods are crafted from the wood of the *chikáton*—"stone" trees of the northern plains known for their strong and dangerously acidic wood. The sap produced deep in their branches is powerful—enough so to burn through clothes, skin, and almost anything else it might happen to touch on a human body. Unless carefully maintained and regularly re-lacquered, even the metal sheaths of the sénsin rods become hopelessly corroded after bearing the burning weapons for only several years. As a young girl, Hamara was once foolish enough to momentarily snatch an unsheathed sénsin at its middle, rather than at the metal-banded handle or ringed tip. Nearly three months passed before the burns began to fade in her palm. It was a mistake she never intends to repeat.

Some say the sénsin rods are too difficult and dangerous to be bothered with. But to Hamara, few things have ever looked so powerful or graceful as the smooth, practiced dance of a skilled sénsin bearer in motion. Father took up his training during his first years in Remertrei, and he's been Hamara's teacher from the year she turned eight years old. Now, at nineteen, Hamara can give her instructor a fair fight. And until recently, she had no reason to doubt her abilities. Until recently, practicing sénsin defense was just an interesting pastime.

Nearly falling victim to murderous attackers was nothing short of terrifying. But more than anything, the experience was revealing. Disappointing. How could someone trained in a form of self-defense be so easily knocked to the ground and dragged helplessly away? It's a thought that's tormented Hamara for nearly twelve days now. But no one else seemed to question it. Not even Father.

"You had no way to know. And it happened so fast. There's nothing you could've done differently." He's always assuring her, and he's always so certain.

It's true that Hamara never knew that the creatures from the northern woods could somehow mimic the appearance of human beings. Neither did anyone in Remertrei—after all, the humanlike beasts are a rare subject around the cities of Igretho. But Hamara can't seem to shake the hot embarrassment from her face when anyone asks what happened that evening. She could've done more to fight. Getting caught off guard was no excuse for her failure to defend herself. But at the very least, the failure was a valuable lesson. Next time, Hamara will know what to expect. She'll know to watch for the pale complexions, the odd-colored eyes, the strange clothing, and the thick, slanting accent. Next time she'll be prepared.

* * *

The fruit trees near the back of the house are always ready for harvest not long after the first frost falls and stays through the morning, at a time when the air is persistently cool, yet the sun's warm midday rays seem to fool the land into prolonging autumn. Hamara never tires of the sweet scent of *kifara* fruit. And it's fortunate. This year, the summer was kind. It's taken several weeks to clear the trees' sagging branches of their heavy loads and pile the fruit into crates for the market in town. Mother and Father planted the trees ages ago, when their house was completed—hoping to sell fruit when their sometimes hectic lives as volunteer doctors gave them a chance. The efforts have paid off nearly every year. This year will be no exception. Hamara's taken over the majority of the work herself for several seasons now, hoping to expand the humble garden into an orchard in the years to come—maybe even moving into a home of her own when the funds permit.

Today, only a few baskets' worth of kifara remain to be harvested. Hamara uses the rickety old stepstool from the garden shed to reach the last fruits that dangle from the highest branches, smiling mildly at the sweet perfume that still rises up through the vacant leaves below. It's the same scent the trees carried when she was a tiny girl. The signature scent of autumn in Remertrei.

The sun has begun to retreat to the west now, skipping its rays over the hills and shining into Hamara's eyes as she kneels to lift the last half-filled crate at her feet. It makes her squint, and it turns the man sitting on the nearby hill into a blackened silhouette. Hamara turns and takes several steps toward the shed before her thoughts seem to hiccup back to the figure on the hill.

Is someone sitting on the hill?

She turns to give the slope a second glance. But the tall grass there ripples and sways in an uninterrupted dance, following the slow rhythm of the wind. Empty. Did she only imagine it? She stands watching the scene for a moment longer, wondering. Waiting—as if the silhouette might randomly reappear.

"Hamara!"

Mother. Her voice is raised, anxious. Hamara lets the crate drop from her hands and sprints to the back corner of the house, peering toward the road.

Mother's running back from town. "There's been an accident!" She slows her pace as she reaches the edge of the property. "I've got to grab a few rolls of wrap bandaging—go and fetch clean water!" She disappears into the house without another word.

Hamara sighs. Who's hurt this time? She dashes to the pump at the north side of the house. The water's only beginning to flow into the little water cart she tosses beneath the spout when Mother can be seen running back toward town, clutching a pile of bandaging in her arms. Hamara gives the pump twelve good heaves, not waiting for the flow to stop entirely before clapping the lid onto the water cart and hauling it to the road.

A small crowd of people has gathered when she reaches her mother's side several blocks into town. They stand in a loose circle outside the only leather shop in Remertrei. Some kneeling, some standing. Children dodge to peek curiously between the waiting figures. At the center of them all, a man roughly

Father's age sits wincing on the ground with his left leg stretched out over the dirt. The bloodied gashes running along the side of his knee and calf send an unpleasant shiver over Hamara's skin. It's Mr. Ha'Mesavo, the leatherworker. The remains of shattered roofing tiles are strewn all around him, and overhead, the shop roof has a wound of its own—a gaping hole in its tiles that reveals the aged framework beneath. He must have been trying to mend it.

Mother takes the water and pours it slowly over Mr. Ha'Mesavo's torn leg, dabbing the dust and dirt gently away with a pale washing cloth. Now she takes a violet-green paste from a little jar in her belt and paints a thin layer over the bruising skin. "Do we have the splint?"

"Right here. I've reset the bone as well as we can, for now. But I'll need to make a trip to Tagrei for more *dehalu* gel, for the swelling."

Hamara recognizes her father's voice and moves to spot him between gathering shoulders. They're out of dehalu? While she hasn't taken much interest in her parents' medical expertise, she's at least gathered a few useful facts over the years. For soothing an open wound and reducing excessive swelling, no herb works nearly as well as dehalu.

"We don't have any in storage?" Mother gasps as she wraps the wounded man's leg against a splint in two layers of bandaging.

"Not since the shipment ran short last month." Father shakes his head, then turns to Mr. Ha'Mesavo. "We'll need a few days to get back with the right herb. Fortunately, the last bit we had was enough to cover your leg for now. That should help you get through until we return. Now let's get you onto a couch."

"Thanks, Doctor. Guess I made a real mess of myself." Mr. Ha'Mesavo makes an attempt to smile as Father helps him rise on one foot and hobble into the shop. His leg must be agonizing.

Mother takes Hamara's arm. "I'll go with your father to Tagrei. Stay here with Elein, all right? Don't go *anywhere*. And keep your sénsin on hand. We don't know if any more of those terrible assailants might still be lurking around."

Hamara nods. "We'll be fine."

Mother and Father stop by the house only long enough to gather what they need for their trip. Shawls, money, dried provisions, and a large bag for filling with medicinal herbs. Elein doesn't come peeking out from behind the dining table until after they've shut the door behind them.

Hamara eyes the tall stack of plates near her sister's face. "Weren't you supposed to be washing those? It's your turn today."

"I was just about to! And anyway, where are they going? To Tagrei?" She leans to peer carefully at the scene beyond the window, perhaps catching a final glimpse of her parents as they disappear down the street.

"They're off to get dehalu gel. Mr. Ha'Mesavo fell from the roof of the shop and broke his leg."

Elein raises her eyebrows and wrinkles her nose, but doesn't ask for details. She's always been the squeamish type. "So, it's just us for a while?" She's still watching the window, as if expecting Mother and Father to suddenly return.

"Yep." Hamara shuffles to the pantry, wondering if anything appetizing may have appeared there since morning.

Elein brandishes the half-dressed doll that was hidden at her back and settles down at the table, carefully stitching together the sleeve of a tiny, traditional *kopachue* dress. "Well, I'm glad you didn't go with them. A man was hanging around here when you ran into town, you know. He stood under the tree across the road and stared at the house. He didn't go away until he heard you coming back. It was making me nervous." She doesn't look up from her needlework.

Hamara turns around, glancing out the window herself. "He was probably just another traveler looking for lodging."

Elein shakes her head. "I don't think so—he didn't look like a traveler."

"I'm sure it's nothing to worry about." Hamara turns back to the pantry and snatches a jar of salted gourd seeds from the shelf. "I'll scare him off with my sénsin if he comes back, OK?" She does her best to sound aloof and undaunted. Elein is barely twelve years old, and far too easy to spook. When Hamara was younger and crueler, it was a fact that gave her a good deal of entertainment. But these days, things are different. These days, even Hamara sleeps with her sénsin a little closer.

They eat beside the fire that night, and Hamara waits until her sister has climbed into the loft and fallen silent before double checking the locks on the doors. Everything's secure, but the recurring thought of a strange man stalking near the house can't seem to leave her mind. She lies awake for hours, watching the subtle lines and shadows of the night outside her window, listening to every sound. The creatures who attacked her are still out there, somewhere. What if they come again?

* * *

The air is chilled when the dawn peers through the edges of the curtains the next morning. Hamara crawls hazily out of her blankets and fumbles down the ladder to the main floor, blinking the blur from her eyes. She stokes the fire and dresses in the shadow of its warmth, slipping into fitted gardening pants and her comfiest old blue jolden wrap tunic—the one with ties to hold the front and back folds together, rather than buttons. Buttons are always such a bother. She smirks as she ties her very best hard-backed *hebana* belt at her waist. She's worn it for years. Worn it enough that the leather stretched over the thick backing is rubbed shining-smooth. The front tie has been replaced four times over the years. Mother's been telling her to throw it out for ages, to wear something cleaner and nicer. But new belts are always so stiff and unforgiving. No new belt can compare.

Up in the loft, Elein has yet to stir. Hamara resists the urge to slam and clatter the kitchen cabinets as she rummages for a clean cup. How does that kid sleep so well, anyway? It must have been past midnight when sleep graced Hamara's mind at last. And when it came, it brought dreams so loud and unruly that she's almost certain she didn't sleep at all. It was an exhausting night. One that only a walk in the morning's chill breath can help her shake.

She pauses by the front door to pull a knitted jacket over her shoulders, eyeing the sénsin rod that rests in its usual daytime place beside the window. After a moment, she snatches it down. It's better to be careful.

She was planning to take the usual route. A quiet stroll down Eighth Street and into town, then through the sleeping marketplace and along the riverside docks. But as Hamara steps out into the young morning, pulling the door shut behind her, a better plan arises in her mind. A walk on the hills would be far more relaxing. She rounds the northwest corner of the house, clipping her sheathed sénsin to the eyelets at the back of her belt. And when she looks up, she nearly collides with the stranger that stands in her path. Her heart practically leaps out of her throat. Then she shuffles backward with a breathless curse at her lips, drawing her weapon in one smooth motion.

"Not so human anymore, are we?" The stranger gives a little grimace. His pale gray eyes seem to highlight the whiteness of his subtly sharp-angled teeth and magnify the brightness of his fiery hair. Hair that hangs in short, red-amber waves around his pale face. It's a face Hamara's seen just once before, after a night she's hoped to forget. A deceivingly human face.

"What are you doing here? What do you want from us?" Hamara finds her voice at last.

The creature shows her his empty palms in response. "Maybe nothing."

He shrugs, and Hamara becomes mildly aware of the dark violet wrap lying over his left shoulder. The clothes, the strange eyes, the bright hair. . . . It *has* to be him—the one who rescued her from death. Maybe he isn't exactly like the creatures that attacked that night. But he's still one of them. A stranger lurking too close.

"Don't worry, don't worry. I can wait. We can talk next time." He turns to the northeast and starts off toward the hills, waving over his shoulder as if he were leaving an old friend.

Hamara looks wordlessly on from where she stands. She watches until he vanishes over the first hill, feeling relieved and hopelessly lost all at once. Next time?

Her breath doesn't seem to ease up until she's slipped back into the house and locked the door.

"What's wrong? You look ruffled." Elein peers over the edge of the loft with her feet wagging like tails in the air behind her head.

"What? Oh—I was just out walking." Hamara wanders idly to the fire and pokes the coals, trying to remember how she ordinarily acts, when nothing's amiss—when the hairs on her neck aren't standing on end. She glances impulsively out the back window. There's no one standing beside the fruit trees out back, and the hillside beyond remains vacant as always. For now. But that stalker can't be far. She lets out her breath. Elein can't know. Today needs to be as ordinary as possible.

The two of them spend the morning preparing the ripened kifara fruit for selling—trimming, washing, and packing them carefully into the handcart. Father's usually the one to help heave it into town. Without him, the delivery takes all afternoon. The sisters divide the load and deliver it to the market in two exhausting trips. Hamara pulls with all her weight while Elein pushes feebly—if at all— from behind. Fortunately, the road into town is flat. And the sight of them hauling the fruit by themselves paints a look of ridiculous shock on the market keeper's face.

"I'm fairly certain you only pushed for the last half of the way that time." Hamara gives her sister a sideways glare as she tugs the empty handcart from the market stalls.

"You didn't really need my help anyway." Elein shrugs, as though it were out of her control.

Hamara allows herself to laugh, and for an instant—a lovely, fleeting instant—she nearly forgets about the bright-eyed stranger from the start of the day. Almost.

The afternoon winds fade softly to silence as the evening falls. By the time the twin moons have set their glow in the low east, the air is perfectly stilled. Hamara lies awake, listening through her window for hours. Waiting. Wondering.

Is he out there, haunting the hills? The gray-eyed stranger may have saved her from the edge of death, not long ago. But Hamara knows nothing about him. Can he be trusted at all? And why is he still creeping around Remertrei? Maybe he only saved Hamara from the others so that he could hunt her and Elein himself. Maybe it's all part of some twisted plan. Whatever the answers may be, as long as the stalker's nearby, Hamara won't be able to rest.

The twin moons are high in the cloudless sky, lighting the hills with a soft, silvery shine as Hamara steps out into the night. No need for a lantern. She tightens her grip on the sénsin at her side. She has yet to clip it to her belt. But it doesn't matter. This will just be a quick look. A swift check through the trees and over the surrounding hills. She just needs to be sure.

The front road and surrounding grounds are empty when Hamara searches them. Aside from the uneven rustling of a night breeze over the trees, the scene's entirely silent. And the open lands to the south and north are no different. Then she turns toward the east. The brightness of the night stars catches her eye as she rounds the back corner of the house. Bright, glimmering points of light in an azure-black face. The sight sends a cold shudder through her veins. It wasn't long ago when she was staring desperately up at those same stars—envying their distance from the earth as she was dragged ruthlessly over it. It wasn't long ago at all. But this time she's prepared, isn't she?

Isn't she?

Maybe it's foolish to come out looking for trouble. Maybe she's walking to her death. After all, what chance could she have against a being who can somehow end or save a life with a single touch? But she has to do *something*. This might be daring. But it's what Mother and Father would do. They wouldn't cower in the house, hoping the danger scampers away on its own. They'd come out and chase it away. They'd show it who to fear.

The sharp hillside beyond the kifara trees is the final checkpoint. From there she'll be able to give the entire property one last search. The climb is tiresome. She bends with her nose nearly brushing the tips of the grass, reaching occasionally forward to brace against the slope. But she resists the urge to let herself plop down in the dirt when she reaches the crest at last. Rest can come later. She turns instead to scan the land in all directions. The heart of Remertrei lies to the northwest, calmly lit by a speckling of lantern lights in the streets. Farmers' fields blanket the city's borders on nearly every side—with the exception of the sparse woods and wild, rolling hills to the northeast. And at the foot of the hill, the house remains quiet as ever. No motion in the shadows, no figures stalking in the night. The hills are empty, as they should be. And now, even the wind has gone to sleep. Hamara stands watching it all, feeling the tightness ease out of her shoulders, letting the night cool the fever in her mind. Nothing out here. Nothing to fear.

"The stars are so bright tonight. More so than usual, don't you think?"

The man's voice is soft, but it lands with a terrible jolt in Hamara's unsuspecting ears. She spins in place and spots a familiar figure lying in the grass only several paces away. A pale-faced, strangely dressed figure. It's him. He lies lazily with his hands behind his vibrant head of hair, watching the eastern skies. How could she possibly miss him there? Hamara brings both hands to her weapon, ready to draw it from its metal sheath. But she doesn't. Not yet.

"I suppose you were planning to scare me out of town." The stalker watches the night sky for a moment longer before sitting up to look at her over his shoulder. His grey eyes seem to catch the dim light and throw it back in odd, highlighted flashes of color. Like the eyes of an animal.

"A-Are you stealing people away? Like those others who took me?"

The laughter that erupts from the stranger's throat at that moment nearly startles Hamara off her feet. Loud, genuine laughter. It's not unlike the cackle of the market keeper's husband, when Father tells him the latest jokes floating through town. But smoother.

"*Me?* If I wanted to kill you and take you home for dinner, don't you think I would've done it by now? Kid, regardless of what I am, you've got to realize: I'm not like those murderers. I dissented from that clan ages ago." He waves a hand at the trees, as if the killers hiding somewhere beyond them are entirely old news.

What's going on? A moment ago, Hamara almost thought she knew. She was searching for the stalker who was most certainly a threat to everyone in town. But now . . . now . . .

"Who *are* you?" She had hoped to ask in a more eloquent way—with words that were somehow braver or bolder. But the question flops out of her teeth without warning. And she's suddenly too exhausted to care.

The person sitting in the grass lets out a long, dramatized sigh. "Y'know kid, sometimes I ask myself the same question."

4

-Common Year 178-

High Priestess Kávukrei is lighting the evening candles and narrowing the curtains when a younger priest enters her study. In truth, he's old enough to have grandchildren of his own. But these days, nearly every other soul that roams the halls of Clevyan is young in the eyes of the priestess. The man stands patiently with his hands linked behind his back, not making a sound as his elder moves to stand behind a somewhat cluttered desk. Evening is settling in. It's a time when the families of the sanctuary often gather for little meals in the last hours of the day. A time rarely reserved for councils to meet. Kávukrei glances up at the visitor before reaching to organize the shuffled books and papers in front of her.

"Are you troubled, Talenus?" she asks without pausing.

"Have you not sensed it?" He's a little more disheveled than a leader of his rank ought to be. He must not be sleeping well.

Kávukrei looks up. "You refer to the ongoing imbalance in Claya, caused by the awakened sasarian?"

"We've been blind, High Priestess."

"Oh? How so?" The old woman raises a single eyebrow as she settles back into her ancient, carved chair.

Talenus steps closer. "Fifteen years ago, we sent a young priestess away. Alarei Yu'Ramal. Because she seemed to have some kind of connection to the immortal who had awoken to darkness."

"Yes. We hoped that she would learn to understand that connection and use it to persuade the sasarian against bringing death and destruction into the world. And we've not heard from either of them since. Even the earth tells us little more of them today than it did fifteen years ago," Kávukrei answers, stacking several journals into a drawer. "But for now, it at least means that the world can carry on in peace."

Talenus shakes his head. "The earth has told us more all along. We've only been too naive to see it," he says, and suddenly there's an unstable quaver in his voice. "The more I meditate, the clearer the reality becomes. And I can't keep it to myself any longer."

Kávukrei sets down all the papers in her hands and gives the man before her desk her full attention. Talenus has served as a teacher of histories in the north wing for nearly twelve years now, and has never been quick to heed baseless worries and superstitions. Perhaps something truly is amiss.

"Miss Alarei *did* have a connection to the sasarian. But not because he was any friend or blood relation. She came from Tayd, in North Emér. We all know the immortal appeared somewhere far to the south. Likely in Igretho." The man brings his hands together at his belt.

"And so?"

"The earth directed us to Alarei because she is a second sasarian immortal."

Kávukrei's mind momentarily blanks at the thought. Could it be so? But how could all the elders of Clevyan fail to recognize such an impactful reality? The people of the sanctuary have studied the records of the sasarian immortals for generations. Wouldn't they know if one lived among them?

She eyes Talenus more closely. "The records tell us that the sasarianë do appear in male-female pairs, and that they seem to be born as mortal individuals. But we also know that even before their transformation into immortal beings, the sasarianë of ages past carried unique abilities—such as a stronger ability to hear the voices of the earth, wind, and trees. Miss Alarei never mentioned or exhibited any such gifts, in all her days at Clevyan. You truly suspect she is one of them?"

Talenus gives a slow, heavy nod. "She *must* be. She likely never knew it herself. We sent her away unprotected. If she were to assume her immortal state, she would be the only existing threat to her sasarian brother. But as far as I can sense in my meditations, she has yet to awaken to her potential."

Kávukrei gazes down at the marbled stone surface of her desk. If Alarei truly is a second sasarian, her counterpart would most likely know it from the start. And if he has chosen to bring death and darkness into the world, getting rid of her sooner than later would certainly be wise on his part. He wouldn't hesitate to rid the world of the only individual capable of interrupting him.

"You fear that we've put a future sasarian in danger?"

"It was a grave mistake on our part. He may've already taken her life. Unless we were focused and listening closely to the earth at that moment, perhaps we'd never sense it." Talenus's words nearly fall to a whisper.

The high priestess takes a moment to close her weary eyes, letting the reality settle like dust over her mind. How could the keepers of the sanctuary make such a foolish error? Such a glaring, far-reaching mistake? It's a failure that could cost them—cost the *world*—very dearly. And the thought stings. If the second sasarian is killed before she can rise to her potential, who will remain to oppose the reign of her potentially ruthless counterpart?

The high priestess shakes her head. "I'll gather the counsel. We need to meditate and search for Alarei together. Perhaps there's still hope."

5

-Common Year 178-

"I have a question." Hamara sits on an overturned basin beside the smallest of the kifara trees, peeling the thick husks from the vegetables stacked in the bowl beside her.

Iro throws a handful of husks into the pile that's growing between them, glancing up. "And that is?"

"The two who attacked me wore dark wraps over their shoulders. But the one you wear is a different color. Does it mean something?"

Iro lets out a sound that's somewhere between a laugh and a scoff. "They're mostly used for carrying daily supplies," he tells her, and he pats the violet wrap that lies loosely over his left shoulder. "But aside from that it's a custom that goes way back. The voránjevin people come from ten different clans. Some wear emblems or colors to show it. Members of the Iftav clan made the dark sashes their symbol generations ago. I've never stayed with any one clan for long. But lately I live among the Taufeth. They gave me this one years ago."

"And you said your people don't actually look like humans? In their natural form, I mean?"

"That's right."

"What do you really look like, then?"

Iro looks momentarily up at her with a smirk on his fair face. "Small, thin. Covered in fur. Big eyes and flat ears. I'm sure you'll see for yourself, eventually. No use trying to describe it more than that."

"And you . . . transformed somehow, to look the way you do now. Right?" Hamara tries to imagine what such an event could possibly involve, doing her best to think of something that isn't horrifyingly grotesque.

"It's called *ek'let'eh*—the changing process. We trigger it by channeling energy through certain points in our bodies."

Hamara frowns at the nearly bared vegetable in her hands. "I can't believe I haven't heard more about your kind, all these years. Most people around here think you're some kind of animal predators that only live in the north."

"Well, most clans prefer to live among trees where the stags and boars and rodents roam. Open plains like this are no good for our hunting style." Iro shifts his shoulders, and Hamara can hear a subtle pop in the joints there.

She tosses her veggie into the bowl and reaches for another. "OK, one last question. You mentioned before that you've stayed in this human form for years. Wouldn't you be more comfortable in your original shape?"

At first, Iro doesn't answer. His gray stare floats down to his moving hands. "Maybe in some ways." He shrugs. "I guess this shape just feels natural to me, after all this time."

Iro. Four days have passed since the night Hamara found him stargazing on the back hill. He's come to visit several times since, never shying away from questions. And Hamara's had many. He's shown her how he can channel the strength in his body at will—even pull strength from the bodies of others, if he chooses. He says it's how his people hunt. The voránjevin people. With a single touch they can tear energy from the vital organs of their prey. He says it's how Hamara was knocked so easily off her feet—and nearly killed—the night she was attacked. She was only saved when Iro shared his own strength, directly into her dying heart.

Iro tosses another vegetable into the bowl before looking up again. "Well, what about you? Your family lived in this town for long?"

"My whole life," Hamara answers as she wedges her thumb beneath another peel, prying upward. "But I'm all right with that. We have a good home here. Better than my parents ever had."

Iro opens his mouth as if he's about to ask something more, but Elein's shrill call interrupts him.

"Hamara! The water's boiling! Mother says you need to bring in at least six!" she calls from the corner of the house, watching Iro carefully.

"All right, we'll be right in," Hamara calls back as she snatches the heavy bowl at her feet. She takes several steps toward the house before looking back to catch Iro creeping toward the hills in the opposite direction.

"And where are *you* going?"

Iro nearly stumbles as he glances up. Caught. "Well, kid, I, uh—it's just—" He glances around, running a hand through his sunset hair.

Hamara laughs. "It's all right. It won't be weird. My family's grateful to you. I told them you saved my life that night."

The voránjevin man comes shuffling stiffly back to the house, wearing a toothy grimace on his face that almost makes Hamara snort. And he lowers his voice. "Your family *does* eat more than just vegetables, right?"

* * *

Another two days have passed when Iro appears again. Hamara finds him sitting on a rock just over the crest of the back hill as the sun sinks in the west. It's a spot where the house and nearly all of Remertrei are hidden from view, and the plains and plateaus stretch out like a crumpled canvas into the horizon. Hamara pauses a few feet away, enjoying the view that never seems to grow old.

Iro's the first to speak. "Hamara, you're a good kid. I need to be honest with you." He tips his head to peer at her through the corner of his eye. "It isn't random that you've run into me here."

Hamara shifts her weight. "What do you mean?"

"I was coming to Remertrei with a purpose the night you were attacked. I came to find the family that carries the name Kajon'Mihana."

"The Ka'Mihanas? My family?"

Iro pulls his knees up onto the rock and pivots to watch Hamara directly. "Has your father ever told you where he's from? Before he came here, I mean?"

Hamara blinks. "He's from the south, by the mountains."

"Not Berkerin, I imagine. That's too far to the east. Am I right?"

Hamara shrugs and settles down in the grass, leaning back and letting the dirt prickle her palms. "I guess."

"Did his family live alone—like farmers?"

"No, no, it was a village. A small one, I think. What's so important about that?" Hamara looks up, and Iro stares back with a wild shine in his silvery eyes that ruins any human façade he might be wearing.

"A tiny village to the south. Do you remember the name of it?"

Hamara bites her lip, tipping her chin in thought. "I'm honestly not sure he's ever mentioned it."

"You don't know the name of the place? Anyone in your family gone and visited there?"

Hamara shakes her head. "No. I guess that might be a little odd. But why do you care about it, anyway?"

Iro's stare remains unbroken. "Hamara, do you know of *any* Igretho town further south than Berkerin?"

"Well—" Hamara tries to spout an answer, but her mind falls shamefully blank. "Well, not directly south. No, I guess not. But why—"

"That's because it's not there anymore. It's gone now."

"What?"

Iro glances out over the plains. "You know, with my people, news travels. We've got scouts and messengers in every nation of this Glesian continent. If even one or two of us witness some event, the word will spread from coast to coast before three days have passed." He lowers his voice. "Listen. About twenty years ago, there was a human village by the southern mountains—tiny, a few days' travel from the farthest branch of the Nakuë, for my people. I don't know a lot, but I *do* know that Kajon—your father's family name—was a name in that village. An unfortunate name."

Hamara leans closer, staring back. "What do you mean, 'unfortunate'?"

Iro glances fleetingly to the house before looking back. "People believed the family was cursed—that one of their sons was cursed, specifically."

"And that village is gone now?"

"The place is a blackened crevice now. Destroyed."

"A fire?"

"More than a fire. It's like the earth was torn open and slammed together again. And to this day, nothing grows where the ashes fell."

Hamara folds her arms. "Are you making this up?" It sounds like something from the myths the old carpet weaver in town loves to tell the children who visit her shop.

But the grim expression on Iro's face doesn't crack. "Look, kid, until now we figured no one survived from that little village. But your family carries the name Kajon. I came to Remertrei to look into it."

"Why?"

Iro slides off the rock and raises his arms in a long stretch. "For my own reasons. I can tell you more after you've talked to your father. I'm guessing he knows more about it than he's ever told you."

6

-Common Year 178-

The city lets off a soft glow, reflecting across the shores of Emér and joining with the image of the stars upon the water's surface. Alarei stands at the edge of the woods, wishing she'd worn a thicker jacket. The autumn's nearing its end, and the evening breeze seems to carry a fresh chill from the north. She turns and heads westward into the trees, stepping slowly.

It's her first glimpse of Jaker in over fifteen years. The city has grown. It spreads like speckled moss over the land, with docks crowding the north shore, and shops and houses springing up where once only empty forest groves could be found. Lorith still lives somewhere in its midst, in a little house he built years ago for his wife and three daughters. Or so his last letter described. Someday soon, Alarei will see it herself. But not today.

In fifteen years, Alarei's traversed nearly every seaside town and riverside city in Tayd. She's spent years exploring the far northern cities of Sketza, and even returned to the sun-scalded settlements in the desert lands of Ketsa, at the edge of the Sand Sea. She's searched everywhere she could imagine and asked anyone who would listen. But in fifteen years, she's come no closer to finding him—the only person she seemed to belong beside. The only person who could distract her from the inexplicably persistent hole in her heart. The one person she wanted to give all the joy in the world—even if he wasn't human.

The day she lost Asei was long ago. But his last words to her have yet to fade. Voránjevin. He told her what he is that day. And she's spent countless years since learning everything she can about his kind. The keepers of the woods. The people of the forests. The wild folk. In most Glesian countries, the voránjevin clans are a topic seldom discussed and rarely understood. The nation of Tayd is no exception. Despite having peaceful trade relations with a number of the clans in North Emér, the Tayds are quick to mistrust their neighbors. After all, the clans are considered to be little more than intelligent predators. And like any animals, they can be unpredictable. Dangerous. Or so many believe. Maybe Alarei should've continued to believe the same. But she couldn't—not after Asei.

She first laid eyes on true voránjevin faces at the outskirts of Nakurei, the capital city of Tayd. It was scarcely a month after she left Jaker, when the memories of her final weeks at Clevyan were still achingly fresh in her mind. She wandered with wide eyes through the city streets. Wandered until she nearly walked into the back of a man with a petition clipped to his belt and a colorful banner over his shoulder. An activist, advocating greater trade and friendship with the clans. He didn't hesitate to direct Alarei to the nearest trade post at the far western border of the city when she asked where to find the people of the woods.

"Straight through to the start of the trees. Impossible to get lost," he told her.

Nearly an entire morning of walking brought her to the place, well beyond the lively commotion of the city. The post stood at the very end of the twenty-second lane of the textile district, where the paved road gave way to weed-mottled dirt, and the ancient trees of North Emér replaced the three-story textile warehouses of Nakurei. It was a rough-built barn occupied by only a handful of merchants who strolled between tables of goods. And at the southern door, there were three voránjevin *filíl*—women—leaving furs and woven goods at the post in exchange for metal clasps and utensils. They were tiny—no taller than children eight years of age—and were covered entirely in short fur that varied in color from one filíl to the next. They wore short blue and violet and scarlet dresses with pale wraps across their shoulders. And the wide, flat ears that hung down the sides of their heads were almost as distracting as the massive eyes in their furred faces.

Alarei approached them like a timid child. She could almost feel the weight of their unblinking stares when they turned to see her. Only the filíl with golden-brown fur could speak Moi-Sketzan, the primary language of Tayd and Igretho. The one dressed in scarlet, with eyes that matched the yellow-gray hues in her wrap. She was kind, and gave a little bow before saying anything at all. And her eyes seemed to glow when Alarei mentioned that she was in search of a voránjevin friend. But when she heard the name of Asei's childhood clan, she only shook her head.

"I am sorry. We do not speak with that clan."

Alarei spent nearly ten months in Nakurei that year, working as a record keeper in the city's hulking library. The crowded streets, the voices, the music—all were so contrary to the quiet life she had known at Clevyan. But the change was somehow exciting, *liberating*. There were days when the noise of the city nearly masked the emptiness in her heart. But in time, it wasn't enough.

It was a kind of dream that led her back to Jaker at last. It came to her mind at the stillest moments— often during the deepest hour of the night or in the stillness of the early morning, when the dawn had only just begun to peer in golden slivers over the rooftops. The image of a forest grove. It came as a persistent daydream, and began to fill any open space in her thoughts. It trickled like rainwater between every motion of her day, hovering at the front of her mind despite her efforts to focus on anything else. Sometimes, the grove in the dream was empty. Other times, it was overflowing with marvelous white light. But it never truly left her mind. The vision persisted for weeks. In time, Alarei could no longer hope to ignore it. And so she followed it to the woods west of Jaker. Somewhere in the heart of the trees there, the grove awaits. The grove from the visions. Somehow, Alarei knows it.

For fifteen years she's searched for a friend she once lost. But now it seems as though her search began long before the day she met Asei. It's a search for something that was always missing—something that couldn't be found at the capital, or the cities of Sketza far to the north. She couldn't find it in Jaker as a child, or anywhere along the dusty road to the east, or in the marble corridors of the sanctuary at the end of that road. Now, she'll find it at last.

She steps westward through the trees without any plan at all, watching the cloudless evening sky as it slides between the reaching fingers of the trees. She walks for hours. Maybe more. There's no telling what hour the night has come to when the trees open at last into a little grove before Alarei's face. The grove from the vision.

Or was it a memory?

As she steps into the gap of the trees, she's suddenly no longer certain. It's a place she's never visited before, and yet every detail of the moment seems arranged exactly as she would expect it, as if she's walked this path countless times over.

The grove is nearly swallowed up in the white light that streams from its center. The source of the light is a creature more peculiar than any found in the mortal realms of Claya. But it doesn't frighten her. It's a creature she once saw nearly every day, in the aging stone murals of Clevyan. The Farian, a timeless guardian of the sasarian immortals. Its body is tall and slender. Limbless, and shining like the scepter of the goddess herself. Its single eye floats within the open curve of its head like a pearl tucked into the arc of a crescent moon. Now that Alarei stands in its presence, it seems as familiar to her as the face of an old friend— as if she once walked beside it throughout a lifetime long forgotten.

"Child of gods, the time has come." The Farian speaks with words from long ago, words Alarei has always known. Words from eternity. "The duty to which you are called, the calling of those in the heavens, lies before you. To protect the free will of the children, to stand as a messenger before them, and to present the fate of Claya at the footstool of the goddess. That it and all its realms may become whole and eternal. Do you accept this call?"

Alarei stands motionless at the edge of the grove. And for the first time since she left Nakurei, she smiles. She remembers now. This is it, isn't it? This was the missing factor all along—the reality she's hoped so desperately to remember, the hole in her heart that was impossible to fill. For so many years the elders of Clevyan taught her of the sasarian immortals, claiming to be the keepers of all the knowledge the world has of the immortals and their nature. But it seems they failed to recognize a sasarian of their own day—even when she lived in their very halls. Alarei was born to be immortal. The longer she watches the white glare of the Farian's presence, the clearer her memory becomes. How had she forgotten? There was a time, long before the world was born, when the plan was laid out. A time when Alarei made promises that only now can be fulfilled.

"I accept." Alarei's answer flows with perfect serenity, as if she's waited all her days to utter it.

"Reach out your hand."

The Farian floats effortlessly over the grasses to meet Alarei's outstretched hand. A blaze of light erupts from its edges at the touch of her fingertips, pouring through her veins and flooding her mind like unquenchable flames. Blinding, consuming, *purifying* whiteness. It gusts in a merciless torrent over her frame, and when it fades at last, Alarei's no longer the same. The evening chill has lost its sting. The mild fatigue that lingered in her bones from several nights of poor sleep is lifted instantly away. And the grove is lit with new light—the pure light that streams from her very own presence.

"Rise, sasarian daughter. This Farian is thy servant. It will uphold you in all things."

At some point, Alarei had sunken to her knees. Now she returns to her feet, watching as her long, glimmering robes fall into place at all sides.

And that's when she hears it. The sound that all the elders of Clevyan have dreamed of hearing. It comes as an overpowering orchestra to her newly opened ears, chiming and thrumming and ringing from every corner of the world. The songs of every living soul in Claya. Songs of rejoicing, songs of sorrow, songs of anguish and longing, songs of love—Alarei hears them all. The weight of it nearly returns her to her knees. Such a vast world! So full of lives! And ringing above them all, the sound of a heart more precious to her than any other. The heart of someone she's longed dearly to find.

But can she go to him?

"Wh-Where do I begin?" For a moment, she nearly lacks the breath to ask the guardian at her side.

"Come. This servant will guide you. You must come to master the abilities bestowed upon you." The Farian's single eye seems to pivot in place.

Alarei nods. But now a new presence becomes suddenly obvious at the edge of the trees. Two hearts beating wildly to a tune that differs from that of the human souls in distant Jaker. They're crouched low in the grass just within the shade of the leaves when she turns to see them. Two of them. Voránjevin males. They stare back at her with eyes as round as the greater moon in the night sky above. They bow their heads in reverence. Or perhaps fear. They're hunters, or scouts—clad in only waistcloths—whose dark fur and vibrant eyes ensure they could never be mistaken for human beings. And yet, there's an undeniably familiar light within their souls. Long ago, maybe they were . . .

"Come, you must learn." The Farian's whisper pulls Alarei softly from her thoughts.

"Yes. Let's go."

7

She waited for months—waited all winter. She let the question idle in her mind for ages, never entirely certain why the thought of voicing it left such an unpleasant twinge in her heart. Maybe she was afraid of the answers. Afraid that her father might turn out to be someone entirely different than the man she knows and trusts. Maybe those risks are real. Even so, she can't delay any longer. Today, the perfect opportunity has finally risen.

"Father, what was the name of that little village you were born in?" she asks him as they rake fertilizer into little circles around the bases of the kifara trees.

Father pauses fleetingly with his rake in mid-stroke. Then he returns suddenly to motion, clearing his throat. "Have I never told you?"

"No, actually."

"What brings that up all of a sudden?" He finishes the circle on the first tree and moves to the second. Hamara moves to the third.

"Just wondering. A while back, Iro told me about a village down south where a family had the name Kajon, just like us. He said . . . he said the village is gone now."

Father looks up, and the shadows around his weary eyes seem suddenly darkened. "Havetsu'Kajon. That was my family's name. We lived in Kasántos."

Hamara tries to keep him going. "Was that *your* family, in that village?"

Father lets out air, raising a hand to scratch a most-likely pretend itch at the back of his head. He glances to the road before nodding to the house. "Why don't we go inside?"

Mother took Elein to the market, and the house feels oddly vacant in their absence. Father makes his way to the dining table and settles down in the farthest seat, reaching for the cup he used at breakfast. It's still nearly halfway full. He takes a sip, then leans forward on his elbows the way he often does during family discussions. And his hands make fists beneath his chin.

"Hamara, I should've told you about this years ago. I'm sorry. I just—I just didn't want to trouble my little girls with the things I've seen. But you're a grown woman now. You deserve to know."

Hamara stares wordlessly back at him, unsure how to react.

Father sighs. "Years and years ago, I had a family—just like ours here. I had a mother, a father, and a younger brother. And my brother, he . . . he wasn't like the rest of us." Father sits back in his chair and folds his thick arms. "He was born with completely black eyes. People thought it was some kind of omen. The blackness faded eventually, but it was too late. One of the midwives must've whispered to the people in Kasántos, and soon enough everyone knew. They all called it a curse. Said it was some ancient curse that once plagued our ancestors."

"Wait, so you were *persecuted*?" Hamara leans closer.

"You could call it that." Father frowns at the tabletop. "By the time my brother was about fourteen years old, things got pretty bad. We made plans to move away."

"And that was the end of it?"

"I wish it was." Father's gaze flicks up to meet his daughter's, and for an instant—a terrifying instant—Hamara can hardly recognize him. "As long as I live, the memories of that day will never leave me. I was just about your age. One night, a mob came and overtook us. My father—your grandfather, Kóron—he tried to talk to them. He fell when someone knocked his head with a rod. My mother did everything she could to stop them. So did I. But I saw her fall lifeless to the ground before I could fight my way to her side. Just like that they were gone. Both of them. Then I . . . then I ran for my own life." His voice wavers, and he pauses to stabilize it, swallowing hard. Fresh redness paints the edges of his eyes.

Hamara's mouth falls unconsciously open. From the time of her very earliest memories, Father has always been proud. The kind of man who fears nothing and questions everything. A man who never seems to tire of his demanding profession, who's only satisfied at the end of the day if his arms and legs are aching from exertion. But who is *this* man? Never in all her days has Hamara seen her father so broken. So humbled. And it steals the breath from her chest. "Did—did they kill your little brother, too?"

Father shakes his head. "We sent him ahead of us, before the mob arrived. Sent him to hide in the woods. I spent ages looking for him. That day, after everything, I crept back to the remains of our father's work shed. I was looking for any supplies that could help us trek to Berkerin. That's when I saw him."

"Your brother?"

"It *looked* like him." Father's words fall to a whisper as he leans over the table. "I have no idea what I really saw that day. He stood in the air like a ghost, covered in flames. But the fires didn't harm him. They *obeyed* him. He wore the fire like a coat. And when he raised his hand in the air, the earth cracked open. It knocked me to my feet so hard that I tumbled head over heels down the hill and nearly broke my arm a second time. Nearly all of the town fell into the crevice—houses, shops, gardens, barns, people—it swallowed them whole. Then the entire place was suddenly engulfed in flames. I was on the very edge. I wouldn't have survived if the quake didn't knock me down the hill."

"Did he see you?"

"Don't think so. He was gone before I could think to look again. Vanished."

Father might have said more, but a shout comes echoing in from outside the open windows. It's Mother, returned from the market.

"Marntrei! Mr. Dre'Samor is looking for you! He needs another medicine packet prepared for his daughter's cough!"

"I'm on it!" Father answers, and his voice snaps abruptly back to its usual tone. He rises to his feet and throws open a cupboard of herbs without another word.

At the table, Hamara still sits in astounded silence. Iro was right. All this time, Iro was right.

8

-Common Year 179-

Her feet touch down without a sound on the cold stone, and the light of her presence lays a brilliant white shimmer over the balcony's columns and handrails. It's a balcony Alarei's visited several times before, when the teachers of Clevyan brought all the young children to gaze at the western stars. Those days are such a faraway memory to her now. Like the memories of a lifetime long laid to rest. How could she have ever imagined then—ever *wildly* imagined—what she is now? They say that even as children, the sasarianë of ages past were endowed with gifts. That they could hear the earth speaking or could see spirits roaming the realms. But Alarei was always as ordinary as any child could be. So ordinary that even the elders of Clevyan never knew what she truly was. Only her vision of the boy in flames served as a clue. Now, more than twenty years later, the vision glows again like windblown embers in her mind. She needs to find him—the sasarian who turned to darkness.

"The goddess! Look, the goddess!" A young voice erupts in the corridor.

Alarei peers through the balcony's archway and into the wide marble hall beyond, where mounted candles cast flickering shadows, and the echoes of faraway footsteps are only faintly heard. The halls of Clevyan. After all these years, they've hardly changed. A young boy in ceremonial robes stands only several paces down the hall with his hand raised and pointing.

"Over here! The goddess!"

A class is passing by. Now they come rushing with gaping eyes and wonder at their lips, flooding the entrance to the balcony like little fish at feeding time. Their instructor falls to her knees behind them.

"I'm no goddess. Only her servant. Haven't they taught you?" Alarei kneels to look into their marveling faces, and the innocence in their staring eyes nearly melts her undying heart.

Now the Farian appears soundlessly in the air at her back, and the crowd erupts anew.
"Iba, go quickly to the council of the elders! Tell them the sasarian has come!"

A girl sprints away down the corridor at her teacher's command. When she returns a short while later, the crowd at the western balcony has swelled and spilled into the surrounding halls. It parts only narrowly for High Priestess Kávukrei to pass through.

"Sasarian, please forgive our folly! We never should have sent you away years ago. We should have aided you, helped you prepare for this time." The voice of the priestess is coarser than Alarei remembers, but her face bears the lines of the past twenty years with impressive vitality. She gives a gracious bow, and the grayed locks of her braided hair seem to reflect Alarei's warm shine.

Alarei returns to her feet, shaking her head. "It wasn't within these walls that I found my way, but in the lands of Tayd. It's good that you sent me away."

"We all felt the heart of Claya shift at the moment of your awakening, months ago. What brings you to Clevyan?"

"I heard my name spoken in the elders' hearts."

Kávukrei's eyebrows jump sharply upward in her face. "Oh, yes, of course—we've concentrated very carefully these past months, hoping to learn whether or not you were able to calm the sasarian who appeared years ago."

"He remains hidden, for now. But I'll find him." Alarei keeps a serene face, but her words assure herself as much as they do the high priestess.

She's had a handful of months to begin learning the skills her new body possesses, and in that time she's traversed the world over more times than she could ever care to count. She's leaped across continents with a single step into the wind, visited the borders of hundreds of cities and ports throughout the Glesian and Ataran continents. She's practiced speaking to the elements and learned to understand the voice of the earth itself. She's even begun to venture through the ethereal barrier that hangs between the physical world and the realm of spirits. But in all her learning, she has yet to find any evidence of another sasarian in Claya.

Kávukrei smiles. "Hidden is good. So long as he remains hidden, our world can be at peace. We are honored to have a sasarian grace our halls once again. This sanctuary is yours, however often you care to visit."

Alarei looks over the sea of faces that watches her every motion. Adult faces, children's faces—all staring in speechless wonder at the woman whose countenance shines like the rays of the noonday sun.

Perhaps in their eyes, she truly is no less glorious than a goddess. But behind the shimmering grandeur of immortality that cloaks her presence, has she really changed?

"Thank you." Alarei nods to the high priestess before turning northward. She steps into the wind, and the crowd vanishes abruptly out of view. When her feet touch down a half-breath later, she no longer stands on the western balcony, but in the arched entrance of Clevyan's northern gathering hall. It's a massive, cavernous space, full of dark stone floors and towering pillars that rise like the arms of giants to support the slanted ceiling overhead. The Hall of Prayers. It's entirely unoccupied. Another porch can be seen at the far end of the columns, where the roof yawns at its widest angle from the floor. It's a balcony at least as broad as the one Alarei's just left behind. She walks the length of the hall, watching the way her light seems to slide and blend with the marbled colors of the stones. The Farian drifts mutely at her side.

The sounds of the sanctuary have fallen entirely away when she comes to the balcony, and the hills of Clevyan that stretch out beyond the railing ahead are alight with the pale sheen of the setting sun. They come to an abrupt end in the west, falling sharply to the Sand Sea below. Alarei sits at the center of the sweeping stone porch, closing her eyes and letting the cool surface of the floor pull her mind away from the unending chorus of beating hearts that barrages her ears. The sounds of every living heart in Claya. Someday soon, she can devote herself to them all. She can do all in her power to aid them, to better their world. But for now, she must focus elsewhere—on the sound of the only heartbeat that may be a threat to all others.

That is, if she can find it.

The presence of a fellow sasarian immortal should be easy to find—no matter where on the earth he may roam. But after nearly an hour of concentration, Alarei opens her eyes.

"Farian, I'm wasting time. I can't hear his heartbeat. Are you certain he still exists?"

The question sounds odd the instant she utters it. He *must* still exist. Aside from the power of another sasarian, they say nothing on all the face of Claya can slay the immortals.

"He is alive. He has gone to darkness." The Farian's whisper is echoless, despite the nearby vastness of the Hall of Prayers.

"Darkness?"

Perhaps it's a place beyond the mortal world. Alarei was taught all about the spirit realm as a child in Clevyan. A place where goodhearted people live on in peace after the death of their physical bodies, awaiting the end of time. But the home of the spirits is a place of light, not shadow. The Farian seems to speak of a different sphere entirely. One that somehow exists in neither the physical nor spirit realms.

"Is he trapped?"

"No. He entered the shadows of his own will, and can return to the realms by his own power," the Farian answers. "You must have caution. He may seek your life."

Return to the realms? The Farian speaks as though the immortal has left Claya altogether. Alarei sighs. Wherever he may be, perhaps her counterpart should remain unfound. He may be a danger to the world. But he's already hidden himself away for more than two decades. What if he never returns? Maybe the high priestess is right. Maybe Alarei should wait— should just forget about this other sasarian and focus on learning to fulfill her purpose in the world. The idea is tempting. After all, this other sasarian's had years of practice with his abilities. And he's apparently shown his murderous tendencies in the past. How could Alarei, who inherited her abilities only four short months ago, hope to stop him?

But even so, an enemy unseen and unknown is the most dangerous of all. So long as an unpredictable immortal exists *somewhere* in the realms, will the people of Claya ever truly be safe?

The debate rattles from one end of her thoughts to the other, shaking loose what little concentration remains there. But it all falls softly aside when a sudden memory rises from the depths of her mind. The memory of a name. It's the name of someone she must have known long ago, in another life. A name that's overwhelmingly familiar.

"Skéisono."

She murmurs the name aloud almost without realizing, and a shiver leaps down her spine. Is that *his* name? There's hardly time to wonder before her ears are filled with a sound that couldn't be heard only moments ago: the echo of a heart that thrums above the sound of all its mortal siblings. Alarei's still rising to her feet when a golden, fiery light suddenly floods the gathering hall at her back, rivaling the silvery brightness that streams from her own body.

"Here you are at last."

The man's voice is level. He's standing in the archway that leads to the corridor at the far end of the hall—watching her with eyes like glowing coals. Lustrous robes hang from his perfect frame like the gowns of a god edged in flames. A god of demons. It's him. The boy from the vision, now a man whose presence is far more sinister than Alarei ever anticipated.

"You're back." Alarei makes a valiant effort to sound unafraid, to silently remind herself of the abilities at her disposal. A sasarian should fear nothing. So why is she struggling so terribly to calm her trembling heart?

"Of course. How could I ignore my sister's call?" Skéisono begins a slow stroll down the length of the Hall of Prayers, leaving a trail of flames along the dark floor that flutters and fizzles out in his wake. A guardian much like the Farian hovers soundlessly at his side. "Have you enjoyed your first immortal breaths?"

"I suppose it seems natural."

The shining man comes closer—stopping just beyond the halo of Alarei's glow. "And what are you going to do now?"

Alarei returns his stare. "I'll try to fulfill my purpose as a sasarian."

"Is that so? You want to toil for this world? To somehow heal its wounds?"

"Whatever I can do to create a better world for all people."

"And do they deserve it?" Skéisono turns to step in an idle circle around the nearest pillar.

"Why would the goddess send us here if they didn't?"

The man in the flaming robes lets out a laugh that rings like startling chimes through the hall. "Don't you see, my sister? Claya can't be fixed. Our predecessors have tried and failed. They wasted their time. I've had years to think it through. There's only one way to mend the imperfections of this world." He leans casually against the column he's just circled. "End it. All of it."

Alarei watches the shadows behind the fires in his eyes—watches the way his dark, flawless smile defies the sunlight's relentless attempt to lighten it. When she speaks at last, her voice feels hopelessly quiet. "You know I can't let you do that."

Skéisono's smile fades. "I doubt you can stop me."

Then the sasarian man moves—bolts more rapidly than any mortal being could leap. One moment he's standing beside the pillar, several paces away. Now he stands directly before Alarei's face with his arm somehow encased in a flaming blade. He spears at her heart with unreal speed—almost too quickly to be seen. Alarei hardly manages to react. She raises an arm impulsively over her chest, and the stone from the floor at her feet leaps miraculously up to shield her. The attacker's blade is driven sharply sideways, and flames billow out in all directions as Alarei stumbles momentarily backward in the wake of the blow. Skéisono follows swiftly after her with fire wrapping like a flowing cloak across his shoulders and trailing in thin, glowing wisps along the edges of his robes. Alarei backs away, and the sound of all the mortal hearts that live within the walls of the sanctuary becomes suddenly obvious to her ears.

So many lives!

She calls desperately to them in her heart. With luck, they'll hear it. "People of Clevyan, the hidden sasarian has returned. He's here. You must all flee the sanctuary! I'll do everything I can to stop h—"

She can scarcely finish the thought before Skéisono appears at her back, swinging a curving, fiery blade that only barely misses her head as she pivots and leaps into the wind beyond the balcony's edge. She's got to lead him away. Or at least attempt to. The sasarian man is strong—and fully acquainted with his abilities. How can she possibly catch up now? At the very least, she can give the people time to flee. She turns midstride and lands on the Listening Hills, far from the walls of Clevyan.

"This way!" the Farian whispers at Alarei's right shoulder as soon as her foot touches the grass. A warning.

She leaps to the right and narrowly escapes a volley of flaming stones that comes hurling out of the earth at her feet. Now Skéisono appears to the left and sends a wave of flames and burning earth rolling over her. There's no time to dodge.

Come!

Alarei ducks beneath the surge, calling desperately for the winds to aid her. They heed her voice without delay, parting the molten wave at all sides. Alarei doesn't wait for the heat to settle. She turns eastward and leaps several hilltops away in the time it takes to draw her next breath. And she marvels. Not long ago, she was only an ordinary woman of Tayd. A woman with no particular gift or promise. And no enemies. Now, she struggles to survive the ruthless attacks of an immortal being who wields every element of the earth itself against her. And the battle might be hopeless. Or perhaps she can learn from it.

From where she stands, she calls to the stones and soil at the feet of her enemy. They spring up and encase the burning man on all sides. For an instant. But they obey the man's command as much as her own. He sends them hurling back at her before the words have ended at her lips. Alarei steps aside, calling a single stone into her hand.

"Be my blade," she murmurs as she moves to appear at her enemy's side.

She nearly plunges her newly formed weapon into his back. But the sasarian man pivots promptly in place and catches her wrist, bringing his own flaming blade down toward her head. It nearly brushes Alarei's forehead before she's able to vanish from his grip and reappear several paces away.

Skéisono laughs, and the smile returns to his strangely angelic face. "You're fast, at least." Then he glances over his shoulder to the stone sanctuary that sits in the distance. "But they aren't."

He disappears into the wind, and Alarei's heart plummets.

No!

She darts in a single step over the hills, chasing desperately after the chorus of living hearts that echoes out from Clevyan's sprawling grounds. They must have heard her warning. Most have left the sanctuary walls and gathered in a panicked crowd near the northeastern entrance. Their voices turn to gasps when Alarei appears with a burst of light in their midst. And their exclamations have only just begun to ring out when the towering wall of the sanctuary turns suddenly red beside them—then orange and seething yellow. It comes raining down in a torrent of molten stone, threatening to blanket over all in its path. The people erupt into screams.

"Farian, please—help me protect them!"

Alarei raises her hands, hoping to call the wind or earth to her aid for a shield against the heat. And for a moment, the world becomes slow. Halted, like a nightmare momentarily interrupted. All is silent beyond the sound of the Farian's murmuring voice.

"The flames are no more his than the stone and wind. They only need your direction. Direct them."

Alarei gazes up to the white-orange mass overhead. *Direct them.*

"Be calm!" she calls out to the flames, and her voice seems to clap and reverberate with a deafening volume against the sanctuary walls.

Overhead, the massive molten storm breaks suddenly apart, dissipating into wisps of hissing smoke only a short reach over the people's terrified faces. Their deaths are at least temporarily averted—but there's no time to comfort them before a fiery figure appears at Alarei's side. With another breathless command, she manages to stop the stone blade that's heaved again at her heart. The sharpened tip halts only a finger's width from her robes as her white glow clashes and collides with the golden haze of her enemy's presence. Flickering rays of light leap out from the scene to illuminate the hills with strange, amber light, and the people can be heard shrieking and scattering on all sides, helplessly terrified.

Alarei sends the stone blade to the ground and stares into Skéisono's hellish eyes. She's no closer to defeating him than she was moments ago. But now he's threatening innocent lives—hopelessly defenseless families. It's a reality that unexpectedly melts away the fear in Alarei's bones, leaving something entirely different in its place. Something closer to anger. If only she had more time! If only she hadn't said his name!

"*I* am the one in your way. Not *them!*" She nearly shouts into the immortal man's face as the crowds disperse at his back.

"You're right." Skéisono's hand rises sharply to catch Alarei by the neck, forcing her jaw upward. A new blade appears in his free hand, made of the same pale stone as the sanctuary wall at his back. "I suppose I should end this now. You're brave to stand in front of them, sister. But you know I've got to kill them anyway, don't you?" He leans closer, and his words slip suddenly into a quaking whisper—as if it pains him to speak them at all. "It's—it's the only way to free Claya from the darkness and suffering. The suffering humanity creates for itself. Don't you see?"

Alarei struggles to move at all, suddenly feeling as though her limbs are held by some invisible power. A force that pushes her earthward. She's got to break free. Skéisono's grip is strong, but it's not unbreakable.

Rise!

She calls in her heart to the stones, and a sharpened spike of earth juts abruptly up from the grass to spear through her captor's back. It tears into his shoulder before he manages to stop it. The shout it forces from his throat sends a jarring quake through the earth, and for a fleeting, marvelous instant, his grip loosens. Alarei slips away into the wind without looking back. He'll follow soon enough.

The world flows in a blur of color and light beneath her feet as she passes over it. She journeys northwest over sands and mountains, prairies and sparkling rivers, until she comes to the only place that seems right—a grove buried deep in the heart of the ancient forests of Sketza, far from the sound of any human heartbeats. When she comes to a stop, the clifftop hills of Clevyan are replaced by a maze of towering, colossal trees. They reach far into the azure depths of the sky and spread their dark branches like a vast pavilion overhead. It's a place almost entirely covered in dark moss, lit sporadically by the soft glow of tiny, violet flowers. Somehow, it's a place where Alarei belongs.

"I planned to draw him to the Sand Sea. But this forest called to me. Why do I feel so at ease in this place?" She breathes out—perhaps for the first time in a long while.

The Farian drifts idly before her face. "This is your realm. The place where your spirit connects most directly to the heart of Claya. So long as he carries ill will against you, your sasarian brother cannot enter this place."

Alarei wonders. It seems too fortunate to be real. A safe haven? There's little chance to ponder the benefits. A wild flame appears at the edge of the forest. Billowing, churning. Although it's far away to the south, behind countless acres of bark and leaves, Alarei can see it like a waking vision in her mind. The sight of a man cloaked in ravenous fires, with a stare more potent than that of any demon. He stands at the edge of her realm with his scalding rage lapping and slithering along the intangible barrier before him, singeing the grasses. There's no longer any sign of a wound in his shoulder. And his voice, though far away, comes like a hiss to her ears.

"So you found a hiding place. Hide, then! Hide as long as you like, dear sister. I can cleanse the world without you."

9

-Common Year 179-

It's a windless morning when the city of Koska still stands in its usual place beside the curving fourth branch of the Nakuë River. But well before the sun reaches its highest seat in the peak of the sky, the city is gone. Every rooftop, every painted wall, every brick—every beating heart—gone. A flattened, blackened field is all that remains of what was once one of the most festive and lively cities of Igretho. The desolation is swift. It comes like a summer storm. Raging. Merciless. It comes when the people would least expect it. When the land is free of war and the sky lacks all but the thinnest clouds in its wide face. And the destruction is so ruthlessly complete that the first outsiders to happen upon the scene that afternoon can scarcely tell where the city once stood. Thousands of lives are brought to an abrupt end that morning—winked out like lantern lights in the wake of dawn. And the shock of their inexplicable deaths leaves the people of Igretho reeling with questions.

Questions, and no time to search for answers.

Word of Koska's fate has yet to reach the outer borders of Tayd before the devastation finds another victim, far from the plains of Igretho. The oasis city of Edanehn, deep in the heart of the Sand Sea. Some say they glimpse the god of death standing in the air above the city, sending the flames like a merciless gale from his outstretched hand. But this time, the flames don't last. The oasis has only begun to quake and flood with screams when the fires wither suddenly away into smoke. And the god of death vanishes with a flash of brilliant light at his heels. Edanehn is left terribly wounded in his wake. Shaken, but still standing.

The great city of Hileit is next in his path. Cloaked in morning twilight far beyond the Atayu Sea, the ancient capital of West Ataran is still waking when destruction comes boldly to its gates. A single shudder tears through the earth, and an entire district is shaken to the ground—reduced to heaping piles of crumbling stones well before the people can wake to scream. Nearly the entire southwest arc of Hileit is razed before a spectacular burst of light can be seen over the western city wall. Then the quaking earth is calmed, and the ancient city is left strangely alone with its wounds.

Each hour that passes finds a new city in flames. And with each new day, more reports of death and terrible desolation are heard throughout the nations—in the city streets, in the markets, and in the council halls of every government. Whispers of entire towns suddenly swallowed into the earth, of city districts lighting up in a sudden blast of flames, of ships—sometimes entire fleets—vanishing inexplicably at sea. Each day, more tales are heard. And each day, new fear spreads like a rampant virus among the people of Claya. Some say it's the beginning of the end of days—that the god of death has come to finish the history of the world. Others say they've seen the goddess herself appear in the heart of the chaos to calm the flames and command the earth to be still.

All hold beliefs. Some dark, some hopeful. But one thing is certain among all who dwell beneath the twin moons. A strange and perilous age has come to Claya.

10

-Common Year 179-

"We'll send you word each week. Try not to get into trouble." Mother gives her a tight hug as she and Father shoulder their travel bags. "There's plenty of everything in the pantry."

"We'll be fine—*you're* the ones heading into a disaster. Don't get yourselves killed out there," Hamara replies with her arms folded tightly.

Nearby, Elein looks up with suddenly widened eyes. Mother kneels to give her hand another squeeze. "Your sister loves to exaggerate. Don't you worry. We'll be back in a few short weeks."

"But don't the people in Salialo have doctors of their own? Why do *you* have to go?" The girl's whine rises up from a whisper.

"They've got more injured people than their doctors can handle," Father tells her as he reaches for his walking stick. "They need every doctor in Igretho over there. So you'd better tell everyone in town to be extra careful while we're away. No sprained ankles, all right?"

He winks, trying desperately to be positive. But Hamara can see the anxiety behind his smile. In the stiff way he swings the door open. He and Mother step out onto the road, waving.

Four days have passed since a horrific earthquake tore through the capital and opened a gaping crevice through the streets of its innermost district. They say more than ninety people have already been found dead beneath the collapsing rubble. Likely hundreds more are terribly injured. Hamara's parents talk like they'll be back in a week or two. But Hamara knows they're likely to be away for much, much longer.

"Good luck," she murmurs after them, wondering if she should've tried harder to convince them to take her along. At least she'd be useful over there. Doing something more than babysitting a sister who's more than able to take care of herself. And she wonders if the summer will be over before she'll see them again.

* * *

The afternoon is bright but blustery, tossing the kifara trees into a relentless dance and gusting Hamara's short hair into her face as she steps between them. Useless hair. It's such a bother. Maybe Mother's long absence is a wonderful opportunity to trim the itchy stuff off, the way Hamara's always wanted.

"I don't want my daughter going around with hair shorter than a man's," Mother's always insisted, and Hamara's always followed suit, reluctantly keeping her dark hair hanging just below her shoulders. But now, Mother won't be around to voice an opinion. The wind gusts anew, and Hamara pulls a tie from her pocket to gather the wild clumps of hair beneath one ear. And she sighs. It would be nice to be rid of it. But she can't do that to Mother. At least she can tie it out of the way.

Iro's standing beside his favorite rock at the crest of the back hill when Hamara looks up again. It's the first time he's appeared in weeks. The wind catches his fiery hair and tousles it like flames atop his head.

"It's been a while," she calls to him from the steep foot of the hill. "I finally asked my father about his hometown, like you suggested."

"About time," Iro answers over his shoulder, waving for her to join him in the tall grass. Hamara takes her time scaling the slope. When she reaches its peak at last, coming to a stop beside her friend, he turns to show her a silvery-eyed smile. "So? What did he tell you?"

"You were right. He's from the town that was destroyed, down in the south."

Iro turns to lean into the boulder at his side. "And did he know *how* it was destroyed?"

"He—well—" Hamara shuffles her father's words in her mind, unsure how they could ever be repeated without sounding like thorough madness. "He said it was—that his brother was disliked, and that he became a . . . er . . ." She fusses with the hair tied beneath her ear. There really isn't any ordinary way to tell it.

"Became some kind of god?" Iro doesn't wait for her to finish.

He stood in the air like a ghost, covered in flames. But the fires didn't harm him. They obeyed him.

Father's words echo like a fireside fable in Hamara's ears. They sound no less fantastical than the ancient stories the merchants bring from the far west. Hamara looks back to her friend. "How did you know?"

"A handful of voránjevin hunters witnessed it."

"So you came to Remertrei looking for a survivor from Kasántos? Why?"

Iro sighs. "Well, it might be a pretty desperate plan. But it's all I've got."

"A plan for what?"

"Let me start with the basics. Your uncle became an immortal. One of the sasarian immortals my people have always watched for, through the ages. The sasarianë are sent to protect the free will of all people. Or so I was always taught. But it looks like they can choose to do otherwise."

Hamara brings her hands to her hips. "My uncle must've been looking for vengeance, for the death of his family. They killed his parents. Maybe he thought they killed his brother, too."

Iro nods. "And now he—" He pauses midsentence to stare off toward the northern trees. What does he see? Hamara follows his gaze, squinting in the rising light, and spots a figure standing just outside the shade of the woods. A small figure, with the largest eyes Hamara's ever seen. It raises a dark, slender arm into the air as she looks on, and Iro nods in response. It's some sort of greeting. Iro glances back to the girl at his side.

"A messenger," he tells her. "From the Taufeth clan. He wasn't sure if he should deliver his message with an arai present."

"An arai?"

"A human."

The stranger comes creeping silently closer through the tall grass. It's the first time Hamara's laid eyes on a voránjevin. Or at least, a voránjevin in his true form. Somehow, it's unsettling. She shifts her weight and makes an effort to act as though the sight were entirely ordinary. But is it?

The messenger is male, a *heln*, as Iro calls them. His head is only a little taller than Hamara's elbows, and his petit body is covered entirely in short, blackish-gray fur. He bears all the characteristics that Iro's mentioned idly before: the massive eyes, the broad ears that hang down at the sides of the head. Aside from a skirt-like bit of clothing that's tied at his slender waist, the stranger wears only a gray wrap over his shoulders that ends in a large knot at his back.

The two voránjevin exchange a few words in their own fluid language before Iro's speech returns abruptly to words Hamara can understand.

"She needs to know this too. Tell us in Moi-Sketzan, as well as you can," he insists.

The dark-furred stranger looks up at Hamara and gives a sheepish attempt at a toothy smile, then turns back to Iro. "*Ipheha fe*—I try," he says, and Hamara marvels. Suddenly Iro's accent seems remarkably mild. "Some city, some village. They burn. They be . . . ruins. Man sasarian destroy arai cities. New sasarian come. Try to stop. But need help. Now we gather. Try help some arai. Heal arai."

Hamara's heart drops. More destruction? Just yesterday, the streets of Remertrei were flooding with terrible news. News from the capital, from Koska, from cities in Tayd and beyond. The disasters are happening everywhere. And no one can explain it. Now, Hamara may be the only human person in Remertrei—or even all of Igretho—who can.

"Is it really all because of him? Is my uncle the reason behind all the destruction—the deaths of so many innocent people?" She brings her hands together, unable to ignore the odd tremble in her stomach.

For a moment, Iro simply stares back at her, maybe watching the realization unfold in her face. Maybe wondering when Hamara will stop asking so many questions. Then he turns to the messenger, murmuring softly in his native speech. The stranger nods and slinks soundlessly away, disappearing down over the next hill and back into the cover of the trees.

Iro motions for Hamara to sit down. She does, still trying to make sense of it all—of *any* of it.

"Only another sasarian immortal has the power to stop your father's brother." Iro lowers himself softly down beside her.

"And there *is* another one?"

"A woman who only recently attained her immortal state."

"Have these immortals always existed?"

"As far as we know, they've existed in the world since history began. But more than six generations have passed since anyone's seen them last. The voránjevin clans have attempted to watch out for them, through the ages."

"Why? To worship them?"

Iro shakes his head. "Because they can be very dangerous—like the one who once destroyed our ancestral home. The clans have always thought that if our people looked after the sasarianë as soon as we could find them as mortal children, we could ensure that they'd one day use their godlike abilities to bring good into the world. Obviously, as far as your uncle's concerned, we failed this time around."

With only a moment's warning, the clouds overhead begin to let their tears slip down in a subtle peppering over the hills. Rain. It touches down with a soft pattering in the grass at all sides, leaving chilled spots of moisture across Hamara's uncovered arms.

"And according to your messenger friend, the other immortal needs help stopping my uncle? If my father's long-lost brother truly is capable of bringing an entire city to ruin with the close of his fist, what chance would even the greatest warriors of Claya have against him? How could any of us possibly help the other sasarian stop him?"

"She just needs more time. I can feel it. Alarei's always needed more time to find confidence in herself." Suddenly, Iro's voice loses its usual tone and becomes entirely new. Softer.

Hamara turns to give her friend a closer stare. "You . . . *know* her?"

When Iro looks up, his orange-red hair is beginning to shine with wetness and cling to his pale face, hanging partly over his eyes. The rain's getting heavier now. It splatters atop the boulder at Iro's back and drums along the nearby rooftops of Remertrei.

"Let's get out of the rain."

He returns to his feet. Hamara doesn't argue. The two of them trudge down the hill and into the shelter of the garden shed, leaving the door hanging lazily open as they find seats on overturned crates. The rain falls in a gray curtain just beyond the threshold.

"Look, kid, until recently, no one had seen or heard of your uncle for over two decades. I came to Remertrei because it was the only way I could think of to prevent any other cities from suffering the fate of Kasántos, if your uncle ever appeared again." Iro flicks the wetness from his hair, leaving a dark speckling on the earthen floor. "And now that he's back, it's the only way I can help my best friend stop him."

Best friend? Hamara raises an eyebrow, folding her arms against the chill. "You're gonna need to explain. *What's* the only way?"

"Your uncle might not know that his only brother's still alive. Or maybe he's just been ignoring the fact. Either way, I think your father's the only one who could reach him—maybe even convince him to stop all the killing. At the very least, he could distract him for a while. And a little distraction might be all Alarei needs to get an advantage."

"But my father's gone to Salialo to help the injured. They're in desperate need of doctors over there. I can't possibly tell him to abandon those people just because of some theory we have."

"They say the sasarianë can hear when someone calls for them, no matter where in the world that person may be. You could send a letter to your father and tell him what you know. Tell him to call his brother."

"But apparently my uncle's the one who destroyed half of Salialo! What if he comes back and decides to finish the job?"

"I guess it's a possibility." Iro gazes off into the rain for a time before sitting suddenly forward, eyes alight. "Or maybe you could call him instead! From somewhere out in the hills, where there's no one nearby for him to hurt."

A chill bolts through Hamara's veins as the thought sprouts an image in her mind. "No one but *me*, you mean?"

"I'd be there too!"

Hamara allows herself a genuine laugh. "No offense, but I don't think either of us would last more than a few breaths in front of my uncle. Not if he's as terrible as my father described. And anyway, I don't even know his name. My father never told me."

Iro sits back on his crate, letting out air. "We've got to do *something.*"

Somewhere far to the east, the low grumbling of distant thunder can be heard. Its voice rises in a fleeting, triumphant din before falling back beneath the persistent rhythm of the rain.

"So, how do you know the other immortal, anyway? You called her Alarei?" Hamara scoots her crate a little deeper into the dry depths of the shed as a mild breeze gusts the rain onto her sandals.

Iro smiles without looking up. It's the kind of smile that only the fondest thoughts and memories can awaken. A smile Hamara's never before seen on his face.

"I met her when I was just a boy," he tells her. "I've suspected that she might be one of the sasarianë ever since. She had a dark flicker in her eyes when I looked at her. It's something I always heard about in the sasarian legends, in my clan."

"You must've spent time with humans as a kid."

"I lived at Clevyan."

"Clevyan?" Hamara leans forward. "I've heard of that place. Way out east, right? On the other side of the Sand Sea. It's like a giant temple, isn't it? They allow voránjevin people to live there, too?"

"No, actually. They don't. I was only able to fool them for a few years." Iro's smile turns bitter at the edges. "The elders there were constantly watching me, always trying to keep me out of places."

"Did Alarei know what you are?"

Iro gazes down at his slender hands, slowly interlocking his fingers. "Eventually." Now he rises and steps to the very threshold of the rain, letting the stray droplets paint his toes. "Alarei was the closest friend I've ever known. When I found out that the clan I once belonged to was responsible for her mother's death, I thought she'd want me gone. I was wrong. Ultimately, I left Clevyan because I thought it'd be best for her future as a sasarian, to grow up in a place where her kind are idolized. I didn't want to tarnish her status in their eyes. I thought they'd kick her out because of me. But I never should've left her side—especially not the way I did. That was all about sixteen years ago, now. I was your age."

"Sounds like you haven't seen her since." Hamara lowers her voice, mildly aware that the topic deserves some kind of reverence. Or at least gentleness. Father sometimes teases that Hamara doesn't always have the best tact in conversation. And he's probably right. Maybe she shouldn't ask Iro so many probing questions. But there's something about his old friendship with the sasarian woman—something about the way his entire countenance changes when he talks about her—that pulls Hamara to the edge of almost unbearable curiosity.

Beside the rain, Iro gives a slow nod. "Guess we all have our regrets."

* * *

It's Hamara's turn to gather and wash the dishes that night. Luckily there aren't many of them. Not with Mother and Father away. The sun's slipped well beyond the horizon as she stacks the last bowl for drying, and the outskirts of Remertrei beyond the shuttered windows have long since fallen silent. Up in the loft, Elein plucks noisily away at the stringed instrument she's been learning to play for several weeks now. It's a strangely calming sound, despite the occasionally awkward pitches. Hamara smiles, and has only just tossed the wet dishrag over the pump handle beside the sink when a sudden rap sounds at the door. A visitor? At night? Hamara lifts her sénsin rod from its place on the wall almost without realizing as she crosses toward the door, listening.

"Kid! Hamara! It's me. I've got an idea." Iro's muffled voice comes drifting through the doorframe, and the tension falls away from Hamara's shoulders.

Of course. Who else would come knocking at this hour? She's reaching to unlatch the door when the nearest window shutter swings suddenly open.

"I know someone we can ask for advice." Iro's face bares a vivid grin when it appears in the window, and Hamara finds herself silently thanking the gods that Mother's not present to chide her for always forgetting to lock the shutters. Iro waves a hand toward the north. "He lives about a three-day walk from here, near the southeast shore of Emér. A man named Vehn."

Hamara hangs up her weapon and shuffles to the window, whispering just beneath the sound of Elein's dissonant chiming. "What, you think he knows how to stop my uncle?"

"He might. I've never known anyone like this guy."

"What makes him so special?"

"You'll see." Iro glances sharply at the darkness that surrounds him before gazing back to the light of the window. "When can you leave?"

"Iro, I can't just leave my little sister home alone—or insist that she travel for days to see some stranger."

"Isn't there anyone she can stay with in this town? Why do you human families always keep to yourselves so much?"

Hamara frowns. "Because—well, we—ugh, I don't know, Iro!" She lets her hands float into the air, suddenly exasperated.

"There's really no one?"

"Well, she does spend loads of time with her friend on the third lane. I guess she might be able to stay with them for a time. But I'll need time to ask—"

"Perfect! We can leave tomorrow."

"What? But—hey, why don't you just go and find this Vehn guy yourself?"

Iro's smile fades as he folds his arms along the window ledge. "Because you are the sasarian's *family*. Your father's not here, or I'd tell him to go. But you're still the sasarian's niece. You might be able to do more than you think. And besides, *I* won't be walking much longer."

"Won't be walking? What does that even mean?"

"I'll explain later. Come find me on the hill when you're ready to head out tomorrow!" Iro calls over his shoulder as he slips away into the night.

Hamara sighs, shutting and locking the window before glancing to the loft, where Elein softly hums the notes as her fingers find them.

Fine. Tomorrow then.

11

-Common Year 179-

The blanket of flames at the city wall whirls and billows away at the sound of her voice, then flickers out at her fingertips, leaving only a whisper of heat in its absence. And as the quaking bedrock beneath the city threatens to leap from its bounds, Alarei closes her eyes.

"Return to your sleep."

The earth falls still at her command. And when she opens her eyes, the people of the city have begun to gather like astonished children on all sides. Marveling, falling to their knees with their faces illuminated by the brightness of her shining countenance. Adoring the being who somehow dispelled the imminent death that lingered over them only moments ago.

"The goddess! Come to protect us!" They begin to shout, to sing and exclaim with their hands held high in the air.

But Alarei raises her own hands to quiet them. "Listen to me, please! I'll do what I can, but you *must* leave the city! You'll be safer if you separate into smaller groups. I can only protect this place for so long." She helps them to their feet and sends them into the countryside in every direction. "You can come back for supplies when the attack is over!"

The crowds are still dispersing in a panicked rush as Alarei turns to face the man who stands grimacing through the flames that shroud him, far across the city. Skéisono. For more than three weeks now, she's fought him. Through bright daylight and cloud-cloaked nights, through rain and wind, through sand and snow, through every nation of the world. Never resting, retreating to her realm for only fleeting moments when absolutely necessary to escape his deadly grasp. With nearly constant practice, she's learned to more effectively redirect or dissipate her enemy's attacks. She's found ways to save more lives wherever possible—and even made efforts to return her opponent's attacks. But in all her tireless efforts, she has yet to wound him again. At best, she's only ever slowed him down. And after three weeks of desperate efforts—weeks of spending every fiber of her concentration—the reality of the struggle weighs down with the heaviness of all the world on Alarei's shoulders.

So much struggle, so much effort! And yet so many lives lost! How will it ever end? Alarei sends her most furious stare to the man in the flames, resisting the urge to let her own rage boil out and destroy what remains of the city around her.

"Farian! My efforts are nearly useless! How will I ever stop him before all the lives in this world are lost?" The tears begin to pour like molten drippings of the sun from her radiant eyes.

The Farian hovers just beyond her shoulder. Its single eye shifts and shimmers as it turns in place. "You carry the same abilities as the sasarianë who came before you. The power to stop him is in your hands. You must only learn to wield it."

Same abilities? The Farian is incapable of speaking anything but truth. But how much time did the immortals of old have to learn their skills? Decades? Centuries?

Alarei shakes the trembling from her hands. If the ability truly is somewhere within her, waiting to be discovered, she had better learn faster. Or there won't be a world left to save.

12

-Common Year 179-

The evening is closing in when they spot the lichen-clad mooring jutting out from the shoreline ahead. The waves that beat and thrash against it send their spray high into the wind, leaving dark, splattered signatures across the aged wooden boards. Looking on, Hamara's unsure how the rickety old thing still remains in one piece. The Emér Sea is restless.

"Is this the place?" she nearly shouts over the clapping of the waves against the rocks.

Not far ahead, Iro turns to nod beneath his hood. "I haven't been this way for a while, but I know it well enough!" He pulls his coat more tightly over his arms, cursing loudly at the biting wind. "I've never truly understood how you humans stay warm without fur!"

They've travelled on foot for just over three days along the southeastern shore of Emér to reach this place. And all the while, Hamara's doubted her decision to come on the journey more times than she cares to count. She doubted it when a howling wind kept her awake in her cramped tent for nearly half of the first night, and when she ran out of drinking water the following day—and again when she woke to the sound of an enormous rodent nibbling a hole through her bag of dried fruits. Fortunately, Iro knew where to find every spring and creek along the way, and was terrifyingly swift at killing rodents. He seemed entirely at home in the wild. Throughout the day, he'd often tell Hamara to continue onward toward a certain tree or plateau in the distance before vanishing away into the surrounding shrubs—sometimes looking for herbs or certain types of stone, sometimes snatching up an unsuspecting prey for supper. He slept with nothing between him and the night sky, and tended the fire well beyond dusk each night, singing soft melodies into the glow. At times, Hamara would lie in her tent listening in, wondering. She'd wonder how her mother and father were faring at the capital, and if Elein was behaving herself. She'd wonder if this spontaneous journey was worth undertaking at all. The Et'Fadei family on the third lane in Remertrei was more than willing to have Elein stay with them and their only daughter for a few days. But what if Remertrei faces the same fate as Koska, in Hamara's absence? It's possible. Hamara would never be able to forgive herself for leaving her sister behind—and neither would her parents. But despite all the risks, Iro remains right about one reality. As one of the few blood relatives of the sasarian immortal behind all the death and destruction dotting the land, Hamara might have a better chance at doing *something* about it than most. At the very least, she can try.

A dark rooftop becomes visible over the curve of the next hill, nestled in among the jagged rocks and seaside trees ahead. Finally. Hamara's hood is gusted off her head as she crosses over the last slope and steps down into the well-worn walking path that leads to the cabin's entrance. The sea air is frigid—even for springtime. And when the cabin door opens unexpectedly in front of her, Hamara can't help but smile at the sight of the blazing fireplace in the hearth beyond. The man standing at the threshold looks only slightly older than her own father, with weary eyes and a dark, silver-crested beard.

"The soup's been ready for ages." The man's eyes move between Hamara and Iro. "Well, come in before the heat escapes."

Hamara feels Iro's hand nudging gently at her back, pressing her into the cabin before she can fix the puzzled stare on her face. The door falls shut behind them, and the cozy warmth of the cabin washes up like hot bathwater on all sides.

"You're still as hospitable as ever, I see. Our apologies for burdening you, Vehn." Iro gives the man a little bow, wind-tossed hair floating like static-drawn feathers atop his head.

"You're no burden." Vehn shuffles over to the little stove in the corner. "It's good to have guests, now and then."

"Was he expecting us?" Hamara asks through the corner of her mouth as they lay their coats on a little bench beside the door.

Iro shrugs. "He's probably known we were coming for weeks."

Weeks? Iro only happened upon the idea to visit this man three days ago. How could anyone possibly know about his plan before he created it? It makes no sense. But for now, there's no time to question.

The three of them sit on cushioned benches beside the fire and sip hot spoonfuls of soup, letting the steam rise up and warm their noses. It's a bold flavor, with spice that leaves a little tingle at the lips. It's nothing like the soups of Remertrei. But after days of trekking through the wilds with only simple breads, kifara fruit, and wild-caught rodents to eat, it's nothing short of wonderful. Hamara takes her time, cherishing the warm bowl in her hands and eyeing the impeccable craftsmanship of the space that surrounds her. On every side, the walls seem to reach into the room— whether by an intricately carved and painted bookshelf or a built-in desk that tucks and hides entirely away into a nook. Delicate murals embellish every open wall. The portrait of a massive tree in mid-bloom along the north wall is the most stunning of all. It rises from the floor to the roof beams, full of nesting birds and open blossoms. Its branches open in a wide spread beneath the high ceiling, reaching up to finger along the edges of the loft at the cabin's east end. A setting sun sends its painted rays along the kitchen walls in the west, and rolling desert dunes conceal the woodgrain surrounding the tall hearth in the south wall. Each window sits in a curving, colored frame—*glass* windows, unlike the shuttered windows of Remertrei. And every chair and stool in sight is carved with the subtle shapes of vines, leaves, blooming flowers, and birds' feathers. Even the bowl in Hamara's hands is engraved with tumbling sea waves. It's no secret that the man named Vehn is a man of skill.

"Did you build this house yourself?" Hamara gazes to the high loft where a rocking chair sits beside a window that must be nearly as tall as she is.

Vehn gives a humble nod. "With the aid of the Taufeth clan. It's much easier to lift roof beams into place when you can borrow the strength of thirty individuals at once."

Nearby, Iro grins over his bowl. "I remember that. It was just after I started hanging around the Taufeth, ages ago. We found our strongest hunters and lined up together, pushing all our spare strength into one set of arms. You should've seen this guy," he tells Hamara, pointing to their host with a dripping spoon. "Lifted these roof beams like they were broomsticks!"

"You can do that, with that energy-sharing ability your people have?" Hamara nearly chokes on a bite of vegetable.

"Of course—the voránjevin people can channel their strength into others. If many do this at once, the result can be impressive." Vehn finishes his soup and sets his bowl on the bench beside him, looking up at Hamara with a suddenly sharp stare. "It slipped my mind for a moment, but I remember now why you've come."

"You know why we've come?"

"You're hoping to distract the sasarian who's destroying the world's cities. You're correct to assume that seeing his brother alive would distract him."

"How do you know all this?" Hamara glances warily to her red-haired friend, but he seems entirely focused on finishing his stew with loud, unashamed gulps.

"I know because I've seen it. Just as I saw that the two of you would arrive at my door, sometime last week," Vehn answers as he pulls a kerchief from his pocket to dabble soup from the edges of his mustache. "Sometimes I see things many months ahead of time. And I can tell you now that despite his ability to sense every soul on this earth, your uncle has yet to realize that his brother still lives. He's chosen to shut out and ignore the mortal children of Claya. I suppose it's easier to eradicate them that way."

Iro looks up from his empty bowl at last. "Then is there any chance of reaching him? What if he hears his brother calling his name?"

"He won't hear. You need to go to him." The question was Iro's, but Vehn answers without taking his gaze from the girl who sits across from him.

Hamara's stomach drops. Is she really going to do this? Go walking up to the immortal being who's demolishing the world to see if he'd like to chat about his long-lost brother? What could she possibly say to him, if she even managed to catch his attention? "Oh, hey, Uncle! I don't believe we've met!" The thought's daunting at best. But Vehn talks as though it's the only option. Or at least, an option worth trying. And it almost gives her courage—a pitiful spark of it.

"You mean *me*? But shouldn't I try to get my father to go with me? And how will I know where to go?"

"Your father's skills are needed in Salialo. And there's no time to wait for him to catch up, even if a letter could persuade him. But you can carry the same message that he would." Vehn rises to collect the empty stew bowls and stack them in a basin just beneath the rising sun on the kitchen wall. "Your uncle is most often appearing in the north, along the southern edge of the Sketzan forests. He hopes to break the barrier there that keeps him out of his opponent's safe haven."

Hamara stares blankly after him, momentarily speechless. No one's said anything about her father being a doctor, or about him helping at the capital. How much does this stranger truly know?

"So we need to head north," Iro announces.

"Yes." Vehn nods with his finger wagging in the air. "You're likely to cross his path in a city somewhere between here and Sketza, if not at the border of the Sketzan forests. And when you do, catching his attention could give his counterpart the opportunity she needs. A chance to end all the destruction." He turns suddenly away again. "If you follow the shore of Emér northward from here, you'll find Klauskeht, a merchant post. Less than a day's travel away. Trade ships from all the surrounding nations pass through the docks there." He pulls his coat from a hook by the door and digs in one of its pockets, pulling out a string of *sirlene* rings. The currency of Tayd. Enough to buy three weeks' worth of food from any market Hamara's ever visited. "Take this. The ferries can be pricey. And you'll need a map . . ."

He drops the string of money into her hands before turning to rummage in a nearby desk drawer. Hamara gives Iro another wide-eyed stare, but the heln simply nods contentedly in reply—as if it were all entirely ordinary.

"Ah-ha! Found it. Drawn by a Taufeth scout. The best topographer this side of Emér. You can stay here to prepare as long as needed. I'd come with you, if I wasn't needed in the west," Vehn tells her as he lays the folded map on the bench beside Hamara, who's nearly forgotten how to speak.

"But even if I find him, what am I supposed to do then—assuming I'll still be alive?" The question leaves her mouth, and Hamara finds herself wondering grimly if she'll ever see her mother and father again. Maybe she should get out of this while she still can— should slip out the door and back over the countryside to the town where she belongs, where nothing ever happens.

But Vehn seems to read the thoughts in her eyes. He pours a new drink for himself and settles down in what appears to be his favorite chair beside the fire. And he smiles. "You'll know exactly what to do. Trust me, Hamara. I've already seen it."

* * *

After dusk, the twin moons light the cabin's high windows like gray street lanterns, casting a sleepless glow into the loft where Hamara sits writing letters on the hand-trimmed papers Vehn provided. One to Elein and another to her parents, explaining everything she's discovered—about the role of Father's brother in the destruction of Salialo and countless other cities throughout the world, about Vehn's advice, and about the planned journey she's about to undertake. It takes ages to find the right words to describe it all— especially the potentially pointless, highly dangerous plan to distract an immensely powerful, raging immortal. But she assures them that Vehn seems to be some kind of seer, and he's confident that the plan's worth trying. The least Hamara can do is try. She dates the letters, then sits staring at the numbers, wondering how long it will take to reach Sketza, and if she'll truly manage to find her uncle at all. Wondering what date she'll write on her last letter home, before she returns—if she returns at all.

Iro climbs stiffly up into the loft and settles down on a rug against the opposite wall as Hamara's folding the second letter and laying it atop the first. His hair's still wet from the washing he's just given it, and he holds a thick blanket like an oversized cloak over his shoulders. He leans back into the wall, and the moonlight seems to glimmer and shift in his silver eyes.

"So, you're really going to do this, then? Head off into the unknown in hopes of momentarily distracting the sasarian immortal responsible for destroying half the world's greatest cities?" His voice is oddly tainted by the grin on his face, as if he's about to reveal a joke that's too clever to hide.

"Do I really have much choice? What else could I do—go home and wait for the world to end? But it *does* sound ridiculous, doesn't it?" Hamara tosses her hands in the air before letting herself flop onto the floor.

Iro laughs. A defiant, hopeless laugh with the potential to light even the darkest moments.

"What's so funny over there? *You're* the one who brought me into this! If it's ridiculous, then why bother? Is there some other, better plan in your head?" Hamara struggles to control the sharp edge in her voice.

But Iro doesn't seem to mind. "Nope! I've got nothing." He laughs again, and when Hamara turns to give him her most exasperated glare, he shows her a simple smile. "You're a brave kid, Hamara. I think you can do this."

"And what about you? Why can't you come along?"

"I will—just not right away. I've got to get into a faster body first."

"You're changing into something . . . else?"

Iro nods. "The winged form is one of the most common transformations among all voránjevin clans. Wings are faster than feet, you know. Once I'm airborne, I can be your lifeline along the way. I can bring you supplies while you travel, take the letters you write to the nearest carriers—whatever you need." He shivers, then pulls his blanket more tightly across his knees. "I always feel colder than usual at the beginning of a transformation," he mutters.

"You've already started it? The changing process?"

"Of course—you think I'm always this stiff?"

Hamara sits upright again, wearing her confusion in the lines that gather across her forehead. "But didn't you tell me that it takes more than a month to transform into another shape? Maybe I'll reach Sketza by myself in that time!"

"Usually it does take weeks, yes. And yes, I should've thought of all this sooner." Iro sighs. "But don't worry. I happen to know a few talented minds in the Taufeth clan. They've been experimenting with *hitérian* energy flows during the changing process for ages. And they're certain they've found a way to speed things up, once a person falls into the deep sleep stage of the transformation. I'll be meeting up with them in the morning."

"Well, I hope their wild experiment works. For both our sakes," Hamara tells him, and she wonders what Iro could possibly look like with wings—and how long she might end up traveling alone. The strangeness of it all sinks in anew. She looks at the darkened hills and trees beyond the window. "I can't believe I'm really about to try this. Just a few days ago, I was like everyone else—assuming the destruction in the cities was because of random earthquakes and fires. Not long ago, I'd never heard of sasarian immortals. Even now, I can't help feeling like it's all a dream."

From the moment she finished her soup that evening, Hamara's tried to imagine the road ahead, to visualize the path she'll take and the places she'll see. But there's so little experience to build from. She's never been to Tayd—never been outside Igretho. Northern cities might be nothing like the riverside towns of the south. And how can she possibly predict what the immortals will be like, if she finds them?

"I feel it too, kid. You're heading out there on a whim—following the desperate hope that we can make any difference." Iro closes his eyes. "But if this plan works, every soul in the world will have reason to thank you."

* * *

The winds have settled down to a mild gusting as Hamara gathers her hair beneath her left ear the following morning. She hefts her shoulder pack into place after organizing and counting its contents three times over, grateful for the lightness of her father's spare travel tent. Last of all, she buckles her metal-sheathed sénsin rod to her lower back. And for possibly the thirtieth time since breakfast, she takes a deep breath, attempting to breathe away the nervous tightening in her chest. What's she really doing, anyway? This could be the beginning of the end of her life. But it isn't pointless, is it? There's a chance that her effort could help an immortal woman bring an end to the desolation plaguing the world. A chance that could save lives—many, many lives.

She takes several steps out the cabin door before turning back to Vehn, who stands with his arms folded in the doorway. "Guess I'm ready for Klauskeht. Thank you for all your help."

The man gives an assuring nod. "You'll find your way, Hamara. You won't be alone."

Hamara smiles in reply before turning to the path ahead. He seems so certain. Hopefully he's right.

Iro stands waiting when she walks beyond the first hill, looking weary and paler than ever. The transformation must be taking its toll. But his eyes are still bright. "I'll be right behind you. Just be careful, kid."

"I'll try to be." Hamara shuffles her shoulder pack as she passes by. She's gone several paces more when his voice calls after her.

"And Hamara, before you go, I want you to know my real name."

His real name? Hamara stops midstep to look back, briefly unsure which question to ask first. "What?"

"Iro was an old friend of mine, from a northern clan. My name is Asei. Asei Toh Ifaneis. I needed to put some distance between myself and the clan I came from for a while. I've done it for years."

"And why are you telling me this now?" Maybe Hamara should be upset. Maybe she should be shaken to realize she's put her trust in someone who didn't even give her his real name. But somehow, she isn't.

Asei lowers himself slowly down to sit on the hillside. "You deserve to know who I really am. You're putting your life at risk, and I'm the one who dragged you into it."

Hamara smiles. "Well, if this plan works, every soul in the world will have reason to thank you. Me included."

Asei attempts to laugh, then winces and lets out a curse as he clutches a hand to his side. Hamara laughs in his stead, about to turn away. But the silver-eyed heln raises a hand.

"One more thing. If you see her before I catch up to you—if you see Alarei—tell her I'm sorry. For everything." There's a subtle light in his eyes when he says her name. The same light that first revealed itself to Hamara on a rainy day in Remertrei, not long ago. And though she can't quite define it, one fact is certain: it's a shine that couldn't possibly be fabricated.

Hamara nods, closing her fist before her chin the way all Igretho people do when they enter an agreement. Then she turns northwestward, where the Emér Sea spreads as a shifting, shimmering blanket from the shore to the distant horizon. The first of many new views to come.

13

-Common Year 179-

The air feels heavy. Too heavy. It's warm and wet, lying like slime on his skin. Each bone in his trembling body seems to throb and ache in rhythm with the racing of his heart. But this time, his back and shoulders are the sorest of all. A good stretch might help. He turns onto his side, hoping to sit up, but a sharp bolt of pain in his supporting arm sends him gasping onto his stomach. Someone comes running now, laying warm palms to his spine and sending a soothing surge of energy into the aching bones and tissues. The relief will only last a short while. But in the meantime, it's heavenly.

"*Byt helave dov*—try to lie flat. It reduces the stress on your joints," a voice murmurs softly at his side.

"Thanks." Asei doesn't bother to lift his face from the straw mat he's collapsed onto. In that moment, he decides he doesn't want to move at all. Even speaking is exhausting.

The changing process is never particularly comfortable, just before the deep sleep begins. But having fellow voránjevin nearby to help manage the soreness can make it better. Much better. Only this morning, he was seeing Hamara off on her journey. Now, as the night closes in, Asei can feel his mind slipping softly from consciousness. Preparing for the deep sleep. He swallows the odd taste in his mouth, wondering if his stomach is still there.

So many years have passed since he last transformed. He'd nearly forgotten what it was like. And how much he hated it. It was twenty-three years ago when he managed to change into the humanlike *virsevin* form. He was alone then, with no one to help him through the aching, and no one to bring him food or water when he woke up weeks later. He hardly survived. He was an outcast. A runaway who abandoned his clan the morning after he convinced a hunter to help him initiate his transformation. Last time, he was desperate. This time should be easy. He has help. And at least he has a greater purpose this time around. Something worth enduring for. Something more than simply a desire to escape the life he knew.

The Taufeth clan has counted him as one of their own since the day he arrived among them years ago, and it's fortunate. Without their aid, this transformation would be difficult at best—hopelessly too late at worst.

A hot flurry rushes up his throat and spine, and he coughs—a wet, rattling cough that sends an awful quake through his frame. Now heaviness cloaks his thoughts, as if a tremendous weight were anchored at the front of his mind, pressing him down. And the darkness it brings is so inviting. So warm. Hopefully, it won't last too long.

I'll catch up to you, Hamara. Just don't get killed in the meantime. The thought flutters fleetingly through his fading mind just before he lets go, and the shadows sweep over him like a swift and silent tide.

14

-341 years before the start of the Common Calendar of Glesia (520 years before Common Year 179)-

"Sekýnteo, young sir, your father's come to the west lounge to speak with you."

He was given the news as he left the last of his evening classes, at the time when the school's lanterns had just begun to cast their warm orange and yellow glows along the corridors—at a time when Kyvóike had little more than disdain for the man they called his father.

The west lounge of Mihinehn's Boarding School was rarely occupied on a midweek evening. Buried with studies and endless assignments, the students nearly all spent their weeknights bent over the desks in the study dens of the library or strumming perfect pitches in the symphony hall, or working tirelessly over new creations in a corner of the sculpting studio. Few had time for idle talk and games in the lounge. As one of the highest-marked students of his class, Kyvóike was no exception. He was nearly nineteen, and only weeks from the graduation he'd toiled toward for ages. But this night was different.

"You have no reason to be here."

He wasted no time with idle talk when he entered the lounge. His father stood waiting beside the grandest of the seven west-facing windows, staring with the same stony stare he had worn for years. It's a face young Kyvóike once revered—once esteemed to be the face of the rightful king of Tekéhldeth. The face of power and unquestionable authority. Once, not long ago, it was the face of a man Kyvóike trusted.

"There's nothing to fret over, son. You really must learn to better control your childish emotions." The man brought his hands together with a patronizing tilt to his eyebrows that bristled the rage in his son's darkening heart.

"It was you. You had her killed. The house guards were here. They told me everything." Kyvóike could hardly contain the quaking in his pointing hand, could hardly see through the anger that seethed through his veins and clouded his vision.

"It makes no difference. It needed to be done."

"Is that so? To clear your path? Because you knew her bloodline was purer than yours? You got her out of the way—just like you got rid of your uncle and your brothers."

"I've only done what I must to ensure our family's eventual rise to the throne."

"Family?" Kyvóike nearly laughed as he came stepping across the ornate rug on the floor between them, pausing near the center. "All these years you've talked of our royal family. The same family you've slain, because you were afraid it would rob you of the throne you craved."

The face of the man beside the windows became suddenly sharp angled. "How dare you speak so to your father, the rightful king of this land—"

"*I will be king!*" Young Kyvóike's voice erupted with startling volume, quaking and reverberating within the walls of the lounge like the clamor of the hulking city bells beyond the school walls. "I will be a *god*! I alone will rise, without aid from you or your precious followers. No one can stand in my path. I've seen the visions. I will reign over the Ten Regions with power so swift and terrible that all the world will hear of it. All people will be under my feet. And you—you disgusting boar—you are no exception."

"Foolish, contemptible child! You never could've come this far without my blessing, my wealth!" The man nearly spat.

Kyvóike didn't wait to hear anything more. He hefted a chair from beside the table at his left and sent it hurling at the enemy. The wooden frame burst with a splintering snap across the man's flinching figure and sent him stumbling to the ground, cursing. Kyvóike stepped closer. Close enough to grasp the aging man's throat in his own vein-streaked hand. And he let his voice fall back to a murmur.

"Wealth? Blessing? You're no longer my father. Mother was the only person I ever cared for in this world. She gave me life. And you took away hers. When the time is right, I'll be sure to take yours."

He left the west lounge without looking back that day. Three long years faded by before he saw the face of his father again, in the council of the House of Voices, where all the laws and affairs of the Ten Regions where debated. Three long years before the lord of the house of Sekýnteo—the man they called his father—came to regret the day his son was born.

15

-Common Year 179-

It's a cloudless night. The first in weeks that isn't plagued by the relentless onslaught of flames and shuddering earth. This night, for the first time since the day she met her enemy, Alarei can finally focus on something more than simply calming the storm that rages over the world. It's a break that may not last the night. But Alarei plans to cherish every breath of it.

The sun was only beginning to set over the far western coasts of Glesia when Skéisono vanished from the realms. He vanished so completely that Alarei could no longer hear his fiery heart, could no longer sense his presence at all. Somehow, he's done it again—hidden himself the way he hid for decades, beyond the reach of even Alarei's most diligent searching through the heart of the earth. The Farian says he must be hiding in the gap between the mortal and spirit realms. A place where darkness has hidden in ages past. But it makes no sense.

From what Alarei's seen so far, the spirit realm lies like fog over the physical world, and the two spheres are continually stirred and interwoven. The idea that a gap exists between them is bizarre—if possible at all. But it's the only explanation. And for now, Alarei doesn't concern herself with trying to understand it. For now, she just thanks the gods for a moment free of her counterpart's attacks to aid the people who are suffering in his wake.

She's spent hours in a city of West Ataran, far across the Atayu Sea, healing the wounds and mending the broken bones of more people than she dares to number. Light-skinned people, with hair that matches the pale sands on the sea shores and the shifting colors of the trees in autumn. They gather in massive crowds, some cradling bleeding loved ones, some limping with mangled limbs, others riding in carts with life remaining in little more than a single breath at their lips. All desperate. And somehow, Alarei knows how to help them. With a single touch of her hand, she sends the energy of life into their broken bodies—sends a healing surge of light into their veins that mends shattered bones and pulls the torn tissues back into place. She heals the people long into the night, hardly hearing beyond the shouts of praise and wonder that ring out from their grateful hearts. Then she leaves without a farewell, stepping over the world to aid a city in an island nation that's suffered the same fate, tears sliding like crystal rain from her eyes all the while.

"These wounds never should've happened. I should've been able to stop him the day he appeared." Her tears are swept violently away in the wind at her feet as the world passes swiftly by. She crosses over a jagged wall of mountains, moving southeastward toward the sea. "Lives have been lost. Far, far too many lives."

Gliding at her side, the Farian gives no answer. When a response comes at last, it's given in a voice Alarei's never heard.

"The power to stop him lies within you. It always has."

It's a woman's voice. Alarei turns sharply in her path, stepping out of the wind and touching down to the earth in an unfamiliar forest. The owner of the voice stands only several paces away—a woman more glorious and full of light than the shining twin moons at her back. Her hair cascades like deep-scarlet waves over her shoulders, and she stands clothed entirely in striking white brilliance that seems to outshine even Alarei's own glow. She isn't the goddess. Somehow, Alarei knows it. But whoever the stranger is, she's fast. Fast enough to talk with a sasarian traveling at a speed that no mortal frame could endure.

"Are you . . . another sasarian?" Alarei asks, hoping. It's a wonderful thought.

The woman in white smiles. "I was, long ago." She steps closer, leaving a trail of crystal-like shimmers in the grass at her feet. "My name is Faliéhl."

The name is familiar. The sound of it revives a memory of ancient days in Alarei's unsuspecting mind. Days that passed well before even the birth of Claya itself. The memory of figures standing in a circle at the feet of the goddess—and among them, a woman with deep-scarlet hair and eyes like an evening sky in the wake of a storm. Faliéhl.

"Have you come to help me stop him?" Alarei avoids speaking his name. Let him stay hidden.

"I've come to remind you of something you already know." Faliéhl stands a single step from the draping ends of Alarei's gown. "You stand before a challenge that few sasarianë have faced. When our own kind turns against us—against the world—our very purpose in Claya is compromised. But you have the power to end this."

"So far I can't find any way to stop him." Alarei shakes her head. "He's had *years* to perfect his abilities."

The woman in white smiles again. This time, with subtle bitterness at the edges. "Many generations ago, I watched over all the world as a sasarian immortal. I served Claya alone for many years. When my counterpart obtained his sasarian abilities at last, he used them to become a tyrant over the once great nation of East Ataran. He brought great corruption and darkness into the world, and many suffered because of it. I had the power to stop him then. Now, that same power rests upon you."

Alarei's heart nearly leaps from its place. She's struggled hopelessly long against her enemy's attacks. But now she stands with a being who once succeeded at the very same challenge. Someone who's done it before.

"How did you do it? Will you please teach me? I've tried moving faster, but it seems useless—"

Faliéhl raises a hand to interrupt. "Alarei, you don't need to be faster. You only need to more fully utilize the strength you possess."

"That's what the Farian tells me. But the elements obey my enemy's voice as much as mine. He throws aside my every attack."

"Which is why you must defend Claya using elements that only *you* can master." Faliéhl's words hush Alarei's mind to silence. But what could she possibly mean? She takes Alarei's hand and lifts it up between them, palm skyward. "These hands are stronger than

- 196 -

you think. The day I was forced to slay my brother was the same day that I discovered something remarkable about our abilities as sasarianë. We can not only command the elements. We can *assemble* them."

"Assemble?"

"My weapon that day was a blade I formed by tearing apart the matter I sensed in the air and stone around me. I created something new. Something that obeyed only my voice."

"You created new matter?" Alarei can feel her eyes widening.

"I simply reorganized the elements that were already there. I surrounded myself with matter I had organized, like a hidden shield at all sides. And because it was my own creation, my fellow sasarian had no power to control it. He was helpless against my attack." Faliéhl gently closes Alarei's open hand, folding it into a loose fist. "You must learn to sense the elements in their purest, most fundamental states."

Alarei stares down at her shining fist and marvels. Day after day, week after week she's done all she could to outrun her opponent. Done everything she could think of to gain the upper hand in any way at all. And she's made no real progress. But now, it's as if the curtain's been thrown back from her eyes, and an entire world of possibilities lies suddenly in view, waiting to be tested and explored. Now that it's in front of her, the answer seems so plain.

"Of course," she wonders aloud, unable to contain the smile at her lips. "How have I not thought of this before?"

It's a marvelous concept. One with limitless possibilities. Mastering it could make her perfectly untouchable—could make the task of ending Skéisono's reign of terror an almost laughably simple task. For an instant, she can nearly imagine what the devil's reaction will be when he finds himself powerless against the sasarian he once tormented. When he's no longer able to stop her from doing what she should have done the day he appeared at Clevyan.

What she should have done.

The thought freezes in her mind, and the smile falls away from her radiant face. She should be relieved—*thrilled*—to know that she'll finally have the tool she needs to end the immortal who's brought so much grief and suffering into the world. And she truly is. But now that the solution lies at her fingertips, it feels strange. Almost sour.

"I need to kill him, don't I?" she asks her own hand. That was always the intent, wasn't it?

. . . Wasn't it?

"The paths that lead to the best outcomes in this world are rarely the easiest."

Faliéhl's words come like the gentle guidance of an elder sister. She's right in more ways than one. Learning to disassemble and reorganize the elements isn't likely to be easy. Where should one even begin?

"Can you show me—" Alarei begins, full of questions.

But the space between the trees ahead is empty when she looks up again. The woman in white has gone.

16

-Common Year 179-

The ship gives a mild shudder as it meets the docks, shuffling Hamara on her feet. It would've been a softer ride in the padded seats of the passenger deck, but she prefers the roughness of the wind in her face and the chilled spray of the sea that leaps occasionally up over the railing—anything to keep the world from spinning. Just under a week of living on a trade ship has left almost unceasing, mild nausea in her stomach. Back in Igretho, the branch of the Nakuë that flows by Remertrei is slow and mild. No wild rapids, no tumbling waves. But the inland sea is different. Day and night the Emér Sea is sleepless. Now, after six days of enduring the tossing waves, Hamara will be the first to exit the boat. She stands waiting on the deck as the crew scrambles to fasten the ship to its moorings, admiring the sight of unmoving streets and rooftops in the port town of Dasva. Solid ground! She'll never take it for granted again.

The city feels strange the moment Hamara steps into it. Foreign smells of spice and incense waft up from every alley and open window, and on all sides the peoples' voices seem to speak an oddly tainted version of the Moi-Sketzan language. Even the clothing varies more from person to person than Hamara's seen in even the busiest festivals of Igretho.

The lane from the docks widens after only a handful of crowded blocks, pouring its traffic into a broad, open plaza. The masses weave and disperse in every direction, all seeming to know exactly where to go. Hamara does her best to mirror their confident strides, leaning here and there to peer between sauntering shoulders. Where to now? The street vendors are the first to catch her eye.

"Do you know where to find the best inns? Not too expensive?" she questions the cook as he hands her a freshly seared basket of *imdafa* rice and vegetables.

"Light on the sauce, Igretho style for you." He smiles. "The best places are two blocks down that way. Affordable, but not shady. Stay out of southwestern districts when evening comes." He points almost directly across the plaza to a broad lane that vanishes away to the east.

"Thank you, sir."

She finds the inns exactly where the cook suggested, just two blocks down the lane, all arrayed with painted shutters and colorful signs in multiple languages. The rooms they offer are cramped, but at this point, Hamara's simply thrilled at the thought of sleeping in a place that doesn't rock with sea waves. She'll enjoy it while she can. When morning comes again, she'll be looking for a ferry along the river Held, heading north.

She finds the washing yard in a little court outside the inn's back door after reserving her room, just as the evening is beginning to slide over the city. It's nearly vacant when she enters at the west corner—occupied by only a woman and her child wringing out sopping skirts in the far corner. They don't seem to notice Hamara dropping the dirtied clothes from her bag into the nearest trough and giving the pump handle a gentle heave. The stranger's daughter couldn't be more than four years old. She looks up a moment later and stares the way children often do at foreigners—with an emotionless, almost unblinking stare that only breaks when her mother chides her softly from behind. Hamara lets out a sigh as she lathers the soap in her hands against the dirt-mottled knee-length trousers in the water before her. Who can blame the kid for staring? Hamara most probably *does* look strange, here in the backstreets of Dasva. She's young, traveling alone, dressed in rather boyish Igretho clothes with a sénsin rod clipped to the back of her belt. But there's no sense in trying to fit in.

She rinses out the clothes with a few sloppy presses under another fresh pour of water before laying them on the wringer nearby, moving with an odd quickness in her hands. There's no reason to rush, is there? There shouldn't be. But there's an uneasiness that seems to creep into Hamara's bones alongside the growing dimness of the sky overhead. One that makes her cramped inn room—a room with a locking door—feel overwhelmingly appealing.

The woman and her daughter have vanished when Hamara looks up again, although the light of their lantern can still be seen dancing along the eastward alley walls as they hurry away. Hamara's finished as well. She shoves the damp laundry into her bag before turning back to the little street she entered in by only moments ago. The night has yet to come, but it isn't far. All throughout the streets and weaving alleyways the evening lanterns are beginning to be lit. The hum of the distant plaza can still be heard in the falling sunlight— quieting down, spreading out. And as Hamara rounds a corner, all the ordinary sounds of evening town life come echoing to her ears: doors closing, muffled voices, someone shaking a rug over the edge of a balcony. Familiar sounds. Maybe the disquiet in Hamara's stomach is as uncalled for as she's repeatedly told herself. Maybe the bustling port city of Dasva isn't so unlike Remertrei after all.

The inn's backdoor is as brilliantly painted as its twin at the front lobby. But the hinges seem to be stuck in place when Hamara reaches for the handle. Has the keeper locked it already? Hamara frowns, and is about to find her way to the front door when a sharp shove comes to her shoulder, nearly knocking her to the cobble path at her feet.

Thugs! Robbers!

Hamara's thoughts explode as she scrambles to catch her balance. She flings her bag to the ground and draws her sénsin from behind her hip in one practiced motion, ready to battle whatever scum of a man would dare face her. But there's no one to fight when she scans the narrow street ahead. No one at all. Hamara lets her breath slow, glancing again in all directions. Strange. Maybe it was just some kid running down the alleyways. Nothing to startle over. Or so it seems. She re-shoulders her bag and steps back to the door with her weapon still in hand.

And this time, she sees it.

It sits little more than a stone's toss down the alley to her right, almost directly across from the inn door—in a spot where the light of the nearest street lantern peers down at a sharp angle against the stone walls of the shops and falls like a blade into the shadows, starkly dividing them. There's an object highlighted against the darkness there that Hamara can't recognize. Something smooth, pale. Something *alive*. The longer she stares, the more obvious its misshapen features become. Unnaturally bony shoulders; a hunched, rigid spine; a terribly long, narrow neck. And its face—

The inn door swings abruptly open now, and a handful of strangers come sauntering out with drinks in their hands, chatting idly to one another. They take no notice of the young Igretho woman who stands wide-eyed with her back to the inn wall. Their clamor breaks the silence of the scene like stones tossed into still waters. But it's a welcome relief. Hamara waits for the strangers to disappear around the next corner before glancing back to the alley. It's empty. The lantern light falls uninterrupted to the ground, illuminating the dust as it floats in the cooling air. Whatever haunted the space there a moment ago has vanished.

17

The first breaths are coarse and wet. But they're nothing a good cough can't solve. He blinks impulsively—almost constantly—hoping to clear the haze from his eyes as the heaviness of the deep sleep falls away from his limbs. Now he lets out another cough, shifting his shoulders. It's like he's been cramped in a little box for months. His bones are aching to stretch out and unwind.

It's night. Late night. Asei can smell it in the fresh air that welcomes him as his foot tears through his thinning cocoon. He only struggles for an instant before the hands of others appear at all sides, helping him to scrape away the wet remains of his shell and bringing fresh water to his chin. He drains the bowl in one gulp. Someone's brought a cool rag to his now-furred face, wiping away the sticky remains of the changing fluids.

"How . . . how long did it take?" Asei leans forward to rise on trembling knees.

"Easy now. Only about seven days," someone answers from the left, audibly impressed. It's a voice Asei knows well. Theud. One of the many Taufeth clan members who's studied mid-transformation energy exchange for ages.

Asei curses under his breath, almost laughing. "You serious?" He would've been surprised to wake up in three weeks. But seven *days*?

"Serious. Looks like our first attempt to accelerate the ek'let'eh process worked far better than we hoped. And it seems like your skeletal and muscular structure formed normally. But we need to be careful. Do you have any pain?" Theud steps in a slow circle around the newly awakened, eyeing him closely with a vibrant green stare.

"Not at the moment." Asei shakes his head, and the surrounding scene begins to slide into focus at last.

The two voránjevin faces that watch him are lit by the warm glow of nearby torches, their wide eyes capturing the light and throwing it back like colored gemstones in the night shadows. For the first time since his boyhood, Asei finds himself looking *up* to speak to his fellow clan members. It's an undeniably disorienting feeling, after spending more than half of his life in the tall, humanlike virsevin form. But it's also expected. Built to soar with the eagles in the sky, the winged *virit* form is the smallest, shortest transformation any voránjevin can assume.

Asei hobbles onto his clawed feet and extends his newly formed wings out from his sides. They nearly span the halo of light cast by the torches on the cool earth. Massive, powerful wings. It's a magnificent feeling, to stretch at last. And the motion seems to trigger a swell of strength in his now-feathered chest.

"Such a gorgeous plume!" Akyla gasps at Asei's side, a wet rag still clutched in her hand. "Unlike any I've seen—sunset colors!" She brings a palm to his chest, sensing the flow of energy and nodding slowly. "Your energy seems as balanced as ever. You've even grown your tail feathers in full. No one would ever guess that you were in the virsevin form just seven days ago."

"It's marvelous!" Theud stands back, smiling broadly. "The clans will be thrilled! This will change everything!"

He goes on, talking excitedly about their newfound success, about how it could revolutionize the transformation process for all voránjevin people. But Asei doesn't care to listen. For now, the stickiness that coats his new feathers and the gaping emptiness of his stomach are far more pressing matters. He steps carefully between Theud and Akyla, following the scent of roasting meats that floats from elsewhere in the camp. There isn't much time for delay.

* * *

He doesn't wait long before setting off on a northward path. After only a single day of flight training with virit messengers from the Taufeth, Asei finds himself rising alone on the thermals and gliding rather comfortably on the high winds over the Emér Sea—grinning all the while. The wind whips and glides like rushing waters beneath his newborn wings. Wild and pure. *Exhilarating*. His flying skills are still rough, but they'll have to do. There's no telling how far Hamara could've travelled in a week's time.

He flies more than halfway along the length of the Emér Sea in a single day, keeping the shoreline visible in the west. The winds gust eastward for the greater part of the afternoon, and now, as the daylight begins to shrink away, they've almost slowed to a standstill. Asei glides to a lower altitude, maintaining his speed with only an occasional beat from his long wings. The canopy of the woodlands flows beneath him like a billowing river of green, and he wonders momentarily how long it would've taken to travel so far on foot. Fortunately for Hamara, the arai are excellent shipbuilders.

The sound of another set of wings soaring in the wind nearby is so subtle that Asei almost startles and loses his level glide when he finally spots the stranger flying beside him. The newcomer couldn't be more than half Asei's age, by the span of his wings. A dark-feathered heln, with only hints of gray at the tips of his flight feathers.

"You must've come from far away." His stare drifts along Asei's colorful right wing. "I don't recognize you."

"Just from the south." Asei gives the wind beneath his feathers a single beat.

The youngster flaps twice to keep up. "Where are you headed?"

"I'm looking for a friend of mine. A young arai woman. Though I plan to find the Vilfirehn scouts who've tracked her for me first."

The youth flaps again, tilting in his glide with his left wing angled toward the treetops. He glances up to meet Asei's gaze. "You must've come from the Taufeth," he says. "I remember hearing that someone asked us to watch over an arai traveler for him."

"That's me. I can accompany her myself now. But I need to know where she is."

"Follow me." The boy tips sharply to soar in a tight loop before veering to the northeast.

Show-off. Asei follows without a word.

The night has already begun to spread its subtle fingers over the hills when Asei and his guide reach a humble Vilfirehn camp. From the air, it looks like no more than a single, flickering campfire. The young virit circles slowly over the trees ahead before sweeping down between them in a smooth, practiced landing glide. Asei does his best to follow behind with nearly twice the wingspan and no practice at all. But the gap in the trees is slightly smaller than he had momentarily hoped, and he's forced to come at the ground at a sharper angle than is comfortable. It's an awkward show, but he manages all right—fanning out his tail feathers and coming to a hopping stop a short distance behind the boy. He's still giving his long wings one last stretch and bringing them in at his sides when the boy can be heard reporting softly to his elders.

"From the Taufeth . . ."

He speaks to the handful of virit scouts and messengers who stand within the glow of the fire. Now several other figures come stalking from the shadows of the trees. Hunters in their original voránjevin forms, dressed in only waistcloths and wraps that cross over both shoulders and finish in knots at their backs. One of them—a lone filíl among the males with fur the color of clay—comes stepping closer. She takes a moment to stare at the guest, tipping her head to one side as a mild, sharp-toothed smile appears on her face.

"We're told you come from the Taufeth. But looking at you, I can't help wondering otherwise."

Asei shifts his weight, suddenly grateful that assuming a virit form involves returning his face to its original scarlet-orange fur-covered appearance. It's a perfect camouflage for the hot blush at his cheeks. The clan he once left behind has come to be known for more than its murders among the arai. It's no secret that vibrant colors in the eyes, fur, and feathers of the Iftav people is a trait few other clans share so predominately.

"I've left that heritage behind me," Asei assures his onlookers.

"Good. Every dissenter from the Iftav is a blessing to the clans." The hunter nods with quiet approval. "You're looking for that girl from Igretho, then?"

"Yes. The one I sent a message about."

"Our scouts most recently spotted her entering the arai city called Dasva, at the northeastern edge of the inland sea. A single day's flight from here, but a long one." The hunter snatches a strip of freshly roasted meat from the fire and leaves it in a little bowl at Asei's clawed feet, squatting to look into his eyes. In her natural form, she stands noticeably taller than all the virit in the grove. "What makes you so interested in the travels of random arai, anyway? Especially at a time like this?"

Asei plops down in the grass and makes a valiant attempt to skewer the meat on the talons of his left foot. He's seen virit do it for years. But bringing the food to his mouth with his now remarkably short legs is far more difficult than he would've imagined. He's moved onto his knees and is about to bring his face to the bowl when the hunter squatting before him lifts the food to his mouth. A subtle laugh escapes her teeth.

"You're certainly new to the virit body, aren't you?"

Asei tears a grateful mouthful from the savory offering, not caring how helpless he may look. "Just woke up two days ago. And this arai isn't random. Her

- 210 -

father's the brother of the sasarian who's destroying the arai cities." He talks through his food.

The hunter's broad ears twitch forward. "And what use is that?"

Asei swallows his mouthful. "The sasarian's family was murdered when he was a boy. But he doesn't seem to know that his brother survived. If we could use that to distract him—even for just a single breath—it's worth trying."

"Why is that?"

"Because his counterpart, who fights to defend us all, has yet to stop him—or has that changed since I woke up a few days ago?" Asei sends a glance over the surrounding company, only to be answered with shaking heads and downward glances.

"Nothing's changed. Just this morning our fastest messenger reported that the sasarian woman was seen defending an arai city on the shores of the Atayu."

Asei breathes. "If we can distract the enemy, bring his attention away from her for even just a moment, it might be all the time she needs to take control of the fight."

"You really think that could work?"

"I have no idea." Asei's wings come briefly away from his sides in an attempted shrug. "But it's at least a chance to stop the destruction our world faces."

The little camp falls momentarily silent, giving audience to the few birds that remain awake in the shade of the canopy. Asei downs the last of his food, and the clay-colored hunter passes his bowl to a heln at her back.

"Give him plenty more. He'll need it for his flight." Then she turns back to the virit with the sunset colors in his plume. "I admire your hope, my friend. A few of our scouts have been heading north in and alongside the river Held. If you follow its length, I'm sure you'll find this arai friend of yours. Likely on a boat. Best of luck to your efforts."

Asei smiles. "Thanks. We'll need it."

The camp is mostly still and unoccupied as the night comes along. And the virit hammocks strung up between the low branches of the trees are certainly comfortable enough. But Asei's second night as a bird is hardly restful. He dozes off for only a handful of hours before his racing thoughts leave him wide-eyed and hopelessly awake.

The twin moons are high in their thrones when he leaves the camp and rises on eastward winds, curving in a slow glide to the north. The greater moon has grown since he saw it last. Watching it makes him feel as if he were gliding in place—as if the wind is only an illusion, sweeping like a whisper over his feathers. And the night sky is flawlessly silent.

Silent, like the beast when it comes.

It appears first in the image of a man, standing impossibly in the air ahead. A faint figure that hangs with perfect stillness in the night air. A ghost—scarcely a wing's length away from Asei's face. Every nerve in his sleepless body seems to light at the sight of it, and his wings tuck impulsively inward. The wind stutters in his feathers, and he barrels abruptly toward the earth. He lets out a curse as he struggles awkwardly to find his balance mid-stall, nearly plummeting into the treetops below before recapturing the air in his wings. But he scarcely manages to give a single, solid beat against the chill winds before something hooks his leg from below, jerking him sharply downward. A rope. Or an arm. The attack sends Asei hurling through the leaves, bringing him down atop a thick bough with a force that steals his breath away. And the creature that lands on the bough beside him a moment later is unlike any Asei's ever laid eyes on. A long, hunched being with unnaturally thin limbs. Its little head rises at the end of a dramatically elongated neck as the virit scrambles to gather his feet beneath himself. Then the monster comes lunging closer, and Asei sweeps his massive left wing across the bough as fiercely as his little chest can manage. The effort is enough to send the beast toppling loudly through the branches below. Asei doesn't care to see if it recovers. He leaps from the branches and rises in an exhausting climb through the canopy, beating his wings until the light of the twin moons falls once again in an uninterrupted glow on all sides.

He flies at top speed for nearly an hour before allowing his aching chest and shoulders to rest in a slower glide. And he draws a much-needed deep breath. Whatever the beast was, it wasn't friendly. But the sight of the ghostly arai that preceded its appearance was somehow worse. A sight that left a horribly sour sensation in Asei's heart. He's got to keep moving.

18

-Common Year 179-

The moment is fleeting. It's little more than a thought between Alarei's motions as she calms the towering waves that threaten to immerse a seaside city. She pauses on the shore while the sea buckles and folds into itself by the command of her outstretched hand. And she listens. Not to the cries of relief and rejoicing that pour out from the city at her back, not to the spray of the sea as it returns to its bounds—not even to the whispered threats of the sasarian who stands in a rage out over the tossing face of the ocean. But to the elements themselves.

"Elements, please. Hear my voice." She dares to close her eyes for a single breath. Waiting, feeling. All around, the land and sea are teeming with organized matter. Some living, others simply saturated with energy.

. . . a blade I formed by tearing apart the matter I sensed in the air and stone around me. I created something new.

Tear apart? Alarei opens her eyes and kneels to grasp a little stone from the sand at her feet. It's cool to the touch, smoothed by millennia of wind and rain and rising tides. She could command it to move, to take any shape she desires. Until now, that ability has been her only way to defend against Skéisono's attacks. But Faliéhl spoke of something more—of sensing the elements in their purest, most fundamental state. How is it done? It's a question Alarei's pondered for days. She grips the stone more tightly in her hands, tracing every curve and angle.

To the north, a tremendous quake begins to tear through the earth, shuddering a city tower to its knees. Another attack.

"Be still." Alarei calms the tremors in the land with little more than a whisper, without turning to see the damage, without taking her eyes from the stone in her hands.

And then it happens. Somehow, for an instant more fleeting than ribboning lightning in the night, the stone reveals itself. The presence of infinitely smaller fragments of matter within it becomes suddenly obvious to Alarei's fingertips. They cling together like millions of tiny bricks in a city wall. Each fragment is melded to the next, and each carries properties that somehow give the stone its firmness, color, and every other characteristic. It's marvelous. Magnificent. The building blocks of creation. But could they possibly be commanded to separate? To rearrange?

A blast of hurricane winds arrives without warning and engulfs the seaside city in a cloud of flying sand. Alarei rises to shout into the chaos, calling the winds to sleep with a single command. And she turns reluctantly to the shaken city in need of healing. There's no time to experiment with new skills today. Not yet.

19

The sky is bright, with the dark edge of a retreating storm in the eastern horizon the only blemish on its sunny face. Looking up, Hamara tries to forget her queasy stomach in the drifting shapes of the clouds. If she's learned anything on this journey thus far, it's that long boat rides are something she'll avoid for the rest of her life. The steam-driven riverboat she now rides is at least large enough to ease the general sway of the river's current, but Hamara's sure that she'll sense the subtle rocking again as she tries to sleep when night returns. Even after the lengthy sail along the Emér, her stomach has yet to master the waves. And the river Held is lively at its southern end.

The riverboat left Dasva in the chilled hours of the morning, heading northward along the river, which flows north and south through the lands once inhabited by the ancestors of Igretho. Hamara's heard a handful of tales about the river Held, which welcomed the ancestors as they fled from the far north. She's heard stories of bravery and tragedy, toil and honor. It should be a privilege to see its waters herself. But now, as she finds herself riding for a third day along its flow with a hand to her stomach, it's difficult to admire. She can hardly stop fantasizing about the moment she'll leave it.

Not far beyond the roots of the Held lies the Ádenlal—a vast plain that stretches far to the north until it begins to ripple and collide into the forested lands of Sketza. Vehn suggested that a travelers' caravan would be the safest and most affordable way to cross the plains. And though the idea of riding in a cramped wagon by day and camping in the dirt with complete strangers by night sounds admittedly unpleasant, Hamara looks almost constantly forward to it. At least it won't involve boats.

Fortunately, the riverboat is clean. The living quarters are dim and cramped, but they lack the awful fishy smell of the trade boat that carried Hamara along the Emér. And its top deck is massive. The mild spring evenings have lured many passengers to spend their nights in the open air. Tonight, Hamara joins them. She finds a decent seat atop a large stack of crates at the front of the boat, where the view of the oncoming river is wide and uninterrupted. The sinking sun seems to melt into the slightly westward bend of the waters ahead, dyeing them with blazing orange, red, and pink hues. Looking on, Hamara wonders again how much farther she'll travel alone. If Asei will ever find her at all. She's sent four letters to her family since leaving Igretho. And she's considered writing to Asei more than once. But how would a note ever reach him?

Darkness falls, and the river's breath seems to cool in the absence of the sun. Most of the passengers light lamps and converse over simple coin games in the dim light, holding shawls and thin blankets over their shoulders. Near the stern, someone plays idly on a hollowed stringed instrument. Hamara leans against the crates and listens to the sounds of the night. Calm, but sleepless. Now the dark breeze stutters and sighs, pulling the chilled air from the river's face and sending a shiver across Hamara's uncovered arms. She reaches impulsively for the overcoat at her side. But her hand meets only the bare wood of the crate beneath her. And she sighs. The bag. Her coat's with the bag she left in the passengers' quarters below the deck.

The corridor to the lower decks is narrow, lit by only two lanterns that swing somewhat precariously on their hooks as Hamara steps past them. The steps are thick—bowed at the center and worn smooth by ages of use. Hamara moves down them with her arms held out from her sides, her fingertips sliding along the coarse walls. And her stomach gives a mild lurch. Just a moment longer! She wills her insides to endure as she ducks swiftly into the cramped passengers' quarters, shuffling to nearly the last cubby in the hall. She wastes no time pulling the coat over her head after she snatches it from an upper bunk, not bothering to secure the sleeve ties. And she nearly leaps back to the steps at the end of the hall.

But the sound that greets her there makes her pause in her steps. Two low, heavy thumps come echoing up from the shadows below—like the toppling of a massive stone, or crates of bricks dropping to the wooden floor. A sound from the cargo deck. It sends a mild quake along the length of the stairs and rattles the bunks in the passengers' hall. Hamara bends to peer down into the darkness at the foot of the steps, momentarily forgetting her sour stomach. A box of goods must have fallen over, somewhere in the black belly of the boat. Heavy goods. Hamara shrugs, letting a yawn capture her breath. It's likely nothing to be concerned about.

Or is it?

She turns back to the upper deck and is about to make her way to the fresh air that awaits there when something rams mercilessly into her stomach, knocking the air from her lungs and sending her tumbling down the narrow staircase at her back. The world reels and spins until she lands heavily on her hands and knees beside the entrance to the cargo deck. She struggles to regain her footing, blinking in the darkness that's fallen on all sides. Someone attacked—again. But the stairway above remains obviously empty when Hamara looks back to it. Empty like the alley in Dasva. And there's no time to wonder how. There's scarcely time for the girl to rise on her knees and draw her sénsin rod from its sheath before a wild thumping erupts in the dark depths of the cargo deck to her left. Footsteps, racing closer. Hamara's only just raised her weapon defensively across her chest when a dark blur comes lunging from the shadows. It lands with startling weight across the sénsin's middle, knocking Hamara backward before recoiling and tumbling away. A burst of sand and dirt showers over Hamara's head and shoulders as she scrambles to her feet with her heart hammering in her ears.

Climb! Run!

The instinct jolts through every muscle in Hamara's body. She leaps for the staircase and stumbles blindly up the first several steps before the attacker's footfalls come thundering after her.

"Get away from me!" Hamara swings her weapon into the darkness at her back with all the force her father's always taught her to use. The rod makes contact, sticking and tugging as its acidic surface burns into its victim. But the attacker—whatever it is—gives no scream. It jerks and pulls away into the shadows, dropping what sounds like thick clumps of wet clay to the floor as it moves. It must be injured. But Hamara doesn't care to see the details. She rips her sénsin free and bolts up the steps without looking back. The top deck isn't far. But now it seems impossibly far—a distant escape that hangs just beyond reach, beyond the swaying glow of the lantern light. The boat takes a little dip as Hamara climbs past the passenger bunks, tossing her to the right as she throws out an arm against the wall for support. And her outstretched hand finds something else where it lands. Not the worn, humid walls of the staircase, but something else. Something smooth and cold. The sight of the creature that now sits on the steps above seems to freeze the blood in her veins. It's a pale, naked beast. Hairless—with long, impossibly thin limbs and rigid bones that protrude like spines from its hunched back. Its almost featureless face glares down at Hamara from the end of a neck that's at least as long as a sénsin rod, and its eyes sit like tiny, shining black marbles in their sinking sockets. There's no mouth, no ears—no other features at all. Hamara shrinks back in horror, stumbling backward into the slender doorway of the passengers' quarters. The monster comes slinking after her, holding its horrible face level to hers all the while.

"I said get away!"

Hamara heaves her weapon at the beast's awful face. And she nearly topples to her knees when the rod swings through empty air instead, clattering loudly against the wall. Somehow, very suddenly, there's nothing in the hall to interrupt her swing. The beast is gone. But how? Hamara breathes, looking up and down the narrow passage, glancing into every open bunk.

Empty. The creature has vanished again. Vanished without any sound at all. And Hamara fights to subdue the lightning that pulses through her nerves. It's gone. But what *was* that thing?

She scrambles up the steps to the top deck without looking to the cargo level below. The open air lays a cool mist over her face as she sprints to the boat's stern, where nearly all the passengers still sit chatting by the soft glows of their lamps. Hamara returns her weapon to its sheath and slips soundlessly into the crowd, settling down in a nook between two stacks of rugs. No one seems to notice.

Deep breaths, deep breaths. Hamara closes her eyes and fights to think past the raw fear that still rattles her bones. What just happened? She was attacked. Again—but by what? Some kind of heaven-forsaken beast that's native to the lands of North Emér? How has she never heard of it before? And has no one else on the boat seen it? Its shape was undeniably similar to the silhouette that appeared in the alley in Dasva, not long ago. Did it *follow* her? The thought sends a new shiver through Hamara's spine.

The string instrument whose voice sprinkles the air is played by an old woman sitting beside the starboard railing. Despite ringing noticeably louder, the delicate notes are no less calming here than they were when Hamara heard them from the bow. They dance in a gentle, swaying melody that seems to lay tranquility like a blanket over the deck. A false sense of security. For whatever reason, the monster hasn't followed Hamara out into the open. But there's no telling how long it will hide. She'll have to tell someone.

She rises warily to her feet and returns to the bow of the boat, where the captain is often found bent over maps and schedules and inventory lists in his tiny office. But the office is empty when Hamara reaches it. She sighs and turns in place, wondering where to look next. The man's got to be somewhere nearby. The lantern beside his desk is still lit. Wherever he went, he's likely to return soon.

Hamara leans idly against the nearby railing, staring down to the river. The waters are nearly black in the evening light, speckled by the flickering reflections of the many lights aboard the boat. Like stars in a watery night sky. It reminds Hamara of the festival seasons back in Igretho, when her family would carry flags and colorful lights aboard a slender riverboat to ride to the neighboring city and join the evening celebrations. It wasn't long ago. But it feels like ages ago.

The sound of a nearby footfall pulls Hamara from her thoughts. She turns, relieved that she hasn't waited long. But the man she turns to see is not the captain—or any man she's ever seen. He's pale, and stares down at her with a terrible, unnerving glare—a black-eyed glare with no shine, no whiteness at the edges of his eyes. And he stands close. Too close. He stands so near that Hamara's insides can't suppress a subtle leap at the sight of him. Before she can think to say anything at all, the man raises a thin blade. Hamara draws her own weapon and takes a swing at the stranger's neck without hesitation—and lands it perfectly. Or at least, she *should* have. The weapon passes through the stranger's body as if he were nothing but an image cast in smoke. It shouldn't be possible. But Hamara's given no chance to wonder. The man comes rushing abruptly closer with his blade, and Hamara finds herself shrinking instinctively backward to avoid it. The boat's thin railing meets her lower back, and before she can react at all, her balance tips. The world spins, and the river comes to meet her in a burst of frigid wetness.

The current is merciless. It pulls and tosses her relentlessly along its path. Hamara's hands flail out in every direction as she fights for the surface—fights to grasp hold of anything at all. But the river is deep. The breath's nearly exhausted from her chest when strong hands catch hold of her at last, pulling her to the open air where she coughs and hacks the river from her lungs. Then supporting arms appear at both sides, keeping her afloat and pulling her swiftly to the shallow bank. She crawls onto the rocky shore like a nearly drowned animal, gasping uncontrollably.

"Tha-thank you. Thank you so much. I have no idea—" Hamara swipes the wet hair from her face as she looks up to her saviors, then blinks in silent confusion. There's no one beside her. No one stands in the shallow waters, or along the stony riverbank, or anywhere in sight. No one. Again.

Northward in the river's flow, the boat Hamara left behind has become little more than a cluster of lantern lights. Out of reach. It's going to be a very long night.

20

-Common Year 179-

The screams can be heard from the far edges of the world. Screams of terror, screams of agony and loss that ring like mourning chimes in the failing light of dusk. The sound emanates from a city at the heart of West Ataran, echoing over mountain and sea and wrenching Alarei's heart where she stands. Time is short.

The city of Thelian has already lost its glory when Alarei comes to its aid. At first glance she can see that it's been lifted entirely from its foundations, only to be throttled down again with terrible force. And now, as a distant, glowing figure stands over the westward foot of the mountains with a single hand held high, the wounded remains of Thelian become suddenly alight with wild, ravenous flames. The fiend Skéisono at work once again.

Destruction. Death. Suffering. Alarei's seen it all before. More times in the past weeks than she would've cared to witness in a lifetime—and every instant of it has shaken her soul with unspeakable sorrow. Now, after weeks of desperate battling, weeks of enduring the soul-tearing cries of the families she's not fast enough to save, the blade can plunge no deeper. The sorrow sinks deep into her undying bones, burying and kindling itself into a scalding white blaze. Today, the sasarian woman is filled with a rage that could light all of Claya with its glow.

"ENOUGH!"

She stands in a fury at the edge of the ruin, gathering every flame in the city with the clap of her hands and folding them into a massive, billowing cloud of whirling scarlet overhead. She sends them hurling back to their maker. Skéisono's still moving to redirect the churning flames when Alarei appears beside him, spearing her stone-encased hand at his back. The devil flinches aside, managing to save his heart—but the blade dives swiftly into his side. The horrible cry that erupts from his teeth sends a quake through the mountains and nearly mutes the roar of the molten stone he calls up to defend himself. Alarei steps clear of the danger, and the wounded Skéisono vanishes from her grasp—only to appear at the north end of the city a moment later, entirely unharmed.

"You must pierce his heart," the Farian whispers at Alarei's ear. "Or he will not fall. His guardian heals his body so long as his heart beats."

Alarei stares at her opponent's distant, infuriating grin. His body. Immortal or not, it's a body built of matter. Just as the stones, the trees, the water—everything in Claya. And if it's matter, a sasarian can command it.

The power comes without any struggle at all. Alarei raises her hands and takes hold of the very elements that compose the body of the flaming man in the distance. They lock obediently into her command—resistant, but yielding all the same. And the captured power of his presence seems to ripple and hiccup like violent static in the air between them.

"I have you!"

Alarei can hardly speak through her clenching jaw. She whips her arms westward with all the strength in her being and sends her enemy ramming into the face of the mountains. His impact leaves a raw trench through the stone—uprooting trees and nearly causing an avalanche of boulders and sand and earth. Then she appears in the air over the trench, staring mercilessly down at the battered immortal who lies beneath her. Skéisono was shielded only partly by the stones he called to protect himself. Bright, shimmering blood pours from the pulverized remains of his left shoulder and drenches his entire left side. But he's still alive—and he'll heal at any moment. There's no room for delay.

"You've robbed thousands of their lives and their free will. Now I'll rob you of yours."

The matter in his body seems to writhe and repel her grip when she takes hold of it again. But it can't stop her.

"You—!"

The man has no time to speak before Alarei sends him barreling down into the valley below like a leaf in a hurricane wind. She bolts through the air and appears in his path with a newly formed spear in her hand, only an instant away from catching him like a fish on a skewer. But a single word escapes the sasarian man's lips as he plummets—a word that sends a whip of sand to snatch Alarei by the ankle and rip her from the air. She meets the earth with a jarring snap in her right side, and a terrible pain tears through her nerves. Terrible, but fleeting. The Farian appears overhead, and the agony melts instantly away. Mended—before Alarei can react with any sound at all. But there's little time to marvel. A massive stone blade comes jutting out from the earth when she rises to her feet, aiming for her face and nearly pinning her to a tree. And when she commands it away, her fellow sasarian stands glowering only an arm's length away, restored to his perfect, flaming glory.

"So you're strong now, are you?" The rage seems to burn in his eyes with a more spectacular splendor than ever before as he opens his palm to the sky. A twisting, darting pillar of lightning leaps down from the clouds to meet his open hand, coiling submissively over his arms and shoulders. "You've learned a new trick?"

He sends the lightning shooting outward with terrible force. It sparks and explodes over the land, setting trees and mountain grasses aflame. Another bolt leaps into the boundaries of Thelian's remains and detonates in the metal shingles of an already blackened tower, sending fiery debris through the air with a deafening boom.

"Come!"

Alarei gathers the scattering bolts with a single hand at her back as she rushes her opponent. *Stay!* She wills the matter in Skéisono's figure to remain in place as she closes in. But the resistance she finds there is greater than before. Much greater. He's learning. He pushes back with unyielding force as she brings her gathered lightning forward to meet him, and the bolts are sent rebounding away to the east with another earth-trembling bang.

Then the two sasariane become as fast as the light that flashes from their countenances. They bolt and dart in flashes of light over the land—each spearing, jabbing, and ramming every kind of attack they can muster at the other. Each struggling to grapple with the elements that make up their opponent's body, each dodging with marvelous speed. They clash in bursts of flame and silvery blasts of light in the sky for what seems like ages before Skéisono slips through a gap in Alarei's defenses without warning, landing a terrible blow on her hip. The attack shatters the bones and forces Alarei to stagger backward with a breathless cry, bracing for the inevitable follow up. But it doesn't come. She looks up, taking no notice of the way her wounds mend as quickly as they were given. Skéisono no longer stands beside her, but far to the south, at the edge of Thelian. He's gone to finish his work.

The god of death raises his arms out from his sides. The earth obeys. A massive, gaping crevice opens through the heart of the city, and the already crippled structures in its path begin to collapse and cascade into the open depths. Houses, halls, broken steeples, and towers full of shrieking, scrambling human figures—all begin to buckle and topple to pieces. Alarei's heart collapses along with them.

And then, like a sudden summer breeze, the answer to it all becomes as clear and bright as the morning sun to Alarei's eyes.

We can not only command the elements. We can assemble *them.*

At every side, the world seems to come abruptly alive, filled to overflowing with living matter. Matter that moves, bends, and shifts. Matter that clings together in predictable patterns and glints like shattered stardust in every surface. Matter that can be reorganized. Every particle of the world is built of it. And now, at last, Alarei knows how to truly wield it.

Without moving at all, she calls to them—not to the elements, but to their very roots. She calls to the building blocks in the air at all sides, calls to the matter in the earth at her feet, in the swaying grasses and blackened trees. She calls, and the elements melt to pieces at the sound of her voice. They break apart and gather in a gliding, shimmering cloud around the woman who stands weeping with the brilliance of the sun in her falling tears. Now they come together, reforming, reorganizing—forming a haze of new air that cloaks its creator like tinted, circling winds. And in her outstretched hand, by her command, they form a blade. Not of stone, not of fire or of water. A crystalline blade, created from the strongest roots of all the elements that sleep in the foothills of Thelian. A blade that only its creator can command.

Thelian can wait no longer. Alarei rushes to the enemy's side with the speed of the lightning that so recently passed beneath her fingertips. She sends her blade like a flying arrow to the heart of the man in the flames. The immortal man who attempts to call the crystal blade to his own hand or direct it away—whose eyes fill with unnameable terror when his commands fall uselessly into the air. The blade tears through his ribs as he moves desperately to avoid it, ripping through his body as though it were little more than a stray leaf in its path.

And then the flaming man is gone. He vanishes from the realms entirely without leaving so much as a heartbeat in his wake. Gone to hiding.

Breathless, speechless, Alarei turns alone to gaze at the suffering remains of a once great city. The city of Thelian. It could take days to unbury and heal the survivors of the ruin. To reform the foundations of their city without causing further trauma to buried victims could take much longer. But looking over it all, there's an indescribable peace like fresh air in Alarei's soul. The kind she's longed for—sought for—for years. Now, for the first time since the moment her enemy came to her in the halls of Clevyan, she isn't afraid. Not anymore.

She smiles. Thelian can have her for as long as it needs.

21

-Common Year 179-

Hamara sits in a daze beside a humble campfire near the bank of the river. She sits for what feels like hours. Shivering, endlessly reliving her last moments on the boat with terrifying clarity and wondering what it all could possibly mean. A horrible beast in the cargo hold? Some kind of murderous ghost? The details sound ridiculous. But it's all real. Or at least, it all *seemed* real.

It's fortunate that her supply of spark stones was in her coat pocket when she fell from the boat. Otherwise it'd be harder—if possible at all—to make a fire on the freshly misted ground. And the fire is desperately needed. The night's chill. Too chill for someone who's just taken an unplanned evening dip in the river. And after shivering for ages in her dripping clothes, Hamara's beginning to wonder if the night will ever end. Above, a cloud sails hastily by. The lesser moon falls briefly into view before hiding away again. There must be wind above the treetops.

The river's calm when Hamara finally finds the energy to step back to its bank. She leans to stare northward and southward along the watery road, searching for any signs of traffic. No boats. Not yet. But something should come along eventually. *They'll come; they'll come,* Hamara assures herself as she marches in place and wills the warmth to return to her feet. Another boat is what she should hope for, isn't it? Maybe it is, but the more she imagines climbing aboard another boat, the less she wants to be rescued. After all that's happened, walking the remaining length of the river Held seems like a much more comfortable option. Assuming she can find food and supplies, of course.

"Hamara, is that you?"

The voice startles her, echoing down from high overhead and falling like rain through the leaves. It's a familiar voice. No one sits in the treetops when she turns toward the sound. But the massive eagle circling in the dark sky beyond steals her breath away. Such an enormous bird! It's clearly far larger than any she's ever laid eyes on, though it's little more than a silhouetted shadow against the soft light of the twin moons. It comes gliding closer as she watches, descending in a slow spiral. Now its broad tail feathers fan out as it sweeps gracefully down between the trees and lands with a gust of wind and a little hop in the tall grass.

"*Tye ts'payei!* What in all the world has happened to you, kid? You look terrible!" The bright-eyed eagle folds his long wings and comes stepping into the light of the fire. And Hamara's jaw nearly falls from its place.

"Ir—I mean, Asei? Y-you really did grow wings!"

He told her he would. But how could she possibly know what to expect? Now that the result is standing before her, it's almost too bizarre to believe. Every detail of Asei's appearance has radically changed.

He stands only as tall as Hamara's mid-thigh. Where there was once a pale face and loose, fiery waves of red hair, now there's a rounder, red-and-orange-furred face with flat, broad ears that hang down on each side. The heln's once humanlike eyes are now wide, shining spheres that reflect the light of the fire and moons above with stunning sharpness. But they've retained their unmistakable silvery-gray hue. Asei's eyes.

The eagle laughs. "What, did you think I was making that part up?" He waddles closer, eyeing Hamara's dripping trousers. "You must be freezing! Did it occur to you that a cold spring night isn't ideal for swimming in the Held, with a human body like yours?"

Hamara laughs. Genuinely. It awakens a stiff ache in her chest, but she doesn't mind. It feels terribly good to be at ease. Somehow, everything's going to be all right. She draws a long breath. "I don't even know where to begin." She returns to the fire, arms folded tightly against the chill.

Asei follows. "I heard you made it to Dasva after taking a trade boat along the shore of the sea, and that you left on a giant riverboat a few days ago, heading north. I was expecting to catch up to your boat." He glances around. "But—uh, Hamara, this isn't a boat. This is a random patch of woods in North Emér."

"Something attacked me. Something that was hiding in the storage deck of the boat."

"What do you mean, *something?*"

"It was like some kind of . . . some kind of"— Hamara stares at the fire, wondering what words could possibly describe the monster's horrible face— "deformed creature."

Asei gives a subtle shudder, and all his bright feathers fluff softly outward before lying soundlessly flat again.

"What did it look like?"

"Unlike anything I've ever seen. It was a grayish color. Thin and bony all over. Hairless. With a long neck and horrible beady black pits for eyes," Hamara tells him.

Asei steps closer. "And it attacked you?"

"Thank the gods I had my sénsin, or the thing may've killed me."

"But how did you end up here, looking like you've gone for a swim?"

The image of the black-eyed man on the boat returns as a cold, merciless shock to Hamara's mind. It's a sight that won't fade from her memories anytime soon. "I went to find the boat's captain, to tell him about the monster. But then some stranger attacked me. Came at me with a knife."

"What?! What kind of boat did you pay to ride on?"

Hamara shakes her head. "I don't think he was an ordinary thug. He had unnatural eyes. Entirely black eyes. And my sénsin caught him on the neck—it's a hit that would bring any man to his knees instantly. But my swing went right through him. Like he was just . . . just . . ."

"Just made of smoke?" Asei finishes the sentence.

Hamara looks up at him. "How did you know?"

"He came after me too, when I was flying north to find you." This time, only the feathers along the back of Asei's neck rise momentarily on end. "He's a ghost, I think. Then something knocked me out of the air. I never got a good glance at the beast that attacked me, but it was long and thin, like you said. And I can tell you that it didn't have muscle. It might've been made of sand."

"Made of sand?" Hamara wonders aloud. It was sand—not blood—that showered over her in the darkness by the cargo bay.

Asei lowers onto his stubby knees, watching the fire. The entire blaze is framed like a dancing portrait in his wide eyes. "When I was just a tiny boy, I sometimes heard the older kids tell stories about the *kadanto*, a sand puppet that dark spirits use to torment the living. I always thought those were just ghost stories they told to scare us." He turns to show Hamara a half-mouth grin. "Maybe it's real after all."

"But why would it come after you and me?"

"Maybe it's random. Or maybe it has something to do with our reason for journeying north."

"You think it wants to stop us?"

"Not sure we'll ever know. But one thing's certain. We've got to keep an eye out for it from now on." Asei shuffles his wings. "So the ghost somehow pushed you off the boat?"

Hamara nods, glancing warily to the dark trees that surround the scene. "I got too close to the edge, trying to move away. Lost my balance. Thank the gods someone was there to help me to shore."

"Someone helped you? Who?"

"No idea. Two people who were stronger swimmers than I'll ever be. They vanished before I could thank them."

Asei partly opens one wing into the air at his side as he stares up to the canopy in thought. "Y'know, it was probably just a couple of *virkepa* fishers from the Vilfirehn clan."

"Virkepa?"

"Voránjevin people. Transformed into a shape that helps them swim better." Asei returns to his talon-clad feet and moves to stand at Hamara's back. "I don't have hands at the moment, but I can use my foot. Sit up straight," he tells her. "I promise I won't claw you."

"What? What are you—"

"Just sit up straight, kid. It'll help."

Hamara straightens her back, looking curiously over her shoulder. Asei balances carefully on one foot, raising the other to lay it gently along her spine. A sudden rush of warmth floods into her chilled back and spreads to the edges of her shoulders. After shivering for hours, it's a wonderful relief.

Asei steps back to his place beside the fire. "Energy shifting can generate a lot of heat—especially when it's channeled into a body that can't receive it as efficiently as ours. Like a human body."

"Thanks," Hamara says, and she huddles her knees to her chest, hoping the warmth will somehow flow through her core. "How much farther do you think we'll need to go? I haven't seen any sign of my uncle. I was a little nervous to stay in Dasva, with the way all the cities are going up in flames. But he never showed up."

"I guess he's busy starting fires elsewhere."

"What if there's no way to get his attention?"

"I'm sure there will be. If Vehn saw it happen, it'll happen. At the very worst we'll end up travelling all the way to the forests of Sketza before we can catch your uncle's eye."

Hamara brings her cheek to her knees, staring calmly at the eagle beside her. "So, are you looking forward to seeing her again? Your sasarian friend?"

Asei gives the fire a pained smile. "I don't plan to be seen. I don't think she'd want to see me again."

"Of course she would! You're the kindest voránjevin guy I've ever met!"

"And how many voránjevin 'guys' have you met, again? Two?"

"Come on—what, you mean you're going to hide or something if we run into her?" Hamara puts on her best scowl.

Asei laughs. "Look, I wish I could undo the mistakes I made years ago. But I can't. She's moved on, now—to a new kind of existence. A life beyond old hopes, old friendships. And she's got a lot on her agenda. She doesn't need pointless distractions right now. It's best if I stay out of her path."

A moment of silence floods the air between them, broken only by the soft crackling of the sticks in the fire. Maybe it should make Hamara uncomfortable. But it doesn't. In fact, for some reason she can't entirely understand, it sets loose a little flutter in her chest. A lively spark that urges her to know more. She leans to look more closely into Asei's massive eyes. "She obviously still means a great deal to you. More than someone who's just a friend ever would."

Asei meets her gaze. "Well—I—" Then he shifts his wings again, briefly returning his shape to a round poof of vibrant, ruffled feathers. "You sure like to pry, don't you, kid?" He shakes his head. "You up for a walk yet? There's a little camp of scouts less than a half-night's travel from here."

Hamara's mouth drops open. "What? Why didn't you mention that sooner?!" Although walking through the shadowed woods to join a voránjevin camp doesn't exactly sound cozy, it sounds better than sitting in the dark waiting for her clothes to dry. And besides, with Asei as her guide, she has no reason to fear the clans.

Asei pretends not to hear her complaint. "They can help us plan the best route north from here. If we have to cross the Ádenlal plains, we had better be prepared."

* * *

The dawn is just beginning to peer through the trees and paint lighter tints into the sky above when they reach the camp at last. Asei comes down through a gap in the leaves and shuffles ahead with his wings still partly open, hopping over logs and bushes. From behind, he looks like a bird of prey scrambling after a fleeing rodent. A voránjevin filíl with vibrant green eyes and stormy-gray fur comes to meet them, calling softly. Asei answers. Hamara doesn't try to follow the foreign conversation—she's too distracted by the sight of a humble fire surrounded by woven hammocks. Fantastically comfortable-looking hammocks.

"She says they've got a few blankets you can use. And she's just come back with a fresh kill," Asei translates without looking back.

Only three scouts seem to occupy the camp. Each is a voránjevin in his or her natural form, which is noticeably taller than Asei's eagle body. But standing among them, Hamara still feels like a hulking giant. She huddles down beside the fire at the green-eyed scout's invitation, wondering how to act. Someone lays two little hands on her back, and a soft surge of heat floods through her bones the same way it did when Asei used his foot. Then a blanket appears over her chilled shoulders, and Hamara turns to see a black-and-gray-furred stranger murmuring softly at her back.

"Uh—thank you." Hamara tucks the blanket into the bends of her elbows.

"It's *ha'oa*," Asei whispers from nearby. "And she says you're too big for the spare clothes they have."

Hamara shrugs. No surprise there. She looks to her sandals, eyeing the chilled hue of her ordinarily darker, clay-colored toes. "It's all right. I'm mostly dry now, anyhow." She snatches the hair clasp that spent the night clipped to her sleeve and reaches to pull her hair back into a tiny bunch at the crown of her head. Moving to sit across the fire, Asei chatters with the others. After a moment he nods, then looks back to Hamara.

"They say the human city of Tavehlik is about a two-day hike from here. We should head there next. I can gather supplies while you sleep."

"How soon will we leave?" Hamara asks through a yawn. A long one.

"As soon as you're rested enough to keep your eyes open while you talk," Asei tells her.

Hamara stirs, looking up and blinking impulsively. When did her eyes fall shut?

"Good idea."

She lies sideways on the blanket beneath her, letting her breath ease out. It's a heavenly feeling to lie down on something soft by the fire. Normally, she might feel a little odd relaxing so readily in the camp of voránjevin strangers. But today, she's too exhausted to care.

22

-Common Year 179-

The tall bell tower of Tavehlik is the first structure to catch Hamara's eye as she follows Asei to the edge of the Ádenlal plains. The morning light reflects off the four bells there with a startling luster, combining with the unrestrained brightness of the plains and forcing Hamara to shade her eyes. After traveling for days beneath the thick cover of trees, the plains are shockingly bright.

It took the greater part of two days to walk to this point from the voránjevin camp. And in two days' time, Hamara's become almost delirious with the thought of all the fresh foods she'll most likely find in the city. Cities in the north may not have the same pastries as the towns in Igretho, but they're bound to have *something* more enticing than the dried meats she's been eating for two days.

"It's a bigger city than I expected!" Asei calls down from high overhead, hovering momentarily on the wind before sweeping down to land in the grass just over the crest of the next hill. "You head on into the city and get what you need. We can meet back here at sunset."

"You're not coming along?"

"Those streets are no place for a giant eagle. Besides—I should fly ahead to get a feel for where we're headed next."

"All right, all right. But if you're not here by sunset I'm finding a cozy inn to stay in." Hamara fingers the sirlene currency in her coat pocket, smiling at the thought.

The city's as lively as Dasva, but much less open. Rather than wide, open squares, Tavehlik's streets are crowded and narrow from the moment Hamara passes through the southern gate. A world of smells hits her breath as she follows a crowd of basket-bearing women into the nearest lane. At all sides, the vendors hang their wares like flags from ladders and tall poles. Clothing, artwork, carved bowls and serving spoons—the variety is endless. The third lane is heavily cloaked with the gray steam of searing meats and simmering soups. Hamara floats between the open restaurant tables, leaning here and there to peek at the meals in guests' bowls. So many choices! She debates between the savory options for ages before settling at last for a hearty stew that's served with freshly baked flatbread. It's nothing like the stews of Igretho—creamy, with a hint of sweet. The kind of food that should never be rushed. It might be Hamara's new favorite.

She goes in search of a posthouse next, debating all the while if she should tell her family any of the details from her last night on the riverboat. After all, they've already got enough stress to deal with. Piling on a little more wouldn't do them any good. And besides, if Hamara ever does manage to return to Remertrei alive, it'll be tremendous good fun to see Elein's reaction to the harrowing story in person.

A kind stranger directs Hamara to a place five blocks to the east, where a humble posthouse sits nestled between two overflowing entrances to a jewelry market. It isn't entirely what she's accustomed to, but like the posthouses of Igretho, it has letter-folds—single sheets of parchment that are pre-marked for postage and double as their own envelopes—and ink stacked neatly in shelves. And the prices are surprisingly low. Hamara's fumbling for change when a sudden quake rips through the pavement, knocking nearly everyone in the surrounding streets to the ground. Hamara flails and stabilizes herself against the nearest wall as paper launches from the shelves nearby, flooding the room with a flurry of cream-colored leaflets. The clerk lets out a curse as little wooden ink jars tumble from their places and roll out onto the posthouse floor. All around, the city erupts with screams and panicked shouts.

"An earthquake!"

The air of the city transforms in an instant. The natural flow of the crowds turns to startled, congested panic. Storekeepers scramble to snatch up the goods that have been tossed into the lanes; cooks dance around spilled stews and overturned crates of vegetables. Adults rush to gather their children in the commotion. Hamara scarcely has the time to find her balance and step to the door of the posthouse before another fierce jolt quakes the cobble at her feet, and she finds herself stumbling forward onto her hands, nearly ramming her nose into the ground. The screams of the city grow sharply louder, and when Hamara looks up, she can see the bell tower teetering in the distance. It tilts over the surrounding buildings, swaying side to side as if blown by a casual breeze. Now the bricks near its middle begin to buckle and crack. Then the tower's top half shifts abruptly sideways. Hamara holds her breath, waiting for it to fall—but a blast of intense heat that comes billowing abruptly at her back takes her attention elsewhere. She scrambles onto her feet and turns to find the entire posthouse—the entire east side of the street—suddenly blanketed in flames. The fire comes roaring down like molten rain from the sky, igniting every rooftop, every wall and lamppost. The screams of the people are nearly muted by the deafening rumble of collapsing stone and brickwork and the loud snaps of wooden beams bursting and splintering in every direction. It all happens so swiftly, so suddenly. In the length of a single breath, the city of Tavehlik descends into horrific chaos. And standing at the heart of it, Hamara can hardly think to move.

But she *must* move.

Hamara breathes deep and wills her feet into motion. Out of the city. She's got to get out. The gate isn't far. She darts back down the nearest street that isn't broiling in flames, retracing her steps to the southern gate as well as she can remember. But every step of the path is flooded with terrified faces, bloodied bodies, and darting, burning figures.

"Keep moving! We've got to get out!" Hamara shouts over the deafening roar of the city as she stoops here and there to jerk collapsed strangers back onto their feet. She's forced to battle her way through the shrieking crowds every block of the way, leaping over the chaotic spread of city rubble that's begun to clutter the ground.

Three more streets . . . two more blocks . . . just a little farther! Just a few steps more!

She's within sight of the gate, where the people are pouring out onto the plains like fish freed from a catcher's net, when white light erupts in a blinding burst in the sky overhead. The flames that consume the city flicker and die instantly beneath the glare, leaving only blackened scars in their wake. Hamara glances hurriedly over her shoulder as she comes to the gate, then stops in her place. The bell tower has vanished. But a figure has appeared in its place. A figure that stands in the air, shining as brightly as the rising sun over the city. A glowing, radiant being whose outstretched hands seem to carry all the light of the dawn in their palms. Hamara's heart drops like a stone into her stomach.

They're here. The immortals are here.

She runs breathlessly out through the city gate, stumbling away from the crowds and over several hills to the southwest, to the place where Asei planned to meet at dusk. She nearly collapses at the spot, turning to stare out over the crippled city with her mind spinning in place. This is it! The immortals are here—right here, in Tavehlik. But what was the plan, again? And how many people just lost their lives?

Breathe!

She shakes her hands in the air and steps in a quick circle, fighting to keep calm, to clear her thoughts. Such chaos! Such death and destruction! She's heard of it happening to cities all over world. Heard of it for weeks. But now that the devastation is before her eyes, it's almost too much to comprehend. It's a sickening new awareness—a rattling, choking sensation in her lungs.

It must all be *his* doing—the earthquakes, the fires—all the doing of Father's immortal brother. And now, he must be somewhere nearby. At last, after journeying all the way from the Igretho, Hamara has a chance to reach him. But *how* will she reach him? What could she possibly say to distract him? And will she survive it?

You'll know exactly what to do. Trust me, Hamara. I've already seen it.

Vehn's confidence rings back over Hamara's trembling thoughts, and she plants her feet more squarely on the hillside.

"Uncle, I've come here to find you." She watches the ethereal flames and white light clashing together in spontaneous flashes over the city. A band of lightning tears through the air, quaking the hillside. "I know you're here. I've come on behalf of my father, Marntrei. Your *brother*, Marntrei. He's still alive. Uncle, please listen to me! Can you hear me?"

A massive balloon of fire billows up from the northwestern corner of the city, but its expansion pauses miraculously in midair, as if the very flow of time were stopped in motion. Then the flames flicker hurriedly away, suppressed by some unseen force. And another quake tears through the earth, forcing Hamara to brace against the ground on all fours. The sasarian immortals must be battling. And every minute that passes is another minute for people in Tavehlik to die.

Hamara returns to her feet.

"UNCLE!" she shouts with all the breath in her lungs. *"Brother of Marntrei, son of Kóron! Stop this killing!"*

She's raising her hands to her mouth, about to shout again, when a sudden glare of brilliant light erupts across the hilltop and nearly startles her back to her knees. She raises an arm against the extraordinary brightness, wondering helplessly if the final moment of her life has come without warning. When she lowers her arm a moment later, she's no longer alone on the hilltop. But the angelic being who stands only several paces away isn't her uncle—isn't a man at all, but a woman. A woman cloaked in a marvelous, shimmering gown, with eyes full of stars and a presence that beams like searing white flames. She stares back at Hamara with a gaze that seems able to pierce every human thought that ever dared to exist.

"His name is Skéisono."

The immortal's voice rings like heavenly chimes through the air. And her words have scarcely reached Hamara's ears before another presence arrives at the hilltop. A man. He appears in a flurry of amber flames and golden light, a dark, jagged blade clutched in his raised hand. It's him. He's come at last, and he raises his weapon over the shining woman's head—

"*Skéisono! Marntrei's alive!*" Hamara's shrill scream leaves a sting in her throat.

And the man in the flames pauses abruptly in place.

He turns to the Igretho girl who dared to call his name, lowering his blade, and the terrible burning of his hellish gaze seems to send a jolt through Hamara's bones. Her heart leaps, and every instinct in her blood screams for her to somehow shrink into the ground and vanish away. But the moment doesn't last. A silvery-blue crystal appears like a circlet at the fiery man's left wrist, then his right—

"What—?!" He scowls, unable to break free as the glassy stones pull him to his knees. Then they expand, springing suddenly outward to encase his entire frame in their rigid grip. Only his head and shoulders remain uncovered as the sasarian woman moves to stand in front of him, staring bitterly down into his eyes.

"Brother, I wish I didn't have to do this."

The captured immortal says nothing at all. But the rage shines with horrific brightness in his eyes.

Hardly a stone's cast away, Hamara looks breathlessly on. The two immortals shine like twin stars on the hilltop—one a rising dawn, the other a fading dusk. Their glows meld and shimmer together like glinting reflections on a river's face. Both glorious, both terrifying in their own way. But the longer Hamara stares, the more the face of the captive sasarian man seems to pull strangely at her heart. A familiar face. A face that turns to look back to her now with the same strong jaw, the same sharp stare that Hamara's known from the time she was a tiny child.

Brother of Marntrei indeed.

The thought whispers through her mind, and somehow, the man encased in crystal begins to change. Not with startling blazes of light, not with claps of thunder or raging flames. But with silence. The grimace melts away from his shining face. The burning fades from his gaze, and his once ravenous flames flicker soundlessly out. Then a whisper scarcely louder than the wind in the grasses escapes his lips.

"Marntrei?"

The angelic woman beside him kneels down now, watching her captive closely. She brings a single palm to the crystal that imprisons him, and all at once the blue stone shimmers and melts away into the earth. The sasarian man who arrived in a fiery rage only an instant ago rises to his feet, staring southward, suddenly unconcerned with the two women beside him. He could fight—could seek revenge for his humiliating capture, could resume his vicious campaign of destruction against the city of Tavehlik. But he doesn't.

He turns to the south and vanishes into the wind, saying nothing at all. Only his counterpart remains behind. And by nothing short of a miracle, something Hamara agreed to do comes flitting back to her hopelessly dazzled mind.

"Oh—um, I—I'm supposed to tell you." Her voice sounds like the squeak of a rodent, in the presence of an angelic immortal. "My friend—*your* friend, Asei, he wanted you to know that he's sorry. For everything. He told me he never should've left your side."

The words come out so feebly. But the goddess-like woman who stands atop the hill still listens. And she turns to smile at Hamara with a magnificent brightness in her face that could turn night to day.

23

"**S**tay off your feet as much as possible, you hear? You've got to let the swelling go down and let the bones reset." He shakes his finger at the slender boy the way he often did at his own misbehaving daughters in years past. "Too much movement will only delay your recovery. I'll be back to check on your progress in a few weeks. And don't be afraid when those little furred people come by again. I don't know much about them, but I saw their medicine work miracles last week. They could help you heal faster."

"All right," the boy answers with a dejected sigh as Marntrei finishes attaching the last strap to his leg brace.

Nearby, the boy's mother struggles to contain the moisture that wells up in her eyes. "How can we ever repay you for your kindness, sir?"

Marntrei gives her hand a firm squeeze. "By taking care of yourselves," he tells her.

The sun's begun to set when he returns to the inn at the river's edge and begins gathering supplies for the journey home. He and Chimai plan to leave for Remertrei with the first boat that departs at the light of morning. It's a comforting thought. After several weeks of helping the wounded citizens of Salialo, Marntrei's relieved to be heading home again. Leaving his daughters alone during such uncommon times as these was already stressful enough, and Hamara's strange letters have only made his anxiety worse. Leaving her sister and journeying north alone? At a time like this? What was she thinking?

He stuffs his emergency medical supplies into their usual carrying bag, then slips it into an open space in his shoulder pack. He's turned to snatch his canteen from the table beside the window when the sharp light of the setting sun along the face of the nearby Nakuë River catches his eye.

Or was it something else?

He looks again, stepping closer to the window and pushing away the half-opened shutters for an uninterrupted view. This time, he spots a figure standing at the water's edge. A man dressed in long, gleaming robes like the glorious king of an angelic kingdom. Or a demonic one. His presence shines like fire, and his golden aura lays a radiant pool of light over the moving surface of the Nakuë. And his face, though as luminous and perfect as the face of a god, bears the same mild frown and stern stare that Marntrei knew so well as a boy. Could it possibly be?

"Great gods." Marntrei's wonder escapes his teeth as he steps to the doorway left open at his entrance.

Maybe he's worked too hard these past few weeks. Slept too little. Maybe it's all a dream—the product of an exhausted mind. But when the godlike man at the water's edge speaks, Marntrei's heart takes a heavy leap in its place.

"So you became a doctor after all, like you always wanted. It's been a long time, hasn't it, brother?"

The voice no longer belongs to a boy, as it did when Marntrei heard it last. But he would recognize it anywhere. He brings a hand to his forehead in disbelief, a storm of emotions boiling up in his chest and threatening to drive him abruptly to madness. He nearly laughs. "Is this some kind of dream?"

The man by the river shakes his head. And he shows a bitter smile. Skéisono's smile. "Years have passed, haven't they? Time's gone on without me. And here you are—alive. An aging father with a life full of tales."

Marntrei stares into the eyes he once knew so well, wondering what remains of the soul that flickers behind them. "What happened to you, Skéisono?"

"I've become a god of death. I've become the curse the people always wanted me to be."

The answer comes flatly, and there's a burning in the glowing man's eyes that makes Marntrei's stomach twist into knots. Hamara's letters talked about Skéisono being responsible for the fires, earthquakes, floods, and destruction that have ravaged the world in recent weeks. Despite what he saw decades ago at the edge of Kasántos, Marntrei's remained admittedly skeptical. But now, the sight of Salialo's devastated inner districts flashes with horrible detail through his mind.

"Was it really you, brother? All this destruction? All this—this"—his hands float up to his temples as he struggles for words—"all this *death*?"

"The world is too broken to save, brother. I must cleanse it."

"What does that even mean?"

Skéisono doesn't answer. He comes stepping over the grass with bare feet that shine like polished stone, letting his long robes spread and glimmer like trickling waters in his wake. He steps until he stands only an arm's length away, and Marntrei can see the golden flecks in his eyes.

"You're afraid, aren't you, Marntrei? I can hear it in your heartbeat. I can see it in the color of your soul. Afraid for the people you watch over. The people you want to protect." He pauses, staring, and Marntrei's certain he can feel the man's glare counting every fiber of his being. "Hamara has her father's eyes, you know."

The words send Marntrei's heart racing to the sky and back. Hamara! Did he find her? "If you hurt her in any way—"

"Marntrei! I've got to snatch the last of your gauze wrapping. Got one last broken hand to set and I'm out."

Chimai's voice comes echoing from around the corner of the inn, and Marntrei's shoulders stiffen.

"Chimai, stay back!" he calls hastily over his shoulder before turning back to the being who stands before him.

But the riverside grasses are empty when he looks again. The golden man—demon, ghost, or vison—has vanished.

24

-Common Year 179-

It's possible that only a few minutes have passed. Or maybe it was hours. Hamara's entirely unsure. She's wandering in a stupor through the disheveled crowds outside the walls of Tavehlik when Asei finds her again.

"What in the name of the gods has happened here?!" he shouts as he comes gliding down to the earth. "Was the city on fire?"

Hamara scrambles up the hill to his side and waits for her breath to return, unsure where to begin. "You—you should've seen it! They were here! The immortals!"

"Both of them? Here at Tavehlik?" The eagle's eyes nearly leap from his head.

"Yes, yes! You should've seen it! And our plan actually *worked*. I yelled after my uncle, and the other sasarian—your friend—she heard me." Hamara talks too rapidly for her breath to keep up, and she can't seem to stop her arms from drifting up and waving in the air as the scenes run through her mind for what must be the thousandth time. "My uncle was attacking the city. The goddess must've heard me shouting and came to me, and my uncle followed. She told me his name, I distracted him, and she was able to capture him."

"Goddess?"

"Well, I guess she's not *the* goddess but she sure looked like one. I can't remember her name. Al . . . ala . . ."

"Alarei."

"Yes, Alarei. She looked like a goddess. My uncle was like some kind of fiery demon. I thought she was going to kill him right here in front of me. But when he heard my father's name, my uncle somehow changed. And, and—" Hamara looks up now, taking a breath, and finds Asei staring off at nothing in particular.

"Like a goddess . . ." he murmurs, and a subtle smile appears at his teeth.

"Yes! She stayed around here for a while, healing the wounded. But she's gone now."

"Good, good. That's best." Asei opens his wings and gives them a little shake before folding them again. "I can't believe that plan actually worked. And what do you mean, your uncle changed? He's still running free?"

Hamara shrugs, glancing to the nearby hillside where two glorious immortal beings stood not long ago. "I'm not sure how to describe it. It was like his fire went out. He seemed to forget all about destroying the city, and about attacking Alarei. He just became . . . calm. And Alarei let him go."

Asei blinks. "Well, I've got no idea what that means for us, but I hope it's good."

"I think it is. But what do we do now?" Hamara folds her arms. "It seems like your friend has taken control of things."

"Now? Now I guess I help you get back home." Asei uses his clawed foot to satisfy an itch on his feathery side. "We can start by heading to the primary camp of the Vilfirehn, just a little southeast of here. If you walk swiftly we can reach it by nightfall."

"Good enough for me." Hamara nods in agreement, checking the water supply in her canteen. Fortunately, she was able to refill it at the shack that served her the stew, before the city fell into chaos. It's smaller than the one she left behind on the riverboat— the kind the voránjevin scouts and hunters carry in their wraps. But she's grateful to have it. "I guess I won't need to worry about supplies, then?"

"Nope."

Heading back home. Home, to Remertrei. The thought leaves such an odd, floating sensation in Hamara's heart. Not long ago, she set out from Remertrei still wondering if the immortals really existed. And in a few weeks she's traveled farther from home than ever before. Now, she's seen the sasarian immortals with her own eyes—witnessed a portion of the spectacular power they carry. Now the world seems to have transformed into a different place entirely. The sort of world where almost anything could be real and possible.

"Do you think this is really it? The end of the destruction?" she wonders aloud as Asei prepares to leap down the slope of the hill and catch the wind in his feathers.

He gives Tavehlik a careful glance before looking back to his human friend. "Seems like it's too soon to say for certain. But I sure hope so."

* * *

The night forest doesn't carry the same ominous mood that it always did before. It was once the perfect setting for every terrifying story Hamara ever told her sister, Elein. A scene full of shadows, of fingering branches and strange, distant echoes in the darkness. But after spending so many nights among the trees, Hamara struggles to remember why the woods would ever be frightening on their own. It's only a bunch of trees, after all. The same trees that shield against the sun's rays in the light of day. Of course, spending each night in the company of Asei and other voránjevin has helped. To them, the night forest is a spectacular hunting ground, and nothing stalks its paths that couldn't be conquered by their life-stealing touch.

Hamara can't help smiling to herself as she watches Asei's slow-gliding figure through the gaps in the canopy above. How will she describe all that's happened when she returns home? Will Mother and Father even believe it? Or will they simply be furious at her for leaving Elein for so long? Even if they will be, the thought only makes her laugh. They'll understand, in time. After seeing her immortal uncle, nothing seems frightening. And it's a wonderfully comfortable feeling. While it lasts.

"Hey, I forgot to tell you," Asei calls out as he comes swooping abruptly down through the treetops and lands a few paces ahead, "if you want—"

There's no chance for his words to finish. A sudden commotion erupts in the leaves nearby, as though someone were barreling through the woods, slowing for nothing. Asei's only just turned toward the sound, ears perked slightly forward, when a pale shape flies out from the shadows of the trees. It slams into Asei—erasing him instantly from view. The attacker is lit for only a fleeting instant by the nearly full greater moon above, but Hamara sees enough. And her stomach takes a sickening drop.

"Asei!"

She bolts through the trees, wrestling her sénsin free from its sheath at her lower back as she runs. It's that monster. The beast from the riverboat. That disgusting, horrible thing has found them again. She swallows the panic that's planted a ball in her throat and tears through the trees until the beast comes back into view, hunched over Asei's limp shape in the foliage. It turns, raising its featureless face at the end of its grotesquely long neck. Hamara doesn't hold back. She leaps at the monster and brings her weapon down on its left shoulder with all the strength she can muster. The acidic rod burns and sinks into the beast's torso like a hot knife in a pile of cream, and dark clumps of its body fall in heavy globs to the ground. It's an effective hit, but the monster jerks and twitches wildly, pulling the sénsin sharply aside and knocking Hamara flat to the earth. She's only barely managed to re-grip her weapon and scramble back onto her feet when the attacker comes charging toward her, one arm slumping and falling off entirely along the way. Then it leaps into the air, and Hamara fails to suppress a scream as she moves desperately aside, taking a heavy swing at the creature's distorted legs. She aims too high, but the force of the beast's leap gives the strike more power than Hamara could have given it alone. The sénsin rod tears entirely through the monster's pale middle. A burst of sand showers down on Hamara's head and shoulders as the beast's remains fall in a pile nearby. Hamara wastes no time darting after it. She lands with two feet on the creature's disgusting head, crushing it into nothing more than a pile of thick sand. And she does her best to kick and scatter the remaining clumps in all directions, letting more curses escape her mouth than she's ever known was possible.

"Get away! Leave us alone, horrible, disgusting beast! Stay away from us, or I'll bash your head in again!"

Asei's lying on his side with his wings partly unfolded when Hamara rushes back to him. She kneels and puts a hand to his neck, then lowers an ear to his feathered chest. Shallow breath. A heartbeat. Thank the gods. But he can't stay here. She slides an arm beneath the giant eagle's head, then another beneath his legs, and attempts to stand. But the massive wings make it awkward, brushing heavily along the ground. Hamara's forced to lay him down again to fold his wings in against his sides. He's small, but a massive armful. It can't be safe to remain here and fend off the beast alone all night. Hamara peers to the moons and stars beyond the tips of the trees and turns toward what appears to be the east, shuffling off through the shadows as well as she's able. She's only taken a few steps when a warm, wet sensation meets her stomach. She glances down, holding her breath. A dark, shining patch has already begun to grow in Asei's feathers, clumping them together and soaking Hamara's clothes. Blood. Lots of it.

25

Winters atop the cliffs were always so mild. Often they were less like winter and more like an extended autumn, which gradually warmed again into spring. Even so, the open colonnades and wide marble halls of the sanctuary seemed to have a talent for gathering only the chilliest winds and funneling them through the far corridors, prompting everyone along their paths to hide beneath shawls and hoods as they went on their way. Winter was Asei's favorite time of year at Clevyan. The only time of year when he could walk the halls beneath the security of a hood without looking strange. The only time of year when he could even hope to blend in.

It was midwinter when he first began to sneak into the librarian's special collection at Clevyan. The room was in the far corner of the library, and small— no more than a study with a hearth, a little shelf of carefully bound books and records kept in carved boxes, and a humble desk beside the window. Only those with permission from the librarian or the high priestess were permitted to peruse the old, weathering records there. But it was a simple task to watch the librarian's daily routine. Every single day, like clockwork, he would leave his papers at the sound of the noonday bells, gather his notes, and head off to the central courtyard, where he'd spend the next hour chatting with the gardeners and enjoying a simple lunch. It was during this hour each day when Asei began to explore the special collections—the room where all of Clevyan's oldest, most precious records could be found. These were records made back in the earliest days of the sanctuary, when the sasarian immortal who built it came often to visit the people and teach them about his kind, the nature of the realms, and countless other things. And Asei read about it all.

It must have been his fifth or sixth week of sneaking into the special collections when he first read of the fallen sasarian. The once powerful immortal king who was cast out of his body as punishment for using his heaven-bestowed power for evil. A being who became a demon to the world, tormenting the people of every nation and striving to steal men's bodies. More than anything, he wanted to disrupt the mission of all sasariane to come. The records told that the last immortals to walk the earth revoked this dark spirit's ability to directly touch or possess the bodies of the living. But they couldn't destroy him.

"I figured I'd find you here." Alarei's voice came like sudden music at the doorway, and Asei nearly leaped from the seat behind the desk.

"*Yteo ha*, you don't need to sneak like that!"

"Well, I learn from the best, don't I?" She was smiling when he looked up.

Asei made a false scowl, silently watching the black shadow flicker over his friend's eyes. It lasted for only a fleeting moment before giving way to a natural greenish-brown hue—the same way it always did whenever he looked at Alarei. In the old records, it was called the dark shimmer. It was said to be visible in the eyes of youths who became sasarian immortals later in life. But for some reason apparently never entirely understood to anyone who kept the records, after a sasarian was more than eight days old, the dark shimmer was only visible to certain onlookers. *Voránjevin* onlookers.

"You hungry? I'm heading to the orchard now." Alarei lifted the basket in her hand and gave it a subtle shake, showing him the smile that always set his heart afloat. She always loved to picnic beneath the canopies of the massive orchard trees, and Asei didn't mind it at all.

"You already know you don't need to ask that. I'm *always* hungry," he reminded her as he rose to his feet. And he wasn't exaggerating.

It was his last winter at Clevyan when he first read of the fallen sasarian spirit, a ghost of malice that might still haunt the dark places of the earth—a tale he tucked away in the back shelves of his memory. After all, it was a random bit of knowledge that would most likely never be important. Or so he hoped.

26

-Common year 179-

He lets himself sink into the very darkest space between the realms. A place where the unceasing clamor of the world and all its souls is shut away behind a curtain of silence, where time and distance no longer have any meaning. Where the sting of daylight can never reach. And for perhaps the first time since the moment he became immortal, Skéisono stands perfectly still and just *breathes*. Breathes out all the ideas that have cluttered his mind until now—breathes out the anger and the logic that had become so deeply lodged in his heart—and holds it all in his hands. His quaking hands.

Until a moment ago, the plan was flawless. It made complete sense. The world could never be whole and perfect, because the beings who crowd its face are flawed and corrupted by nature. There's no sense trying to mend something that simply can't be fixed. And there's no way to change the very nature of the world, is there? Until a moment ago, Skéisono was so certain of it all. Now, he's seen the face and heard the beating heart of a brother he once lost. It should mean nothing. But somehow, it's shaken him.

Why does it matter?

For so long, he's chosen to shut out the voices of the world—the world he never seemed to belong in. A world full of darkness and corruption that only a cleansing flame could redeem. He was the bearer of that flame. He *had* to be. There was no one else with the power to save Claya from its own fevering sickness. Or so it once seemed.

Marntrei's older than he was years ago. But he's hardly changed. The way he angled his shoulders, the way he stepped with his weight at his heels—all were as they were ages ago, only yesterday, when he was just a stubborn village boy in southern Igretho. A boy with passions and dreams like any other.

Why does it matter? Even now, the memory of his face seems to jerk at something painful in Skéisono's heart. And the more he resists, the more horribly it pulls. Marntrei's nothing but a mortal man. A flawed man, like the millions that roam and corrupt Claya's face. The first living mortal Skéisono's spoken to since obtaining his power. The first mortal heartbeat he's ever allowed himself to hear in decades. It was a heavy heart, full of hopes and fears for others. Now that Skéisono's heard it, the sound seems to drown his soul. And it isn't the only heart that beats in Claya.

Alone in total darkness, the immortal man who once held the world in the flaming palm of his hand falls silently to his knees. Choking.

How many fathers like Marntrei lived in the city of Koska? The city of Thelian? How many mothers; how many sons and daughters? How many children? How many Marntreis have lost their lives since the god of death began his reign? And why does it matter now, after all that's been done?

"*Skéisono*—'altered winds.' They named you well, didn't they? You alone have already achieved far more than any sasarian before you. You've altered this world forever."

The ghost comes striding from the shadows, trailing embroidered robes at his sides.

"Leave me be. I need to think." Skéisono doesn't look up.

But the ghost king appears immediately before his face, a shallow frown at his mouth and a suspecting squint in the shineless black voids of his eyes.

"She learned to organize elements of her own, as my enemy of old once did. But she's still no true threat. You can easily learn the same. You must get rid of her, before she grows any stronger."

"I'll deal with her as I choose." Skéisono stares unafraid into the dark spirit's bottomless eyes. Then he turns away without saying anything more, raising his hand to tear an opening in the blackness before him. An exit from the shadows. He steps through and is expelled sharply back into the mortal, physical realm, at a place where the land sinks and heaves itself into the sea. A shoreline where the waves toss relentlessly into the air and shatter against the cold earth without end. He stands motionless at their edge, watching.

Until it hits.

It comes down on his shoulders like the weight of all the world's mountains together, pressing him mercilessly down to his knees in the sand and threatening to strangle the very life from his undying bones. It's a burden no longer muted by the blackness he's just left behind. One he's managed to shut out and ignore for decades. The weight of all the sorrow in a horribly torn and injured world. The suffering of Claya's children. So many souls! Thousands, *millions*—more living beings than could ever be counted. All crying out at once. All weeping, all wailing with the pain of broken hearts, broken families, and broken lives. Ruined, like their homes and cities that were laid to waste. Shattered beyond any ability to heal. The sound bombards Skéisono's ears like the roaring of ten thousand earthquakes. Deafening, agonizing. It can't be silenced, can't be fixed, can't be undone. And the weight of it all is more than he can bear.

The woman comes without making any sound at all. Skéisono doesn't turn to see her. But the glow of her countenance lights the stones of the shoreline. And the unending rhythm of her beating heart sounds like a nearing drum over the seaside grasses. Alarei. That's her name, isn't it? She pauses only a short pace away, saying nothing.

"What have you done to me?" Skéisono's voice is coarse and choked. Hardly more than a gasp.

"I was hoping you'd tell me."

"Is that so?" Skéisono watches the way the sands beneath him seem to shimmer and sparkle as the waves slip over them. "You should finish the task you took upon yourself on the hilltop. End this. I won't stop you."

"I'm not sure if that's best. Not anymore." Alarei steps closer and kneels down in the sand at his side, her guardian floating closely behind. "Did you think your brother was dead?"

"It shouldn't matter whether he is or not."

"But it *does* matter. Doesn't it?"

There's an extraordinary light in her eyes when Skéisono looks up at last to meet her gaze. A wonderful shining that he's never noticed before—never cared to see. It's a familiar shine. One that makes him suddenly aware of an awful emptiness in his chest. Something's missing—something that's been missing all along.

"Can nothing fill this emptiness?" He gasps.

"I think you already know the answer, my brother. You just need to let yourself remember."

Brother. Not long ago, Skéisono was fighting with all his power to destroy this woman, who now sits peacefully beside him, calling him brother. Her guard is down. Perhaps he could easily slay her now, with a single piercing strike to the heart. But somehow, the battle no longer matters. He looks back to the sea. The Palarian floats silently out in front of him, hovering just over the waves. He'd nearly forgotten it was with him.

"Palarian, what have I forgotten?"

The guardian's single eye shifts and glows more brightly at the sound of his voice. And as Skéisono looks on, something ancient returns to his mind. Memories. They come like distant torches in the fog of his thoughts. He finds them drifting at the edge of his awareness, untouched. Scenes from long ago. Promises made before the world was, at a time when these days were only a future yet to be had. *Promises.* His role was sealed long ago. The duty of the sasarianë. A mission he was sent to fulfill, but had long since forgotten—or was too blinded to see.

How could he forget? He wonders, and the full voice of the world comes storming again into his ears. The sound of every living heart on Claya's face. *His* people. The people he once loved, in the beginning. He was sent to give them a better world. But what has he given them? Their sorrows rise up like a bitter song in Claya's winds—a song once sung by the heart of a boy in Kasántos, when he watched everything he loved vanish away into flames.

What has he given them?

He's destroyed their cities, their homes. Killed their dearest ones, robbed the young and the innocent of life. He's destroyed whatever peace they once had and given them only death and terror in exchange—gifts from the being sent to protect them. He's haunted and tormented their world as a god of death. A god now so filled with agony and regret that he can scarcely bear it.

27

Vehn's nearly asleep when the vision comes to him. He's only just allowed himself to slump lazily back in his favorite chair after finishing a sorely needed fix on his back porch. It was tough work, refitting the decking that was splintered when the last storm sent a massive tree limb collapsing atop it. And now that it's over, nothing seems lovelier than a nap in the afternoon light. The weather is perfect for a nap. Sunny, but not too hot.

But the vision spoils all hope of sleep when it comes. It erupts like a sudden fountain of light in his mind's eye and floods every corner of his consciousness with consuming brilliance. It's a vision among visions. A glimpse not simply into the distant future, but into another reality. And for an almost overwhelming instant, Vehn the seer finds himself peering into what can only be another world entirely. An earth born of gemstones, with crystal towers and cities that shine like glass in the morning light. Its inhabitants shine like the evening stars, roaming and filling the land like darting points of light. A land entirely void of darkness.

28

-Common Year 179-

More than seven days have passed when Alarei returns to the seaside. The man she finds there nearly blends into the golden rays of the sun that sinks beyond the waves. A glowing man who has yet to step from the place where he fell to his knees over a week ago. An entire week. It's a massive span of unfettered time that Alarei never would have imagined herself having, not long ago. Time she's spent in the aid of every nation in Claya—healing wounds, freeing survivors pinned beneath mountains of rubble, and mending the gaping crevasses that remain in city foundations and town centers. She leaps from one horizon to the next each day and night, doing all she can to soothe the fresh pains of the world. But much remains. There's much more to be done—more than even a sasarian immortal can hope to accomplish in a week of tireless efforts. Even now, she shouldn't turn away from the needs of the world. But something pulls her to the western seashore of Glesia today, to the place where her immortal brother has sat like a carved, motionless figure gazing out to sea.

"Do you plan to wait here for the end of days?"

She comes stepping to his side, genuinely curious. She pauses just beyond the lapping of the waves, where she can see the perpetual shimmer in the sasarian man's sleepless, expressionless face. For a time, he doesn't answer—doesn't react at all. And Alarei wonders how long she should bother to wait. The Farian drifts soundlessly out over the shallow tide nearby, seemingly unfazed by the cold spray that occasionally leaps up to dot its slender body. Its sibling floats idly over the sand, not far behind.

"I was afraid of the dark as a little child." Skéisono's words break the silence at last, falling like a warm hum over the voice of the waves. But his gaze is unmoving. "Until my father taught me not to fear. He took me out to his workshop one evening and closed up the door behind us. Not even a sliver of moonlight could slip in. And in the consuming blackness, he lit a single candle no larger than my finger. A miserably tiny flame. But the moment it appeared, it chased the darkness. All the blackness in the room fled from that little flame. My father explained to me that as weak as that flame was, not even all the darkness in the world could extinguish it. He told me that no amount of darkness has power over light. It can only exist where the light has yet to shine."

He turns at last to face his fellow immortal with tears like delicate diamonds in his weary eyes, and the sorrow that floods his dark gaze shocks the breath from Alarei's chest. "Claya is broken, wounded. More full of pain and darkness than ever before, because of me. We carry light. But after all I've done, the scars in this world are too deep to be healed."

Alarei stares back, almost questioning if the being before her truly is the same sasarian man she knew a week ago. The flames are gone. The callous gleam in his eyes has faded entirely away. Somehow, he's no longer the raging god of death and destruction Alarei once knew, but a shattered soul. A man as broken and wounded as the cities he destroyed.

"You . . . you really have changed, haven't you?" She steps closer. "It's true that you created much of this suffering. But somehow you've changed. You finally feel the pains of Claya. Now you can help me mend it all."

"You really think this can be fixed?" He laughs. A bitter, hopeless laugh.

Alarei kneels to take his hand in hers. "I know it's worth doing everything in our power to try. You can either let this burden destroy you and leave me to battle alone, or we can rise above it. Together."

* * *

The forests of Sketza are dimly lit. The stars and twin moons peer down through only narrow gaps in the towering canopy above, shining with startling sharpness in the black face of the sky beyond. Until the sasarianë appear like the dawn at the heart of the woods, the forest floor is illuminated only by the night flowers that grow like little lanterns at the feet of the ancient trees and let out their sleepless, violet glows.

"I wasn't sure if you'd be able to enter my realm. But it looks like you can now." Alarei smiles. The Farian must no longer sense any threat in the man's presence. "Why did you want to come here? We can talk anywhere."

Skéisono glances over the scene before looking back to her. "Because dark spirits can't come here. I didn't want anyone listening in." He closes his eyes for a single breath. "They know me. I made the darkness my haven for years. The gap between the realms. It's a place beyond all feeling, outside the sights and sounds of the world."

"You were still a child when you became immortal. I saw it in a vision, the night it happened. How did you manage to find the gap on your own?"

"I didn't. I was led."

"Led? By who?"

"By a tortured soul. A man who was once a sasarian immortal himself, ages ago. Kyvóike. He once ruled over a mighty kingdom. But his fellow immortal defeated him, and he became an outcast from the worlds of light. Now the shadows of the gap are his only palace." Skéisono steps to the nearest tree, allowing himself to lean against its massive, deep-grooved body. "He told me all about his day, and about the sasarianë of ages past who failed to mend Claya's broken nature despite their very greatest efforts. He told me not to waste my time doing the same—that there's no sense trying to fix a world that simply can't be mended. And I believed him. I'd seen the darkness and cruelty of the world with my own eyes. It made perfect sense to me that the only way to mend the earth was to cleanse it. To erase all those who would ever be capable of corrupting it. I thought it would end all the pain."

"Why did you wait for so many years? You could've finished the deed long before I ever found the Farian." Alarei tries not to imagine what the possibility would have looked like.

Skéisono folds his arms. "Time works differently in the gap. Unpredictably. But besides that, I wanted a battle. That ghost told me about you. Told me that he'd watched you for years, that you didn't have the confidence to defy me. He wanted me to take your life before you ever rose to claim your sasarian power. But I wanted a challenge."

"Thank the gods that you did. Or Claya would already be lost."

The sasarian man looks up to meet Alarei's waiting gaze, and the broken remains of his once fiery heart seem to melt anew before her eyes. "The world I've created is little better. I turned against the very nature of the sasarianë. Against my own people. I've killed thousands. There's no undoing what's been done. Now I can only await the judgment of the goddess."

Alarei shakes her head. "You'll face the goddess with your mistakes someday. We all will. But not today. There's still hope, Skéisono. The power to heal this world is in our hands. We can work together, as the immortals of ages past have done. We can heal the people's injuries and rebuild the cities, just as a sasarian once built the sanctuary of Clevyan—"

"You must not do as we did. You must do *more*."

The voice comes like a sudden wind through the trees, interrupting Alarei's words and startling the stillness of the scene. The woman it belongs to comes striding like an angel through the shadows. She's pale, dressed entirely in brilliant white with hair that tumbles in thick amber curls over her shoulders. Another messenger, not unlike the woman who visited Alarei weeks ago. But this isn't Faliéhl.

The stranger pauses several paces away. "We used the gifts inherent in us as sasarianë to bless and aid the world in every way we could imagine. But it wasn't enough."

Now another figure appears beyond the first—a man as angelic as the woman who preceded him, with the darkened skin and hair of someone who may have once been a native to the nations of Glesia. "We never found our true potential as sasarian immortals. Now the task is given to you, to succeed where others have failed. The power is in you."

The two beings vanish as suddenly as they appeared, leaving without so much as disturbing the grass at their feet. Without any sound at all—just as any sasarian would depart. But these were not sasarianë. Or at least, not anymore. In their wake, Alarei stands momentarily breathless.

"Our . . . our predecessors. You saw them too, didn't you?" She glances to the shimmering man beside her.

"They came to deliver a message." Skéisono still stares at the open space where the visitors stood, speaking with little more than a murmur. "To tell us to find our true potential. But how do we find it? Where could we possibly begin, after all that's broken?"

The Palarian gives an answer. It drifts out from behind the nearest tree with a new glimmer in its shifting, silvery eye. "By considering all that you have, which you are able to give to Claya."

"All we have?" Skéisono looks down at the shimmering robes that clothe his undying body, at the palms of his glowing hands—hands that once belonged to an ordinary, heartbroken boy. Now, more than twenty years later, the same hands are responsible for the deaths of hundreds. *Thousands.* And he's more heartbroken than he ever knew was possible. "After everything I've done, I have no right to wield the power that's in me. I want to give it all back."

"Give it *back*?" Alarei repeats softly, glancing to her guardian, which glides patiently in the air beside her. "Can we do that?"

"As it has been said, the power is in you. You may give it freely, if you choose. These guardians will uphold you, so long as the gift of immortality remains with you," the Farian answers.

"Then I'll return my gifts to the children of Claya. It's the only true option I have." Skéisono steps away from the tree with his hands in fists, ready to act.

But Alarei moves to stand in his path. "There's no sense rushing. We need to consider this carefully. Maybe we *can* somehow share our sasarian gifts with the people of the world. But what if someone chooses to use that power for evil?"

"Like I did?" Skéisono stares back in momentary silence as the thoughts churn through his eyes, and Alarei watches the way her own light seems to shift and slide like wavering sunlight across his face. "No one should be enabled to repeat the wounds that I've already left in this world. Maybe there's a way to restrict the power we give. Reserve it for those who carry only good intentions. People who would never use it to hinder the free will of others."

"You mean, give a gift of power that's somehow only activated by good will? Is it possible?" Alarei can't help wrinkling her nose at the thought. Even after becoming a sasarian immortal—after learning to tear apart and reorganize the very building blocks of the earth and its elements—the idea of giving such a gift to all the living souls of the world seems dangerous and unreal, if possible at all.

The Palarian turns slowly in place. "There is no limit to the gifts you can give the world, or to the conditions you set upon those gifts—so long as you do not rob the free will of the people. Claya will hear your offering, and receive it according to your command. Speak your command, and the realms will obey."

"And what will happen to us if we do this? If we give up our sasarian abilities?" Alarei wonders aloud, and neither guardian answers immediately. They each drift idly in their places, twitching their glassy eyes as if they hadn't heard the question at all. But there's no way they didn't. Then the Farian lets a soft shimmer of light flicker along its slender body.

"None have attempted the plan you speak of. You might suppose that to lay down your sasarian power is to return to a mortal state, to become as all other children of Claya. But it is not known what may truly become of you. This mystery even these guardians cannot answer."

"I don't care what happens to me." Skéisono waves away the uncertainty like an annoying insect from the air.

But the question leaves a subtle twinge in Alarei's heart. It's a mystery, then? Returning to a more ordinary human state wouldn't be terrible. But if she and Skéisono truly do attempt to give up all that makes them sasariané, it's possible that their fate at the end of the entire endeavor could be something wildly different. There's no way to know for certain. It's a risk—a brave guess in the dark. One that her fellow immortal has no trouble accepting on a whim. After all, he has little left to lose. But what could Alarei lose? She wonders, and the memory of a face comes fluttering across her mind. A face she's ached to see again—even one last time—

"You're worried. I can see it." Skéisono's words slide calmly between Alarei's thoughts.

She looks up. "Maybe. But it won't stop anything."

"I couldn't kill you when I wanted to. And even now I can't force you to join me. You can choose another way."

Alarei shakes her head. "I choose to do whatever's best for our world. We're in this together."

Skéisono brings a gentle hand to her shoulder, and the smile that appears on his face is more radiant and gloriously bright than all the stars and moons in the night sky combined. The first true smile to grace a once fiery face. "For so long, I chose to shut out the world and all the people in it. I refused to hear them. It was the sound of my brother's beating heart that opened my eyes. A brother I thought I'd lost," he tells her, ignoring the single tear that escapes down his cheek. "As sasarianë we can sense every heartbeat on the face of the earth. Maybe that could be our first gift to the world. Let every soul be given the ability to hear the hearts of those most important to them, no matter the distance."

Alarei smiles in return. "It'll be a marvelous gift." She lifts her hands before her, palms to the stars. "We can bestow it together. Give me your hands."

"You already know how to do this?" Skéisono lays his hands carefully over hers.

"No, but I have an idea. The leaders of Clevyan sometimes meditated in groups when I was young. They said it magnified the reach of their minds. Maybe if we concentrate, focusing on the sound of all living people, we can send the gift to them all at once."

Concentrate. The two of them close their eyes, listening. They listen to the overwhelming symphony of living hearts that floods every corner of the world. They listen to human hearts, voránjevin hearts, to souls young and old—all full of sorrows and joys, hopes and fears, and every vibrant emotion in between.

I don't deserve this power. Please, take it back.

The words come to Alarei's ears like a half-whispered promise. Not spoken, but somehow audible. Words that fall like rain from Skéisono's quaking heart and sink deep into the earth.

"Take it back."

Now the words come from Alarei's own voice, and in a moment too surreal and too fleeting to comprehend, two immortal beings become one voice, uttering one request. Where their hands meet, a sudden burst of light streams out in all directions with the brightness of a thousand sunsets. And a gale force more violent than all the earth's winds follows after it. Roaring, merciless winds that seem to erupt at the heart of the scene and drive the sasarianë apart.

"Sleep!"

"Be still!"

They call out to the storm, commanding it to cease, hoping desperately to calm it. But the hurricane yields to no one. It lifts Skéisono from the earth and sends him hurling away—over forest and prairie, over rivers and hills and sweeping plateaus. It tosses and whirls for ages all around him. When the winds die away at last, leaving him shaken and breathless on the ground, he no longer stands in the forests of Sketza, but at the crest of a hill in an open, rolling plain. An emerald sea of swaying grasses expands out from his feet toward every horizon. And he recognizes the place, though he never saw it as a child. His sasarian realm. The hills of Igretho.

Part 3

1

-318 years before the start of the Common Calendar of Glesia (490 years before Common Year 179; the ninth year of the reign of Sekýnteo the Golden over the Ten Regions of East Ataran)-

The towers and golden-domed rooftops in the City of Glimmering Lights always shone most spectacularly at dusk, when the sun's dying rays came peering narrowly over the peaks of the western mountains. Looking over the proud cityscape from the highest, most private balcony of the House of Voices, Kyvóike couldn't hide the smile at his lips.

For generations, those carrying the bloodline of the ancient kings were forced to live among the commoners. Generations of royalty robbed of their rightful inheritance—all because the people sought to set up a foolish new government for themselves. Ungrateful, unruly peasants. They took the rule of the Ten Regions into their own hands, supposing themselves wise enough to replace the experienced wisdom and grace of the kings of old. Wisdom that was perfected over ages. And their plan was childish. All of it. The House of Voices was no exception, filled with its so-called representatives—a pitifully contrived excuse for a government, riddled with holes and leaders who were easily persuaded by the promises of gold and silver. It had its time. But now, the reign of the kings had returned. The reign of the *final* king. For with the elements at his command and the gift of immortality bestowed upon him, Kyvóike Sekýnteo—Sekýnteo the Golden—could have no foe in all of Claya. And he would rule to the very end of days.

His guardian floated motionlessly in the air at his side. An inhuman, marvelous creature that came to him in the king's study only moments before, bringing power untold. Power that only the rightful king was worthy to bear.

"At last, the heavens themselves have given their approval of my reign. Come, Palarian. The people must see the glory of their king. They must know who to fear."

2

It's roughly a three-day journey back to Remertrei, with the little steam-driven boat pressing against the southward flow of the waters. But it's still faster than walking. The rising dawn shines brightly on the Nakuë's face, forcing all aboard the slender riverboat to squint and tip their hats against the glare.

Marntrei raises a hand to shield his eyes as he gazes northeastward along the river's path. The reflecting light of the morning along the water's face is bright indeed. Dazzlingly so. But it has yet to surpass the brightness and splendor of the image that Marntrei can't seem to dispel from his anxious mind. The sight of his own immortal brother's face.

Hamara has her father's eyes, you know.

Skéisono. His words were calm when he spoke them—far from malicious. But they sprouted more anxiety in Marntrei's heart than the many long days he spent among the wounded of Salialo ever could. Hamara! Where is she now? He must have seen her somewhere up north. But why? And what happened? Was she safe? Is she safe now?

Marntrei turns to Chimai, who's sat taking inventory of their medical supplies at the rear of the boat for the past hour. To his mild surprise, she's already staring back at him. Her hands have fallen away from the nearly finished chart in her lap, and subtle wetness makes a shimmer at the edges of her dark eyes. Has something happened? They've just come from a terrible scene of death and suffering in Salialo. But Chimai's always handled her job with her hands on her hips and an indestructible smile on her face. Never shaken. It's odd in more ways than one to see her at the edge of weeping now.

Marntrei crosses the deck and is about to sit down beside her when a subtle sound comes hiccupping to his ears. A sound that seems to reverberate into his very bones, despite its softness. And somehow, it's overwhelmingly familiar. It's the echo of two young, beating hearts. One ringing out from toward the head of the river, from Remertrei. And the other sounding from far away to the north, from somewhere deep in the woods, not far from the Ádenlal plains. It's the sound of two hearts that Marntrei's looked after since the moment they began to beat.

"O-Our daughters." He sinks slowly down onto the bench beside his wife, putting an arm around her shoulders as he fights the lump that swells up in his throat. "Somehow, I can hear their hearts beating. Safe."

Chimai reaches to grasp his hand tightly in hers, beaming. "Isn't it wonderful?"

3

-Common Year 179-

Styóka's only just arrived back at his cabin and shouldered the door open when a sudden realization comes to his mind: his daughter is about to arrive. He knows it with perfect certainty, although none of his senses can explain it. He doesn't see her down the road, doesn't hear her voice calling. But she's coming—the daughter he once sent away. The daughter he hasn't heard from in months. Somehow, he can just *feel* it.

He steps into his single-room cabin and sets his canteen on the table. When he turns hardly a moment later to find his daughter standing in the doorway, he almost isn't surprised. But the sight of her splendor shocks every thought from his mind. She stands clothed in sunrays like the goddess herself, with a gaze as bright as the twin moons and a shining countenance that floods the cabin with white, ethereal light.

"Alarei, my beautiful daughter!" He shuffles backward into a chair, nearly forgetting how to breathe.

"I would've come sooner if I had the chance. I'm so sorry, Father."

The angel smiles gingerly—smiles the way Styóka's little girl always did, with mild dimples creasing gently into view. It's a sight that threatens to melt his heart.

"What's happened to you?"

"I've been given power from the heavens." Alarei draws a slow breath, gazing to the floor before looking back to her father. "We're going to try something. Something that might change our entire world. The change has already begun. I don't know what will happen to me when this is over. I wanted to thank you one last time, for doing all you could to give me the best possible life."

Tears spring up without warning in Styóka's eyes, and he struggles to swipe them hurriedly away with his dirtied sleeve. "I should've done better for you, my sweet girl. Your brother and I should've gone with you to Clevyan."

But the angel shakes her head. She crosses the room, trailing her long robes like sparkling glass at her heels. When she kneels at her weeping father's feet and takes his calloused, quaking hands in hers, the light in her eyes is more spectacular than any words could hope to describe.

"No, Father. You did all you could. And despite whatever happens after today, I'll always be your daughter."

The warmth of her hands lingers at his palms, even after she's vanished like a breath of wind from before his face an instant later. Then Styóka is left alone in a daze, wondering if he's just seen a vision—if the angel he just witnessed was real at all. Wondering if he'll ever see her again.

4

-Common Year 179-

Hamara lets out a content sigh as she slips into a newly hemmed, knee-length kopachue dress and fastens the ties. It's a rich violet-blue color that seems pleasantly completed when she dons new calf-length fitted trousers underneath and her old black hebana belt over the top of it all, above the small of her waist. The coarse fabric flows out from her frame like a flower blossom hung by its stem, folding and curving over itself on all sides. The local voránjevin seamstresses had spare fabric and were oddly thrilled to dress an arai girl. They worked incredibly fast. Hamara isn't usually one to wear a kopachue. But after traveling for days in her only remaining—and now very stained—set of clothes, she's relieved to have a chance to wash clean and wear something that doesn't reek of river water and sweat—or Asei's blood.

She carried him for ages before voránjevin scouts found them, the night the monster attacked—

more than long enough for his blood to seep through the makeshift wrap she'd made out of her coat and thoroughly soak her clothes, leaving an unpleasant wetness on her stomach. When she looked up at last to see the scouts coming her way through the trees in the early light, she thought she was dreaming. They sent bursts of strength flooding through her aching arms and, by some kind of miracle, got Asei's bleeding to slow. The central camp of the Vilfirehn clan wasn't far. It sits like a hidden city deep in the woods of North Emér. An intricate tangle of treetop lofts, rope crossings, hammocks, and slender wooden platforms built between the trees. Little gardens can be found throughout the ground level, sometimes elevated in humble wooden boxes. And at the heart of it all, a canopied grove beside a little stream that flows through the center of the camp. A quiet place, where voránjevin individuals passing through the "deep sleep" of the transformation process lie concealed in large, glossy cocoons. The sleeping grounds.

It's still morning when Hamara returns to the little raised platform where Asei's lain since the night before. It's a spot not far from the southern edge of the camp, and sits only a short step off the ground. Hamara's glad—there's no telling if the little treetop ledges and rope bridges of the camp could hold the weight of someone so much larger than their usual occupants.

"Looks like the eagle has awakened at last!" She grins.

Asei sits with his right wing partly open as a rust-colored filíl carefully changes the bandaging on his side. He looks up, and his silvery-gray eyes catch the full brightness of the midday light that beams down through the leaves.

"Thanks to you more than anyone, kid. I hate being in debt, you know." He shuffles his clawed feet. "First you risk everything to potentially distract your crazy uncle, and now this?"

Hamara laughs, stepping up onto the platform and settling down on the nearest thick-woven straw mat. "You don't owe me anything, bird man. I'm just glad that nasty thing didn't come back and attack again when I was trying to find help."

"I could hear you coming as I passed out. To be honest, I thought that monster was about to kill us both."

"Not this time." Hamara shakes her head.

"You're a brave girl to fight the kadanto so fearlessly." The filíl at Asei's side finishes his bandaging before turning her gaze to Hamara. She speaks Moi-Sketzan surprisingly well—easily as well as Asei.

Hamara feels her checks flush. "Fighting back just helps me feel less afraid." She sits forward. "So, your people have seen that creature too?"

"Now and then. Though I haven't seen it myself for many years." The stranger presses the old red-and-brown-stained bandaging into a little bowl of water for soaking. "It appeared to me several times in the south. Our clan once dwelt near the southern mountains of the land you call Igretho. Skéisono visited our camp from time to time, when he was a boy."

"You mean my uncle? The immortal? You knew him?"

The voránjevin nods. "We tried to look after him when he came to us. The clans have watched for the sasarianë for generations. But one day, I needed to change into a virit messenger. When I woke weeks later, he had vanished. He and all his village."

"All but my father," Hamara adds. And somehow, mentioning her father seems to trigger an odd sensation in her mind. A warm flurry that brings sudden, breathtaking clarity to her thoughts and leaves her feeling as though she could cross over the world in a moment's time without leaving the place where she sits.

My father, Marntrei. My mother, Chimai.

She remembers their faces, and their living presence becomes suddenly obvious. As if they stood nearby—as if she could *see* them, where they sit in the riverboat. The river. That's where they are, isn't it? Riding along the Nakuë, far away to the south. Thinking of their daughters. Somehow, Hamara knows it. But how could that possibly be?

The sound of trickling water pulls Hamara abruptly back into the camp of the Vilfirehn. The filíl wrings water from the cloth she just used to dab blood from Asei's matted feathers and lays it over the edge of another bowl. "I've often regretted not doing more for Skéisono. If I had just waited one more day, maybe I could've looked after him. Could've prevented all the ruin he's brought to the world. But there's no sense regretting now. The past can't be altered." She brings a hand to Hamara's shoulder. "And now we have new hope."

Hamara smiles. "You can thank Asei for that. It was all his idea, Miss—er—"

"My name is Vayeka."

Hamara might have asked something more, but Asei rises sharply to his feet with a wild look in his giant eyes, interrupting any words that were about to be spoken. "It's him. It was him all along."

"What?" Hamara blinks.

"The kadanto. I think I know what it is." Asei lifts his left wing awkwardly in the air in front of him, as if he's forgotten that a hand no longer exists there.

"The records at Clevyan spoke of a sasarian whose power was taken from him because he used it for evil purposes."

"Like my uncle did?"

"I guess so. But he became a ghost. A dark spirit. I read that he haunted and tormented the people of Claya until a few hundred years ago, when the sasarian immortals of the time revoked his ability to touch or possess living bodies."

Hamara thinks back to her last night on the riverboat, remembering the horrible black-eyed stranger who cornered her with a knife—a being seemingly made of smoke. "Now that I think of it, the stranger who attacked me before I fell off the riverboat never actually touched me."

"He was once a king. But now he's a ghost. An angry ghost." Asei nods.

"And he can somehow control the sand and dirt to make a puppet for himself?"

Vayeka shakes her head. "The ghost cannot command the elements in his fallen state. He shapes the sand puppet with his own hands. I've seen him do it."

Hamara wonders at how strange it all sounds. A ghost puppeteer? But then, as of late, almost anything seems possible. "Maybe Asei's right about the ghost's identity. But I still don't see why he would be angry with *us*."

"The kadanto seems to appear most often to those who strive to aid the sasarian immortals." Vayeka lowers to her knees near the center of the mat. "It only stalked me during the years that I watched over the sasarian child. Now, it seems to be attacking the two people who were hoping to interfere with the destruction that same immortal was causing."

"Yep. And he must be creating the kadanto out of whatever physical materials he can move, just to attack us." Asei bobs his head again in agreement.

"Did the records say anything about how to get rid of him?" Hamara raises an eyebrow. It'd be tremendously useful information.

"No. But if he truly is an outcast spirit, he must obey the law of the realms—former sasarian or not," Asei tells her.

Hamara looks between the two voránjevin, wondering if either one will explain what was just said.

Vayeka notices. "The law of the realms is that all outcast spirits are subject to the living. If we command them to leave us, they must leave. For a time, at least."

Subject to the command of the living? On the riverboat, the kadanto had Hamara cornered in a hall below the deck. But it vanished before touching her. At the time, she was too terrified to contemplate why. But now she remembers the words that left her throat at that moment with all the volume she could produce.

Get away from me!

Is that all she needed to do? Yell for the beast to leave her alone? It's a strategy that seemed to work again, when the monster nearly killed Asei in the woods. But how long will that horrible creature continue to return?

* * *

That night, the lanterns throughout the camp of the Vilfirehn set a warm glow in the trees, lighting the walking paths with soft halos of yellow light. It's an impressively calm night, without even the slightest breath of wind to quiver the leaves. Asei curses the wound in his side as he waddles slowly through the camp. He'd much rather be flying. Stubby virit legs, with their long, curving talons, are no good for walking. He walks only halfway to the gardens when Vayeka appears in his path, frowning curiously down at him.

"You're supposed to be resting."

"I needed a change of scene." Asei gives his best attempt at a shrug with hulking wings in place of ordinary shoulders. "And anyway, I need your help with something."

Vayeka raises two fingers to point back down the path. "We can talk while you rest."

It's only a short journey back to the platform where Asei's spent most of the day. He scrambles back onto it with a hidden wince and plops down on the mat that's scarcely cooled since he left it moments ago. "OK, I'm resting." He looks back to Vayeka. "Now I need you to help me trigger an ek'let'eh. I need to change back into the virsevin form. Or even my original form. Something with arms."

Vayeka's pointed front teeth become momentarily visible as her mouth falls open. "Begin a change? Now? But you're injured—and I hear you woke as a virit scarcely a week ago!"

"Yes, yes, but something's happening with Alarei. I can feel it. She might need help. I need to take on a stronger form."

"The sasarian woman?"

"I don't know how to explain it, but she's changing. I can feel it. I can feel her presence becoming less and less powerful." Asei stares blankly down at the mat beneath him. "It's almost like . . . like she's becoming more like an ordinary person."

"More like a mortal being? But why would that be?"

"I don't know. But if she's about to be in danger, I don't want her to be alone."

A moment of silence passes over the mat, and somewhere out in the camp, the sound of children chasing through the trees can be heard. Their laughter skips and leaps in the evening air, delicate and fleeting.

Vayeka kneels down at Asei's side and carefully raises his wing, bringing a gentle hand to the still darkened feathers near his wound. "You're healing well, but your injury's still very new. My sons weren't certain you'd make it to the camp alive when they found you. Not after all the blood you'd lost. Beginning the ek'let'eh again so soon is likely to strain your body in more ways than one. If you don't take in sufficient energy and nutrients for the transformation, your bones may not reform with enough strength. You'll become frail."

Asei looks back into the dark eyes of the filíl beside him. "It doesn't matter what happens to me—so long as I can be the help she needs for now. Vayeka, I left her alone before, when I thought it was best. And I've regretted it ever since. Please, don't force me to make that mistake again."

Vayeka stares. Sternly, at first. But the edges of her frown soften a moment later. Only subtly—as if one of her own boys has misbehaved. "You're a stubborn heln, Asei. It seems your Iftav heritage shines through in more than just your brightly colored feathers." She folds her arms across her chest. "We haven't practiced the rapid ek'let'eh as the Taufeth have. Your transformation will be natural. Slow."

"That's OK, I think. As long as I can make the change."

Vayeka shakes her head in silent dismay, then moves to sit directly behind Asei's feathered back. She lays her palm along his spine, gliding along its length and pausing briefly at points where his strength seems to swell in little eddies—places where a pulse of energy from her hand could trigger each of the transformations. Asei can feel the gentle surge of heat and power wherever her hands rest. A sensation that seems to ripple through his every nerve.

"Your original form, then?" Vayeka's whisper is partly muffled by the mass of feathers she speaks into.

A moment ago, Asei may have told her yes. But now the idea of returning to his original form—a shape he hasn't taken in decades—seems off. Even wrong.

"No. Virsevin form. If I see Alarei again, I want to see her with the face she knows." He glances over his right wing to find the filíl shaking her head yet again.

"I can't believe I'm helping you with this. Are you sure you want the risk?"

"I'm sure."

Vayeka lets out a slow breath. "All right, then." She reaches to bring one hand to his chest, laying it nearly over his heart. The second lies along his upper spine, following the curve at the base of his neck. "Take a deep breath," she warns him, as is the custom. And he does. But the energy that surges from her palms sends the air in his lungs bursting immediately out again. The surge swells like a fiery bolt of lightning through his nerves and rattles his bones. It's the same sensation that always accompanies the start of the ek'let'eh. But with Asei's weakened state, it seems somehow more overwhelming than ever.

"Ihyait!" Asei curses, leaping up and nearly stumbling over backward.

Vayeka steadies him with a single arm across his back. "You better make it through this one, or I'll never forgive myself," she tells him.

"Th-thank—thank you for all your help." Asei wheezes and settles down onto his knees, wondering for an instant if he really *can* get through it—if the effort's already too late. But there's no sense worrying. No turning back now.

5

She appears like a leaf in the wind among the blackened remains of Clevyan's northern balcony. The stone is chilled when her feet touch down. And blackened. There was a battle here, not long ago—the evidence of which remains brutally obvious in more ways than one. The once pale stone columns and marbled walls now resemble the charred confines of a cavern, and the simple elegance of the floor is harshly interrupted by a crumbling, gaping hole that opens into the halls below. A mild breeze rises through the new space, carrying all the subtle scents of ancient stone corridors and distant courtyards.

Something's changed since the moment the two sasarianë were separated in the heart of the forest. Alarei stands at the center of the once grand balcony, closes her eyes and listens. Just *listens*. Less than a day ago, she was able to hear all the living souls on Claya's face. It was a relentless, unending tide at her ears. But now they've fallen silent. After living for weeks with such a constant chorus of sound at the edge of her mind, the silence is almost stifling. Perhaps the gift they hoped to bestow upon the world has worked after all.

The few sounds that reach her now are undeniably familiar. The echo of birds down the marble halls, the sleepless whisper of morning wind through the archways, and the occasional, far-off chime of voices in the corridors of the sanctuary. They're sounds she heard constantly as a girl. It's all exactly as she remembers. But it lacks its centerpiece—the sound of a voice that accompanied her every day in the halls of Clevyan. A voice she's since heard speaking her name in Igretho, and in the forests north of Emér. The voice of a friend dearer to her than any other. She's heard each time he speaks her name. And each time she's resisted the almost crippling urge to go to him—to see his face again, to witness the smile that she's missed so terribly for years.

It was nearly eighteen years ago when he left her alone on the hills of Clevyan. He left with words that made no sense to her then. Words about a spectacular future that the elders of Clevyan would know how to help Alarei realize. Now that future has come to meet her, and everything Asei said that day becomes suddenly clear. Somehow, he knew. He knew that Alarei was destined to awaken as a sasarian immortal when the time was right. And it made sense to assume that the elders of the sanctuary—the world's greatest scholars of the immortals and their histories—would eventually recognize it as well. In reality, they didn't. But it was an outcome that Asei had no way to anticipate. He must have simply hoped to give Alarei the best possible chance of associating with those who could help her reach her sasarian potential.

It was hardly over a week ago when the events at Tavehlik left Alarei inexplicably freed from the burden of executing her sasarian brother. A little over a week ago when she dared allow herself to draw momentarily nearer to Asei—only to watch him desperately from a distance. Hidden. It was a night when the person most precious to her nearly lost his life. His heart let out a horrible shudder the moment he was injured near the Ádenlal plains, and it was impossible for Alarei to stay away entirely. She could have gone instantly to his side, could have healed him in the time it takes to speak his name. But somehow, it didn't feel right. She couldn't allow herself to touch him. Not yet. Not when an entire world ached for healing. Even so, she made certain that Asei received the aid he needed—visiting the dreams of a voránjevin scout who slept in the woods nearby and urging him to rise and go in search of the travelers in need. And she watched like a ghost in the wind as they carried Asei into their camp—watched with an aching heart and a tremor in her breath until the cries of the world wrenched her sorrowfully away. He'd be all right. Somehow, she knew it. But the assurance hardly helped.

Until recently, taking her focus away from the voices of the world for even an instant came with a terrible price. A cost measured in lives lost. But now, the destruction has ended. Now Alarei has time to think, to breathe, to listen. And now it takes every fiber of strength in her soul to resist spending every day and night beside the friend she once lost. But she *must* resist. The world still needs all the aid it can get. And as the elders of Clevyan have long taught, the heart of a sasarian immortal can only belong to Claya. The world deserves no less.

Doesn't it?

Alarei opens her eyes, shaking her head and turning to gaze again over the burned and scarred remains of the Hall of Prayers at her back. It's the place where two sasarian immortals met for the first time. The place where one made his first ruthless attempt to take the life of the other—and nearly succeeded. It wasn't long ago at all. But now, standing again in the battleground, Alarei feels as though it all happened *ages* ago. That day, it was an idle whisper that called her fellow immortal to her side. A name murmured entirely by accident. Today, she'll call him here again.

It's a far simpler task now, to clear her mind. And despite the new silence of the world, her fellow immortal's heart can still be heard from afar. She focuses, and the sound comes fluttering to her ears. A subtle drumbeat buried far away in the plains of Igretho. She's scarcely let his name escape her lips when a new wave of white-golden light floods through the dark columns of the hall.

"So much has changed since I last visited this place." He's standing several paces away, gazing down at the gaping hole in the stone floor. Skéisono. The being who once hunted her here. But the flames that cloaked his shining figure that day have long since extinguished.

"Changed for the better, I think," Alarei answers. "The world's become so silent. Do you think the people of Claya truly received our gift?"

The Farian answers first. It glides into the space over the broken floor. "They did. Though many have not yet recognized it."

Alarei steps slowly along the edge of the fractured stones. "Some hearing has remained with us, it seems. I was still able to hear Skéisono's heart, when I focused. And I can hear a few others. My father, my brother, and . . ." A name reappears in her mind, but she shakes her head, pushing past it. "It seems like we can hear the hearts of those closest to us, just as all people now can."

"And we still have so much more to give." Skéisono turns to stare out over the nearby balcony, to the cliff-top hills and the golden, rolling dunes of the Sand Sea to the west. "I once commanded the earth to take innocent lives in this place. No one should be allowed to misuse that power again."

"Then let's give it back." Alarei holds out her hands, palms to the sky. "Maybe here, outside each of our realms, we won't be separated again. Farian, do you know what caused the winds to oppose us yesterday?"

The Farian pivots its single eye, catching the sharp light of the beings who surround it. "You offer a gift of power to the world. To receive it, Claya must change its nature—just as you were changed when you obtained your inheritance. But these servants cannot say for certain why the winds may not heed you."

"Whatever the reason for yesterday's winds, they can't stop us from moving forward." Skéisono brings his hands to Alarei's. "Just like last time, we'll give the power back. Let the pure-hearted souls in the world be given our power over the elements. If they ask with good intent, the elements will obey."

"So long as they don't hope to destroy the free will of others." Alarei nods, and she closes her eyes. But this time, there's no sound to focus on. No endless symphony of living souls to enshrine at the center of her thoughts. Now, there's nothing—nothing but a handful of echoes from the hearts of those dearest to her. "But . . . how will we do this? We can't hear them anymore."

"No, but we can remember," Skéisono answers without opening his eyes.

He's right. Alarei pulls her mind back into focus, pushing to recall the way the world so recently rang in a merciless din at her ears—remembering the sorrowful dirges, the joyous shouts and desperate hopes. Remembering the songs of celebrating hearts that clamored with such dissonance against the wind-rending cries of suffering souls throughout the world.

This time, the light comes slowly. It begins as a warm stirring between the hands of the sasarianë, then rises into a white glow that escapes in bright rays between their fingers. When Alarei opens her eyes, the swelling light is reflecting with striking brilliance off the polished walls and columns of the Hall of Prayers.

"I think it's working—"

Her words are swept away by a raging wind that bursts abruptly into the scene. It whips and throttles against the immortals in its midst, drawing them in opposite directions until they can no longer stand against it. And this time, it sweeps both of them away. The world spins and hurtles by on all sides, and Alarei loses sight of Skéisono—of Clevyan, the cliffs, and the Sand Sea altogether.

6

The first reports that come in with the scouts that morning seem like little more than vague rumors. Whispers of distant, miraculous events. Rainstorms appearing abruptly over drought-stricken lands, or ceasing altogether where their floods were threatening lives in arai villages. But as the day moves along, more tales come drifting into the camp of the Vilfirehn—stories that become more marvelous with each passing hour. Some scouts bring word of hurricanes suddenly ceasing at the southern coasts, or of maimed and missing limbs that were suddenly restored in nearby clans. Others tell of a mountainside in the east that heaved open by its own power to free a handful of miners trapped inside. They say it peeled open like a thick-skinned fruit. But perhaps the most spectacular report of all is the tale of a voracious wildfire at the far northeastern edge of the Ádenlal that raged for days, only to abruptly fizzle out and vanish sharply into smoke when a little child requested that it do so.

By the afternoon of Hamara and Asei's third day with the Vilfirehn, the stories are too numerous to count and too remarkable to comprehend.

"Something's happening to the world."

Hamara sits watching a group of young hunters preparing to depart into the woods with their instructor. Many of the young voránjevin are wearing nothing over their furred bodies, and are most likely only a few years younger than Hamara herself. But with such slender, tiny statures, they look like little more than toddlers.

"Something incredible. *Everyone's* feeling it. I feel it too." Asei leans to snatch a thick slice of cooked meat with his teeth from the tray beside him, then tips his head to let it slip like a fish into his jaws.

Hamara frowns idly at the canopy above, wondering. "First we all started knowing where our family members are. Now all these wild stories are going around. Do you think it's related to the immortals?"

"Absolutely. Alarei's got to be behind this. Who or what else could it be? And if he's still around, your uncle must've changed his agenda." Asei pauses to swallow. "I can't say exactly what's happening now, but whatever it is, it's changing the sasarianë as much as it's changing the rest of the world."

"How do you know?"

"Because . . ." The silver-eyed eagle stares momentarily to the grass beyond his little shelter. And his voice loses its usual buoyant melody. "Because I can feel the life energy leaving Alarei every day. Each day a little more slips away."

Ordinarily, the claim would seem bizarre. But after spontaneously acquiring the ability to hear the heartbeats of her own family echoing from far away to the south, Hamara's hardly surprised.

Asei finishes one last bite of his feast before looking up. "This wound is healing fast. It might not be terribly comfortable, but I think I'll be able to handle flying by tomorrow. Then we can get you back on your way. We'll take a route that leads by each voránjevin camp along the way. You'll have all the supplies and protection you could ever need."

"You really shouldn't fly until you're more fully healed." Hamara tips her chin like a nagging mother. If she's learned anything from being the daughter of two doctors, it's that bodies need plenty of time to heal—more time than most people have the patience to allow. "It's not good to—"

She stops midsentence to stare blankly at her winged friend, who's suddenly teetering on one stubby leg and clawing strangely at the air with the other. He wobbles to remain balanced, holding one wing partly open with his chin tucked to his feathery chest. The sight of it frees an unavoidable laugh from Hamara's throat. "What in the name of Claya are you doing? Some kind of bird dance?"

The plume along Asei's neck fluffs outward like broad hairs on end. "Curse my lack of arms! I'm going to lose my mind if this bandage gets any itchier! I can't reach it!" He scowls. "Kid, just rip it off for me, will you?"

"Are you sure that's OK?"

"It's fine, it's fine! The bleeding stopped long ago. The wound is closing up."

"All right, I'll take a look, at least."

Hamara shuffles to the virit's side and reaches to gingerly untie the bandaging secured around his middle. It's similar to the absorbent padding her parents have always used against open wounds, but thinner. Almost stretchy. When she loosens the knot and carefully unravels the double layers, the wound it exposes seems far more severe than she expected. It's the sort of deep gash that her parents would've insisted on stitching together. But the voránjevin ways are not like human ways. Vayeka's mentioned that the regular application of hitérian energy causes the wounded tissues to rebuild themselves, quickly mending broken veins to stop excessive bleeding. Looking now, Hamara can already see how new skin and muscle is growing in to replace what was torn. But the complete process must still take time.

"Asei, this still looks pretty painful."

"It's not as bad as it looks. I only need another day, trust me."

He sounds so confident, so unconcerned. But Hamara isn't convinced. An oddly sour sensation sprouts in her throat, and she becomes all too aware of the urgency that's tugged at her heart since the morning they reached the Vilfirehn. An undefined sense of urgency that hangs like a massive pendulum over her head—and doesn't seem to make any sense. What could possibly be urgent, now that Asei's getting the help he needs? He and Hamara accomplished what they set out to do, didn't they? Now Hamara just needs to get home. Or at least, that was the plan. But kneeling beside her friend and staring into his still undeniably fresh injury, the girl from Remertrei can't seem to dispel an odd thought from her mind.

Is there something more? Something they've forgotten that has yet to be resolved? But what else could possibly need doing before Hamara can return home? Maybe Asei knows the answer. He's been dying to get back onto the road. And more and more, so is Hamara.

"Come on now, can you heal up already? We've got places to go!" Hamara murmurs to the wound as she removes the last wrap of bandaging. She's turned to fold the bandaging on the mat beside her when Asei nearly knocks her to the floor with his suddenly outstretched wings.

"What the—? Hamara, what did you *do*?!" He hops in a little circle with a shrill voice, bending to eye his side.

Hamara jumps to her feet. "I—I just took off the bandage, like you asked! Is it hurting worse? I'll get Vayeka—"

She's about to leap from the platform and bolt down the walking path. But Asei calls her back.

"No, look! Look!" The massive smile on his face is beyond confusing.

"What? What's wrong? What's going on?!"

"Just *look* at this, kid!"

The virit is leaping in place, and the wind from his massive wings gusts the straw mats and stacks of bandaging to the edges of the platform beneath him. Hamara returns to her friend's side with her hands held up in confusion, kneeling again to see the deep gash in his side. And her mouth drops open. The wound is gone.

"Gone? It's *gone*? But—but how is that possible? Just a moment ago it was, it was—"

Hamara sits unconsciously down. Her hair nearly blows free from its tie when Asei gives a triumphant beat with his wings.

"I feel *amazing*! Hamara, it was you! What you said! It had to be—just like all the rumors!"

"What? What do you mean? All I did was—I just—" Hamara gestures loosely to the bandaging that

Asei's wild flapping has just blown off into the walking path.

"My body healed because of what you said. That's got to be it!"

Could it be? Hamara wonders. The stories they've heard from the scouts these days are nothing short of fantastical. Mountains cleaving open? Storms and blazes ceasing at the request of ordinary people? Now, one of the stories is right in front of her. Even so, how could words alone heal an injury—heal it *instantly?* The question is impossible to answer. But as Asei launches into the air, beating his wings to rise up through the canopy in a gust of wind and thrilled shouts, the answer no longer seems to matter.

And Hamara can't help but laugh out loud.

* * *

They rise as the sun's only beginning to peer over the horizon the next morning. At a time when all but the youngest residents of the camp are already awake and darting from one daily task to another. It seems like all the voránjevin are early risers, if not entirely nocturnal. After living among them for this long, Hamara's almost beginning to feel like one of them. A tall, furless one of them.

She tucks her water canteen into the folds of the maroon wrap that's tied in the traditional voránjevin style over her shoulder and around her waist. Ordinarily, as Vayeka explained, a traveler would lay it over both shoulders before circling it around the waist and ending it in a knot at the lower back. But Hamara's a bit larger than the usual wearer. It was a gift that Vayeka insisted on giving. A strong fabric made with open weave, for the warmer months.

"You can use it to carry supplies," she told her.

Now, looking down at the dark folds of the wrap atop the lighter violet-blue of her voránjevin-made kopachue dress, Hamara wonders if her family will even recognize her when they see her next.

"I don't feel like I thanked Vayeka enough for all her help these past few days." She leans lazily into the tree she's come to, glancing back toward the heart of the camp.

Asei's voice falls softly down from the branches overhead. "It's the culture of the clans to care for all people. Only the extremists of the Iftav wouldn't do the same," he tells her. "You ready? We'd better get you back to Remertrei while I can still fly."

Hamara peers up through the leaves, spotting only random patches of Asei's vibrant plume. "Where will you go after that?"

"To find Alarei."

"So you've changed your mind, then? About seeing her? You seemed so adamant about staying away before."

"She didn't seem to be in danger before. Or at least, not danger she couldn't handle."

A mild breeze slips through the trees, reminding Hamara to tie back the hair that dances loosely at her neck. "Do you think more wild changes will come to the world?"

"I don't know. I just want to be waiting nearby if Alarei runs into trouble. Just in case."

"But you just started another transformation, didn't you? Won't you be stuck in one place for a while, once you enter the deep sleep?"

Asei shuffles along his perch, sending little bits of bark sprinkling down to the earth. "I'll get horribly stiff and sore in the days leading up to that, too. But I'll manage all right. It won't be the first time I've done it alone."

Alone. The thought makes Hamara's feet shift stiffly in place. It doesn't seem right at all. And before she can finish contemplating why, a solution comes blurting abruptly out of her mouth. "Remertrei can wait. Let's go to your friend's aid. I'll go with you. Just let me write another letter to my family to let them know I'll be away for a bit longer."

"What? You want to come with?" Asei leaves the branches with a sudden rush of wind and comes leaping down into the grass, staring with eyes as wide and silvery as the greater moon that's still sinking at the horizon. "Hamara, you've done enough. Why should I keep dragging you along?"

Hamara folds her arms. "Your wound healed when I asked it to. Maybe I can help speed up the changing process for you."

"How? By asking my body to hurry up? Now why haven't I tried that before . . ."

"It's worth a try, isn't it?"

"Maybe I can speed it up myself."

"Maybe—but what if that kadanto thing comes again and attacks while you sleep? You'll be helpless! And I'm the only one here who's got nothing keeping me busy."

The virit opens his sharp-toothed mouth, about to speak. But no words come. Then he tips his head to stare at Hamara through the corners of his narrowed eyes. "It won't be a pretty sight, you know, when I wake up. Blood; sweat; a giant, slimy, soggy shell . . ."

Hamara shrugs. "I'm not squeamish."

Asei gives his wings a rough shake. "All right, fine. You've convinced me," he tells her, and he lets out an exaggerated sigh. "Let's see what your magic words can do."

7

-Common Year 179-

The winds are a raging envelope on all sides. Tossing, whipping, folding. They whirl and heave Alarei for ages over the face of the earth until she can no longer hope to distinguish up from down. When they cease at last, leaving her collapsed on the ground, the world falls into shocking silence on all sides. And darkness. The black stone beneath her hands is hot and flawlessly smooth. It extends endlessly outward in all directions like an ancient, breathless sea. And no sky looms overhead. Instead, the mortal and spirit realms can be seen shifting and churning endlessly like pools of fogged and glimmering liquid, far beyond reach. What is this place? Aside from the occasional soft glows of gold and amber light in the blackened distance, the scene beyond Alarei's own glow is almost entirely void of light. And the air is warm. *Uncomfortably* warm— a sensation that sasarian immortals wouldn't usually be able to experience. The world and its laws are changing.

"You don't know this place, do you? The sasarianë of ages past were well acquainted with the heart of the earth. It's a shame that you've chosen to abandon your abilities long before you ever learned to fully appreciate them."

The man's voice is a startling rupture in the silence. And the sudden presence of another being is jarring. Not long ago, Alarei would have sensed if any soul in all the world was approaching. Not anymore. She turns to find a black-eyed stranger standing in the darkness. A spirit.

"And you are?" she asks, but the ghost only shakes his head. Dissatisfied.

"What kind of fools choose to throw away the power of the gods? It can't accomplish anything. And now look at you. You're becoming more and more like pathetic mortals with every breath you take." The man sneers, stepping closer. "Now the light of Claya won't even carry you, and you'll be forced to crawl like vermin along the ground. Shameful."

Alarei backs soundlessly away. Who is this ghost? His image brightens and fades like a flickering flame as he speaks, and Alarei catches occasional glimpses of long, ornate sleeves hanging from his nearly invisible arms. Whoever he is, he's not her priority. Almost without thinking, she turns to step away into the realms, trying to recall the sound of Skéisono's heart. She should still be able to hear it—to go to him in an instant, as always. But nothing happens when she brings her destination to mind. And the sasarian woman is left standing motionless in the dark.

"What did I tell you? The ways of the immortals are leaving you. Now you'll walk like the rest." The stranger comes circling closer in three long strides. Then he pauses, tipping his head to one side. "How lovely. I can come closer to you now than I ever could before. I wonder, do you bleed like a mortal now, as well?" The dark spirit comes leaping abruptly closer like a ravenous beast from the darkness, suddenly melting into a mass of shadows that wears a horrible, twisted grin.

"Farian, take me from this place!" Alarei shouts, and all at once the overwhelming heat and darkness of the scene vanish away. The mortal realm blooms in a rush of color and daylight at all sides, and with little more than a flinch, Alarei finds herself standing in an empty plain. And she waits to find her breath.

A ghost! He was simply a ghost, nothing more. So why did his presence cause such a terrible tremor in Alarei's bones? After facing Skéisono at his raging worst—after learning to wield unstoppable power that few immortals have mastered in ages past, Alarei assumed nothing could frighten her again. Apparently, she was mistaken.

An afternoon wind leaps playfully over the hills now, stirring the tall grasses and tossing the immortal's short hair against her jawline. A breeze. Soft, from the northeast. It's something entirely ordinary. A phenomenon that occurs nearly every day of any mortal lifetime. But the winds of Claya have long been known to part ways for their sasarian masters—rising to aid them only when commanded to do so. Or so it has been, since the beginning of the ages. These days, few things remain as they once were. How many months have passed since Alarei last felt the wind toss her hair? She glances down to the halo of light that still emanates from her presence and lights the roots of the grass at her feet. It's dimmer than before.

"That spirit." She talks to her faintly glowing palm. "He said the light of Claya will no longer carry us.

He seemed to know what's happening to us as we return our gifts to Claya."

The Farian materializes just beyond her shoulder, turning slowly in place. "He watches the motions of all sasarianë with great envy. He has done so ever since his own power was taken from him, since the day Faliéhl defeated him in his wrath."

Alarei turns to watch her guardian's shining eye. "It was him, wasn't it—the one who turned Skéisono against us decades ago?"

"The same."

"Are we truly becoming mortal again? Is that what's happening to us now?"

"This servant cannot answer for certain. But with your second gift to the world you chose to forsake your command over the elements. The light of Claya once carried you wherever your heart desired, more rapidly than any mortal bodies could travel. Now, it seems you must walk as mortals walk."

Walk? Alarei turns to stare in all directions, hoping to make sense of the world that surrounds her. Days ago, the deep rhythm of the earth's soul and every being who lived on its surface served as unmistakable place markers. Landmarks that helped Alarei pinpoint her exact location at all times—and the location of anyone else—with perfect speed. It was impossible to become lost. Now, few things are so simple. She closes her eyes, focusing. To the southwest, the sounds of her father's and brother's hearts beat softly along—in the Tayd cities of Hadón and Jaker, as usual. Nearly straight south, the heart of a dearest friend still resounds like a tireless signal in the forests of North Emér. A strong beat that pours relief into Alarei's anxious mind. Asei. He must be recovering well. Only one other heart can be heard beyond his, down in the rolling hills of Igretho.

The heart of a sasarian man. Alarei turns to face the sound of his presence, watching the softening hues of the southern skies. She must be standing somewhere in the great expanse of the Ádenlal plains. Without warning, the world has grown suddenly vast. *Hopelessly* vast.

"We have more gifts to return to Claya. This isn't finished. I've got to reach Skéisono, even if it takes a little time," Alarei tells the distant hills, burying the odd numbness in her stomach. There's no reason to worry. It could take weeks to reach even the northern shores of Emér on foot. Maybe more. But it's only time—a resource that can never run short for immortal beings.

. . . Can it?

8

The visions rarely come at convenient moments. And they always arrive with startling clarity, striking like lightning in Vehn's often unsuspecting mind and scalding away any other thought that dared to dwell there. This time is no exception. The vision jolts the man to his feet so suddenly that he startles the voránjevin children who sit quietly on the rug before him, practicing their handwriting with commendable diligence. They look up from their little slates, wide-eyed, ears twitching.

"What's wrong, Teacher Vehn?" One of them voices the question that paints every pupil's young face.

Vehn snatches a kerchief from his desk to mop the sweat that's appeared at his forehead. "My good students, we won't be having class tomorrow," he tells them. "I've just realized that I need to make a visit to the west shores of Emér."

Gasps and whispers of excitement erupt over the young ones, and they begin to wiggle in their places, showing one another their broad, toothy smiles.

"A hunt! Are you going on a special hunt?"

"Can we come with you, Teacher?"

Vehn waves his hand. "No, no. I'm afraid this journey will be far too boring for adventurers like yourselves. You'll be much better off with the clan." He stuffs the kerchief sloppily into his pocket. "Now, which one of you would like to be excused right now to deliver a message for me? Who's the fastest runner here?"

Several little faces light up, and young voices flood the room from one wall to the next.

"Me, me!"

"I am! I'm *always* the fastest!"

"No, Teacher, it's me!"

Vehn laughs, then raises his hand to calm the clamor. He tips his chin to a green-eyed heln at his left. "Shosaiyo, how about you? Will you take a message back to camp for me?"

The student nods and rises to his feet, grinning. "Yes, Teacher. What message?"

Vehn kneels down to look into the child's bright eyes. "I need to send a message to one of our virit scouts. It's a message they must carry to Vayeka of the Vilfirehn. Tell her there's someone who needed her years ago, who'll need her again. Very soon. I'll be ready to leave when she arrives here."

"Got it." The boy gives a stiff nod before turning to bolt out the open door of the cabin, trailing the envious stares of his classmates at his heels.

Vehn lets a smile crease his bearded face before turning back to his class. "Right, then. Now, who would like to share the practice sentences they crafted using today's vocabulary?"

9

-Common Year 179-

The sound fades in and out of earshot as he walks—sometimes clear, sometimes almost entirely muffled by the rushing voice of the winds over the hills. The sound of a heartbeat that was once too loud to ignore, no matter where in the world he stood. The only other immortal heartbeat in the world.

He's followed the sound on foot for what seems like hours, now. Walking northward one rocky hill at a time with his long robes trailing in the breeze. He gazes onward, eyeing the distant shadow of the mountains that guard the southernmost edge of the Sand Sea. Yesterday, he could've gone there in a single breath. Yesterday, there was no travel—only thought, and an instant arrival. The ability to move with such speed was a gift indeed. One Skéisono took entirely for granted.

Now a heavy sensation begins to crawl along his lungs—his feet, his legs. It's something he hasn't felt for decades. Not since his boyhood. A sensation he had all but forgotten. Could it be . . . exhaustion?

"Palarian, has the world received our gifts?"

"Yes. The pure-hearted people of Claya are discovering them even now." The guardian drifts effortlessly beside its immortal's shoulder, moving like a pillar of smoke over grass and stone.

Skéisono pauses in his steps, letting his breath ease. "I wish I could see it. Or at least hear it." He smiles bleakly to the horizon. It's a terribly long way to the Ádenlal plains, where Alarei's heart echoes endlessly on. The journey could be well over a month on foot. But perhaps there's a faster way. There's *got* to be. He looks down to the dry earth at his feet.

"Sands, earth—I've forsaken my right to command you. But I can still ask, can't I? As all good-willed people now can?" He shakes his head, feeling foolish. It's worth a try. "We sasarianë have more to give back to Claya. But my fellow immortal is far away. Will you help me travel faster?"

Without delay, the sands begin to stir at the sound of his voice. They churn and gather at all sides, rippling and folding like little waves at his heels.

Skéisono kneels, watching them closely. "Will you give me speed?"

The answer is swift. The sands harden and rise up as a solid slab of stone beneath the glowing man's feet. The earth below begins to roll and shift, shuffling the slab smoothly forward. Slowly, at first. But it picks up speed. In moments, Skéisono finds himself gliding rapidly over the hills like a slender boat over waves. And he smiles. It isn't instant, but it's faster than walking.

* * *

The night is cloudless and luminous when it comes. The greater moon has waned into a slender crescent, and the starry curtain beyond seems to have grown bolder and brighter in response. The silvery glow seems to lie like frost on every stone and every blade of grass in the rolling hills. Stepping from his traveling stone and nearly stumbling onto the unmoving ground, Skéisono wishes he had the energy to admire it all. But the man who was once the indestructible terror of all the world can hardly keep his eyes from falling shut. And the cold stone he's ridden atop for hours hasn't helped.

Such weariness, such drowsiness! For the first time in twenty-one years, Skéisono struggles to fight off the heavy pull of sleep that creeps along every edge of his body. Why would he need to sleep? It's a ridiculous concept. Sasarian immortals have no need for sleep or rest. Or at least, they never have before. But the exhaustion is maddening.

He glances around, seriously considering where he might lie down on the stony earth. But the sudden sight of a figure on the hillside nearby brushes his weariness momentarily aside. The darkened figure of a woman. She stands only several paces away, where the starlight and brightness of the lesser moon should easily light her face. But her features remain oddly shadowed—hidden, as if she wore a veil. A spirit.

"You really think you can hide it?" Her voice is coarse, echoless.

Skéisono stares, unmoving. "Hide what?"

Now the ghost seems to quake in her place. Her outline blurs and trembles like dark fire in the delicate light. "You dare pretend, you foul demon? Murderer!" She raises an accusing finger in the air, pointing to the immortal whose light has faded to little more than a humble glow at the edges of his figure. "My children died because of you! You robbed us of life! Robbed nearly all those who once lived in Thelian, the great western city you tore apart and burned to the ground!"

The words rip a jarring, fiery trench through Skéisono's already badly wounded soul. Words that revive the awful reality that's plagued his undying mind from the moment he first heard the cries of a suffering world, not long ago. It's a realization that left him paralyzed by the seashore for days on end—that even now only lets him breathe when he focuses all his power on the desperate task ahead.

He breathes. "I know I brought horrible suffering into this world. But those days have ended. We're going to make it all right again. We're giving up our power to the world—"

"You really think it can be mended? The world you've broken? The lives you've shattered? Heartless fool!" Another voice hisses from behind. Skéisono turns to find the spirit of a tall, broad-shouldered man shaking his head in dismay.

Now the spirit of a teenage boy stands on the hillside to the east. A boy with tousled hair and a condescending stare that Skéisono recognizes from days long past. A boy his brother Marntrei once fought off with a shovel. "You can pretend to make it better. Pretend all you like! But we all know the truth. You've always been a curse. You curse everything you touch. Nothing will ever change that."

"It's true that what I did can never be excused. I don't expect forgiveness. Not now, or ever." Skéisono stares at them each in turn, fighting to quell the wrenching ache in his heart. "The goddess will be my judge, when the time comes. For now, I'll do all I can to ensure that my mistakes can never be repeated—that

Claya will become something greater than ever before. A world where the people themselves carry the power of the immortals."

"How many cities did you burn, again? Thirty? Fifty?" A fourth spirit speaks up from the next hill over.

"Hundreds of us have lost our lives because of you! You think you could ever bring any good into this world?" another calls out.

"Just *listen* to me—" Skéisono begins, but the voices on all sides seem to rise up and drown his words like a merciless tide. What began as a handful of spirits has multiplied into a massive crowd. A mass full of pointing fingers, of jeering shouts and eyes full of seething retribution. All staring, all accusing.

"Murderer!"

"Demon!"

"Beast of hell!"

They shout and hiss on all sides until their words thicken like foul poison in the night air, until the glowing man who stands at their center raises his voice above them all.

"ENOUGH! LEAVE ME!"

Skéisono's shout echoes and rolls off the surrounding hills like a rebounding clap of thunder, and all at once the prairie returns to perfect stillness. The crowd has vanished. In its absence, a sasarian man falls alone to his knees, cradling his head in his quaking hands.

10

-Common Year 179-

Hamara can't withhold a satisfied grin as she builds a humble fire for the evening. She sits with her back to the massive cocoon that lies at the edge of the heat, marveling again at how quickly it's all happened. It was only two days ago when she and Asei set out from the camp of the Vilfirehn and headed north. Two days since Hamara first began to plead with the elements to hasten Asei's transformation. By evening of the first day, Asei was already too stiff to fly. The following morning, he fell into the deep sleep almost midstep. Hamara did her best to follow Vayeka's instructions, insisting that Asei keep eating and drinking until the moment he collapsed.

"He'll need all the fuel he can get," she had warned. She suggested that the two of them wait at the camp of the Vilfirehn until Asei's change could be completed. But Asei was too anxious to head north. He was certain they could make progress while he still had wings. His expectation wasn't entirely accurate. But how could he have known? Until recently, the ek'let'eh process took no less than a month. Now that a hard-shelled cocoon has grown over Asei's entire body, it'll be a simple job for Hamara to keep watch for a few days—especially with the Vilfirehn scouts occasionally passing by with news and supplies. There's no telling how long the transformation will take. But Hamara has every reason to expect a short wait.

All around, the sparse woods have grown dim. There was a time when Hamara would've been unnerved to spend the night in the dark with only a little fire and Asei's strange cocoon to accompany her. But now, it feels almost as ordinary as an evening by the fire in Remertrei. Almost.

She watches the fire and counts the early stars for quite some time before a gray stone in the leaves just outside the glow of the fire catches her eye. She may have gone long into the night without noticing it if she didn't happen to glimpse it shifting subtly sideways through the bushes. It isn't a stone. Hamara sits suddenly straighter, watching the pale shape with her hand hovering over the grip of her sénsin rod. For a time, the object doesn't move. But it doesn't remain hidden for long. A tall, narrow limb begins to rise from the shadows. A neck—and at its top, a featureless face appears over the bushes, peering down with horrible black, beady eyes that would send a terrible twisting into the stomach of anyone unfortunate enough to be caught in their gaze. The kadanto. It's back.

Hamara doesn't wait for it to come slinking any closer.

"Go! Get away from us!" she shouts at the beast, and it melts before her eyes—its rigid shape collapsing into a shower of sand and dirt that cascades over the leaves. Gone. Hamara rises and turns to scan the darkness between the trees on all sides. It might come again, at any hour of the night.

"Stones, sand, and earth," she whispers into the night air, not feeling half as strange as she most probably should, while talking to the ground. "Will you help us? Will you make some kind of shelter for us? Something the kadanto can't enter?"

The words have scarcely left her breath when the dirt at her feet begins to stir and rise in a gentle swirl. It encircles the little camp—even Asei's cocoon and the crackling fire—in a ring of compacting earth and whirling dust. Hamara crouches silently down to her knees, watching with breathless wonder as a thick, circular wall rises up to enclose her in a cramped and windowless earthen dome.

"Wait—a chimney! We'll need an opening at the top!"

The sloping roof of the hut pauses mid-construction at the sound of Hamara's words, then abruptly resumes its motion, carving out a little opening in the crest of its thick scalp. The fire's dry breath wastes no time finding the escape, and Hamara lets out a mild hack as the excess smoke billows momentarily into her face. Below, the ground trembles and shuffles until every loose grain of sand is tucked away into a solid, stony floor. And then the little shelter falls still. The wind, the distant calls of birds—all become muted behind dark earthen walls. Only the whispering crackle of the fire breaks the newfound silence in the air. And Hamara sits wide-eyed at the center. Did the dirt really just build a shelter upon request? She presses her palm to the wall beside her. Although compacted into almost stonelike firmness, it seems like ordinary dirt and sand. Could it really stop the kadanto—a beast made of dirt itself? There's only one way to know. Hamara sighs and returns to her spot by the fire. And she smiles. At the very least, the hut will make the night less chilled.

* * *

She isn't sure what wakes her first. Maybe it's the slight whistle of the wind over the rough-hewn chimney, or the fact that her coat has slipped off her shoulder. Or maybe it's the subtle sounds of the forest waking on all sides that pull her gently from her dreams. When Hamara opens her eyes at last, the dawn has only just begun to peer over the tips of the eastern trees.

And nearly half of the shelter's walls are no longer standing.

The sight jolts Hamara to her feet. She turns on her heels and scans carefully over the surface of Asei's tawny cocoon. It shows no sign of distress—no cracks, no punctures. It looks no different than it did the night before. Nearby, the fire lies in an amber-speckled pile of simmering coals, encircled by powdery ash and the crumbled remains of the wall that stood behind it. Did the shelter just . . . collapse? Hamara shakes her head and pours a little water onto a kerchief, dabbing the sleep from her face and struggling to wake up entirely. Despite whatever happened, no one seems harmed. She steps outside the broken remains of the hut, searching the ground for anything amiss. Were there strong winds in the night? A fallen tree limb? She's hasn't stepped far when the loud snap of a twig nearby sends a sudden stiffening down her spine. The sound of a footfall. She turns, reaching instinctively for the sénsin sheathed at her lower back. But the weapon is gone.

What? But where—?

There's no time to look for it. Something rams into Hamara's stomach and sends her staggering backward. Her back meets a tree with a force that explodes the breath from her chest and leaves her doubled over on the ground, gasping and struggling to see through the wetness that's sprung up in her eyes. When she raises her head at last, the attacker stands at the spot where Hamara was lying asleep only moments before. It looks no different than usual. But it's no less sickening, either. The pale, elongated beast that seems to trigger tremors in Hamara's insides each time she sees it. It's back again. It rises to its full height over Asei's cocoon, stretching out its horribly long neck and fusing its thin arms into a single pointed spear. Now it hefts its weapon high in the air, ready to pierce through the voránjevin who sleeps helplessly in its path. Hamara's heart lurches, resurrecting her voice from the pit in her stomach.

"Get out of here, you disgusting pile of dirt!" she shouts, making an effort to return to her feet with her middle still throbbing and her head still full of buzzing.

But beside Asei's cocoon, the kadanto doesn't vanish. It doesn't burst into a shower of sand the way it did the night before, but turns toward her. And Hamara's heart drops. What's happening? Why is that thing still here? And where's her sénsin? How can she possibly fight the sand beast without any weapon at all? She swallows the tightness in her throat and takes a step closer.

"Do you hear me? I command you to go! *Be gone!*" She raises her voice, waving her hand as if shooing a pesky rodent.

This time, her words send a violent tremor through the monster's frame. But it doesn't leave. Instead, it melts slowly down, seeping like mud into the ground and leaving only a dark shadow in its place—

the shape of a man with black eyes, cloaked in darkness. The ghost from the riverboat.

"You think you can command me? I have more power than you know."

His voice is little more than a rasping hiss. And though he stands several paces away, the sound is like a feather at Hamara's ears—as if the man were whispering at her side. His image flickers in and out of sight as he speaks—sometimes visible as little more than a rippling disturbance in the air. But now, as Hamara watches on, the spirit transforms. Without warning, the ghost of a shadowed king is replaced by the image of a pale woman in blood-mottled clothes. A woman whose head is tilted sharply to one side. Too sharply. Shining, vibrant blood drizzles like a red ribbon from her mouth and rolled-back eyes—and from the severed remains of her left arm. She comes hobbling closer, and suddenly the air becomes thick with unseen blackness. Suffocating, bitter malice that threatens to choke the life from Hamara's shaking breaths.

"I've killed many like you." The ghost king's voice comes hissing from the woman's otherwise lifeless mouth. "Are you any stronger than they were, Hamara, rat of Igretho?"

Hamara blinks, fighting to suppress the horrible shuddering that's erupted in her bones. Now the dead woman transforms into an elderly man with nearly half his head missing. All his remaining features are cloaked by caked and drying layers of black and brownish red.

"Will you scream, like the others? *Will you beg?*" the old man shouts with the remaining half of his jaw, and the sound sends a quake through the trees.

Then he comes creeping closer yet, and all the warmth seems to leave Hamara's toes and fingers as she looks on, suddenly too horrified to move—to *breathe*.

If he truly is an outcast spirit, he must obey the law of the realms—former sasarian or not.

Asei's words come drifting back like a warm breeze into the girl's frozen thoughts. He must obey. Sasarian or not.

"You—you're only a ghost." Hamara struggles to push the words from her throat. She draws a deep breath. "I command you to leave this place!"

The ghost flickers back into the form of a black-eyed king. A king who holds his fists out from his sides and lets out a horrific, deafening wail.

Hamara claps her hands to her ears. "I COMMAND YOU TO LEAVE THIS PLACE! NOW!"

The dark spirit vanishes at last in a chaotic mass of thrashing shadow and blackness, letting out one last scream that could stop the blood in the veins of anyone in the whole of North Emér. And then Hamara is left trembling alone in the silence of the morning woods.

11

-318 years before the start of the Common Calendar of Glesia (490 years before Common Year 179; later in the ninth year of the reign of Sekýnteo the Golden over the Ten Regions of East Ataran)-

He stood atop the highest of the seven spires of the House of Voices. Unmoving, like an eagle at attention. An idol cloaked in living flames that curled and coiled along his shining figure. Far below, the streets of Tekéhldeth flowed with motion— hundreds, thousands of people crawling like ants between the walls and towers of the city. His subjects. Simple, skittish creatures whose loyalty could never be assumed. It had to be tested.

The sun had nearly settled beyond the western mountains, and now the somber call of the tower bells rang out from the four edges of the city. A sound that quaked every living heart within the walls of Tekéhldeth.

One toll, and the sea of ants came to a sudden halt. Two tolls, and all within the sound of the bells fell to their knees. Any traitors still standing were bound by the guards who stood like sentinels in every lane. Three tolls, and every head in the city bowed in unison to honor the king of the Ten Regions, Sekýnteo the Golden, who reigned with the power of the gods themselves.

The king watched it all from atop the House of Voices, listening to the marvelous thrumming of terror in the hearts of the people and the pitiful screams of the revilers bound and taken to the North Wall. It was a jarring dissonance that always brought a smile to his glimmering face. But it was never enough.

There was a hot hunger in the blood of the king of Tekéhldeth. A fever that tormented him since long before the beginning of his reign, since before he first entered the House of Voices as a young representative. A hellish fevering that never seemed to subside. There was a time when he felt certain that the death of the eviskyóneh, the last elected leader who once governed over all the House of Voices, would quench it—or the carefully arranged execution of his own traitorous father. There was a time when he supposed that the dawn of his triumphant reign over the Ten Regions would at last extinguish the gnawing burn in his soul. But it didn't. Nothing did.

It wasn't enough to hold all the nation in his hands, or to see the people bow in fear beneath his feet. It wasn't enough to be worshiped as their god, or to hear the prisoners beg for their lives at the North Wall. It wasn't enough to wield command over the very elements of the earth. *Nothing* was enough. And after the slow burn of decades, the flame in the heart of Kyvóike Sekýnteo had seared away all hope of peace in his soul. It carved a gaping void into the core of his fiery being—a raw sensation that kept him wide-eyed and closefisted as the days and nights rolled numbly by.

Something was missing from the start. Something that lingered forever beyond the reach of the only man who had all the world at his fingertips.

The answer remained hidden. But now the Golden King held his fist high in the air, swearing a curse into the winds. He would find the cure to his unending thirst. Even if he must overtake every nation in Claya to find it.

12

-Common Year 179-

He's still alive. He *must* be, somewhere far away to the south.

Isn't he?

Two days ago, Alarei was absolutely certain. But after traveling in silence over the Ádenlal plains for nearly two days and two nights—sometimes walking, sometimes riding the stones that would carry her along at her simple request—her straining ears can hardly detect Skéisono's heartbeat at all. The sound is fading. And the silence that replaces it lies like a shade over Alarei's once far-gazing mind. In some ways, the immortal is blind—blind in a world that's become hopelessly vast. She's spent hours wandering in what seems like the best general direction, following the guidance of the sun, the moons, and the few remaining heartbeats that flutter in and out of earshot. Wandering might be better than standing still. But could it possibly work, in the end? Could the two sasarianë unknowingly pass each other by as they wander through the same valley or wood? Such pitiful circumstances seem more possible with each passing day. And if Skéisono isn't heading north from his realm in the south, Alarei may need far more time to find him than she ever would have anticipated—far more time than her increasingly weary body may be able to endure.

"Farian, are we still immortal, Skéisono and I?" She pauses near the crest of a stony slope, letting her bare feet rest on the cool earth.

Her guardian hangs behind. "Yes. But the light of Claya seems to be leaving you. The weakness of mortal blood and bones may soon return to you. This servant will remain with you as long as it is able."

Is it true? Mortal again? Alarei wonders at the strangeness of the thought. Soon, she might be required to return to the mundane tasks she once performed daily. Eating, sleeping—things that seem strange to her now. Things she once never imagined living without.

The wind shifts over the plains, gusting Alarei's hair from her forehead and carrying a kind of bitterness in its folds that's difficult to name. It's a cold, empty sensation. Overhead, the clouds are gathering with darkened shades at their edges, muting the shadows on the hills. But one shadow remains oddly distinct. A shadow that flits and flutters along the profile of the next hill, where the rocks jut out like exposed ribs from the sloping earth. A presence hovers there. A spirit. One that carries bitterness and malice—not unlike the being that cornered Alarei at the heart of the earth. But this one is different. Weaker. And full of pain.

A little hiss escapes from the shadowed being that cowers behind the stones. "What do you want, dying sasarian?" The shadow's voice is thin.

"Darkness has no place in the light. Why are you here?" Alarei steps closer.

The shadow flinches. "This light burns me. You think I come willingly into its glare?"

"Then why are you here?"

The dark presence flashes in and out of sight, sometimes appearing as a dark figure several paces away, sometimes suddenly standing just beyond the glow of Alarei's presence. "We had a place. A place of emptiness, nothingness. A place between the realms too dark for shadows to cast. Now that place has collapsed, and all who sought refuge there are made outcasts." The spirit hides its head beneath its hands, rocking like a drunkard on its feet. "Now we're doomed! Doomed to wither here in the open light!" It wails, and the sound rises to a horrible, piercing screech that leaps and clamors like shards of glass over the plains.

Alarei winces, about to command the screaming shadow away. But before she can speak, the clamor abruptly ends. She glances in all directions. The plains have returned to windswept silence—even the cold bitterness that soaked the air only a moment ago has vanished like dust in the breeze.

"It's gone. Such a miserable spirit."

A captive of the darkness. One of the many human souls who committed unspeakable evil in their lifetimes. Alarei learned of such spirits during her early days at Clevyan. Unable to endure the brightness of the spirit realm after death, they're cursed to crawl from shadow to shadow—powerless to progress into the eternities with the remainder of the Clayan family. Ever thirsting, never finding. This one deserved no more pity than any other. But something it mentioned makes Alarei's thoughts churn. She turns to her guardian.

"It said they once had a place to hide, between the realms. Is that the same gap Skéisono vanished into for all those years?"

"Yes. There once was a gap between the realms. Now, the gifts of the sasarianë are returning to Claya, and its realms seem to be colliding. This servant can feel the shifting, even now. If the final gift is given, it is possible that all realms may become one."

Two realms as one? It's a thought that's difficult to picture. If the spirit and physical realms truly could merge, what kind of world would be born in the wake of their collision? A world where spirits walk among the living? Or a world of chaos?

"Farian, what will happen to our world if the realms combine? Do you know?"

"No. This servant cannot foresee the result of such an event."

Can *anyone* know the answer? Without entirely knowing why, Alarei makes her best attempt to smile. The uncertainty leaves a sour weight in her chest. It's too late to turn back, to retake the power they've forsaken. But must the plan continue forward? Maybe the sasarianë have given back enough. Maybe they should stop now, before the realms collapse around them. Maybe they've found the limit of their potential at last.

But then, what's this terrible urgency that burns in her heart—an urgency that threatens to drag her onward in search of her counterpart until her very last breath?

13

-Common Year 179-

The morning sunlight lies like a thin blanket of warmth over the stones. It settles in a warm sheen across his face where he lies, shocking his waking eyes with the sharpness of its glare. Sunlight. It's a kind of warmth Skéisono hasn't felt in many, many years. He sits up, moving like the old men he remembers seeing on porches as a child. Stiff, slow. And there's a growing emptiness in his stomach.

"Palarian, I honestly think I might starve out here. Is that possible?"

No answer comes. Skéisono rises wearily to his feet. The eastern mountains are a darkened silhouette against the gleam of the rising day. The hills and rigid plateaus of Igretho roll out indefinitely in all other directions, full of the pale morning hues of green, brown, and gray. Empty. The Palarian is gone.

"Alone then?" Skéisono gives the empty hills another glance, then lets out his breath, looking north, where Alarei's heart still echoes in and out of earshot. Alone then.

For days, he's asked the stones and sands to help ferry him along. And there's no reason why he couldn't do so now. But today, he walks. There's something mildly gratifying about feeling the full weariness in his steps and the straining in his hungry body.

"Earth, could you spare me a little water?"

The morning dew stirs at the sound of his request, gathering from the stones and grasses at all sides and pooling soundlessly into his lowered hands. It has a pure taste, with a hint of sweet prairie grass at the edges. And Skéisono finds himself staring blankly down into the wet shimmer in his palms. Who would've thought that everything would come to this? Not long ago, he was a god. A god who reigned with fire and terror over the earth. Now, the memory of it all brings nothing but agony to his soul. Now his immortality slowly fails him. He's dying—thirsty, hungry, alone in the wastes. But it's still far better than what he deserves.

He returns to his feet with a mild quake in his knees, raising his sights to the distant trees that stand sparsely along the northern horizon.

Or at least, to where the trees stood a moment ago.

Somehow, in the time it took to quench his thirst, the entire scene has changed. The Igretho hills are now cloaked in a white mist and dotted with lofty, ancient trees that seem to shed golden hues like captured sunlight from their leaves. The mist between them is marvelously lit—as though a million white lanterns hang suspended and unseen in the air. And where a few young trees grew on the northern horizon only moments ago, a pale tower now rises like a sentinel above the hills. It stands with perfect straightness, reflecting the morning with its shining, edgeless white walls.

Skéisono stands motionless in his place. The realm of spirits. Somehow, he's wandered into it. It's a place he's been able to enter from the time the Palarian came to him. He visited it now and then out of curiosity, but never stayed long. It always seemed so empty. So boring.

A figure comes stepping through the white haze now, appearing like a glimmering shade against the distant walls of the white tower. The figure of a woman—someone with a calm gaze and a long braid lying over one shoulder. A woman Skéisono never suspected he would see again. She stops to show him a warm smile he hasn't seen in decades. A smile that breaks his wounded heart into pieces. Could it possibly be?

"Mother—?"

Skéisono steps forward, but the ground at his feet seems to gust suddenly away like a blanket caught in wind. When his foot comes down again, it doesn't meet grass, but frigid seawater that spurts and splashes well beyond his waist. The chill saps the breath from his chest. He gasps and nearly summersaults forward as the tide rushes in from behind, urging him shoreward and laying a cold layer of wetness over his back. There was a time when all the waters of Claya would flow respectfully around him—would leave him dry and untouched in their midst. But those days have gone. Now, the cold waters cling to his long robes and soak mercilessly to his skin. He sloshes and stumbles to the sandy shore, struggling to pull away wet layers of clothing and letting them drift away with the waves as he goes. He's peeled away all but his innermost silk tunic as he reaches the shore and lifts his head to take in the surrounding scene at last. And his heart sinks.

Where he stood in southern Igretho not long ago, the morning was young. Now he stands at a place beside the sea, where the light of the twin moons still holds full sway in the night sky. The faint beating of Alarei's heart no longer sounds in the distant north, but in the east. Far, far to the east. Somehow, Skéisono's returned to the mortal realm. But exiting the world of spirits would ordinarily bring him directly back to the point where he left the physical plane—to the very same patch of earth. This time, he's reentered the world of the living far away from the hills of Igretho. Far from *anywhere* in Glesia. Hopelessly far. He's come to a place beyond the great Atayu Sea, somewhere on the western continent. And the reality of the distance sinks down like the weight of the sea's endless waters on his shoulders. He drops to his kness. The journey to his fellow sasarian's side has just become much, much longer.

14

There was a time, years ago, when Hamara was young and her sister Elein was hardly able to walk, when their mother raised songbirds. Colorful, innocent little creatures that sang a vast array of cheerful, warbling songs as the sun rose each morning. They flew free in the sky all the day long, returning on their own each night to the little nest boxes Mother made for them beside the garden shed. Hamara had always loved hearing their sweet voices each dawn and watching the way they glided in wide circles over the hills when the afternoons came. But witnessing the little hatchlings break free of their orange-white shells was by far the most fascinating part of it all.

Now, as she stands watching the shifting motions beneath the shell of the most massive egg she's ever seen, Hamara feels the same childlike wonder spark and flutter in her heart.

After only three days in the deep sleep, Asei's waking. His vague figure can be seen through the increasingly clear cocoon that encloses him—not unlike the shadows of Mother's unborn songbirds in their tiny shells. Shuffling, turning, stretching. He's been at the edge of waking all morning. Now he lets out a wet, rattling cough, reaching wearily to grip his thinning cocoon with both hands. The shell tears like soiled parchment between his fingers, and all at once Asei tips forward onto his hands and knees in the open air, coughing clear fluids into the grass—no longer a feathery eagle, but a man with skin the color of desert sands and fiery hair slicked in wet waves atop his head. Hamara stands blinking, momentarily struck by the bizarreness of it all before suddenly remembering her assignment. She scrambles to pull a canteen of water and a thin blanket out of the little bag Vayeka sent along for the occasion and rushes to her coughing friend's side.

"Here! Here's water for you." She looks politely aside as she kneels to offer the water and blanket on extended arms. "Do you feel all right?"

Asei lets another hack escape his throat before reaching for the canteen and tipping his head to empty it in several long gulps. "Thanks. I think so," he answers, rubbing his eyes and shaking his head. "How long has it been?"

"About three days since you fell asleep."

"*Ivykt kyh'o fa!* Sweet heavens above! Are you sure?" He sits back and makes an effort to rise to his feet without warning.

Hamara scarcely raises the blanket over her face in time. "Will you cover up? And yes, I'm sure. Trust me." She gives her shoulders a shake, as if she could somehow shrug away the terror that visited her several days before.

Asei wobbles back onto his knees with a curse before standing successfully on the second attempt. Then he snatches the blanket, wrapping it as a temporary skirt around his bare waist. "I've never understood why you arai are so sensitive about wearing clothes all the time. Is it the lack of fur?" He laughs, moving his shoulders in slow rotations. "Seems like your magic words really worked, kid. I feel pretty normal so far."

"Thank the gods it didn't take long. I'm not sure how much longer I could've put up with that horrible thing on my own."

"The kadanto? It came again, after all?"

"A few times."

"You're a strong woman, Hamara." Asei shakes his head as he bends to wipe the wetness from his face with the hem of his blanket. "You're not hurt, are you?"

"No. It left when I commanded, as usual. Although it wasn't exactly in a rush last time." Hamara returns to her feet, gathering supplies into her shoulder bag and the folds of her voránjevin wrap.

"Good. But it looks like I'm even further in debt to you now." Asei stretches out his back. "And I'm starved. But first, please tell me there's a river or lake nearby?"

Hamara tips her chin to the northwest. "You spotted a creek over that way, just before you landed and fell asleep. Remember?"

"Oh—right! Perfect. I've got to get rid of all this nastiness before I put anything on." Asei bends to snatch up his bag and starts off to the northwest without another word.

Hamara rushes to finish gathering her own things and kick dirt onto the smoldering ashes of the campfire before following after him. His smile has faded away when she reaches his side—replaced by a cold stare that sends a twinge of anxiety through Hamara's lungs.

"What's wrong? Something hurt?"

Vayeka was sure to warn Hamara about the many possible outcomes of Asei's transformation, if his body didn't have the right balance of nutrients and energy. Some more terrifying than others.

But the heln doesn't meet Hamara's gaze. He continues forward with a sudden rigidity in his steps, his expression unchanging. "No. Alarei needs help. Badly. I can feel it."

15

-In the ages between the fall of the Ten Regions and the start of the Common Calendar of Glesia (a span of roughly 318 years)-

In the beginning, Kyvóike Sekýnteo was bound to the place where his rule ended. Tied to the place that once served as his palace and throne. He roamed its broken, disheveled halls for weeks in unspeakable torment. Torn from his glory, from his immortal body. Betrayed! Robbed by his own wretched sasarian sister—one who should've joined his conquest, not ended it. He was a pained and drifting soul, a ghost too weak to leave the halls of his crumbling castle.

But in time, he found strength again.

First it was the power to venture out into the ruins of the city that was decimated at the moment of his defeat. Then it was the strength to journey farther along the ruined streets each day, straining against the raw force that bound him to his tomb. Soon, he could wander well into the outer lanes with ease. That's when he found them—a remnant of his once glorious kingdom. Survivors from the Ten Regions who were transformed into scampering little beasts. And it wasn't long before others appeared in the ruins. Men. Men who came from the cities of West Ataran with hearts full of superstition and desire. The bodies of the men were especially easy for Kyvóike to enter. But they were too fragile, too soft. The king could only take them for a short while before their living hearts would seize up and fail without warning. Pitiful, detestable excuses for men! They died far too easily. And the body of a dead man was of no use to the ghost king. But he never stopped experimenting. He tested his limits, always pushing for greater freedom.

After only several months more, he was strong enough to focus his energy and move sand with his disembodied hands. He even learned to mold the earth and wear it like a glove—one he used to capture a vermin survivor of the ruins as bait for another whose death was long overdue. With each passing day, the king's abilities grew. But it wasn't long before the survivors of the Ten Regions were nowhere to be found, and the people of the far west no longer dared to venture near the cursed ruins of Tekéhldeth. And the ghost called Kyvóike Sekýnteo was forced to find another escape.

It was eighty-two long years before he built enough strength to venture away from the lands of East Ataran, where the Ten Regions once thrived as the most powerful nation the world had ever known. He spent countless years haunting the lands of the far west, slowly perfecting the skill of stealing into the bodies of living men without killing them. It was always such a delicate practice. Move in too quickly, and the body's heart would fail. But move too slowly, and the man would recognize an attack. And the shamans never wasted time shooing Kyvóike out of his victims.

The final step was always the most difficult of all. The subtle art of expelling the body's original inhabitant in order to quietly take his place. Every time, despite the king's greatest, most delicate efforts, the body refused to live on once its original owner was lost. It was a maddening puzzle. A fruitless and often hopeless effort that required every speck of patience that remained to the wretched ghost king. A struggle that kept him experimenting for generations of time, until the fall of the Ten Regions was more than two hundred years past, and the world no longer remembered the glory of Tekéhldeth.

Sekýnteo the Golden was nearly swallowed up in his torment by the time he discovered the gap. He happened upon it almost by mistake as he pressed near the blinding and impenetrable border of the spirit realm. As an outcast soul, he was condemned to roam the mortal realm, where the light of the sun and twin moons scalded his being without end—never able to enter the brilliance of the spirit realm for rest. The gap between the realms appeared as a merciful escape where one was never thought to exist. It was little more than a flickering shadow at his fingertips when he found it. But he learned to hide away into its depths after less than a day of experimenting along its edge. And the victorious shout he let out when he succeeded was mighty enough to quake the edges of the realms. At long last, after over two hundred years of torment, the king had a refuge from the burning light that plagued the living world.

But the sweetness of victory didn't last. The sasarian immortals weren't finished with their betrayal. Kyvóike had only just managed to find the perfect body—one belonging to a man who possessed unique sensitivities to the spirit realm. It was an effortless capture. The king dragged his living prize into the gap, hoping to conquer his new body with ease. But the sasarianë refused to let the king of old find rest. The ingrates—those who should have honored him as their elder, their forefather—came following after him. Cursed immortals! Traitors! They came to rip the victory from his hands yet again, revoking his ability to touch the bodies of living beings and tearing away his only hope of ever returning to his former glory. And so Kyvóike Sekýnteo, Sekýnteo the Golden, was forced once again to bend to the dirt—to mold sand and clay and create a twisted puppet, an extension of himself in the physical world. A blade to cut where his own hand could no longer claw.

Vile sasarianë! Traitors!

They may have torn his glory away, ripped his kingdom from his hands and destroyed his body. They may have robbed him of his only chance to regain a physical form. But they can never truly slay him. And until the very end of days they will live to regret their betrayal of Kyvóike Sekýnteo. The indestructible being who will never allow them to succeed in their hopeless, pathetic mission.

16

-Common Year 179-

She's lost track of the days when sleep pulls her eyes shut at last. How long has it been since she first appeared on the plains? Days? A week? The Farian vanished without a sound sometime in the night, or she would ask—although the answer no longer seems important. The plains are unending. The elements have helped her along her way—helped in any way they still can. But the Ádenlal is vast. And now, Alarei's body can no longer ignore the reality that its once limitless supply of life energy is fading. Quickly. She hasn't slept or eaten since she came to the plains. It's a fact that shouldn't matter. But it does. Somehow, mortality's catching up to her. As if all the days she spent as an immortal were counted and tucked away for later, waiting to be experienced with the ails of mortality now, all at once. And she lacks the strength to fight it.

A stone catches Alarei's foot and sends her stumbling to her knees. The earth bites like prickling shards at her palms where she lands. Cool, sleeping earth. For a moment, the sasarian woman remains stiffened in place, staring down at the dirt and damp grasses between her spread fingers. The thought of rising to her feet again seems to ignite all kinds of protest in her weary legs. And so she remains where she is. She takes the air deep into her lungs, lifting her head to gaze out over the wide roll of the plains. Dying. She can feel her body quietly dying on every side. And a single question looms like an overwhelming tide on her shoulders.

Was it worth it?

She agreed to Skéisono's suggestion. She agreed to give back the sasarian gifts of power so that the good-hearted people of all nations could enjoy them—use them to defend against the darkness in the world. But at least one more gift remains to be given. And it seems as though the sasariané themselves will no longer survive to offer it. The gift of immortality is slipping away like sand between their desperately reaching hands. A gift that's lost can't possibly be shared. And what will happen to the sasarian line, now that the power of the immortals is broken? Will there be any sasariané at all, in generations to come? Or will the name fade away into myth—become little more than a fireside tale or a whisper in records long forgotten?

Was it worth it?

The thought is oppressive. Stifling. And as Alarei lays her head down on the cold earth, the idea takes root like a weed in her mind.

"Why did you give up on us?"

The voice is young. The girl it belongs to stands only a stone's toss away when Alarei looks up. A girl who couldn't be more than twelve years old. Or so she appears. Spirits seem to take on many appearances. But this one lacks the bitter darkness of the last visitor on the plains.

"Our homes in Koska were destroyed. Our families died before our eyes. Why didn't you save us? Why didn't you stop him?"

The girl sheds no tears. But there's an innocence in her eyes that pulls horribly at Alarei's heart.

"I-I tried. I did all I could—"

"And when you had every opportunity to rid the world of our murderer, you chose instead to join him? To throw away your power—the only tool that could heal what remains of the world?" A man's harsh growl is heard before his subtle figure fades into view beyond the girl. He stands with a furrowed brow, frowning as though the reality were far too terrible to accept.

Alarei shakes her head. "No, no, it's not like that! He changed! We thought there might be a better way to heal the world. I just—I wanted to—" She tries pitifully to explain, but the words seem to form a knot behind her teeth, and she fumbles hopelessly to loosen it.

"The sasarian generations have ended!" a third spirit cries out from behind.

"Who can mend the world now?" another laments from the right.

The voices all begin to question at once, and Alarei abandons any attempt to answer them. It's too late to undo it now. Too late. The world remains incomplete. And it's a world she now has no way to mend. Even the strength of an ordinary human being is leaving her.

And so, no longer able to stand, the last sasarian woman remains lying hopeless in the grass, staring down at her empty hands—weakening hands that still carry the slightest glow, like the light of cooling embers. Fading.

* * *

"Alarei!"

His voice comes echoing to her ears like the sweet melody of a songbird in the still air. A wonderful sound, too perfect to be real. The voice of the only person who ever made her life seem stable.

"Alarei, hang in there!"

His voice comes again. Nearer—sounding as real as ever. But could it possibly be? The sound of light footsteps comes pattering over the earth, a whispering thrum like the rhythm of the beating heart that draws closer along with it. Is it a dream?

The grasses are swaying like a pale curtain before Alarei's face when she opens her eyes at last. And as she rises on shaking arms to peer beyond them, ruthless pain erupts in her bones. Enough to push a sudden gasp through her teeth and send her collapsing back to the earth.

"Just stay there! I'll come to you!"

His voice is older than it once was. But it still carries the same warm tones that captured her heart ages ago. It isn't a dream, is it? The footsteps come to a stop at her side, and she's pulled into warm, cradling arms before she can hope to raise her head. A soft surge of energy flows from the arms and palms that hold her, soothing the cold ache in her lungs. The heart that dances against her cheek plays the same melody that's called to her from the moment she first heard it from afar, months ago. And the face that gazes down at her is as fiery-haired and silvery-eyed as she's always remembered.

"A-Asei?" Her voice trembles as the tears puddle and spill anew from the edges of her eyes. "Is this real?"

The voránjevin man smiles, and the sight of it seems to unravel all the years that have rolled by since Alarei witnessed it last. Nearly eighteen years.

"Of course it is," he tells her, and his gaze drifts momentarily aside. "Alarei, I . . . I know you probably don't want to see me again. But I couldn't just—"

She doesn't wait for his words to finish. It takes nearly all the remaining strength in her bones to throw her arms around him. She buries her face against his neck, taking in the wind-blown scent of his clothes and skin, and the wonderful warmth of his body. "I would've come to you months ago, the instant I first felt your presence in the south. But I had to stop him first. I had to do all I could for Claya."

What stiffness remained in Asei's shoulders seems to melt suddenly away, and his arms close in more tightly at all sides. "I'm so sorry. I never should've left you alone at Clevyan."

"That was long ago. You only did what you thought was best. You're here now."

Asei's hand moves to tuck the wind-gusted hair away from Alarei's glowing face. "We spotted you from hilltops away. You looked like a fallen star."

"But how did you know to find me here, in the middle of the plains?"

"It sounds crazy, but I followed the sound. I could hear your heart beating."

Alarei pulls herself slowly upright to stare into the face she's longed for ages to see, leaning heavily on Asei's arms. The soft radiance of her countenance reflects like warm lantern light over his features. "Our gift! So it really did work. . . ."

"You made that happen? I *knew* you must've had something to do with it! It works for everyone! We can all hear the hearts of people who matter to us. And we can—"

Asei's words fall abruptly short as he leans to catch Alarei, who tips suddenly sideways and nearly falls from his grasp. He pulls her back into a tight lock against his chest. And a slight quiver slips into his voice. "Great gods, Alarei, what's happened to you? You feel so frail!"

Alarei lets her weary eyes fall momentarily closed. "All the power given to us . . . it belongs to Claya. We wanted to give it back. To fulfill our purpose. After all Skéisono did, it was the only way we could imagine . . . the only way to make things right."

"You mean you gave up your sasarian power?"

"Most of it. We had no idea what would happen to us, once we did. Now we're losing our immortality . . . losing everything that . . . makes us sasarianë." Alarei struggles to deepen her breaths.

"Don't worry. I can stabilize your energy. Seems like your body accepts hitérian energy as easily as any voránjevin one would." Asei lays a gentle hand along her spine, then brings the other to her heart. "Just keep breathing. Where's the other sasarian?"

Alarei feels the energy in her body shift and blend beneath Asei's hands. Wonderful, soothing relief begins to flow through her core and into her limbs, dulling every ache in its path.

"The winds separated us. I need to find him again, to figure out the next step. There's something more that must be done for Claya. I can feel it. But Skéisono must be someplace far from here. I can hardly hear his heart at all. And if he shares my struggle, he may die before I can ever find him." She reaches to find

Asei's hand, grasping it firmly. "I don't think the power we gave can ever be taken back. The guardians have left us. The sasarian line will be forever interrupted. Broken for nothing, if we don't finish what we've started."

Asei shakes his head. "Alarei, it hasn't been for nothing. Haven't you seen it? The world's becoming an entirely different place, because of you. A *better* place. People can hear each other's hearts from afar. They can protect their families from any imaginable danger with the help of the elements. They can heal any injury in a single day, and can stop the storms and floods and wildfires that threaten their homes—the possibilities are endless. My friend Hamara here even managed to heal the nasty wound I had, with her words alone! Alarei, the world will never be the same, because of all you've done. It'll be infinitely better."

Is it true? The words seem to sink into Alarei's exhausted heart and kindle a flame where only cold shadows once reigned. A better world. All these days in the Ádenlal plains, she's walked without any view of the nations beyond, never knowing with real certainty whether any of her most recent sacrifices have had any true purpose—despite whatever the Farian assured her. Now Asei's come like a beacon from the mortal world. A witness, able to confirm all of her greatest hopes. The despair that cloaked her mind only hours ago is parting and dissipating like fog in the morning light. And the brightness that takes its place is almost too marvelous to be real.

She peers up into Asei's silver gaze, unable to stop the wet blur that bubbles up anew in the corners of her eyes, and a subtle motion on the hillside beyond his shoulder becomes suddenly obvious. It's a woman—a young woman—dressed in a lovely kopachue dress with a voránjevin wrap over her shoulder and a sénsin rod sheathed at her belt. She stands watching with a curious smile on her young face. A girl the sasarian woman has seen once before, at the city of Tavehlik. Then again from afar, on a dark night in the woods of North Emér.

Alarei smiles. "Hamara, the message you brought to your uncle was the beginning of all this. The changes we brought to Claya wouldn't be possible if Skéisono's heart hadn't been transformed. All of Claya will be forever indebted to you."

"What did I tell you?" Asei calls over his shoulder.

The girl smirks and folds her arms uncomfortably, shuffling in place. "Well, it was Asei who dragged me into it. So it looks like we're all in debt to each other."

Alarei laughs, and it feels like the first laugh in decades. "I'm afraid so."

Asei takes Alarei's shoulders between his hands, holding her out before him and looking closely into her eyes. "We're here to help. Tell us what you need."

"I just need the strength to concentrate. If I could just know for certain where Skéisono is now, I might be able to find a better way to reach him."

"We'll concentrate with you. Can you sit up now?" Asei waves Hamara closer, motioning for her to sit. "We can form a circle, like the old days."

He shuffles sideways as Alarei moves into the upright sitting posture that every child in Clevyan is taught to assume during deepest meditation. Then he assumes the same posture himself, still holding her hand tightly in his own. Hamara sits to the left, glancing silently to her company for guidance. Alarei shows her another broad smile as she takes her hand. The three of them form a humble meditation circle in the midst of the open plains. And with support at each side, Alarei can almost forget the dulled pains in her nearly mortal body. She closes her eyes, letting the wind on the plains level the air in her lungs. And all the thoughts in her mind settle down into one:

Skéisono, are you there?

17

-Common Year 179-

The morning struggles to break through the gathering clouds that stretch out over the darkened face of the sea. Below, the waves seem to toss and roll in a relentless dance, refusing to rest in the absence of daylight. Sitting in the sand with his back to a stone, Skéisono wonders how many mornings await him before the last of his strength drains out into the earth. The sea air is cool. Calming. If he had the strength, he'd go stand at the edge of the waters—would ask them to carry him across their wide face to the shores of Glesia. But the journey would take weeks. And crossing the sea is only half the journey. A journey he's certain he could no longer survive.

Pretend all you like! But we all know the truth. You've always been a curse. You curse everything you touch. Nothing will ever change that.

From the moment he collapsed to the sand, the condemning words of the dead have rung unceasingly through Skéisono's ears. Everything he touches. Cursed.

Maybe there was a time when those words weren't true. But all these years, he's proved them right. Perhaps Claya was never so torn and sorrowful as it's been since Skéisono Havetsu'Kajon came into it. He came like a raging storm into the world and left a scar as deep as the great oceans in his wake. Now he's tried to fix it, to somehow make things better. Perhaps the plan was hopeless. Can such horrific wounds ever truly be mended? Now here he is, dying on the seashore more than halfway across the world from the only person who can help him finish what he started. But at least he tried. At least he changed, before the end.

"You're not giving up, are you, son?"

The voice comes from behind. A tall man now stands at Skéisono's side. A man whose stern gaze the dying sasarian could never mistake.

"Father." Skéisono struggles to pull his voice from a heavy place in his chest.

To the east, the sea has vanished behind a curtain of white mist. A pale colonnade now stands where the shore was visible a moment ago, shaded in part by the canopy of towering trees that loom high overhead. Massive, ancient trees with leaves that shimmer and glisten like dewdrops in the morning light. Trees of the spirit realm.

"You're stronger than that, son."

"Father, I—" Skéisono blinks, and his father's disappeared without a sound, leaving only an uninterrupted view of the shimmering grassy hillside in his place. ". . . It's too far."

"Time, distance, separation. These barriers exist only in the mortal sphere. Even there, they're little more than an illusion. No distance can truly separate us."

A woman's voice sounds from between the white columns. Mother's voice. She stands dressed in a simple white gown. Her hair is braided into a bun below her left ear, and her eyes shine with the light of a thousand stars. Skéisono watches her, at a loss for words, wondering how she can bear to look at the son who brought so much shame to her name. She comes walking like an angel to his side, kneeling down in the grass to look closely into his eyes.

"You can rise above it all, my child. The realms are merging, and a portion of the light of Claya remains in you. The sasarian generations have ended. Now you must rise, or our world will lose its only chance of obtaining its greatest potential. A future more wonderful than words can tell." She reaches forward, letting her fingers hover briefly beside her son's still embodied cheek—as if she might touch him. But she doesn't. Then she lowers her hand, smiling. "I must go. We're needed elsewhere. But we've sent someone to find you. We'll be together soon, Skéisono."

"Mother, wait!"

Skéisono makes a pitiful effort to move onto his knees, hoping impossibly to rise to his feet and follow after her. But the stone he hoped to lean on is no longer at his side. He stumbles forward and lands on his hands and knees in the patch of wildflowers that's suddenly appeared in the stone's place. Flowers of the mortal, physical realm. A young voránjevin boy stands scarcely an arm's length away when Skéisono lifts his gaze. A stranger glaring with massive, vibrant teal eyes that grow suddenly wider.

"*Him?!* Mother, this is the man who destroyed the arai cities! I saw him. He killed *hundreds*. He doesn't deserve our help." The boy's ears turn aggressively backward as he bares his tiny, pointed teeth.

"Maybe he doesn't. But the world does."

The reply floats over Skéisono's shoulder, carried in a voice he hasn't heard in many years. Dark hands appear at his chest and back before he can react. Voránjevin hands. Warm energy pours into his body where they rest, easing the terrible throbbing in his limbs and calming the tremor in his bones. When he turns at last, Vayeka's calm face is waiting—still as rusty-furred and serene as ever.

"Much has changed since I last looked on your face," she nearly whispers.

Skéisono watches the way the swaying light of the grove plays and darts in her dark eyes. Eyes that once contained the only solace in his world.

"Your son's right. I don't deserve your help." He tests his ability to stand, rising slowly to glance through the trees to the east. "Is that . . . ?"

"The westernmost shore of the Emér Sea. Exactly where Vehn said you'd appear," Vayeka tells him.

Skéisono's heart leaps. The western shore of Emér? Moments ago, the Atayu Sea stood between him and Alarei's fading heartbeat. But now, by some miracle, the spirit realm has expelled him back onto the Glesian continent.

"It isn't over, is it?" He gazes to the northeastern horizon. He's been pulled back from the edge of death, at least momentarily. And it's a wonderful feeling. But there's no time to rest. Something more remains to be done.

"Not quite yet, it isn't." A man who stands in the shade of the trees speaks up with a smirk gracing his bearded face. The one Vayeka called Vehn. "Just don't disappoint us again."

"I don't intend to." Skéisono turns to look into the three faces that watch him with stonelike wonder in their eyes—human and voránjevin eyes alike. They stare in silence, waiting to see what the man once known as the god of death will do next.

"All this time I thought I had to somehow undo the mistakes I've made. But now I see. I only need to rise above them." He gives his old friend one last glance. "Thank you, Vayeka. For all you've ever done for me."

The filíl gives a soundless nod in reply. "Now go. Go and fulfill the call the heavens gave you long ago. All the world awaits."

Skéisono turns to the sound of Alarei's heart, closing his eyes. Despite losing his ability to travel instantly in the physical realm, he's unintentionally managed to travel from one continent to another and back again by taking only a few small steps in the spirit realm. Could he do it again? He pulls the spirit realm into the forefront of his mind, calling it softly closer.

Please. I just need to take one step. One step to Alarei.

The white haze of the spirit realm has already replaced the grove of wildflowers when he opens his eyes. A stunning, cascading range of sparkling mountains rises in the southeast horizon, their feet buried in the rippling blanket of the pale trees that covers the land in all directions. But Skéisono can't stay to admire the scene. He lifts his foot, focusing on the place where Alarei waits—doing all he can to imagine the very spot—and steps forward. All around, the trees and mountains blur and melt abruptly away, sliding aside like painted curtains from his view. The mortal world rises to replace it without so much as a whisper of wind. And when the sasarian man's foot touches down, a warm mound of golden-tan sands lies beneath it. Sands along the shore of Emér, seemingly only a few days' journey north of where he stood a moment ago.

It isn't the Ádenlal plains, where Alarei may still be waiting. But it's progress.

He doesn't delay, calling again to the world of white mist. This time, the spirit realm welcomes him into the garden courtyard of some magnificent temple—one with shining, glittering-white spires and archways that throw back the sunlight like flaming mirrors. The sight of it steals a gasp from behind Skéisono's teeth. Then he shakes the distraction from his head, recalling the sound of a sasarian heartbeat in a distant land and taking another step forward. But the scalding rock valley that appears before his eyes when he returns to the physical sphere is far from his fellow immortal's side. Standing near the edge of a jagged plateau that overlooks the Sand Sea, he can glimpse the stone columns of Clevyan rising like brave soldiers along the perilous edge of the cliffs in the distant northeast.

"What?!" Skéisono sends a furious shout over the dunes. He kneels to pluck a stone from the earth and send it hurling down into the valley below. It cracks against the foot of the plateau and explodes into shards that shoot sharply in all directions. "What am I doing wrong?"

He asks no one, expecting nothing. When an answer comes a moment later, it rises from the silent depths of his own mind.

No distance can truly separate us.

His mother's words. They come drifting back like incense on the wind. And they sink heavily into his ears. *Never, Mother?* She spoke of rising above. Above what? The question hovers idly in Skéisono's mind. All his days, life has kept him buried. Sunken like a stone beneath the waves of the sea. Life's pains have choked him from the start—drowned him with suffocating weight that even life as a sasarian immortal couldn't relieve. It's a weight that Skéisono's never tried to lift. One he never imagined he could.

But maybe he never needed to. Maybe he can rise above it.

Above the losses of his childhood, above the pain that drove him to darkness and hopeless rage. Above the shame of his horrific mistakes, above the crippling sorrow that tore his heart to pieces when he first laid eyes on the suffering he brought into the world.

Above distance, above time and place.

Was it always that simple? He thought he already understood. But now, the answer unrolls like a flawless scroll before his eyes. Alarei may still be waiting somewhere far away. But the distance no longer matters. It *never* did.

Skéisono closes his eyes once again, refocusing all his mind on the sound of Alarei's heart—not the place where she stands, not the distance that keeps her out of reach. And the world that surrounds him seems to fade from existence. He no longer feels the hot sun on his brow, the nipping of sharp stone at his feet, or the sound of endless winds gusting over the desert sands. All fades beneath the sound at the forefront of his mind.

No distance can separate.

18

-Common Year 179-

His voice comes like a half-muffled echo, at first. Like a thought floating idly at the back of her mind. But it grows clearer. Louder. Until all other sound seems to fade away behind it. When Alarei opens her eyes, she sits alone. Alone in a vast, open void—a seemingly endless space filled with pale, shifting light. The plains have vanished, taking Asei and Hamara along with them, and leaving behind a realm of perfect silence. Until a man's voice interrupts the stillness.

"I guess you aren't the only one who can learn new tricks, now and then." He stands a single step from her side, wearing only a simple robe with a thick sash folded over his shoulders. And he smiles with an almost overwhelming brilliance in his glowing face.

"Skéisono! You found me!" Alarei rises abruptly to her feet and nearly loses contact with the smoothed ground beneath her. "What—where are we?"

"Somewhere beyond time and space, I think. A place where distance can't separate us."

"I feel so weightless. Seems like we've left our bodies."

"Maybe. I'm not sure."

Alarei finds her footing and looks up to her fellow sasarian—the very same being who battled ferociously to take her life, not long ago. Somehow, he's different. More different now than ever before. More full of light—as if all the struggle of the past years and months were nothing but a distant, fading daydream.

"What happens now? There's something more we need to do."

"I think we can give one last gift to the world. The last of our sasarian power. It'll still work here. I can feel it." Skéisono holds out his hands, palms to the open void above.

Alarei raises her own hands, then pauses with her fingers hovering warily over his. "What do you think will happen this time?" she asks, and a wave of memories floods over her mind. Memories of Asei. His laugh, his shining gray eyes, his warmth, and the smell of the forest in his clothes. Memories that could continue forever on—could expand to fill a lifetime by his side. And the breaking in her heart is almost more than she can bear.

"I don't know. Maybe there'll be nothing left of us." Skéisono closes his fists, watching her closely. "I won't force you to do this, Alarei. I don't know what you might lose."

Alarei shakes her head, pulling his fingers gently open again as three sparkling tears slip through the spaces between them. "Maybe we won't lose everything. But even if we do, the people of Claya deserve all we can give. We can do this for them. For all who now live, and all those who will rise in generations to come."

Skéisono nods. "The sasarianë will fade into legend. But the world will be better for it, I hope."

"It'll be a world that hears and obeys the voices of the good-hearted, where everyone is connected to those they love—no matter the distance."

"A world no longer divided by realms. A home shared by all people, with or without their mortal bodies."

"Where even death has no power to separate." Alarei lays her hands over her sasarian brother's, closing her eyes.

"A world free of corruption. A world without darkness," Skéisono whispers, hands quaking, and the light of his countenance begins to rise.

What begins as a warm glow in the space between two immortals' hands rises swiftly to a piercing, fiery shine. It swells into a burst of light that spreads like glimmering waters over the scene, consuming all in its path. Alarei can feel it radiating through every fiber of her being like hot sunlight through glass, like summer winds through open weave. And as she lets it carry her away, one final thought flutters over her mind.

Goodbye, Asei.

19

They say the twin moons have ruled the night skies for more than ten thousand generations— that their hidden, glassy eyes have witnessed the birth of every river and forest and recorded the dawn of every life and every nation since time began. And every death. For the moons have no age or season. They say the moons have seen all that can possibly be seen on Claya's ancient face.

But now, a new age rises. A new dawn more marvelous than any tale that even the twin moons in their timeless wisdom could tell. Now a bold glimmer of light rises like brilliant mist from the heart of the earth, dusting down and altering all it touches.

In a single breath, the barren black shores of the far west become a sparkling inlet. Its once blackened and jagged stones now peer like gleaming crystals from the flawless waves that crest over them. To the far east, the Sand Sea in the deserts of Ketsa becomes a sea indeed. Where golden dunes once ruled beneath a merciless sun, an inland sea the color of a morning sky now spreads from the mountain gate to the eastern cliffs—a sister to the distant Emér, whose waters now gleam with a radiance that can be spotted from nearly every mountain in the Glesian continent.

As though awakened from a dark dream before the eyes of all who call it home, the entire sphere of Claya is transformed. Its mountains are turned to summits of silver and starry gemstone, and its forests are reborn as vast havens of unending light—every tree set aglow like a lantern in its place. A great wind whips over the prairies of the world, sweeping away all imperfection until every blade of grass shimmers like a sliver of tinted glass on the hillsides. The world is renewed. And the nations are not left untouched in the midst of it. Where dust and ruin once laid in the wake of a sasarian's rage, gleaming cities of marble and gold now rise like sparkling mountains from the ground. Where the crippled remains of Thelian once sat, a floating city of glass now drifts over the valley as if suspended from the heavens on invisible strings, reflecting the light of the new dawn in its massive, crystal towers. Every capital is transformed into a maze of spires and byways and spotless courtyards— sometimes built of pearl and azure stones, sometimes hewn of crystal and silver, sometimes spontaneously grown from the coiled, twisting vines and roots of the undying trees themselves.

The realms have combined, and all across the world's broad face the rejoicing of families can be heard. Mothers and fathers reunited with children once lost, brothers and sisters exclaiming at the sight of faces they once only dreamed of seeing again. Throughout every nation, the spirits of all the good-hearted who were ever born on its face can be seen racing to greet those they once left behind—spirits walking among their embodied kin and adding their voices to the songs of joy and wonder that rise from the earth in all directions. The realm of spirits has collapsed, bringing with it a brightness that no darkness can withstand. For only an instant, the shadows of the outcast can be heard crying out in hidden places. Foul, corrupted souls who once made the darkness their kingdom. They scream in the burning glare of the new world, recoiling and shriveling helplessly away into the depths of the sky, leaving behind a world free of corruption. A world without darkness.

20

The sky is a brilliant, lustrous blue when Alarei looks up to it again. It shines with unreal brightness across its entire face, as though the dawn has left its perch on the horizon and somehow taken hold of the entire world at once with its extraordinary glow. Even the swaying grasses that frame Alarei's view seem to sparkle and glimmer like narrow blades of emerald crystal. She breathes, testing the sensations in her lungs and at her fingertips. It seems real. Physical. A living body. So her body remains, after all. There's no pain, no remnant of the heaviness that plagued her for days on the plains. Her hand looks entirely ordinary when she raises it into sight. Not shining like an angel, not clothed in a gentle glow. But the sleeve that still drapes over her arm has turned to shimmering white—not unlike the silvery-white strands of hair that fall across her face as she rises from the ground.

Skéisono isn't far. She spots him standing only a few paces away on the grassy hilltop, dressed entirely in white—his now frosted hair perfectly matching the diamond tears that streak down his face. What does he see? Alarei follows his gaze, turning to take in a view of the hills in all directions. And the sight nearly knocks her to her knees. Not far to the northeast, a riverside city rests with spires and towers and curving bridges reaching high into the sky. A city built entirely of marble and etched, sparkling crystal. To the south, a massive windmill turns in a slow rotation with blades like gleaming, sapphire wings. And in all directions, shouts and songs can be heard. Songs of heart-bursting joy—of living souls reunited with those they once lost.

"That river. I saw it before, as an immortal. Is it . . . the Nakuë?" Alarei turns sharply back to her company, suddenly feeling as though she could leap to the heavens and back. "It worked! This is Claya! We haven't left, haven't died! We gave the last gift—and we're still alive!"

Skéisono looks back at her with sparkling eyes, a smile just beginning to appear on his face that could last an eternity. But something interrupts the motion. A horrible, agonizing cry erupts in the air, and Alarei turns to see the disintegrating spirit of a man coiling and writhing on the hilltop. A dark spirit. The brightness of Claya's new dawn should have destroyed him in an instant, or sent him hurling out into the darkness beyond the skies. But this one is stronger than most. And in his dying moment, he moves quickly.

"Look out! No—Kyvóike!"

Alarei reaches desperately out, hoping to move into action—to do *anything*. But the speed of an immortal body has left her. She can do little more than scream before the withering dark spirit takes hold of a glimmering stone at his feet and sends it shooting like a spear through the heart of the once immortal sasarian man who looks on. A man who watches calmly, who makes no attempt to move aside. Kyvóike Sekýnteo disintegrates away in a storm of tortured screams even as his strike lands. And when he's gone, the hillside returns to its quiet solitude, serenaded by the passing wind and the songs of joy that echo up from the crystal city. Still smiling, Skéisono remains standing for a moment longer before sitting slowly down in the grass. A soft laugh escapes his lips. Then he falls suddenly sideways as Alarei races to catch him in her arms. The blood has begun to pour in a vibrant red fountain from the gaping wound in his chest—a stark splash of color over his flawlessly white robes.

"I can heal you! The elements should still listen, if I ask—" Alarei scrambles to pull the sash from his shoulder and wrap it around his chest.

Skéisono shakes his head. "No, Alarei. I've done all I can to move beyond my mistakes. But I . . . I have no place in the new world we've created."

"Of course you do. With or without your body. The realms have combined."

Skéisono shakes his head again, struggling to breathe. "She . . . calls me back. The goddess. Beyond Claya. I'll go . . . now . . . to face her judgment. Whatever that may bring." He coughs, and a wet, red shine appears at his teeth.

Alarei takes his hand in a tight squeeze. "You finished well."

She stares quietly down at the once fiery sasarian man that lies dying in her arms. A man with a heart full of scars. A man broken beyond repair—yet somehow more whole than ever before. A man with a face as calm as the morning that swells over the hills.

He shows her one last smile. "Thank y-you . . . for . . . giving me the . . . chance."

Then his face changes. The light escapes from his eyes, his labored breaths slow to silence, and his entire frame grows suddenly still. Alarei lays him softly down in the sparkling grass.

"May the goddess smile upon you, my brother."

A long silence passes before she moves again. And when she whispers at last to the earth, rising to move aside as a gentle rumble awakens in the soil at her feet, the tears have already dried from her face. The stones rise to receive the lifeless sasarian body before her—a body returned to mortality. They roll and shift, colliding and combining until they've encased the remains of Skéisono Havetsu'Kajon in a rough, earthen tomb. The grasses move like blankets over the sinking stones. When the low rumble of the earth returns to sleep, the grave on the hillside is perfectly hidden at the base of a tall, crystalline pillar that now rises beside it. A beacon that catches the rays of the sun and twin moons that share the sky overhead.

21

-Year 10, by the calendar of Eni'erei, the new Claya-

"**K**eep your wrists straight, Ithëa. It helps you avoid injury. Gives you a stronger defense, too."

Hamara demonstrates again with her own sénsin rod, moving slowly into the correct posture. The red-haired girl who looks on adjusts her wrists and attempts to follow suit with her own still-sheathed rod. Her petite hands mimic the motions with commendable skill, despite her minimal training.

She smiles, blushing. "I always forget."

"One sprained or broken wrist would fix that."

"It would only hurt for a second!"

"Well, it wasn't always that way. The world was a radically different place when *I* learned sénsin defense." Hamara shakes her head at the memory.

Her student breaks her pose to skip playfully in the grass. "Yes, Father's told me all about it. He says people used to suffer for ages, waiting for their injuries to heal." She leans into her instructor's view. "And he says you helped him fight off a nasty monster that was always trying to kill you both."

"I did. He nearly died! And back then, death had a stronger sting. It meant separation from everyone who still lived in their body."

Young Ithëa gives a solemn nod, as though she knows all about it. But there's no way she can possibly fathom it. Not at her young age. Death was once a great divider among the living and the spirits. It laid an impassable barrier between them, paving a merciless ravine through the heart of every family it struck. But now the world has changed. Now, the people of Eni'erei, the new earth, live long lives together, unburdened by illness or injury. They grow old, as always. But slowly—much, much more slowly. And after several hundred years of peace, they lay their aging bodies aside to continue living on as spirits among the people they've always loved. Ageless, free of the limits and imperfections of their mortal bodies. It's the natural result of a world made free of darkness—a world where the elements obey every call of the good people who live among them. How could a child of this new reality possibly understand the pain and separation that death once brought into the world?

Ithëa comes closer, and a grin identical to that of her voránjevin father appears on her slender face. But she has her human mother's dark, starlit eyes. "I wish we had monsters like that now! I could learn to battle them like you did."

"Trust me, it's not as fun as it sounds," Hamara assures her, returning her weapon to the sheath at her belt.

"But why do we learn sénsin defense if there's never anything to fight off?"

It's a good question. Ever since the realms collided, creating a new world where the light of the sun and moons never fades, where no darkness can hide, there's little to defend against. Few ill-willed people can be found anymore. And those that do appear are powerless to harm the kind-hearted, who now wield the power of the elements. A good question indeed.

Hamara tips her head to one side, staring through the trees to the glimmering waters of the distant Nakuë. "Because it's good to remember the world we came from, to help us avoid making the same mistakes," she answers at last. And she raises an eyebrow at her student. "And anyway, we should always be prepared. You never know what wild beasts you might find in the woods these days."

Ithëa smiles broadly. "I'll be the wildest beast of them all! Mother says I have hitérian shifting points in my body, just like pure voránjevin people. I'm *dying* to change into an eagle, like Father can."

"I bet you'd be even shorter than he was as a bird." Hamara laughs.

But it's incredible to imagine. It's an indescribably marvelous thought, that where there were once two distinct races, one massive family is now emerging. Now children are born to blended families—with one parent a human and the other a voránjevin in the near-human virsevin form. Children can come into the world with a human shape that carries voránjevin traits and capabilities. A bridge between the races. Ithëa's only begun to learn how to channel her energy at will. But there's no telling what abilities she might discover in the years to come.

"Ithëa, Kynan's just woken from his nap. We'll head up now if you're ready!"

The girl's mother calls her from the crest of the next hill, silvery hair gusting in the mild wind. She walks with a tiny boy clutching her right hand and teetering along beside her. She's mortal—less godlike than she was the day Hamara first laid eyes on her, over nine years ago. But her white hair and near-shimmering clay complexion make her unlike any other mortal in existence. And all who see her know her name. Alarei, the last sasarian. The one they call the Mother of Eni'erei.

"Coming!" Ithëa shouts back far more loudly than necessary. "Come on!" She waves for her instructor to come along as she turns to the hill, clipping her sheathed sénsin to the belt at her lower back.

They've done it every year, since the start of the new world. At the anniversary of the earth's rebirth, the last sasarian and her family climb the hill just southwest of the crystal city of Melvynin, which came to be when the barrier between the realms collapsed and the mortal town of Remertrei was merged with the spirit city that stood beside it. They come each year to visit the shining pillar that marks the grave of a sasarian remembered by many—for many different reasons.

A fiery-haired man dressed in gray with a vibrant, traditional voránjevin wrap over one shoulder appears at Alarei's side, waving. "How are the orchards?"

"Good as ever!" Hamara calls back. "Especially now that a certain heln isn't sneaking in with his little boy to eat an entire tree's worth of kifara each week!"

Asei tips his head in a hearty laugh. "Hey, at least I always left you plenty of gold to cover it!" He takes Ithëa's hand when she comes skipping to his side, and their two heads match like red gems in the same lovely bracelet.

The crystal pillar is catching the rays of the sun and throwing out dazzling beams of reflected light as they come to the hilltop. Alarei kneels at its base, where a handful of violet wildflowers dance playfully in the breeze. She murmurs to the soil, and a new blossom rises up from the grass at the sound of her request. It blooms and sways alongside the others as little Kynan reaches to swat and poke at their petals.

Ithëa comes closer, smiling quaintly at the scene. "Just one? Can't we add more?"

"One every year. That's our tradition, remember?" Her father leaves a gentle pat at her shoulder.

Alarei turns, holding out a hand for her daughter to join her in the grass. "Do you remember why we come to honor this grave each year?"

Ithëa lowers to her knees beside her mother, laughing softly at the sight of her younger brother attempting to sniff the crystal grave marker. "Because a man died here who made all the darkness leave the world. A sasarian man."

"Yes, he was a sasarian, just like me. The Palarian came to him when he was young, just as the Farian eventually came to me."

"But Mother, where did the Palarian and Farian go?" The girl pouts her lip in thought.

"They sit at the poles of the world, upholding our earth with the power they once wielded to support the sasarianë," Alarei tells her, and she reaches to flatten a wild hair on her son's rusty-brown head. "They left Skéisono and I, when we chose to give up our power. Now they bless our entire earth with the immortality that was once bestowed upon the sasarianë alone."

Ithëa leans back on slender hands. "Skéisono. I've heard people say that he was an evil man. They said he killed lots of people."

Asei kneels down at his daughter's side now, warm light glimmering in his eyes. "He made many terrible mistakes, yes. But he changed. He turned around. And without him, we'd never have the world we live in today."

"So . . . was he good or evil?"

Alarei shakes her head. "My sweet girl. We all have weaknesses. And until nine years ago, so did our world. The shadows lived among us—as common as the light. Sometimes life gave us pain. Many of us lived with broken hearts and broken families. The sasarianë were no exception. For some, letting darkness into the wounds seemed like the only way to find relief." She holds her child's hand out flat before her, slowly tracing the lines in the little palm the way she often does when she tells tales of ages past. "There was a time, not long ago, when Eni'erei had a different name. When only the immortals could speak to the elements, and darkness built its kingdom in the hearts of the people. A time when the races were divided, and when families could be separated by impossible distances. When death had power to come between us—a merciless wall between the spirits and those with living bodies."

"But that world was changed, wasn't it? Changed into this one?"

"That's right. And the scars of the old world were burned away in the light of a new dawn."

The wind rises again in a sudden, spirited gust, carrying with it the sweet scents of gardens in the crystal city beyond the hill. It rustles young Ithëa's shawl and tosses her hair over her eyes. But she doesn't notice.

"Mother, where's Skéisono now?"

Her mother lifts her gaze to the shining pillar that rises from the hillside before them, and a smile graces her mortal face.

"Home."

GLESIA (THIRD AGE)

SKETZA

ÁDENLAL PLAINS

ÉRSIV
KEHS
DEIDRO
MIWEDA
HALIK
ATÁYU SEA

TAVEHLIK

TAYD
ONTRAGO
NAKONSIO
HADÓN
JAKER
DASVA

FIRÁL
JENSA
EDANEHN
CLEVYAN
SAND
SEA

OKÓTA
EMÉR
KETSA

NAGEL
TAKLIALÉ
LÁKON

KLAUSKET

REMERTREI
TAGREI

KÓSKA
ATÁYU SEA
RIVEN
SAHALO
SERÍT
BERKERIN

IGRETHO

INDERIT MARSHES
KAÁNTO'S

- 389 -

About the Author

A short introduction: I grew up in the upper Midwest, where the forested hills and cloud-dimpled skies always flooded my heart with the inspiration to write. My husband, Daren, was raised in northern Alberta. He and I live with our children in rural Minnesota.

Now, why do I write?

Since I was about eight years old, I've had dreams of another earth called Claya. These dreams sometimes come at night. But most often, they come to me like sudden, vivid memories as I sit pondering in the middle of the day. Claya is a world full of diversity—from the Black Shores of the west to the vibrant, emerald forests of North Emér, to the blowing sands of Ketsa in the far east. The people who wander between these lands are no less diverse. Claya is home to many tribes and nations—each of which has more history and heritage than I could ever hope to record entirely.

While I've written about the things I see in dreams for many years, *Anamnesis* was my first attempt to share my writings with a public audience. I owe my wonderful husband for all his tremendous support in this effort!

I've created my website as a resource for readers who are interested in knowing more. You can visit the site at memoriesofclaya.com. There, you can take a deeper look into the geography, languages, and cultures of Claya. I plan to expand this site as my other books are completed.

Thank you for your interest in my work!
Whitney H. Murphy